Philosophy and Terry Pratchett

Also by Jacob M. Held

DR. SEUSS AND PHILOSOPHY
ROALD DAHL AND PHILOSOPHY

Also by James B. South

BUFFY THE VAMPIRE SLAYER AND PHILOSOPHY (*co-editor*)

Also edited by Jacob M. Held and James B. South

JAMES BOND AND PHILOSOPHY

Philosophy and Terry Pratchett

Edited by

Jacob M. Held
Associate Professor, Department of Philosophy and Religion, University of Central Arkansas, USA

and

James B. South
Associate Professor, Department of Philosophy, Marquette University, USA

palgrave
macmillan

First published 2014 by
PALGRAVE MACMILLAN

Palgrave Macmillan in the UK is an imprint of Macmillan Publishers
Limited, registered in England, company number 785998,
of Houndmills, Basingstoke, Hampshire RG21 6XS.

Palgrave Macmillan in the US is a division of St Martin's Press LLC,
175 Fifth Avenue, New York, NY 10010.

Palgrave Macmillan is the global academic imprint of the
above companies and has companies and representatives
throughout the world.

Palgrave® and Macmillan® are registered trademarks in the
United States, the United Kingdom, Europe and other countries.

ISBN 978–1–137–36015–1

This book is printed on paper suitable for recycling and made from
fully managed and sustained forest sources. Logging, pulping and
manufacturing processes are expected to conform to the
environmental regulations of the country of origin.

A catalogue record for this book is available from the British Library.

A catalog record for this book is available from the Library
of Congress.

Typeset by MPS Limited, Chennai, India.

*To Sir Terry Pratchett, whose
imagination made this volume possible*

Contents

Contents

Part III Ethics and the Good Life

Part IV Logic and Metaphysics

Acknowledgments

Jacob M. Held would like to thank James South for introducing him to Terry Pratchett, and for encouraging and supporting him early in his career. Without James's support I might not have ever contemplated doing work in pop culture, and now I couldn't imagine doing otherwise. I'd also like to acknowledge my colleague Kim Newman, who has helped me copy-edit other work and who is always up for talking about Pratchett.

James B. South would like to thank his colleagues in the philosophy department at Marquette University for the singular privilege of being chair of the department for eight years. Their conversation, support, and hard work made my life very interesting. I also want to thank Richard Holz, Dean of the Klingler College of Arts and Sciences, who has allowed me the time to work on this book, and the other staff of the College who make going into work a pleasure. Finally, a special note of thanks is due to my colleague Susanne Foster, who provided me with some very helpful last minute copy-editing assistance.

Preface

I read my first Pratchett novel in the later 1980s. While browsing with my partner through a science fiction bookstore in Columbia, South Carolina, I happened upon a copy of *The Light Fantastic* with its literally amazing cover art by Josh Kirby. It was several years later that I read *Guards, Guards* and realized I couldn't stop there. After that, I hung out on alt.fan.pratchett for a while, was there when the famous Ankh/Anorak mistake was made and happily purchased one. From there it just gets worse (or better, depending on your viewpoint). My first wedding anniversary was spent in Oxford watching Stephen Brigg's production of *Men at Arms*. My father-in-law framed a copy of the Ankh-Morpork mappe for me to hang in my office when I got my first faculty position. It's made several office moves since, but it's still there over my desk.

I could continue embarrassing myself by showing what a fan of Pratchett I was (and still am), but instead I'll flash forward a few years when a graduate student named Jacob Held was a student of mine. Somewhere in-between the teacher–student relationship and the subsequent friendship that developed, I handed him a copy of *Small Gods*, suggesting he might like it. He did. That is the story of the origin of the volume you're now reading (whether as a book or on some device Ponder Stibbons could only dream of). He and I have collaborated before, and as was the case previously, he has been an ideal co-editor.

Sir Terry, of course, needs no introduction. Having sold over 85 million books, his work speaks for itself, though those of us who have been fortunate enough to hear him speak, often standing in the rain to get a book signed, know how eloquent and funny he can be in person. Despite his popularity, awards, and the string of "serious" writers who acknowledge the quality of his work, it remains surprising that so few books or essays have been written about him. This book is an attempt to rectify that gap to some extent.

The 13 essays (13 also being the age at which Sir Terry published his first story) herein address Pratchett's work from explicitly philosophical perspectives. The essays are too interesting, and the subject matter too much fun, for me to spoil the surprises that await the reader in what follows. The hope of Jacob and me is that this volume will bring readers and fans of Pratchett who may not know much philosophy an added appreciation of the complexity and depth of his work. For philosophers, we hope this volume will lead them to read Pratchett for the serious man of ideas that he is, as well as for his narrative verve, wicked since of humor, and nice (in the Pratchettian sense) distinctions made in his novels.

While your copy of the book does not come with a banana, there will be a copy sent to a librarian who has a special fondness for them. And if, for some reason, your local bookstore doesn't carry the book, watch for a certain street-corner vendor who will be selling copies at a price that he'll assure you means he's cutting his own throat.

JAMES B. SOUTH

Notes on the Contributors

Jennifer Jill Fellows is an instructor in the interdisciplinary Arts One program at the University of British Columbia and a philosophy instructor at Douglas College. Her research interests are in two main areas: the metaphysics of personhood, and issues of trust and objectivity in social epistemology. To learn more, please visit Jill's personal webpage at https://sites.google.com/site/fellowsjill/. Jill's affinity for Pratchett's witches started at a young age, growing up on the Alberta Prairies, which is in no way like Discworld's Lancre.

Susanne E. Foster is an Associate Professor of Philosophy at Marquette University. Though her main research interest is environmental and animal virtue ethics, she has made a number of forays into philosophy and popular culture, focusing on the work of Joss Whedon. Writing on the work of Terry Pratchett, however, is something she has longed to do ever since she discovered that the Turtle moves. Like countless others, she is Pratchett's biggest fan.

Kevin Guilfoy is Associate Professor of Philosophy and Director of the Philosophy, Politics, and Economics program at Carroll University. He has a chapter in *Mad Men and Philosophy* (Wiley, 2010) and has published various articles on medieval philosophy. He is a realist about the Discworld and spends evenings looking into the heavens for giant space turtles, and teaches his children to lay out porkpies, sherry, and turnips on "Christmas Eve." He would like to thank the Goddess Anoia for opening the stuck drawers of his mind.

Jacob M. Held, Ph.D. (Marquette), M.A. (University of Wisconsin – Milwaukee), B.S. (University of Wisconsin – Madison), D. Thau (Quirm), DMSK (Lancre), D. Thau (Hon. Genua) is Associate

Professor of Philosophy at the University of Central Arkansas, Internship Coordinator (Philosophy), Director of the UCA Core, Chair of Graduate Faculty (PhiRe), Affiliated Faculty Associate (Leadership Studies, UCA), Faculty Advisor to PRISM, Chair of Indefinite but Definitely Indecent Studies (Quirm School for Young Ladies), Affiliated Advisor and Rotating Faculty Associate of Sehr-Significant Importance (University of Uberwald, Hubward Satellite Campus), and Visiting Professor in Chickens and Non-Lethal Domesticated Livestock (Jahn the Conqueror University (Floor 3.5, Shrimp Packers Building (Annex), Genua). His areas of specialty include legal and political philosophy, 19th Century German Philosophy, and Applied Ethics.

J. Keeping fell in love with science fiction and fantasy at a young age and wanted to be Terry Pratchett when he grew up. Since that position was already taken, he had to settle for becoming a Professor of Philosophy at York University in Toronto, Canada instead. He has published scholarly articles too numerous to count (assuming you get bored and give up at six or seven) on topics ranging from Nietzsche's will to power to the phenomenology of animal consciousness. When he can steal the time, he writes science fiction, and you can find his work in SF periodicals such as *The Grantville Gazette* and *Andromeda Spaceways Inflight Magazine*. He also possesses a talent for magic rivaling that of Rincewind.

Tuomas W. Manninen earned his Ph.D. in philosophy in 2007 from the University of Iowa, where his studies focused on an admixture of contemporary analytic metaphysics and the history of early analytic philosophy. He is presently a lecturer at Arizona State University at the West Campus. He teaches courses in critical thinking, philosophy of mind, political philosophy, and other assorted topics. Like some other academics, he suffers from the persistent hallucination that he is sane – although he has achieved this without the use of any frog products. He lives in Phoenix, Arizona with his wife, Bertha (who doesn't get the Discworld novels at all), and two daughters, Michelle and Julia (who, hopefully, one day will).

Erica L. Neely is Assistant Professor of Philosophy at Ohio Northern University. Her research centers on issues in philosophy of technology and computer ethics, although she makes the occasional foray into other areas of ethics and social philosophy. She discovered Pratchett's novels while living in England and has definite opinions on the superiority of Josh Kirby's covers.

Andrew Rayment is Associate Professor of English Literature at Chiba University in Japan, where his colleagues force-feed him dried frog pills every time the words "Pratchett is better than Shakespeare" form on his lips. Rayment moved to Japan a few years back in hopeful search of an improvement in his marital arts, only to discover (like many before him) that a slight misreading had sorely deceived him. His other ramblings about Pratchett can be found in his book *Fantasy, Politics, Postmodernity: Pratchett, Pullman, Miéville and Stories of the Eye* (Rodopoi, 2014).

Jay Ruud is a Professor and Chair of the English department at the University of Central Arkansas. In addition to articles on Chaucer, Julian of Norwich, Dante, and medieval drama, he is the author of three books on medieval literature and one on Tolkien. He has been reading Discworld novels since his son introduced him to them 15 years ago. He has four grandchildren, three dogs, and a cat who resents them, is a long-suffering Chicago Cubs fan, believes that Lee Harvey Oswald acted alone, and is pretty sure that his pancreatic problems are the result of eating something purchased from Cut-Me-Own-Throat Dibbler.

Ben Saunders wrote his chapter while he was Lecturer in Philosophy at the University of Stirling, but from September 2014 he will be Associate Professor in Political Philosophy at the University of Southampton. His professional interests focus on democratic theory, including the "one man, one vote" idea practiced in Ankh-Morpork, and the thought of 19th-century liberal John Stuart Mill, but he has also contributed to popular philosophy books on soccer, Philip K. Dick, and (with Eloïse Harding) *The Hitchhiker's Guide to the Galaxy* (Palgrave MacMillan, 2012). He first encountered Pratchett through the nomes trilogy but his favorite books are those about the Watch.

Dietrich Schotte has studied philosophy and theology at Leipzig and Marburg (Germany). He is now research assistant at the Institut of Philosophy at Marburg, where he also received his Ph.D. with a thesis on the problem of religion in Thomas Hobbes (published as *Die Entmachtung Gottes durch den LEVIATHAN: Thomas Hobbes über Religion*, Frommann-Holzboog, 2013). His main interests are moral and political philosophy as well as philosophy of religion, while he historically focuses on the early modern period and the Enlightenment. He's been reading Pratchett ever since his thirteenth birthday and since he heads for a university career in philosophy, he started taking Thai boxing lessons three years ago (just in case).

James B. South is an Associate Professor of Philosophy at Marquette University. His research covers late medieval and renaissance philosophy as well as philosophy and popular culture. After being Philosophy Department Chair (i.e. Senior Wrangler) for eight years, he is now Associate Dean for Faculty in the Klingler College of Arts and Sciences. Being a vegan, he cannot take dried frog pills, so his connection to reality is a bit shaky. Luckily, he has begun studying Headology at the Michigan Psychoanalytic Institute. His role model is Lord Vetinari, though unlike Vetinari, he sides with Death in liking cats.

Martin Vacek is a doctoral researcher at the Institute of Philosophy of the Slovak Academy of Sciences in Bratislava, Slovakia. His academic interests focus mainly on metaphysical issues of modality, namely possible and impossible worlds. That's probably the reason why he takes every fiction seriously. Martin also runs the www.metaphysics.sk philosophy portal.

Note on References to the Works of Terry Pratchett

All of Terry Pratchett's works have appeared in multiple formats, editions, and reprints. There has been no attempt to make all references depend on any one edition. In the Notes to each chapter, the date of the edition used is given. In the Bibliography to each chapter, the original publication date of the work is given.

Part I Self-Perception, Narrative, and Identity

1 A Golem Is Not Born, but Rather Becomes, a Woman: Gender on the Disc

Jacob M. Held

The Discworld is populated by all sorts of creatures that push the limits of our understanding of what it means to be "human," or rather, a person; vampires, goblins, golems, trolls, dwarfs, Nobbs . . . women. I only half-jokingly include women among the other "monstrous" creatures with which Pratchett entertains his readers. Pratchett's women challenge our understanding of personhood as much as any other fictional creation. According to Michel Foucault (1926–84), the "human monster" is a legal construct, a result of the "juridico-biological" domain. The "monster" is a breach of the law, of the ideas of normalcy. The monster is the limit, the impossible and forbidden.[1] Pratchett's monsters push the limits of our understanding of normalcy. Monsters are the "mixture of two reals, the animal and the human . . . it is the blending, the mixture of two species . . . two sexes . . . of life and death . . . a mixture of forms."[2] Vampires are a mixture of life and death, as are zombies; Igors are a mixture of forms or bodies; trolls mix animate and inanimate nature as do golems in a way; werewolves mix the animal and human; and then there are women. Pratchett's women force us to consider the idea of gender and push the limits of our legal and biological understanding of what it means to be human. And insofar as women deviate from the norm, as so often do Pratchett's women, they are monstrous in the sense above.

So in this chapter I am going to focus on women, or rather the idea of "woman." Some might, therefore, categorize this as a feminist essay and thus anticipate a diatribe against men. Such expectations would betray an ignorance about feminism and the role of gender studies. Consider a working definition of "feminism" as "a set of ideas that recognize in an explicit way that women are subordinate to men and seek to address imbalances of power between the sexes."[3] There is nothing here that is anti-male or, for that matter, contentious. Rather, this definition recognizes the fact that women's subordinate situation in society is a social construct.[4] Anybody interested in social justice then would be negligent were he or she not to seek further understanding of the nature of this subordination.

Gender, or the "cultural meanings that a sexed body assumes,"[5] impacts on every individual. Gender informs one's personal identity and bears significant consequences for one in terms of one's possibilities in society. For example, Eskarina Smith isn't initially allowed into Unseen University because women can't be wizards. This isn't a practical impossibility, even if Granny Weatherwax thinks women can't be wizards in the same way "fish can't be birds"[6] or that women just can't understand wizardry in the same way men can't understand witchcraft.[7] Granny is an essentialist, she thinks that "identity categories [like girl or woman] reflect innate characteristics that comprise the fundamental nature of the members of those categories."[8] But what is actually meant in Eskarina's case isn't that she *can't* be a wizard, but that women aren't *allowed* to be wizards. Yet, Granny is recapitulating the old trope that women's brains work differently than men's, some version of which normally manifests when someone wants to explain why women don't pursue math or science careers at the same rate as men. Math is harder for girls. Or girls are naturally and essentially different from boys in terms of intellectual capacities or interests. Even Pratchett chimes in here with his remark that all girls of age seven are magically attracted to pink,[9] a fact my seven-year-old daughter provides a counterexample to. Although for an essentialist that wouldn't disprove their claim, it would be evidence that there is something wrong with my daughter: a proper girl of seven likes pink.

One can reject essentialism for the view that categories, like gender, are social constructs. But just because gender is a construct, doesn't mean it isn't real. Constructs are real insofar as expectations are imposed and asserted, often through punitive measures on members of a particular group, a pressure Tiffany Aching feels when she recognizes that she can't ever live up to the name "Tiffany," nor does she want to follow her cultural destiny of becoming a wife.[10] And neither will do for a girl that wants to be a witch, witches themselves being women who shirk the conventions of traditional society to become something monstrous that lives on the boundaries. Some people on the boundaries, like Granny Weatherwax, are respected, but, as noted by the incident with Mrs. Snapperly,[11] sometimes society isn't so accommodating to outliers, sometimes they get pushed to the margins.

Yet, when it comes to women and men, "perhaps [the] differences are superficial, perhaps they are destined to disappear. What is certain is that right now they do most obviously exist."[12] Gender matters to and negatively impacts on Eskarina Smith, Tiffany Aching, as well as Cheery Littlebottom and Polly Perks, and the myriad other women that populate the Discworld. So in what follows we'll look at the reality of gender, from its construction and implementation to its enforcement. We'll proceed historically, beginning with the work of Simone de Beauvoir. Here we'll focus on the idea of gender as socially constructed, an enforced normative structure meant to control and suppress women's agency. On the Disc, Gladys and Cheery Littlebottom most clearly exhibit Beauvoir's understanding of gender. Most recently, Judith Butler has advocated the position that gender be understood as performative, that is, gender is a constantly reinforced and tenuous identity made real through the performance of gender norms. On the Disc, we find Polly Perks and Sergeant Jackrum who perform masculinity convincingly, regardless of what parts they have (or fail to have) between their legs. Let's begin with Beauvoir.

What You Won't Find in Lady Waggon's *Book on Household Management*

"One is not born, but rather becomes, a woman."[13] With these nine words Beauvoir defined the terms of a conversation we're still having today, a conversation about the origin and meaning of gender. Beauvoir tells us that one is not born a woman. But clearly this is false. Some humans are born with female bits. Aren't these humans denoted by the term "woman," and so aren't some people clearly born women, namely those people born with the propensity to grow bumpy bits up top and a conspicuous absence down below. In order to understand how it is that a vagina doesn't make one a woman, even if an extra pair of socks does make one a man, one must first distinguish between sex and gender.

Sex is biological. Sex denotes primary sex characteristics like the possession of a penis or vagina, testes, ovaries, and sundry other elements of human plumbing. Sex is about whether you can pee standing up, without acrobatics and a degree in non-Euclidean geometry. Gender on the other hand is about how one presents oneself, how one identifies. Gender is about the meaning a sexed body acquires within society. So gender is about how those who possess vaginas are expected to act. But there is no necessary symmetry between sex and gender. Vagina owners can behave in ways consistent with penis possessors, and vice versa. In addition, since gender is about the meanings our bodies acquire, and since it isn't necessarily tied to our sex, there could be more genders than there are sexes. And it gets even more complicated. The determining of sex itself appears to be culturally determined. For example, what makes one human male and another female? Is it hormones, DNA, the possession of testes, ovaries, etc.? Given the multifarious ways in which we can determine sex, sex itself is ambiguous, and since gender isn't tied to sex, gender is even more so. It's a very complicated matter, but Pratchett can help. Consider Gladys.

Golems are interesting creations in the Discworld. They ask us to engage in deliberations about the nature of servitude, labor, and freedom. But for our purposes, we should ask about their sex and gender. Now obviously they do not possess a sex, unless an idiosyncratic or perhaps especially saucy artisan decided to get creative with a bit of left over clay. But for the most part, from what we're told, they don't have genitalia and don't reproduce sexually. Nor do they possess DNA, hormones, or any other marker we might use to code sex in our scientific or legal discourses. Yet they do seem to possess gender, or at least have it imposed on them. All the way back in *Feet of Clay*, Dorfl is referred to as "he" or "him," and this is done because Vimes thinks "it" wouldn't fit. So he denotes Dorfl as male, as a "him," out of respect.[14] In *Going Postal*, Pump 19 is called "Mr. Pump" by Moist throughout. In fact, every golem is by default referred to as "Mr." or barring that as "he" or "him."[15] It would appear that insofar as golems are to be treated as people, they must be gendered. To be a person is to possess a gender, and the default gender appears to be male.

Now if golems are to be gendered, then golem gender can't be the result of bringing their gender into accord with their biological or primary sex characteristics, for they have none. Instead, gender must be seen as an expression of their identity. Insofar as one is a person, as golems are, one must possess a gender. Everyone defaults to masculine, that is, to "Mr." out of respect or habit. And this is instructive. Men are taken to be the default, the representative of personhood. Women, therefore, are a variation on the theme, or rather a deviation from it. Here, we find Gladys.

Miss Maccalariat raises the issue of golem gender with Moist. She finds a golem in the ladies room and, given that they are all referred to as "Mr." is offended. Moist explains that they are just referred to as "Mr." since "'it' seems wrong and . . . 'Miss' is not appropriate."[16] So the golems need a gender in order to be respected as persons, but not "Miss," since that's not appropriate. But Miss Maccalariat needs a "Miss." That is, her view of society, her understanding of gender roles and expectations demands that only women clean the ladies room. So Gladys is created, or rather a golem is re-christened, "Gladys." Gladys the golem is properly clothed and subsequently fits well into Miss Maccalariat's gendered worldview. Now Gladys can clean the ladies room. But something soon happens to Gladys. As soon as she is denoted a "she," she begins to change. She begins to act like a "she." That is, Gladys begins to adopt feminine behaviors and even identifies as a woman. Beauvoir understands why. Gladys wasn't born, or rather baked, a woman: she became one.

According to Beauvoir, one becomes a woman through being acculturated to adopt, accept, and emulate gender. The myth of the eternal feminine[17] constructs a "natural" binary between male and female, and those that are female possess an intractable nature, one different from men. Expectations are set for them, expectations regarding dress, behavior, etiquette, and general comportment.[18] Thus one's body, one's being female, determines one's cultural possibilities. Once Gladys becomes a woman, she dresses differently, unlike other golems, she adds treble to her voice, she starts to make Moist sandwiches, offer him backrubs, engages in gossip with Glenda and the other counter girls in some sort of "misplaced" female solidarity, develops a crush on Moist, and reads *Ladies Own Magazine* and Lady Deirdre Waggon's *Book of Household Management*, at least until Adora Dearheart introduces her to Releventia Flout's *Why Men Get Under Your Feet*.[19] Dearheart wonders why Gladys should think she's a woman, and Moist is perceptive enough to wonder why she would think she was a man either.[20] And Moist is onto something when he notes that the issue arises from the fact that there simply haven't been emancipated golems before.[21] Being free, or rather being a person, seems to bring along with it being gendered. People just do possess gender, this is how their identities are situated

8

within society. But if we are concerned with freedom, with emancipation, then we must also recognize that gender carries with it baggage. Which gender one is identified with has consequences. "Discrete genders are what 'humanizes' individuals within contemporary culture; [but] those who fail to do their gender right are regularly punished."[22] Gender is a cultural fiction that carries with it expectations, expectations that once accepted begin to appear as natural, as expressions of an intractable essence: expectations such as how to treat one's boss, one's place in the home or workplace, who can or can't do magic, attend university, and so forth. As Butler notes with respect to Beauvoir's insight, "'woman' is a historical idea and not a natural fact, [Beauvoir] clearly underscores the distinction between sex, as biological facticity, and gender, as the cultural interpretation or signification of that facticity."[23] But gender is a construction that conceals its genesis. Our forgetfulness allows gender to get reified into a natural law, an innate order, such that deviations are not new or novel constructions, but flaws in the deviant.

Remember, proper girls of seven like pink. Gladys is learning how to be a proper woman. Gender is a restrictive concept, one that delimits a person's possibilities within a particular society. "As an existentialist, Beauvoir was concerned about the tension between freedom and determinism and believed that there is nothing necessary or inevitable about who a person ultimately becomes."[24] Gender, as the reified expectations of society and as a limiting factor on a person's possibilities, is thus in tension with their transcendence, their ability to be and become whomever they choose to be or become. Beauvoir's existentialism is about enhancing one's agency and gender, at least for women, does not enhance, but rather limits, agency. Gladys seems restricted by the gender chosen for her, at least until she begins to "do it for herself."[25] If one is concerned with freedom and liberation, as golems and others seem to be, then they should also be concerned with gender, a point Cheery Littlebottom brings to light.

Feminism from the Mines: How a Dwarf does Gender

At one time Cheery (pronounced "Cheri") Littlebottom was unique among dwarfs. An out woman dwarf. Even if trends seem to indicate that Dwarf society is becoming more tolerant of out women dwarfs, from micromail fashion shows at Shatta to stylized beards,[26] it wasn't always so. Cheery isn't unique insofar as she is biologically female, otherwise her origins would be hard to explain, and she'd be very, very busy. What distinguished Cheery was that she openly exhibited her femininity. Female dwarfs have existed as long as there have been dwarfs and the need for subsequent dwarfs. But, we're told, dwarfs don't recognize gender: "All dwarfs were he unless they asserted otherwise."[27] But defaulting to male isn't the same thing as not recognizing gender. As Cheery helps to illustrate, by recognizing no gender, dwarfs de facto recognize and enforce only male gender.

Cheery's predicament is expressed clearly in a brief exchange with a fellow Watch woman, Angua. Angua notes to Cheery, "*you* can do anything the men do" and Cheery responds "provided we do only what the men do."[28] Dwarfs may not recognize gender explicitly, but masculinity is clearly reinforced. Thus, dwarfs may not explicitly discriminate, but in assuming all gender to be male they limit the possibilities of someone like Cheery. In dwarf society, we are presented with a hegemonic binary, a case wherein male and female are placed against each other with male assuming the position of preeminence.[29] Cheery finds herself in the position of so many women. She must either conform to the demands society places on her gender or fear reprisal, whether that be through overt discrimination or the shaming and social pressures inflicted by society: "The woman who does not conform devaluates herself . . . socially . . . A woman who has no wish to shock or to devaluate herself socially should live out her feminine situation in a feminine manner."[30] Cheery does not want to conform, however.

She wants to be a female dwarf, and so she doesn't conform, and in so doing she shocks. She wears make-up, women's clothing, and earrings.[31] But in so doing she earns the opprobrium of "proper" dwarf society. In *The Fifth Elephant* she is part of a contingent that travels to Uberwald, and she comes into conflict with traditional dwarf culture. She stands out as a female dwarf, and her willingness to express her gender openly is taken as an affront to everything proper and dwarfish. In fact, she is insulted several times with the inflammatory "Ha'ak."[32] The context makes it clear that she is being chided and insulted for being monstrous, for pushing the boundary and falling outside of accepted dwarfish gender roles. As an out woman she stresses the system of dwarf gender to the breaking point. She must conform or shock. She chooses to shock and must bear the price for that, a price many women wouldn't or couldn't be expected to pay. The problem with this situation is that the system is rigged to punish the expression of female gender, so being a dwarf woman isn't a viable alternative for dwarfs and thus a significant portion of dwarfish society is unable to express itself in any authentic way. I guess, female dwarfs could simply continue to conform. They could just accept that as women they have a specific place in dwarf society. Does Cheery need to rub everyone's face in her gender?

The problem with conformity isn't that it might be unsatisfying to those that are asked or required to conform, it's that conformity breeds complicity and obedience, and thus is in direct conflict with agency and freedom. For a woman, "the less she exercises her freedom to understand, to grasp and discover the world about her, the less resources will she find in herself, the less she will dare to affirm herself as a subject."[33] The more you conform, the more you obey, the less you are able to develop those skills and resources necessary to affirm your own agency. Women are caught in a vicious circle that perpetuates their unfreedom, all under the guise of the mythical eternal feminine, a law of nature that decrees that this is how it has always been and this is the way it ought to continue. This is what Cheery is reacting against, and that is why she is met with such resistance.

This system has worked for male dwarfs forever. But now they are losing their claim to "natural" superiority, to the privilege they have claimed for themselves, all thanks to that Ha'ak, Cheery Littlebottom. This is a challenging situation for women, and so not many will be as adventurous as Cheery. Some, like Dee in *The Fifth Elephant*, will be complicit in their servitude, because they see no other way or have internalized gender norms and identify with the roles prescribed for them. So we see Dee condemning Cheery as a Ha'ak and lamenting "Why should *they* be allowed to do this . . . *I* can't! And I work so hard"[34] In a classic case of resentment, Dee expresses her outrage at Cheery for doing what she wishes she had the courage to. She resents Cheery for being what she could not be, an out woman dwarf. Dee chose to accept and conform, out of fear perhaps, or survival. And now she resents Cheery for her courage. How many other dwarf women are similar to Dee? How many have been protecting and advocating for the "old ways" not out of a genuine belief in these values but out of a sense of comfort, or out of bad faith, affirming an antiquated gender system while denying the possibility of an alternative to mask the fact that they have chosen to live manufactured, inauthentic, or cowardly lives? They fled from the responsibility of their own freedom and now chastise those who demonstrate them to be the cowards that they are. Cheery, and others like her, will bear the brunt of their resentment. How many dwarfish women have found cold comfort in the "old ways" in the belief that it's always been this way, it's natural and so forth, thus relieving them of the responsibility of being held accountable for their complicity in a discriminatory gender system? These women, like Dee, "cheerfully [believe] these lies because they invite her to follow the easy slope: in this others commit their worst crime against her; throughout her life from childhood on. They damage and corrupt her by designating as her true vocation this submission."[35] Here women are complicit in their own servitude, but "complicity is conceived as a condition of an embodied self whose abilities, and therefore options, have been formed by its social circumstances."[36] So perhaps some of their responsibility is mitigated. Women are in an ambiguous situation. A woman can't be expected to revolt continually and shirk societal conventions. To do so would limit her agency significantly by foreclosing many opportunities for her to participate in society. If Cheery did nothing but transgress gender norms, she would limit her ability to function in society significantly. Likewise, women can't simply "go along." To do so is to accept culturally imposed limitations on one's agency. Women must navigate a coercive system, continually negotiating when to revolt, compromise, or acquiesce. Cheery learns this lesson late in *The Fifth Elephant*.

At the end of *The Fifth Elephant* Cheery decides to wear traditional dwarfish garb to the king's coronation, not because she feels compelled, but because she could choose to wear women's clothing. She has realized that she can choose how to perform her gender, and it's not always the right time and place to rebel, to shock. As she explains to Vimes: "I *can* wear what I like, sir. That's the point. I don't *have* to wear that dress. I can wear what I like. I don't *have* to wear something just because other people *don't* want me to."[37] It's not rebellion for rebellion's sake, it's about expressing her genuine self, her genuine gender. Cheery can choose how to perform her gender.

The Ins and Outs of Performing Gender

As noted above, Judith Butler defines gender as "the cultural meanings that the sexed body assumes" as such "a gender cannot be said to follow from a sex in any one way. Taken to its logical limit, the sex/gender distinction suggests a radical discontinuity between sexed bodies and culturally constructed genders."[38] With respect to Beauvoir, Butler notes that she "meant merely to suggest that the category of women is a variable cultural accomplishment, a set of meanings that are taken on or taken up within a cultural field, and that no one is born with a gender – gender is always acquired."[39] Being so acquired, however, does not make gender any less real. Gender is real insofar as people identify with their genders, insofar as gender does form a constitutive element of one's personal identity. In addition, gender is real insofar as it is recognized, reaffirmed, and ossified into social and cultural expectations and practices. Merely pointing out the contingent nature of gender does not remove its importance. But what Butler helps us to appreciate beyond Beauvoir is that this constructed nature of gender means gender itself is simply a performance. We are constantly stylizing and performing our genders. Consider the Ins and Outs.

Sergeant Jackrum's Ins and Outs are a monstrous regiment indeed. It is comprised of an Igor, a vampire, a troll, and entirely of women. At the heart of *Monstrous Regiment* is Polly Perks, who joins the Ins and Outs in order to find her brother, Paul. However, only boys are allowed to sign up for military service, so Polly chops off her hair, dresses as a boy, and enlists. The reader quickly learns that the entire Ins and Outs is comprised of women, all passing as boys. Even their Sergeant, Jackrum, is a woman. And as we find out at the end almost the entire leadership of the military itself is female, all passing as male. Here we have something much more interesting than simply the well-worn comedic trope of cross-dressing. Here we have gender being performed throughout in various ways, each calling into question the stability of gender categories.

We can begin with the simple fact that Polly Perks and Sergeant Jackrum are female. Even though Butler is right that sex is a gendered category—that is, how we determine one's sex already depends on what characteristics we determine to be fundamental to the determination of sex such as genitalia and hormones—both Polly and Jackrum have girl parts and lack boy parts. This explains the need for an extra pair of socks. They also lack secondary sex characteristics attributed to males, which is why they always have such nice clean shaves. Polly and Jackrum are female, but as we'll see this doesn't mean they are also women.

Polly learns quickly that acting male is fairly simple. Polly adopts masculine characteristics easily. She tells herself, "Think young male . . . Fart loudly and with self-satisfaction at a job well done, walk like a puppet . . . never hug anyone, and if you meet a friend, punch him."[40] She figures out that with "care and attention to detail . . . a woman could pee standing up."[41] She figures out how to bulge where she should and not where she shouldn't. Through adopting the outward appearance of a young male, and by manifesting stereotypical masculine behaviors, she performs masculinity convincingly. Now she does not do so as an expression of her "true" gender or personality, but she does exemplify gender as a performance. In fact, she and her cohorts are able to perform masculinity so well that when a military plan calls for them to dress as women and sneak through the washerwoman's entrance their commanding officer, Blouse, claims he's noticed "habits, perfectly normal . . . like the deep exploration of a nostril . . . a tendency to grin after passing wind . . . to . . . scratch . . . your selves in public" that disqualifies them from the mission.[42] Apparently Blouse is the right man for the job, of being a woman, whereas the females are unqualified. These girls so convincing perform masculinity that they are in fact men. Regardless of whether or not they have a pair (of socks) they are men. They behave as men, they occupy the social space of men, they are treated as men, and so in terms of their integration into society, their socially constructed meaning and socially constructed subject position, they are men. "Gender is in no way a stable identity or locus of agency from which various acts proceed; rather, it is an identity tenuously constituted in time—an identity instituted through a *stylized repetition of acts*."[43] Gender should be understood as "the mundane way in which bodily gestures, movements, and enactments of various kinds constitute the illusion of an abiding gendered self."[44]

Polly Perks and her comrades have constructed around themselves the illusion of masculinity through the repetition of masculine acts, and they perpetuate the illusion through the continuous performance of those acts. In this regard they are men. But there is something not quite right about claiming they are men, *tout court*, for they don't identify as men. They know they are performing, and they are performing not out of a sense of authentic selfhood, but necessity. So at the end of the book when Polly rejoins the military she does so as a woman. At root Polly is "cisgender": her gender (woman) is consistent with her sex (female). She performed masculinity, she was a man when circumstances demanded it, but she never identified as a man. Polly helps point out that "gender identity is a performative accomplishment compelled by social sanction and taboo."[45] She had to perform masculinity to be in the military. This is where Sergeant Jackrum is illuminating. Sergeant Jackrum may be Terry Pratchett's first transgender character.

We can't not perform gender. Whether we are Polly performing gender for ulterior motives, or performing our gender because it feels natural or is the identity we have chosen for ourselves, we are always already performing, and performing a role that has been written by previous generations of actors and reinforced by society and societal pressures. When Polly performs as a man, she is performing, and how she performs masculinity is dictated by how masculinity has been written by society. It's okay to fart loudly as a boy. That's gender. When she performs womanhood she does so according to how womanhood has been written as a gender role. "Actors are always already on the stage, within the terms of the performance."[46] In fact, it's not until the end when Polly starts to perform womanhood differently, as an out woman in the military, that we see how roles can change. But Jackrum is a different matter entirely.

Jackrum is female, but has been living as a man for so long that he (and I think "he" is the proper pronoun) can no longer even fathom living as a woman. He notes in several places when they are contemplating the plan to dress as washerwomen that

"You won't get me in skirts. Everyone has their place, right?"[47] This isn't simply about maintaining his cover as a man in order to protect his place in the army. He is a man, the idea of being a woman is ludicrous. "Woman" as a gender no longer fits Jackrum. In fact, when he contemplates leaving the military he adopts Polly's plan of returning to his estranged son as his long lost *father* so that he may be a grand*father* to his grandchildren. At that point, beyond the military there is really no reason to adopt the facade of masculinity, to play act the man, except that being a man is what is befitting to Jackrum. At that point we are given a glimpse into Jackrum the trans-man, a transgender woman who transitioned to a man some time ago and only now fully realizes and accepts it.

Before Jackrum returned to his son he gave Polly a bit of advice: "whatever it is you are going to do . . . do it as you . . . Good or bad, do it as you. Too many lies and there's no truth to go back to."[48] What are we to make of this as Jackrum returns to his son play acting a man? Well, maybe being a man is true for Jackrum, maybe that is his truth. No more lies about being a woman dressed as a man, but the truth, the simple affirmation that Jackrum is a man, vagina be damned. And here Jackrum lets us see the fundamental insight of Judith Butler's theory of gender.

For Butler, all gender is a performance, and each actor is always already on the stage, performing. We are never outside of the play of gender. That doesn't diminish the importance of gender, it affirms it, and it affirms the importance of doing one's gender well. "In this sense gender is always a doing, though not a doing by a subject who might be said to preexist the deed."[49] Underneath it all there wasn't the essence of a male Jackrum waiting to burst out. The performance of Jackrum as male constituted Jackrum as male. That's all there is, the performance. We don't have a latent gender identity waiting to express itself. Instead, we adopt roles and play act our way across the gender stage, choosing, adopting, and altering our roles as they seem to fit. This is why gender is so tenuous.

Gender is "the repeated stylization of the body, a set of repeated acts within a highly rigid regulatory frame that congeal over time to produce the appearance of substance, of a natural sort of being."[50] Gender is a constant restyling of one's sexed body, a constant play of meanings within a cultural space. Over time this style acquires the appearance of a substance, of a stable identity. And in fact it becomes impossible to think ourselves beyond or outside of our gender. "Discrete genders are part of what 'humanizes' individuals . . . [even if] the postulation of a true gender identity [is] revealed as a regulatory fiction."[51] Gender serves a very real regulatory role in crafting and maintaining our identities. "It is through sex . . . an imaginary point determined by the deployment of sexuality . . . that each individual has to pass in order to have access to his own intelligibility."[52] Even as frail, fluid, and tenuous our gender forms part of the foundation of our identities, identities we are able to craft over time. Our gender is a constitutive part of our self-image, how we understand ourselves and our places in society. We can't think ourselves outside of gender. But it is always a construct, always a performance, even if we forget that we are acting. There is no gendered substance at the heart of it all. And this fiction is often coercive; it has power, at least so long as we forget its origin or reinforce the illusion.

Although gender is a performance, it is a performance within a system of power, a punitive system. As noted above, women who perform femininity poorly are chastised, they are bad women. The same goes for men. Other deviations such as those of trans-individuals are downright monstrous, pushing the very limits of the concept of gender and exploding our understanding of it. So "we punish those who fail to do their gender right."[53] But when gender is asserted against the individual the regulatory fiction becomes constrictive, it inhibits the expression of that person, it delimits a sphere of acceptable behavior, the transgression of which leads to that person being ostracized and even the victim of violence. When something is deemed an "abomination unto Nuggan," it's not just moral reprisals one earns. It can lead to punitive legal punishments and violent outbursts from those in society who feel threatened when their fantasy of gender norms is questioned. Consider again how Dee and other conservatives reacted to Cheery. Non-conformity is a threat to the established order, in this case the system of meaning whereby our gendered identities are crafted and reinforced. When this is torn asunder, when this is questioned, the very core of our self-understanding, our values, are put into question. This is uncomfortable, and such discomfort can lead to conservative reactionaries striking out at those who've put their system into question. Motivated by ignorance, fear, and insecurity, gender non-conformity is an easy target, and one it is easy to rally the troops behind. But it is these abominations, these monsters, that lay bare the illusion of gender and in fact open up greater possibilities for all people. "The monster is the transgression of natural limits, the transgression of classifications, of the table, and of the law of the table."[54] And this transgression is in the end liberating. Our forgetfulness conceals the origin of gender as a social construct and its nature as performative. Remembering can be unsettling, but in the end it frees us from the chains of the illusion of gender essentialism and the restrictive social systems predicated thereon.

For Dwarfs, Golems, and even Humans, Gender's a Drag

Mimi Marinucci notes that "one way to challenge a binary opposition is to deny or ignore the distinction it identifies . . . the goal is the proliferation of categories."[55] These monstrous women like Polly and Jackrum, these outliers like Gladys and Cheery, do something through their transgressions: they explode the gender binary, demonstrating its contingent nature, while laying bare the fact that its construction is predicated on a desire to control, to impose a hierarchy that privileges some to the detriment of others. Butler highlights how drag and the drag performer exemplify this type of transgression. According to Butler transvestites are unsettling because they "challenge . . . the distinction between appearance and reality that structures a good deal of popular thinking about gender identity. If the 'reality' of gender is constituted by the performance itself, then there is no recourse to an essential and unrealized 'sex' or 'gender' which gender performances ostensibly express."[56] The question about whether "it" is really a girl or boy becomes nonsensical, "it" is what "it" performs itself to be. The Ha'ak challenges the settled categories of gender and not only unsettles them to the point where other genders must be recognized, but highlights the tenuous nature of gender itself. Jackrum can be a man. Gladys can be a woman.

Drag disrupts the extant system of categories and demonstrates the emperor has no clothes, or is a transvestite. "Drag fully subverts the distinction . . . and mocks both the expressive model of gender and the notion of a true gender identity."[57] Drag shows that all gender is performance and, in fact, a performance or imitation without an original. Consider the rupert in drag near the end of *Monstrous Regiment*. Surely he is performing the role of "woman," and in a way better than actual women, or rather females. But the other females, Polly and her comrades, even as girls, were performing the role of "woman." So the rupert is imitating an imitation, he is play acting a role that is always already a role, not a determined essence. That is why he can be so good at it, and even better than Polly and the rest of the Ins and Outs. When they performed "woman" they didn't know they were performing, they were obeying social pressures and avoiding all abominations unto Nuggan. They weren't at root women, or essentially women. They were females who were coerced to perform as women. The rupert's imitation shows gender to be the charade that it is: "in *imitating gender, drag implicitly reveals the imitative structure of gender itself—as well as its contingency* . . . Indeed the parody is *of* the very notion of an original . . . gender fashions itself as an imitation without an origin."[58] The parody of gender liberates by disavowing the given authority of gender, by subverting its claim to being natural. In that act of subversion drag liberates us from the constraints of a reified gender and the social controls employed to maintain that system of illusion. Polly, Jackrum, Cheery, Gladys, and the rest are radical but probably not in the way Pratchett intended. They aren't radical because they show the reader that a girl can do anything a boy can do; they are radical because they get to the root of gender, they show its contingent nature and how one might employ various strategies to subvert, manipulate, and control gender for their own purposes as agents.

Through his examples in the Discworld Pratchett lays bare both the meaningfulness of gender, its profound impact on one's social possibilities and identity, while simultaneously demonstrating its contingent and tenuous nature. Thus we are offered an account of not only what gender is, but how one can employ it to define and thus realize oneself in society. Destabilizing the concept of gender allows us to see beyond the rigidity of the past and opens up greater possibilities for those individuals who can't or simply don't want to fit themselves into a restrictive gender binary. One isn't born, but rather becomes, one's gender. This is true for golems, dwarfs, trolls, humans, all of us. When it comes to performing gender we'd be wise to heed Sergeant Jackrum: "whatever it is you are going to do . . . do it as you."[59]

Notes

1. M. Foucault (1999) *Abnormal: Lectures at the Collège de France 1974–1975*, edited V. Marchetti and A. Salomoni, translated G. Burchell (New York: Picador), pp. 55–6.
2. Ibid., p. 63.
3. J. Hannam (2007) *Feminism* (Harlow, UK: Pearson Education), pp. 3–4.
4. Ibid., p. 4.
5. J. Butler (2006) *Gender Trouble: Feminism and the Subversion of Identity* (New York: Routledge Classics), p. 9.
6. T. Pratchett (2008) *Equal Rites* (New York: Harper) p. 30.
7. Ibid., p. 9.

8. M. Marinucci (2010) *Feminism is Queer: The Intimate Connection between Queer and Feminist Theory* (London: Zed Books), p. 5.
9. Pratchett, *Equal Rites*, p. 287.
10. T. Pratchett (2011) *The Wee Free Men: The Beginning* (New York: HarperCollins Publishers), pp. 7, 18.
11. Ibid., pp. 34–8.
12. S. de Beauvoir (1974) *The Second Sex*, translated and edited H.M. Parshley (New York: Vintage Books), p. xvii.
13. Ibid., p. 301.
14. T. Pratchett (2000) *Feet of Clay* (New York: Harpertorch), p. 350.
15. T. Pratchett (2004) *Going Postal* (London: Corgi Books), pp. 35, 112, 208.
16. Ibid., p. 262.
17. Beauvoir, *Second Sex*, p. 285.
18. Ibid., p. 592.
19. T. Pratchett (2007) *Making Money* (New York: HarperCollins Publishers), pp. 19, 71, 143, 363.
20. Ibid., p. 222.
21. Ibid.
22. J. Butler (2008) "Performative Acts and Gender Constitution: An Essay in Phenomenology and Feminist Theory" in *The Feminist Philosophy Reader*, edited Alison Bailey and Chris Cuomo (New York: McGraw-Hill Higher Education), p. 99.
23. Ibid.
24. Marinucci, *Feminism is Queer*, p. 69.
25. Pratchett, *Making Money*, p. 363.
26. T. Pratchett (2010) *Unseen Academicals* (New York: HarperCollins), pp. 142–6.
27. Ibid., p. 144.
28. Pratchett, *Feet of Clay*, p. 92.
29. Marinucci, *Feminism is Queer*, p. 76.
30. Beauvoir, *Second Sex*, p. 759.
31. Pratchett, *Feet of Clay*, pp. 180, 208, 249.
32. T. Pratchett (2000b) *The Fifth Elephant* (New York: HarperCollins), pp. 156–281.
33. Beauvoir, *Second Sex*, p. 316.
34. Pratchett, *Fifth Elephant*, p. 282.
35. Beauvoir, *Second Sex*, p. 802.
36. S. James (2003) "Complicity and Slavery in *The Second Sex*" in *The Cambridge Companion to Simone de Beauvoir*, edited Claudia Card (Cambridge: Cambridge University Press), p. 152.
37. Pratchett, *Fifth Elephant*, p. 304.
38. Butler, *Gender Trouble*, p. 9.

39. Ibid., p. 151.
40. T. Pratchett (2004) *Monstrous Regiment* (New York: HarperTorch), p. 3.
41. Ibid., p. 33.
42. Ibid., p. 238.
43. Butler, "Performative Acts," p. 97.
44. Ibid.
45. Ibid., p. 98.
46. Ibid., p. 103.
47. Pratchett, *Monstrous Regiment*, p. 271.
48. Ibid., p. 379.
49. Butler, *Gender Trouble*, p. 34.
50. Ibid., p. 45.
51. Ibid., pp. 190, 192.
52. M. Foucault (1990) *The History of Sexuality—Volume I: An Introduction*, translated Robert Hurley (New York: Vintage Books), p. 155.
53. Butler, *Gender Trouble*, p. 190.
54. Foucault, *Abnormal*, p. 63.
55. Marinucci, *Feminism is Queer*, p. 36.
56. Butler, "Performative Acts," p. 104.
57. Butler, *Gender Trouble*, p. 186.
58. Ibid., pp. 187–8.
59. Pratchett, *Monstrous Regiment*, p. 379.

Bibliography

Beauvoir, S. de (1974) *The Second Sex*, translated and edited H.M. Parshley (New York: Vintage Books).

Butler, J. (2006) *Gender Trouble: Feminism and the Subversion of Identity* (New York: Routledge Classics).

_____ (2008) "Performative Acts and Gender Constitution: An Essay in Phenomenology and Feminist Theory" in *The Feminist Philosophy Reader*, edited Alison Bailey and Chris Cuomo (New York: McGraw-Hill Higher Education).

Card, C. (2003) "Introduction: Beauvoir and the Ambiguity of 'Ambiguity' in Ethics" in *The Cambridge Companion to Simone de Beauvoir*, translated Claudia Card (Cambridge: Cambridge University Press).

Foucault, M. (1990) *The History of Sexuality—Volume I: An Introduction*, translated Robert Hurley (New York: Vintage Books).

_____ (1999) *Abnormal: Lectures at the Collège de France 1974–1975*, edited Valerio Marchetti and Antonella Salomoni, translated Graham Burchell (New York: Picador).

Hannam, J. (2007) *Feminism* (Harlow, UK: Pearson Education Limited).

James, S. (2003) "Complicity and Slavery in *The Second Sex*" in *The Cambridge Companion to Simone de Beauvoir*, edited Claudia Card (Cambridge: Cambridge University Press).

Marinucci, M. (2010) *Feminism is Queer: The Intimate Connection between Queer and Feminist Theory* (London: Zed Books).

Pratchett, T. (1987) *Equal Rites* (London: Victor Gollancz).

_____ (1996) *Feet of Clay* (New York: HarperCollins).

_____ (1999) *The Fifth Elephant* (New York: HarperCollins).

_____ (2003) *Monstrous Regiment* (New York: HarperCollins).

_____ (2003) *The Wee Free Men: The Beginning* (New York: HarperCollins).

_____ (2004) *Going Postal* (New York: HarperCollins).

_____ (2007) *Making Money* (New York: HarperCollins).

_____ (2009) *Unseen Academicals* (New York: HarperCollins).

2 "Nothing Like a Bit of Destiny to Get the Old Plot Rolling": A Philosophical Reading of *Wyrd Sisters*

James B. South

In what follows, I want to explore some themes and provide a philosophically informed reading of Terry Pratchett's Discworld novel *Wyrd Sisters*. There are three features of the novel that I think are important. They both aid us in understanding Pratchett's work more generally and also are themselves philosophically interesting positions. The three topics I want to focus on are (a) the concept of "destiny," (b) the role of storytelling, and (c) what I think is an ethical lesson we can draw from his treatment of the first two topics. One feature of *Wyrd Sisters* is especially relevant in my choice of this novel for a close reading: that it is explicitly about storytelling. A central figure in the novel is the dwarf playwright, Hwel, whose name pretty obviously serves two functions: as a doppelgänger of Will(iam) Shakespeare (as his shortened name shows) and (something that Pratchett wants to emphasize) the importance of human free will in the face of all the forces that we might characterize as "destiny." Of course, I could range across Pratchett's writings to show these themes, but I think a close reading of one novel is a more productive way to get at the way Pratchett thinks about these three topics.

Before moving to a discussion of the novel, though, I do want to start by taking a wider view, remarking upon several facts about Terry Pratchett as he has disclosed himself to his readers in interviews and non-fiction. First, we know that Pratchett does not believe in God, though as a writer he creates gods all the time. As he puts it in an interview: "there is a rumour going around that I have found God. I think this is unlikely because I have enough difficulty finding my keys, and there is empirical evidence that they exist." In the same interview, he recounts a story his mother told him about two families living in London during World War II:

> They lived in a pair of semi-detached houses. The daughter of one was due to get married to the son of the other and on the night before the wedding a German bomb destroyed the members of both families who were staying in those houses in one go, except for the sailor brother of the groom, who arrived in time to help scrabble through the wreckage with his bare hands.

And he continues: "like many of the stories she told me, this had an enormous effect on me. I thought it was a miracle. It was exactly the same shape as a miracle. It was just . . . reversed."[1] In the statements, we can sense his early fascination with the power of stories, but there is something worth highlighting here that will help us to understand a central theme of *Wyrd Sisters*.

The reverse shape of a miracle could be construed as a mirror image of a miracle, and there are two features of mirrors that are interesting. First, they are distorting, that is, holding a mirror up to something shows whatever it's reflecting in reverse. Second, though, there is a sense in which mirrors only function if there's something they can be held up to, as it were. That is, a mirror by itself is a blank surface. As such, looking into one can also be revelatory of what is in front of it. I see myself in a mirror, and while the image may be reversed, I have to look at myself, confront myself. The blankness of the mirror calls to me to think about myself. This feature of mirrors is usually captured by the way we say things such as "he has to look at himself in the mirror every day." That can be a sign of our chagrin about a person, a way of washing our hands of a situation. The emphasis here is on the "he," and I am able to escape responsibility for confronting such a person by more or less simply saying that what I see is there for him to see, if he would only look. But at the same time, holding a mirror up to myself can cause me to see myself. I have to get up every morning and look at myself in the mirror. How do I decide if I like what I see?

Second, as this interview demonstrates, Pratchett has an enormous respect for stories and their affect on human imagination. Elsewhere, in writing about "imagination," Pratchett makes that point emphatically:

> that ability has given us all our fiction and our mythology. Most of our religions, too, because following the success of "What Thunder Is" and its sequel "How We Got Fire," which was breaking pile-of-juicy-mammoth-ribs records all along the valley, some bright apprentice with a forehead like a balcony came up with the incredible "We Can Stop the Thunderer Hurting Us If We Do These Special Things" followed by "We Are The True People And We're Better Than Those People In The Next Valley Because We Do These Special Things."

And he concludes, "suddenly the world was a story. Home Sapiens became Homo Narrans 'Story-telling Man'; the rest was, literally, history."[2]

What I find especially interesting here is the sheer *importance* Pratchett places on the role of stories. While not discounting the significance of our powers to know the world (*Homo sapiens*), he claims that *the* most important quality that makes us human is our ability to tell ourselves (and convince others of the value) of our stories. This contrast between knowledge and imagination is a crucial one for Pratchett, which can be brought out more clearly when we reflect upon his view of the world. That view directs our attention to a specific picture of the relation between humans and the world. When he writes, in the same work, in praise of stories that "a raft of fantasies, 'made-up things,' floats us through the cold, dark universe" we have to pause and catch our breath. The "cold, dark universe" is a striking image and while he does not elaborate on just what he means there, he certainly does elsewhere.

One interpretation of "the cold, dark universe" is present in the well-known passage in *Hogfather*, where Pratchett has Death tell his "granddaughter," Susan:

THEN TAKE THE UNIVERSE AND GRIND IT DOWN TO THE FINEST POWDER AND SIEVE IT THROUGH THE FINEST SIEVE AND THEN *SHOW* ME ONE ATOM OF JUSTICE, ONE MOLECULE OF MERCY. AND YET—Death waved a hand. AND YET YOU ACT AS IF THERE IS SOME IDEAL ORDER IN THE WORLD, AS IF THERE IS SOME . . . SOME *RIGHTNESS* IN THE UNIVERSE BY WHICH IT MAY BE JUDGED.

This is a complex saying, and its complexity suffuses the story Pratchett tells in *Wyrd Sisters*. Here I initially want to note the "as if" in the passage. Humans *have* to tell a story about how they fit into the cold, dark universe, they *have* to try to make the universe inhabitable. As Death continues:

CORRECT. STARS EXPLODE, WORLDS COLLIDE, THERE'S HARDLY ANYWHERE IN THE UNIVERSE WHERE HUMANS CAN LIVE WITHOUT BEING FROZEN OR FRIED, AND YET YOU BELIEVE THAT A . . . A BED IS A NORMAL THING. IT IS THE MOST AMAZING TALENT.[3]

It is this "most amazing talent" that also creates one of the driving forces of so many stories, that of "destiny." This term and our understandings of it take us to the heart of the human story. Destiny is something we use to give our lives a meaning, though it does so from outside us. But, like the mirror, there is a multiplicity of meanings running through its use. On the one hand, it consoles us—what happened was meant to happen. On the other hand, though, as I hope to show, *Wyrd Sisters* makes clear that such a view of destiny is an illusion, or story, or fantasy. It may serve a necessary function in our lives as those who need stories in the "cold, dark universe," but it simply isn't real, any more than justice is, or mercy, or an ideal order. Beds are not normal things in our world, yet they're things we're intimately familiar with and they are real. But these ordinary things are extraordinary. Destiny, by contrast, is an extraordinary concept, one of a host of stories we tell ourselves, but it is on a par with the story we tell ourselves about beds being normal. As Granny Weatherwax, one of the three witches in *Wyrd Sisters*, states, "'Oh, *obvious*,' said Granny. 'I'll grant you it's *obvious*. Trouble is, just because things are obvious doesn't mean they're true.'"[4] As we shall see, "destiny" is obvious, but it isn't true.

Returning to the account of the story Pratchett's mother told him, which had the reverse shape of a miracle, he asks a series of questions: "Did the sailor thank his god that the bomb had missed him? Or did he curse because it had not missed his family? If the sailor had given thanks, wouldn't he be betraying his family? If God saved one, He could have saved the rest, couldn't He? After all, isn't God in charge? Why does He act as if He isn't? Does He want us to act as if He isn't, too?"[5] It's that last question that ties into the topic of destiny. If we act as if God isn't in charge, then it's tempting to replace God with "destiny." But the force of Pratchett's litany of questions is to make us question, and surely God substitutes are as questionable as God. If destiny can be both obvious, but not true, the question that imposes itself on our minds is how we're supposed to act without such foundations as God or an ideal order in the universe. As Pratchett knows only too well, there are lots of stories we tell ourselves that are obvious, but not true, yet provide a basis for our actions: "the mental muscles swollen on the aerobics of gods and heroes have gone on to invent new fantasies 'natural justice,' 'eminent domain,' 'human rights,' which have given something approaching solid form."[6] The paramount problem, then, is to be able to distinguish between fantasies that help us live our lives and those that keep us from living our lives.

"When shall we three meet again?" "Well, I can do next Tuesday"

Let's consider the title of *Wyrd Sisters*. There's an obvious pun, since the spelling of 'wyrd' suggests 'weird,' and there's no doubt that in the everyday sense of the term Granny Weatherwax, Gytha "Nanny" Ogg, and Magrat Garlick, the three witches in the novel, are weird in their own ways. But more importantly, the spelling "wyrd" reminds us that the word "weird" is based on the Anglo-Saxon word "wyrd," which has the connotation of fate or destiny. So, the very title of the book inscribes the notion of destiny as being at the center of its concern. At the same time, the title of the book also reminds us of *Macbeth*, which includes three witches, called "weird sisters," and who inform Macbeth that he is destined to be king. And this, too, has its parallel in *Wyrd Sisters*, where Duke Felmet, the cousin of King Verence, murders Verence to become king of the region known as Lancre. And like Macbeth, Felmet has an ambitious wife, Lady Felmet. Indeed, the references to Macbeth pile up repeatedly throughout the book, most notably in the way that Felmet, once he becomes King, repeatedly scratches at the hand that held the knife he used to kill Verence. "'If he could wash the blood off,' he told himself, 'it wouldn't have happened.'"[7] While that is Lady Macbeth's curse in Shakespeare's play, it is his in this novel. This is fitting since he is the one who murdered the king. This shift tells us something about how Pratchett views human responsibility. No one made Felmet kill Verence, not the witches, not Lady Felmet, and especially not destiny as some sort of impersonal force in the world. He wanted to have a kingdom and now he has one. I'll return to this difference below, but it needs highlighting now.

In addition, it is worth drawing attention to another significant difference between *Macbeth* and *Wyrd Sisters*. The witches in the latter did not tell Felmet he was destined to be king, thereby setting in motion his murder of Verence. Indeed, the witches in *Wyrd Sisters*, through their language, their ordinary lives, and their appearance, bear little resemblance to the witches in *Macbeth*. They are not evil crones, or harbingers of dark news, or connected with the forces of the underworld. Indeed, the very ordinariness of their exchange at their first meeting in the novel is deflationary: "'When shall we three meet again?' 'Well, I can do next Tuesday.'"[8]

Still, there are conventions to story-telling, and *Wyrd Sisters* follows those conventions, even if its ultimate effect is to subvert them. So, this being a story about a murdered king, it turns out that Verence had a son, who was taken by Verence's allies to the witches for safe-keeping. Knowing they couldn't keep the baby without risk of his being found by Felmet's troops, they decide to give the child to others who will take care of him. They find a theater troupe and offer to the husband, Olwyn Vitoller, and his wife the opportunity to raise the child, whom they name Tomjon. Here again, there's an opportunity to invoke destiny. Surely, the story goes, Tomjon will one day return to Lancre and avenge his father's murder and become the King of Lancre. That's the way we would expect the story to go; it's the way the witches more or less expect the story to go.

As the witches go back to their respective cottages, they each bestow a wish on the baby. Magrat wishes that "he will make friends easily." Nanny Ogg wishes: "A bloody good memory is what he ought to have. He'll always remember the words." Granny Weatherwax's wish is the most potent of all: "Let him be whoever he thinks he is. That's all anybody could hope for in this world."[9] Here, again, we see the working of destiny, but in a way that undoes its typical effect. If it's traditional for the witches to bestow these wishes, then there is some sort of destiny at work. But if Tomjon is destined to be whoever he thinks he is, then there's no necessity in fulfilling the story-shaped destiny of becoming king and avenging his father's death. And a further question arises, which I will explore in due course: in what sense is being who you think you are destiny?

"You'd have to be a born fool to be a king"

In his provocative essay on *King Lear*, "The Avoidance of Love," the philosopher Stanley Cavell writes of that play:

> It is a drama not about the given condition in which the soul finds itself (in relation to Gods or to earth) but about the soul, as Schopenhauer puts the vision of Kant, as the provider of the given, of the conditions under which Gods and earth can appear. It is an enactment not of fate but of responsibility, including the responsibility for fate.[10]

What I am suggesting in this chapter is that Pratchett is providing us with a similar representation—simply substitute "destiny" for "fate." The phrase "the soul as the provider of the given" is as good a way as any to characterize what Pratchett means when he speaks of the power of the imagination in creating fantasies by which we shape our lives. Pratchett has Tomjon enact his responsibility, including his destiny to be king, but in ways that subvert our expectations. It's destiny reversed, as it were. As Granny says early in the novel, "You'd have to be a born fool to be a king."[11]

Before I go on to show how that subversion of expectations plays out in the novel, let me add a few additional points. In another essay, "Ending the Waiting Game," Cavell makes the following stark claim in relation to Samuel Beckett's play, *Endgame* (incidentally, *Waiting for Godot* is referenced briefly in *Wyrd Sisters*):

> [It] is about an effort to undo, to end something by undoing it, and in particular to end a curse, and moreover the commonest. Most ordinary curse of man—not so much that he was ever born and must die, but that he has to figure out the one and shape up to the other and justify what comes between, and that he is not a beast and not a god; in a word,

that he is a man, and alone. All those, however, are the facts of life; the curse comes in the ways we try to deny them.[12]

This complex claim has many ramifications, but what is especially relevant to *Wyrd Sisters* is the way that Pratchett seems very aware that the stories we tell are ways to deny these "facts of life." So, while we usually think of witches as cursing us, in the novel we find out that that could be a way to avoid recognizing the facts of life. And using "destiny" to justify what comes between being born and dying is also a denial of the responsibility for our fate.

King Verence, as would be customary in such tales, had a Fool, a professional Fool, that is, a graduate of the Fool's Guild. When Verence was murdered, the Fool was duty bound to follow the new king, Felmet. In the course of talking with Felmet and his wife, the Fool shows that he is no fool:

> "In . . . in the Guild," said the Fool, "we learned that words can be more powerful even than magic."
>
> "Clown!" said the Duke. "Words are just words. Brief syllables. Sticks and stones may break my bones"—he paused, savoring the thought—"but words can never hurt me."
>
> "My Lord, there are such words that can," said the Fool. "Liar! Usurper! Murderer!"[13]

The lesson I want to take from this brief exchange is that the Fool has landed on one way in which we can deny the facts of life: we can redescribe them and, in doing so, come to think about the world differently, and cause others to do so as well. The words we use, the stories we tell, are, as Cavell points out, our responsibility, not dependent on the facts of life such as birth and death, or words that deny our responsibility, such as "fate" or "destiny." That is, we have to justify our uses of words as well as the more complex stories we make out of our words. As *Wyrd Sisters* continues, we see many ways in which the witches work to undo the curse of both words and stories.

"And as for thinking it could be controlled"

A year after leaving Tomjon with Vitoller and his wife, the witches discover that the kingdom is unhappy with Felmet. To be more precise, the land and the creatures dependent on the land are being neglected. As Granny explains:

A kingdom is made up of all sorts of things. Ideas. Loyalties. Memories. It all sort of exists together. And then all these things create some kind of life. Not a body kind of life, more like a living idea. Made up of everything that's alive and what they're thinking. And what the people *before* them thought.[14]

In reading this passage, we hear a colloquial echo of Ludwig Wittgenstein's notion of a "form of life." Wittgenstein writes that "to imagine a language means to imagine a form of life."[15] This is a lesson the Fool knows only too well. The literature on just what Wittgenstein means by a form of life is vast, and adjudicating between the various interpretations is beyond the scope of this chapter. My favorite account of the extensiveness of a form of life, though, is well summed up, again by Cavell, in the following description:

We learn and teach words in certain contexts, and then we are expected, and expect others, to be able to project them into further contexts. Nothing ensures that this projection will take place (in particular, not the grasping of universals nor the grasping of books of rules), just as nothing insures that we will make, and understand, the same projections. That on the whole we do is a matter of our sharing routes of interest and feeling, senses of humor and of significance and of fulfillment, of what is outrageous, of what is similar to what else, what a rebuke, what forgiveness, of when an utterance is an assertion, when an appeal, when an explanation— all the whirl of organism Wittgenstein calls "forms of life." Human speech and activity, sanity and community, rest on nothing more, but nothing less, than this. It is a vision as simple as it is difficult, and as difficult as it is (and because it is) terrifying.[16]

But when in *Wyrd Sisters* Granny comes to realize that the *kingdom* of Lancre has a mind, as she puts it, "metterforically," what are we to make of that? It can't be just the case that humans in the kingdom are upset, though that's partly the case. After all, Felmet has been burning cottages with people still in them and dispatching people he thinks are disloyal to him. These are not actions designed to make subjects happy. But Granny is pointing to a different aspect of the form of life of Lancre, and it's one not just dependent on language. Cavell explains that to speak of a form of life as merely conventional—as the Fool's words imply—is to miss an essential aspect of the notion, one having to do with emphasis—we should not think of *forms* of life, but instead forms of *life*. After all, as Cavell points out, there's a difference between poking at your food and pawing at your food.[17] And who is to say that Granny is wrong when she thinks to herself, "animals had minds. People had minds, although human minds were vague foggy things. Even insects had minds, little pointy bits of light in the darkness of non-mind." It's then that Granny realizes that the kingdom's mind was "made up of all the other little minds inside it."[18]

Once this realization occurs to Granny, she opens her front door and finds herself confronted by birds and bears, rabbits, weasels, vermin, badgers, foxes, and other creatures. She's put out—actually more accurately thrown outside herself by this experience of a kingdom's reality. Still, she falls back on a fundamental rule of being a witch; she can't meddle. But, in the end she does. As Nanny Ogg explains, "as you progress in the Craft, you'll learn there is another rule . . . When you break rules, break 'em good and hard."[19] And here, in Nanny Ogg's rule, we get a good sense of how one is responsible for one's actions and how one can justify what comes between being born and dying.

So, the witches do meddle, and they meddle good and hard: they move time in Lancre forward 15 years so that Tomjon will be old enough to come back and claim his rightful place on the throne, thereby avenging his father's murder at the hand of Felmet. After all, that's his destiny. Meanwhile, thanks to the Fool's suggestion about the power of words, Felmet sends the Fool to Ankh-Morpork to recruit Hwel and his company, now including a 15-years-older Tomjon, to perform a play in Lancre that will show him as the rightful claimant to the throne and cast the witches in a bad light. This confrontation between the power of words and Granny's meddling leads to the conclusion of the play and the undoing of the notion of destiny and the confounding of Granny's meddling.

"Destiny gets it wrong half the time"

As Hwel, Tomjon, and company arrive in Lancre to stage the play Felmet wants, Granny finds herself worried. She senses the power of the theater:

> It changed the world, and said things were otherwise than they were. And it was magic that didn't belong to magical people. It was commanded by ordinary people, who didn't know the rules. They altered the world because it sounded better.[20]

There's something a bit confusing here. Pratchett has said all along that the world is what it is for us because of the stories we tell. But now we find Granny thinking, "I want the world the way it is."[21] But we know the way the world is; Death has shown us that there is nothing to it that is friendly to humans other than the stories we tell. There is no atom of justice or molecule of mercy. Yet we think beds are normal. We are by nature fantasists, so how can Granny slip between "is" and fantasy? The answer to that question will become apparent as the narrative proceeds.

The novel now reaches its climax, as the reader (and characters) wait to see how Tomjon will fulfill his destiny. As Granny watches Hwel's play unfold, she knows that what she sees on stage is not true, but she also gains a new appreciation of the power of words. And then she realizes what is wrong with the theater. She thinks to herself: "this is Art holding a Mirror up to Life. That's why everything is exactly the wrong way around."[22] There is, Pratchett intimates here, a distinction waiting to be made between the stories that we tell, our forms of life, and art with a capital A. I take it that this amounts to both an acknowledgment of the power of art and storytelling, but also a warning to the reader that not all stories are equal to our forms of life; they distort our sense of the reality appropriate to our lives, what Cavell calls our "sharing routes of interest and feeling." Some stories, for example the story Felmet and the Duchess tell themselves about ruling Lancre, are stories that fail the test of responsibility and justification, because they are not in tune with the routes of interest and feeling of the community they seek to inhabit. They are like those images in mirrors that give a distorted image of the world, a reverse image. Other stories, the stories that Granny and all the animal and insect minds of Lancre know, are somehow truthful, responsible, and justificatory because they do share in a communal form of life. They are more fitting for us. But how can we *know* the difference?

Well, one thing we might ask ourselves here is what "knowing the difference" might mean. After all, knowing is only one aspect of *our* form of life. As Cavell notes in his reading of *King Lear*: "the medium [Shakespearean tragedy] is one which keeps significance continuously before our sense, so that when it comes over us that we have missed it, this discovery will reveal our ignorance to have been willful, complicitous, a refusal to see."[23] I think something very much like this effort to keep what's happening continually before us as we read is something that Pratchett is attempting to do as well. His medium is hardly the same as Shakespearean tragedy, but in his persistent effort to see the action of the story through the eyes of the various characters—Granny, Felmet, the Duchess, Verence, the Fool, et al.—he forces us to do the same. In fact, as we will see, no one has truly understood what is about to unfold, though they all think they do. There is a persistent undoing of all the stories lodged in the characters' heads about destiny, kingship, magic, and even themselves.

As the play within the novel progresses, Hwel realizes there's something wrong, as does Tomjon. Tomjon's unease is seen in his thought that "Hwel had said everything about the play was fine except the play itself."[24] As a concrete warning to the reader about the danger of the confusion between reality and its mirror, the king's soldiers arrest the actors playing the three witches in the play; after all, they look the part and fit the false story the play is trying to tell about witches. This action provides Granny, Nanny, and Magrat a chance to slip on stage and "act" the witches' parts. Again, the intrusion of reality within the mirror image of the play can't help but make us aware of the discrepancy and the reverse image of the play's artifice. As the play's "Evil King" and "Good Duke" get ready for their climactic duel, the contrast with what really happened is striking, since the reader knows that the Duke murdered the King; there was no duel. Meanwhile, the witches do ordinary things sitting around the cauldron on stage. Magrat tears at the cardboard fire underneath the cauldron, Nanny starts to clean the cauldron, and Granny just sits with her arms folded staring at Tomjon, who is playing the Evil King, knowing that he is the son of the vilely murdered Verence. He's playing a role that is not true to himself.

"Bugger destiny"

Finally, amidst all this chaos and the various intrusions of reality within its mirror image, all the actors break down, forgetting their lines while watching the witches' behavior. Granny speaks directly to Tomjon whose confusion is graphically represented in his playing not only the role of his own father, but also playing it falsely, as if he were an evil king: "Ghosts of the mind and all device away, I bid the Truth to have . . . its tumpty-tumpty day."[25] (The "tumpty-tumpty" had previously been used by Nanny to mimic iambic pentameter.) At that point, the actors revert to speaking and showing what *really* happened more than 15 years ago, not what the play had been enacting: the Evil Duke, with the urging of the Duchess, murdered the rightful King. Felmet, sitting in the audience, is mortified by the appearance, not of the actor playing Death, but Death himself, who enters the stage knowing someone is about to die for real, not the kind of death that occurs in plays when characters die.

While Felmet and the Duchess deny all wrongdoing, the Fool steps from behind the curtain and confesses that he was present at the king's murder and had seen it all. Felmet proceeds to start stabbing, with a prop knife, first the Fool and then everyone else he can reach on stage. Eventually, going mad, he jumps up onto a castle wall, loses his balance and plunges to his death. On stage, Granny uses her "headology" to reveal to the Duchess who she really is. To Granny's surprise, this does not cause the Duchess to break down, but if anything makes her more determined. At that point, Nanny steps forward and, using the stage cauldron, delivers a blow to the Duchess's head, knocking her out. The guards take her away.

And now we come to the point in the story where "destiny gets it wrong half the time." After all, if the odds are 50/50, there's really no destiny at all; it's a matter of chance. One is always free to do something else. Granny tries to explain to Tomjon that he's the king's son and he *must* now become king. He balks, saying he doesn't know how to be king and that he likes acting. We find the two characters at an impasse. What can Granny do? For all of her meddling, which she has done for the sake of the kingdom and its form of life, destiny refuses to cooperate. Of course it does, because there is no such thing. As with justice and mercy, there is no molecule or atom of destiny in the universe. But still we think that there must be. After all, we tell stories about it, we fantasize about it. It makes our world humanly hospitable and intelligible to us.

Magrat, now sitting beside the Fool backstage, is the one who first recognizes a resemblance between the Fool and Tomjon. When Tomjon, refusing his destiny, declines to accept the crown from the mayor, Magrat drags the Fool over to the assembled officials ready to crown a new king. It transpires, we learn, that Granny convinces the assembled town leaders that Tomjon and the Fool are both King Verence's sons, though by different mothers. And here destiny returns but with a twist. As we learn at the very end of the novel, Granny was truthful, but not honest. The Fool and Tomjon *are* half-brothers. But instead of the usual way of thinking about that in contexts of kingly succession, namely that they have the same father, in reality they're both sons of the former queen. Tomjon *is* the son of King Verence and his wife, but the Fool, now king, is the son of a mere handsome former inhabitant of Lancre who had an affair with the queen while the king was away. So, the new king, the Fool now renamed Verence II, was not destined to be king because he has none of the king's blood in him. The entire idea of a royal destiny is shown to be literally foolish, and Tomjon, who really was the heir of the king, does not have to accept his royal destiny.

There is an interesting exchange after Tomjon, Hwel, and their company leave Lancre. Hwel and Tomjon are talking and Hwel suggests that, between the money Verence II gave them and their successful performances in the countryside, they could afford to either stay in an inn or perhaps take a boat back to Ankh-Morpork. Tomjon will have nothing to do with this plan. Hwel relents:

> "You're your Father's son, and no mistake," said Hwel.
> Tomjon sat back and looked at himself in the mirror.
> "Yes," he said. "I thought I had better be."

The use of the mirror metaphor here is interesting. We know that Art holding a mirror up to life can get life backwards, but in this case what we're reminded of is that the facts of life, and the justification someone can provide for them, are beset with ambiguities and that looking at oneself in a mirror can reveal something about oneself. Tomjon, after all, believes he's King Verence's son, and yet being an actor is the way he decides to live out that inheritance, and he thinks this means he's his father's son. It's the way he chooses to be his father's son.

"Roads don't necessarily have to go anywhere, they just have to have somewhere to start"

In *Wyrd Sisters*, Pratchett has given us a story about stories and their power. He's given us an account of destiny that in fact undermines the concept. He's given us an account of moral responsibility and its hazards. And, finally, he's given us a meditation on the ironies attendant on taking life as it comes, not as it's shaped by us and our needs. In conclusion, I want to return to a couple of particularly difficult questions that have surfaced during this chapter. Perhaps the most complicated issues arose as Granny confronted the reality of the power of the theater and she responded with the thought that she wanted the world the way it is. But death has shown us one way the world is—not an atom of justice, a molecule of mercy, or an ideal order. But is that the only way the world is? After all, we live in a world where beds are normal. To get some purchase on this apparent contradiction, I think we can appeal to a thought of Iris Murdoch as explicated by Cora Diamond. Following a distinction made by Murdoch, Diamond emphasizes the "cloudy and shifting domain of the concepts which men live by" and contrasts that with "the hard world set up by science and logic."[26] Death's view of the universe is the hard world set up by science and logic. But that's not a world in which we invented beds with all of their various purposes. Beds and their variety of uses belong to the cloudy and shifting world of the concepts we live by. We return, then, to the idea of a Wittgensteinian form of life. We know what beds are for. We can also, if pushed, make sense of Granny's view that a kingdom and its creatures might have a stake in how they're viewed by those in charge. That's the reality that Granny recognizes that is left out in the form of theater she was witnessing. Yet it is precisely the imaginative gift of Pratchett to help us see that this is the way our world is, no matter how often we deny it.

Relevant, here, is the way the Duchess meets her end. She manages to escape from her dungeon cell in the castle and goes racing through the forest. But she quickly senses something is amiss. There seem to be too many trees, for one thing. As Pratchett describes the scene: "It was at this point that the track opened out into a clearing that hadn't been there the day before and wouldn't be there tomorrow, a clearing in which the moonlight glittered off assembled antlers and fangs and serried ranks of glowing eyes." As she rushes headlong into this assembly of the kingdom's creatures, they close in on her. In devouring the person who did these creatures so much harm simply by encouraging her husband to kill Felmet and proceed not to care about the kingdom, Pratchett writes, "the kingdom exhaled."[27]

Returning to Diamond, the following claim she makes seems pertinent: "moral concepts in a sense 'set up' a world: they show what sorts of things there are, what it means to recognize them, what it is to live in a world with such things."[28] In relation to *Wyrd Sisters*, I hope this chapter has shown that Pratchett views the world from a deeply moral perspective. Death's "hard" world is a denial of what it is to be human, a rising ape whose essential humanity is found in story-telling and fantasy. But not all stories are equal and some do justice to the complexity of our lives better than others. Felmet and the Duchess see Lancre as a place to be ruled. Fair enough, that's what rulers do. But their vision is too narrow, too inward. It's all about what is in it for them. They can use stories to support that narrow view, but other stories can counter their stories. It may not be the story of destiny, as we have seen, and there may not be a destination to the road we are traveling: "Roads don't necessarily have to go anywhere, they just have to have somewhere to start."[29] In a cloudy and shifting moral universe, though, while the destination may not be clear, the way we make the journey does matter, and in *Wyrd Sisters* Pratchett has set forth a way to tell better stories to make up for the old, tired, and inadequate ones.

Notes

1. www.dailymail.co.uk/femail/article-1028222/I-create-gods-time–I-think-exist.html.
2. T. Pratchett (1999) "Foreword" in *The Ultimate Encyclopedia of Fantasy*, edited D. Pringle (Woodstock, NY: The Overlook Press), p. 6.
3. T. Pratchett (1996) *Hogfather* (London: Victor Gollancz), p. 381.
4. T. Pratchett (1988) *Wyrd Sisters* (New York: HarperTorch), p. 22.
5. www.dailymail.co.uk/femail/article-1028222/I-create-gods-time–I-think-exist.html.
6. Pratchett, "Foreword," p. 6.
7. Pratchett, *Wyrd Sisters*, p. 45.
8. Ibid., pp. 1, 3.
9. Ibid., p. 41.
10. S. Cavell (1969) "The Avoidance of Love" in *Must We Mean What We Say?* (New York: Charles Scribner's Sons), p. 310.
11. Pratchett, *Wyrd Sisters*, p. 24.
12. S. Cavell (1969) "Ending the Waiting Game," in *Must We Mean What We Say?*, op. cit., p. 122.
13. Pratchett, *Wyrd Sisters*, p. 68.
14. Ibid., p. 94.
15. L. Wittgenstein (1958) *Philosophical Investigations*, translated G.E.M. Anscombe (New York: Macmillan Company), § 19, p. 8e.
16. S. Cavell (1969) "The Availability of Wittgenstein's Later Philosophy," in *Must We Mean What We Say?*, op. cit., p. 52.
17. S. Cavell (1989) *This New Yet Unapproachable America* (Chicago: University of Chicago Press), p. 42.
18. Pratchett, *Wyrd Sisters*, p. 78.
19. Ibid., p. 136.
20. Ibid., p. 220.
21. Ibid., p. 221.
22. Ibid., p. 226.
23. Cavell, "The Avoidance of Love," p. 313.
24. Pratchett, *Wyrd Sisters*, p. 229.
25. Ibid., p. 236.

26. C. Diamond (2010) "Murdoch the Explorer," *Philosophical Topics* 38, pp. 53, 57.
27. Pratchett, *Wyrd Sisters*, p. 261.
28. Diamond, "Murdoch the Explorer," p. 62.
29. Pratchett, *Wyrd Sisters*, p. 208.

Bibliography

Cavell, S. (1969) *Must We Mean What We Say?* (New York: Charles Scribner's Sons).

_____ (1989) *This New Yet Unapproachable America*, reprint edn (Chicago: University of Chicago Press).

Diamond, C. (2010) "Murdoch the Explorer," *Philosophical Topics* 38.

Pratchett, T. (1988) *Wyrd Sisters* (New York: HarperTorch).

_____ (1996) *Hogfather* (London: Victor Gollancz).

3 "Feigning to Feign": Pratchett and the Maskerade

Andrew Rayment

Masques, veils, performance, and disguises; masks and masquerading; acting, playing, and play-acting—the novels in Pratchett's Discworld series endlessly vary on the theme of duplicity and doubling, endlessly enact the psychoanalytical truth that nothing is veiled by the veil except another veil. Putting Pratchett in dialogue with the thinking of Ervin Goffman, Joan Riviere, Jacques Lacan, Slavoj Žižek, Edward Said, and Judith Butler, this chapter will explore Pratchett's constant recycling of and riffing upon the notion that not only is the subject always in disguise, but that this disguise *is always already the only reality of the subject.*

It is characteristic of Pratchett, of course, to expose our intuitive understanding of the world as mistaken. Here, he takes on our intuitive understanding that there is an opposition between the fake surface mask and a hidden depth of reality behind it, or between 'being our real selves' and performing the roles that society demands of us. Time and time again, Pratchett dramatizes how our misperception of the mask deceives us into thinking that such simple binaries exist. In other words, he points to the fact that the mask does not hide the truth as such, but, rather, as a screen that points to something *non-existent* beyond itself, functions to obscure the strange relation of truth and lies to mask-wearing and performance.

The Edge of Things: Where Two States Collide

Theaters, theatrical performances, and theatrical performers are the very stuff of Pratchett's Discworld novels. Whole novels take forms of theater as the locus of their action (*Maskerade* (opera), *Moving Pictures* (movies), *Unseen Academicals* (soccer)[1]), while, in others, theatrical groups or performers play crucial roles in (sometimes literally) shaping the dramas unfolding around them: Vitoller's Strolling Players in *Wyrd Sisters*, for instance, or the Lancre Morris Men, who take up acting in *Lords and Ladies* (who are "not even good at bad acting"),[2] or Lady Sybil who performs Ironhammer's "Ransom Song" at a crucial juncture in the *Fifth Elephant*). These are supplemented by the many naïve definitions of theater offered in the novels (we can instance Vorbis's "'A lie. A history that does not exist and never existed . . . the . . . the things . . . like the tales told to children, who are too young . . . words for people to say . . . the'",[3] or Maladict's "'people pretending to be other people to tell a story in a huge room where the world is a different place'"[4]) and, above all, perhaps, by the huge number of those who constantly perform their way across the Discworld stage, ever alert to the fallout that would accompany an ignorant public seeing through their acts (Cut-Me-Own-Throat-Dibbler, Moist von Lipwig, Commander Vimes, Cohen the Barbarian, and Granny Weatherwax to name a few of the more obvious ones). The extent to which Pratchett is drawn to this realm is clear, then, but what exactly captures him? Since Granny Weatherwax is drawn to the theater because it has a kind of magic that is close enough to her own that she cannot leave it alone,[5] it is tempting to say the same of Pratchett (Granny is, after all, one of Pratchett's unofficial spokespersons): that he returns to theater again and again as a place "*at the edge of things*"[6] as a place close to *his* own kind of magic. Theater is a place where reality and fiction are blurred, each constantly spilling out of and overlapping the other. Can we not apply this description to Pratchett's fiction? The microcosm of the theater is, in other words, an analog and metaphor for what happens in the macrocosm of Pratchett's fiction. For on Discworld *theater spills out of the theater* so that the whole flat world becomes a stage. Every location on Discworld, in fact, resembles a set, and every character resembles, well, a character: how, indeed, can we say otherwise when it is made clear that, on Discworld, fretting about one's "performance" is an absolute and unmistakable constant?

Essential to performance is *costume*, of course, so it can come as no surprise either that Discworlders exhibit an extreme anxiety over the clothes that they wear or that their sartorial inclinations are invariably couched in terms of dressing for an audience. Most obviously we can point to the number of occasions in the Discworld series on which it is drawn to our attention that having a pointy hat is essential for a witch or that having a (pointy) hat, robes, and a staff (with a knob on) are essential for a wizard. These items of costume are simply "*statutory*,"[7] and, as Tiffany Aching says, "the witch *was* the pointy hat."[8] Yet, this is a fixation not confined to the pointy-hat brigade: flick through any of Pratchett's novels and you will find an unwavering urge to be dressed *properly*. Magrat is certain that she must wear the proper "queen outfit" (including pantoffle and ruff);[9] Shawn Ogg must have a different hat for each of the many roles he plays in Lancre Castle (including the proper hat for the Royal Historian, to be worn only on Wednesday evening);[10] the plotters in *Going Postal* must be "robed because you couldn't have a secret order without robes";[11] dwarfs must have an iron helmet and a battle axe; vampires must wear evening dress, and so on and so forth—there are an inexhaustible number of examples in Pratchett. "People respect uniforms" we are informed in *Lords and Ladies*, but, given that we are told this in respect of a bandit leader who wears an eye-patch *even though he has two good eyes*,[12] might it not be more accurate to say that, in Pratchett, people respect the primacy of *costume*?

Fretting about one's performance, however, is not simply a matter of donning an appropriate costume. Discworlders are equally concerned that they properly *play the roles to which their costumes pertain.* Once again, there are almost too many examples from which to choose: there is Granny Weatherwax, who is aware that, beyond the pointy hat, she must show gullible villagers that she has powers that they cannot begin to comprehend[13] and occasionally put on "a suitable occult expression."[14] There is Magrat, who is aware that she cannot simply rely on her queen outfit but must also do such things as exercising "noblyyess obligay."[15] Shawn Ogg knows he must adopt a different language depending on the hat he is wearing (for instance, he tends to reserve use of "sire" for when he is wearing the giant, powdered footman's wig but not when he is wearing the helmet that denotes he is Lancre's standing army).[16] In *Thud!*, Mrs. Winkings is aware that she cannot just dress up as a vampire but must pronounce her "w"s as "v"s;[17] Carrot is aware that his Watchman's uniform is never enough but that he must always ask questions "for the look of the thing",[18] and so on and so forth. Costume and play: there is an unremitting evocation in Pratchett of the relationship between performer and the audience.

It is wise to pause at this juncture in order to consider the exact effect of Pratchett's presentation. Just why is it that appearance is represented as mattering to such an inordinate degree on Discworld? Pratchett's aim is, of course, partly to satirize cliché in the fantasy genre: his characters are not only knowingly aware of the fantasy stereotypes to which they conform, but are also actively keen to conform to them *properly*. This is funny in an ironic way on the one hand, but it also gives Pratchett a free hand to keep on using the stereotypes of fantasy (freshened up, no doubt) that are part of his success on the other: fantasy readers, after all, demand a stock set of recognizable types. Yet, as ever with Pratchett, the treatment reaches much further than this.

In his insistence that they must emphatically dress for and play the role of what they are, Pratchett is actually proposing a radical social ontology for his characters. For, on Discworld, costume acting is not something secondary, reduced to that which takes place in the theater, but rather is universalized into *the primary condition for being*. The implicit assertion is that these characters can only become what they are through their recognizable performances of what they are: no one will believe that Tiffany (for instance) is a witch unless they see her perform as a witch, and yet it is precisely because she performs what they believe is a witch that their vision of her as such can be sustained: seeing is believing, but, after all, *believing is also seeing*—"reality is simply what goes on inside people's heads."[19]

Pratchett is exaggerating monumentally, of course; by which we mean he is being his usual self in creating an extreme and distorted vision in which we are invited to recognize the reflection of our own world. He is, in fact, in his presentation of theater spilling into ordinary life, finding resonance with a number of thinkers who regard performance not as an "illusion, the pale imitation of a real life lived elsewhere," but as "fundamental to the constitution of our social and cultural world," "the very stuff of our ordinary lives."[20] The vision of *Homo sapiens* as *"homo performans,"*[21] a performing animal, in Victor Turner's memorable coinage, is precisely what Pratchett seeks to sustain.

The thinker with whom Pratchett finds most resonance in this regard, however, is probably the eminent social anthropologist Ervin Goffman, who, in his seminal *The Presentation of Self in Everyday Life*, posits that ordinary life is essentially a series of role-plays. How, Goffman asks, can one take up any social position, say as a nurse or a university academic, without putting on a recognizable "uniform" (a pinafore for a nurse, say, or a coffee-stained corduroy jacket for an academic),[22] or without adopting the "proper" mannerisms, tone of voice, or vocabulary (nurses, upon greeting their patients must ask how their health is, academics are required to pepper their speech with quotes from Virgil)?[23] It is not that nurses or academics are consciously acting out these roles or that they are aware of pretending—it is merely the fact that the accession to *any* social role requires a performative dimension. Goffman also points out how we perform not simply in obviously public situations but also in what we might think of as more unofficial ones—there are clear roles to be played, after all, even when sitting down to the most commonplace of family meals.[24]

Goffman, then, in harmony with Pratchett, suggests it is difficult to separate the theater of our lives from its reality. "Life itself is a dramatically enacted thing," he says. "All the world is not . . . a stage, but the crucial ways in which it is not are not easy to specify."[25] Yet, we can see from the slight reservation in his language (*all the world is **not** a stage*) that Goffman is not actually prepared to go quite as far as Pratchett. We might say, in fact, that Pratchett supplements Goffman when he dramatizes (in every sense) the notion that people do not role-play just in public or private situations with others, but that they also may do so *when they are alone*. In Pratchett, in point of fact, it is an unusual character who is not a constant audience to him or herself. Archchancellor Mustrum Ridcully, to take one prominent example, will not remove his robes, even in the deep, dark forests of Lance where there is not a human soul to observe him because of the imaginary audience to which he must always play. How, if he takes off his ceremonial robes, he plaintively asks, "'will anyone know I'm a wizard?'"[26] Perhaps this is symbolized best, though, by Sam Vimes who, like a post-alcoholic Evil Queen, constantly muses on his appearance to a mirror on the wall. Altering his "costume" in the act of shaving, Vimes constantly muses on how clothes make the man, his anxiety circling the horrific question of whether being forced to perform by his wife, Lady Sybil, as a nob in a feather-plumed hat will necessarily *make* him a nob in a feather-plumed hat (which, of course, in a sense it will).[27] On insisting that the relationship between audience and performer is present even when the audience is also the performer, Pratchett posits a more fundamental level of performativity than Goffman: Vimes acts "in" and "out" of character to himself, for he oscillates between his own gaze of himself in his room dressing up in nobbish clothes and his gaze of himself playing an ordinary policeman on the streets.[28] This performance sensitizes us to something fundamentally fictional about his character; and in what sense can we locate Vimes as non-fictional if he is performing himself as "in" character to himself?

Pratchett, to sum up this section, is in harmony with traditional sociologists such as Goffman in suggesting that our intuitive sense that there is a difference between what we really are and the role we play, between the "mask"/costume we wear in social situations and the "real" us behind or underneath the veil, is itself a kind of fiction. On Discworld, reality exists on the level of performance—it just so happens that this may be equally true of the real world as well. In shorthand, as Polly Perks in *Monstrous Regiment* says, "put on trousers and the world changes"[29]—this is equally true for you, the person watching you, and *you who are watching yourself.*

This Only Looks Wrong: Appearance is Deceivin'

If Pratchett is aware and keen to show his readers how reality is (at least in a sense) located on the level of performance, then he is equally aware that this is a state of affairs with *consequences.* For in a performative world, "truth" and "lies" and "real" and "false" begin to relate to one another in extraordinary ways; just *how* extraordinary Pratchett illustrates in his constant probing of the extravagant logic of disguise. Discworld is, of course, full of those in disguises of one kind or another: the two Opera House Ghosts and André the undercover detective in *Maskerade*; Sally von Humpeding in *Thud!*, who joins the Watch on false pretenses and who looks "if not like a boy, then, like someone who wouldn't mind passing for one,"[30] hinting at a double disguise; Lord Vetinari, who spends time as the lethal Stoker Blake in *Raising Steam*; Polly Perks, who dresses as a man in *Monstrous Regiment*; Captain Carrot, who hilariously attempts to disguise himself with a false moustache, pink nose, and brown bowler hat in order to 'inconspicuously' break into the Unseen University library in *Jingo*[31] (though he is unsure, innocent lad that he is, why the joke shop from which he got them would also sell fake breasts)—the list is endless. This is both adventure fantasy and comedy, after all, and how can one have adventure fantasy or comedy (à la Shakespeare) without characters gallivanting around, cross-dressing, and glorying in the freedom of pretending to be who they are not?

Yet, Pratchett's interest in disguise goes far beyond a device to create intrigue in his stories. For behind his interest lies a wish to explore a fascinating philosophical conundrum, namely if one accepts that the self is a kind of fiction, or at least partly fictional, and if "fictional" implies a kind of falseness to reality, then just how can one create a false appearance in a world where *everyone always already has a false appearance*? In other words, how can one disguise oneself if one is by default always already in disguise (a disguise that is paradoxically somehow your "real" self)? Pratchett's answer is almost as extraordinary as the question: *one must double the pretense*. Since everyone is always already masquerading, performing what they are, the only way to deceive others into thinking that one is what one is actually not is to *pretend to be what one is*! This is the double masquerade, the pretense of performing that one is acting. And Pratchett is simply, delightedly, crammed full of such examples.

To disguise oneself, then, it is not enough simply to perform the role of being in disguise. Pratchett gives us many examples of those who fail utterly to disguise themselves because they do exactly that. There is, for instance, the hilarious sight of Nobby Nobbs and Detritus trying to "mingle in secret" in the opera house while awaiting the appearance of the ghost. Nobby, wearing a deformed fur hat and a cloak that is far too long, gives "the impression of being a superhero who had spent too much time around the Kryptonite," while Detritus, wearing a surprisingly well-fitting suit, has unfortunately neglected to take off his helmet, so that both give the impression of having the "'words Watchman in disguise flashing on and off'"[32] just above their heads. Or there is Mr. Horsefry, one of the plotters in *Going Postal*, who goes about in a "highly noticeable long hooded cloak."[33] Or we could cite the plotters (again) on the

Hygienic Railway in *Raising Steam* who are noticeable because they try "a little too hard to present themselves as harmless members of the public."[34] Since reality is on the level of performance, to perform the role of being in disguise is to advertise that this is precisely what one is doing—effective concealment, on the other hand, can only occur when one *pretends that one is performing the role of being in disguise*. Take the case of Pratchett's wizards and witches.

A "real" witch or a wizard on Discworld, as we have seen, is but a performance of (fictional) witchiness or wizardiness. Since performance is where both witch/wizard and audience (sometimes one and the same thing) locate "reality," witches and wizards cannot disguise their witchiness or wizardiness by simply taking off the costume. A witch or wizard who does not perform as such is *simply not a witch or a wizard* (they are an audience to themselves at all times, remember). This being the case, when a disguise is desired in order to disappear (as Discworld witches frequently need to do since they are not always popular), or when one is desired so that they can go incognito to a bar to get drunk (as Unseen University wizards often need to do since they are rascally alcoholics), what is required is a redoubling of the deception.

In regard to the wizards, the trick of disguising oneself as a non-wizard relies precisely upon the fact that part of the performance of being a wizard involves having a beard. That all wizards have great, big, bushy beards would seem to be an insurmountable barrier to their pretending to be non-wizards, but, luckily, Discworld wizards are made of devious stuff. The following conversation takes place in *Moving Pictures*, where, determined to break curfew in order to watch one of the new moving pictures (one which promises "ladies not only showing nearly all [they] had but quite a lot of what [they] had not strictly speaking got"),[35] the wizards need to produce quickly some kind of disguise:

"False beards," said the Lecturer in Recent Runes triumphantly. "We should wear false beards."

The Chair rolled his eyes.

"We've all GOT beards," he said. "What kind of disguise would false beards be?"

"Ah! That's the clever bit," said the Lecturer. "No one would suspect that someone wearing a false beard would have a real beard underneath, would they?"

The Chair opened his mouth to refute this, and then hesitated.

"Well—" he said.

"But where do we get false beards at this time of night?" said a wizard doubtfully.

The Lecturer beamed and reached into his pocket. "We don't have to," he said. "That's the really clever bit: I brought some wire with me, you see, and all you need to do is break two bits off, twiddle them into your sideburns, then loop them over your ears rather clumsily like this," he demonstrated, "and there you are."

The Chair stared.

"Uncanny," he said at last. "It's true. You look just like someone wearing a very badly made false beard."[36]

The logic is utterly brilliant: anyone who is pretending to be a wizard would wear a false beard; ergo, anyone who is *obviously* wearing a false beard must be pretending to be a wizard and cannot therefore be a wizard; ergo, the best way to disguise oneself as a *non-wizard* is to pretend to wear a false beard. In other words, the best way to disguise oneself as a wizard is to pretend to be someone pretending to be a wizard.

Pratchett offers another superb example through his witches and their use of "Boffo," the witchy paraphernalia, hats, warts, frogs, black teeth, and so on, that some witches buy from the Boffo Novelty and Joke Shop (no. 4, Tenth Egg Street, Ankh-Morpork) in order to induce their audience to see the witch that they expect. As with the wizards, since a witch is not a witch unless she looks like a witch, a witch without Boffo is not a witch. On the other hand, a witch wearing Boffo (that is, a costume) *is* a witch (reality is located on the level of performance), whereas a witch who is blatantly performing wearing Boffo is a witch in disguise. This, indeed, is the conclusion Tiffany Aching comes to when she encounters Mrs. Proust, the owner of the famous shop. Seeing the stereotypical "witch of nightmares: battered hat, wart-encrusted nose, claw-like hands, blackened teeth," Tiffany assumes that she is "a real witch disguising herself as a fake witch," but, of course, the Pratchettian twist is that the obviously fake witch mask that Mrs. Proust is wearing *is actually her real face*: "'That really is your face, isn't it? The masks you sell are masks of *you*.'"[37]

Pratchett beautifully illustrates, then, how, if the performance of pretense is taken as real, logic demands that "reality" must be located elsewhere. Hence, one's real features can be the perfect disguise: "truth" and "lies," "real" and "false"—they are truly traumatized in this performative arena. And, to link back to the philosophy of performativity, we can say that Pratchett, here, is in harmony with Slavoj Žižek, a philosopher most interested in how mask-wearing and masquerading interfere with the boundaries of "truth" and "lies," "real" and "false." We always expect, of course, a simple arrangement whereby a false mask just covers up the reality beneath it. Yet, as Žižek indicates (and as seen in Pratchett's examples above), the mask and the masquerade allow a "feigning to feign," the telling of "a lie in the guise of truth."[38] In the above examples, the wizards and Mrs. Proust *are presenting their true features in order to tell a lie* and, as such, are pure fantasy demonstrations of how the double masquerade makes "truth" increasingly difficult to locate, always contaminated as it is by the "lie" of the performance.

The double masquerade, then, is premised on pretense and non-existence; it is a *redoubling* of pretense: when one masquerades, one performs a fictional self; when one double masquerades, one pretends to perform that fictional self—*one pretends to perform what one is not in the first place*. Pratchett and Žižek truly are prepared to follow the logic of the double masquerade through to the unsettling point at which the self becomes a kind of semblance of (non-) presence. Yet, perhaps this is not the most disconcerting point of all, for we now turn to Žižek's seemingly scandalous claim that *the agents of such double masquerades are always women*, a claim that Pratchett appears implicitly to endorse given that one of his novels is seemingly designed to underscore that this is so. The logic of this position is, of course, that *women do not exist*; how, then, can philosopher and fantasy author reach this preposterous conclusion?

Monstrous Regiment is the Pratchett novel that is perhaps most about disguise. It is the story of a young woman, Polly Perks, who disguises herself as a man to join the Borogravian army in search of her brother. Scared at first that she will give herself away, she comes to realize that every single one of the other men in the regiment is also a woman (and, in one of Pratchett's finest twists, nearly all the other top men in the army turn out to have been women all along, too). Leaving aside the obvious way in which the novel engages with the idea of gender performativity (more on this below), the most striking feature of the *Monstrous Regiment* is its procedure of constantly confronting the reader with double masquerades. Polly and the other girls frequently *dress up as women* in order to disguise their soldierly "masculinity," and, eventually, the whole squad of women dress up as women in order to gain entry into the impenetrable Kneck Keep, the two best jokes being that they feel *weird* dressed as women ("They felt awkward. And there was no sense in that at all. But they looked at one another in the chilly light of dawn and giggled in embarrassment. Wow, Polly thought look at us: dressed as women")[39] and that their commanding officer, a rupert who just happens to be called Rupert, who is just about the only real man in the whole novel, thinks not only that he is much the better at disguising himself as a woman but that the girls simply do not pass muster as girls:

> "Y'know, a good officer keeps an eye on his men and I have to say that I've noticed in you, in *all* of you, little . . . habits, perfectly normal, nothing to worry about, like the occasional

deep exploration of the nostril maybe, and a tendency to grin after passing wind, a natural boyish inclination to scratch yourselves in public . . . that sort of thing. These are the kind of little details that would give you away in a trice, and tell any observer that you were a man in woman's clothing, believe me."[40]

Despite what r/Rupert thinks (for he is in the line of Pratchettian tragic characters who are always wrong), the most effective disguise for these women is to pretend to be what they are: women. But the importance of Pratchett's joke with the r/Rupert should not be underestimated, for it allows a direct comparison of the gender performances of the men and women: Pratchett demonstrates quite convincingly through his girl-boy soldiers that women can play a man playing a woman, whereas a man cannot play a woman playing a man (and, indeed, when r/Rupert does dress up as a woman, he looks exactly like what he is—a man in drag). Yet, the implication of this, to return to our original point, is that the novel suggests that *being a 'woman' is always already a performance*: a false "real" appearance.

It seems outrageous, of course, but let us point out that the novel actually resonates with a line of psychoanalytical thought that argues that womanliness *is* fundamentally a performance. *Monstrous Regiment* is an example of Pratchett in his playful Shakespearean mode,[41] so given that he and Žižek often appear "in synch," it should come as no surprise that Žižek frequently uses an example from the Bard to illustrate what he means by the womanly double masquerade:

> *As You Like It* proposes a . . . version of this logic of double deception. Orlando is passionately in love with Rosalind, who, in order to test his love, disguises himself as Ganymede and, as a male companion, interrogates Orlando about his love. She even takes on the personality of Rosalind (in a redoubled masking, she pretends to be herself, to be Ganymede who plays at being Rosalind) . . . Truth [is] staged

in a redoubled deception . . . It is no accident that the agents of such double masquerades are always women: . . . because only a woman *can pretend to be what she is*—a woman.[42]

Both Pratchett and Žižek are, in fact, drawing upon the insights of one of Sigmund Freud's disciples, Joan Riviere, who argued that the propensity to masquerade was the key feature of femininity in her seminal paper, "Womanliness as Masquerade." Where should one draw the line between a "woman" and a performance of a "woman," she asks? Answering her own question, she says that *one should not* because "there is [no] such difference, whether radical or superficial: they are the same thing."[43] Or as Stephen Heath paraphrases it, "in the masquerade the woman mimics an authentic—genuine—womanliness but then authentic womanliness is such mimicry, is the masquerade."[44] In Freudian/Lacanian psychoanalytical theory *having* is on the side of man while *being* is on the side of woman, "being" meaning, in this context, *being the sign of the woman*. This is why *la femme n'existe pas*, as Jacques Lacan said.[45]

Just a Lump of Plaster: Still Damp in the Middle

The sense that reality is a function of performance is extended to another of Pratchett's great and recurring questions: how does power ground itself? The Discworld series constantly takes us into the vicinity both of rulers—Lord Vetinari, Rhys Rhysson (Low King of the Dwarfs), King Verence of Lancre, to mention but three—and of those who seek to exert power over others—Sam Vimes, Moist von Lipwig, the witches, the Magpyrs (vampires with a "y"), the elves, the dwarf grags, Lilith de Tempscire, Cosmo Lavish, and so on and so forth. And each time we are taken into the vicinity of the powerful, each time we enter the halls of the mighty, Pratchett allows the same question to keep popping into our minds: exactly how do the powerful convince others that they actually *have* power? Pratchett wants us not to look but to *see*, for his answer of course is that, on Discworld, as in the real world, the Emperor is always already without his clothes: power must *perform* itself as having power—it must maintain its false "true" appearance of power.

The clever rulers in Pratchett each recognize the truth of Karl Marx's dictum that (to paraphrase somewhat) one is only a king as long as one is *treated* as a king.[46] Vetinari, Rhys, Vimes, Granny Weatherwax—all are aware that, as far as power is concerned, appearances do not just matter but *must be maintained at all costs.* Vetinari says that power is a game of smoke and mirrors,[47] Vimes says that policemen must be magicked into people's heads,[48] Verence is aware he must *act like* the king (even though he *is* the king),[49] Rhys knows that kings must take half an hour just to put on a few clothes—"Kings don't hurry,"[50] but they are all aware of the same vital requirement: they must prevent at all costs that moment of what Žižek calls "mysterious rupture"[51] when power loses its pretense of being "up there"[52] and stops functioning because it is no longer recognized as functioning.

Pratchett is well aware, of course, that part of the performance of power relies upon having the correct symbols. Yet, the pertinent question he raises in this regard is: how can a symbol, by definition a *substitute for something real*, ever be "authentic"? Our lack of Pratchettian training in seeing tends to make us think of such things as the crown jewels in England, for instance, as being "real" symbols of a thus authenticated power. Our equation is: possession of the real crown jewels legitimizes real power. Pratchett, of course, has little time for such woolly thinking as, time after time, his novels introduce symbols of power that turn out to be fake. There is Vetinari's "solid gold" throne, revealed in *Men At Arms* to be "'gold foil over wood,'"[53] there is Tomjon's fake "real" crown in *Wyrd Sisters*, property of the Strolling Players, that "no one had ever wanted to wear [on stage] because it was so uncrownly"[54] (Pratchett's joke being that everyone is right all along but for the wrong reason since it is a fake crown masquerading as a "real" crown disguised as a fake crown), and, above all, the Scone of Scones in *The Fifth Elephant*, which turns out to be a simulacra, to use Jean

Baudrillard's idea—a copy of something with no original. Each symbol is revealed to have been a fake, but, of course, the wise rulers know that this simply does not matter. "One is only a king so long as treated as a king"—this is a treatment that must be elicited through *performance*—it does not matter, therefore, if the prop (the throne, the crown, the Scone) is "real" because it is by default *always already a fake* being always already just a prop for this fake performance of "true" power. All of these rulers are aware that they *wear* power, rather than *have* power. Pratchett is fascinated by charades and play of all kinds—up to and including the elaborate performances that power must put on to disguise the fact that it is never grounded anywhere but in its own circuit. And this is a point, we might say by way of summary, that he beautifully captures with the face of the Elf Queen in *Lords and Ladies*. Described as a kind of mirror/mask which exactly reflects what the humans in the novel have themselves arrogated to her, power, glamor, beauty, the right to rule, she wears the face of what one might say is a "true" (that is, *always already fake*) monarch.

A Vision of Heavily but Tastefully Armored Beauty

We have seen in the above sections how Pratchett gleefully undermines our intuitive understanding that there is a gap between the social roles we play, the performances we put on, the masks we wear, and the "real us" behind them. Endlessly evoking a relationship between performer and audience, Pratchett dramatizes how we are always somehow playing ourselves. The logic of this position, of course, is that our very identities are bound up with play and performance. This chapter continues, then, with a look at how Pratchett reinforces his appreciation of the theatricality of our identities by highlighting how our instinctive sense that the identity categories to which we adhere are somehow *inside* us or *prior to* us is also mistaken. As we shall see, Pratchett brilliantly uses the resources that the fantasy genre makes available to make tangible not only that it is delusional to think of one's identity as existing "out there" somehow as a fixed quality of the world, but also that what appears to come from something prior is actually a mere *product* of the performance.

As is so often the case in the Discworld series, Pratchett proceeds to give us insight into the real world of our experience by distancing us from it and by inverting the "common-sense" positions from which we start. In the case of how he gives us insight into identity formation, however, he *massively* distances us from it and truly turns good sense on its head as he presents us with his Igors—proud henchmen to the monstrous or insane whose notions of identity formation are simply *absurd*.

To be a Discworld Igor, one *has to* limp. This is not an optional extra, but is, in fact, *compulsory*. And it is not the only thing that is mandatory: an Igor has to know how to make doors creak, how to lisp, how to extravagantly roll "r"s, and how to turn up directly behind the master/marrrrthster when called for ("'it's a profethional thing'").[55] And Igors, of course, are also obliged to have a head covered in scars and to be a dab hand at surgery. Pratchett is, of course, taking obvious aim at the cliché of the Igor characters from 1930s and 1940s Hollywood horror movies, but the ontological basis of his joke is still worth thinking about. Pratchett generates humor by taking something that cannot be universalized (a name) and characteristics that are downright eccentric (a limp, for instance), and positing them as a positive set of characteristics that exist as a kind of essence of Igordom, a *template*, prior to each Igor. This is the model from which their "appropriate" behavior must spring—according to this logic, one *is* an Igor *therefore* one does Igorly things: the lisp, the limp, the scars: all are *expressive* of any Igor's given identity.

The logic at work is, as already mentioned, quite *absurd* of course—how can *a name* be the precursor of a set of physical attributes or a set of abilities? Does everyone called "John" behave according to a set of a priori characteristics? But the extremity of the example, the ludicrousness of a limp (for instance) being expressive of an identity, surely serves to reiterate the absurdity of the idea that a positive set of qualities or behaviors can *ever* spring from an identity that is posited as being prior to them. Who would be so foolish, Pratchett seems to ask, as to believe that their identity is grounded outside themselves as some kind of essence and that this essential identity governs who they are and what they do? Yet, Pratchett's point is, of course, that some of us *do* believe this: we *do* often unthinkingly assume that our identity, our "being something," is the *cause* of our behavior.

"I am a John therefore I . . ." is a statement that nearly everyone would reject. So why is it any more thinkable to claim something like "I am American therefore I . . ."; "I am Japanese therefore I . . ."? One can *perform* being an American, no doubt; but this identity can only be a product or effect of the performative process rather than an expressive result of a prior grounding. Philosophically speaking, it is total humbug to make claims such as "I am American, therefore I eat hamburgers," or "I am Japanese, therefore I love cherry blossom," yet it is exactly this form of woolly thinking that Pratchett is able to make fun of through his Igors. *I am an Igor, therefore I . . .* Pratchett sensitizes us to the ludicrous logic through which we may justify our actions and attitudes; yet, of course, he is not content to let matters rest here. A real edge enters the comedy when his Igors begin to apply this spurious reasoning beyond themselves. In the mouth of anyone who believes in essential identities "They are . . ., therefore they . . ." is an altogether more alarming assertion.

Just as being a Discworld Igor requires a compulsory set of qualities/behaviors, so too does being a Discworld vampire (at least according to the Igor in *Carpe Jugulum*). It requires the wearing of evening dress *at all times*. It also requires the owning of a castle with *proper* spidery dungeons, *proper* flickering torches, and *proper* guttering candles, not to forget a carriage with *proper* black plumes. Of course, we must not fail to miss another of Pratchett's send-ups of the horror cliché, but, once again, we must also not be blind to the serious point: although the vampires in *Carpe Jugulum* are villains, and although Pratchett's treatment is humorous in the extreme, we cannot fail to notice that Igor treats these vampires as *Others*. "Other" is used here in the philosophical sense first put forward by Emmanuel Levinas of a group different from our own to which a set of stereotypical characteristics are attached.[56] In particular, it can be said that Igor's precise brand of Othering is that he posits a racist view of cultural enclosure based upon a notion of "radical typing" stemming from the notion that the identity of the Other is always posited as being *essential*. In non-technical terms: he expects vampires to behave as vampires *because* they are vampires, and if they do not do so they cannot be *proper* vampires. Bigotry couched in such terms cannot help but put Pratchett in dialogue with Edward Said.

"He is Mohammed therefore he . . ."; "He is an Arab therefore he . . ."; "They are vampires therefore they . . ."—Pratchett here resonates with Edward Said's point that we treat Others as being a homogeneous mass whose actions are determined in advanced by the essence, *the prior characteristics* of the "race" to which they belong: Arabs have a "collective self-consistency such as to wipe out any traces of individual Arabs with narratable life histories."[57] Arabs are all excitable and therefore should we encounter an excitable Arab it is because of the essence of his Arab nature (and not because he happens to be Mohammed who is getting married tomorrow, for instance, because life details will always be "subordinate to the sheer, unadorned and persistent fact of [his] being an Arab").[58]

To bring it back to Pratchett, although, as already mentioned, the vampires in *Carpe Jugulum are* presented as villains, this is tempered by the fact that Pratchett treats their efforts to escape the attempt to Other them with a degree of (comic) compassion.[59] On the one hand, Pratchett savages them for their fascistic tendencies, yet, on the other, he reminds us of their plight. We are surely invited to sympathize with their desire to escape the identity that Igor is trying to coerce them into assuming for his own ends, so much so in fact that it might be said that the joke is ultimately on Igor. The great lengths that Pratchett goes to elsewhere in order to show that vampires do not have to conform to the essential set of prior characteristics that are ascribed to them add weight to the suggestion that Pratchett is sympathetic towards the *Carpe Jugulum* vampires, at least in this regard.[60] And the particulars of the novel must also be set in the context of it being a central tenet of Pratchett's whole *oeuvre* that the "natural" or "essential" identities to which we are supposedly insuperably fixed are *always* open to renegotiation. How else can we explain the sheer number of characters on Discworld who reinvent their identities?

One is an Igor therefore one *does* Igorly things. The lisp, the limp, the scars are all *expressive* of the Igors' given identity. One is an Arab therefore one *does* Araby things: the dishonesty, the excitability, the immaturity—these are all expressive of the Arabs' given identity. One is a woman and therefore one *does* *womanly things*. The lipstick, the dresses, the high-heels—these are all expressive of a woman's supposedly given essence. It is no secret that, beyond the idea that one's name or one's nationality or one's race can in any way be prior or essential to the subject, Pratchett also takes aim at the idea that there are any essential, prior *gender* qualities. And if he harmonizes with Said in regard to the former, then he is obviously in harmony with Judith Butler in regard to the latter. Butler, of course, is indefatigable in insisting that biological sex must be separated from culturally constructed gender, which she theorizes as a matter of pure performance that must be constantly iterated.

That gender must be separated from biology is most obvious in Pratchett's treatment of dwarf females, particularly Cheery Longbottom, a breastplate remolding warrior[61] who attempts forcibly to "overturn thousands of years of subterranean tradition."[62] In Pratchett's dwarf culture (and in a none too subtle dig at Disney's and Tolkien's dwarfs) *everyone must act male*, a fact which is getting Cheery down. Refusing to be crushed by the weight of a culture that demands gender conformity, Cheery, in the face of much opposition to her subversive bodily acts, *begins to perform as a female*. She begins to wear lipstick, put on earrings, hold a sequined bag, carry a small, ornate axe for evening wear, and so on. Through this process *she creates the category of "female."* Prior to Cheery *there are no female dwarfs* in the sense that there are no words in dwarfish for female categories and no performance of anything but maleness.

Pratchett's treatment is straight from Butler, of course; so much so that it is almost as if he were reading *Gender Trouble* and *Bodies That Matter* as he began to tap out *Feet of Clay*:

Identity is performatively constituted by the very "expressions" that are said to be its results.[63]

Dwarfen femaleness is performed by the carrying of, for instance, an ornate battle axe. That dwarfen femaleness is an effect *of this carrying as opposed to the carrying being a result of dwarfen femaleness is illustrated by the fact that dwarfen femaleness simply does not exist before it begins to be performed.*

The naming is at once the setting of a boundary, and also the repeated inculcation of a norm.

Language emerges . . . for the fixing of sexed positions.[64]

Female pronouns emerge in the dwarfish language with Cheery's revolution and their emergence fixes dwarfen femaleness as a new normal category.

The signifiers of "identity" effectively or rhetorically produce the very social movements that they appear to represent.[65]

Performance of femaleness through the battle axe allows "she" to emerge, which, in turn, produces Cheery's social movement. "She" cannot represent anything before Cheery's social movement because "she" simply does not exist prior to it.

Gender can be chosen as a piece of improvised theater; dominant norms can be undermined through transgressive performances of gender; gender is of such transient, mobile fragility that it must be constantly performed, its contingency requiring it to be constantly remade; gender is discursive and must be iterated in language: Butler's ideas can be *palpably* shown in fantasy and, indeed, are through the figure of Cheery, so much so that Pratchett could perhaps be said to give the clearest example in literature of how gender categories are non-essential and must be created.[66] *Femaleness simply does not exist in the dwarfen world before Cheery*—Pratchett dramatizes how it must be constructed from scratch.[67]

Masks: Hiding Only the Face on the Outside

I have outlined above how masks and masquerades trick us into an apprehension that they are hiding some "real" truth. Masks/ masques point to there being something beyond which they cover and suggest that the binary between false surface reality and true hidden depth can be maintained. I have shown, however, some of the ways in which Pratchett suggests that what the mask really allows to be concealed is the fact that it is this very surface reality that must be taken as the only truth—truly, in a performatively constructed world, truth and lies relate to each other in unusual ways. This chapter finishes, then, with a final example that illustrates this most perfectly, as Pratchett asks one final question: What happens in a world where everyone is always already wearing a mask if one dons another mask to escape from oneself? Which is one's "real" identity? How, in short, can one locate oneself between the two masks?

Pratchett offers two examples in dramatizing these questions: Walter Plinge in *Maskerade*, and the clowns in *Men At Arms*. In an obvious analog to the *Phantom of the Opera*, Walter is a mild mannered janitor by day but transformed into the Opera House Ghost at night as he dons the mask and stalks the dark corridors of the Ankh-Morpork Opera House. In the case of the clowns, we are taken inside the Clown Guild and shown how each clown is obliged to wear "official make-up,"[68] a big, red nose, a wig, a deadpan painted face that is unique to the particular clown (his own "face")—"no other clown can use it."[69] Each, then, wears a mask to cover his "real" features, but, of course, Pratchett maneuvers the reader so that we are obliged to ask, just which is the "real" Walter? Just which is the "real" clown?

We intuitively feel no doubt that Walter is real and the Ghost is the fiction he creates just as we feel that the "real" person is the one hiding behind the clownish slap. Yet, of course, Pratchett demonstrates that the opposite is true, at least in a psychological sense. Walter's fantasy Opera House Ghost can closely express the young man's real desires in ways that the "real," socially inept Walter cannot, the fact of which Granny Weatherwax is acutely aware. Tossing him a home-made white mask, Granny understands that it is only when he is the Ghost that Walter can act as he really wants to—he cannot act to save the Opera House unless he is masked:

> "I don't know what you are when you're behind the mask," said Granny, "but 'ghost' is just another word for 'spirit' and 'spirit' is just another word for 'soul'. Off you go Walter Plinge."
>
> The masked figure did not move.
>
> "I meant . . . off you go, Ghost." . . .
>
> The mask nodded, and darted away.[70]

Pratchett makes it similarly clear that the clowns locate their "real" selves on the level of the "face" that they wear, a point that is difficult for the layperson to apprehend. Interrogating the clown Boffo, Angua asks if clowns ever make up their faces in order to look like another clown:

> He looked at her. It was hard to tell his expression under the permanently downcast mouth, but as far as she could tell she might have well suggested that he perform a specific sex act with a small chicken.
>
> "How could I do that?" he said. "Then I wouldn't be *me*."

"Someone else might do it, though?"
Boffo's buttonhole squirted.
"I don't have to listen to this sort of dirty talk, miss."[71]

The reference to "dirty talk" is apt since Pratchett here echoes Žižek's unsettling point that the masks we may don to hide from ourselves may be far more real than the ordinary social masks we wear in everyday life. Think of the question this way: is the "mask" one wears online, one's screen persona, more "real" than one's "real" self? One's social identity is already a mask that involves repression of inadmissible impulses. But when one dons the internet "mask," these very repressed impulses can come out:

Take the proverbial impotent shy person who, while partici-pating in a cyberspace interactive game, adopts the identity of an irresistible seducer or sadistic murderer. It is all too simple to say that this identity is just an imaginary escape from real-life impotence. The point is rather that . . . he can "show his true self" and do things he would never have done in real-life interactions. In the guise of a fiction, the truth about himself is articulated.[72]

Walter can only show his true self from behind the mask. The masks of the clowns, on which their real, repressed agony is painted, are their true faces. We had above an example of a lie in the guise of truth—yet, Pratchett and Žižek are both aware of the uncanny opposite that the mask allows: *truth in the guise of a fiction.*

What Pratchett ultimately teaches us, then, is one final dark lesson: when we knowingly don a mask to hide our identity we may in fact reveal some absolute truth about ourselves. As Nanny Ogg says, "Masks conceal one face but reveal another."[73]

Looking Like an Indifferent Copy of Oneself

Supplementing non-fantastic treatments with fantastic treat-ments that have an even sharper, more radical edge, Pratchett brilliantly marshals the resources that the fantasy genre provides to present what at first appears outrageous and simply ludicious, before it dawns upon us that he is actually, in a profound sense, *right*. While the world we find in Pratchett's Hall of Mirrors is a distorted representation of our own, it is one that is not only recognizable but also somehow *truer*. Pratchett's fantasy presentation of the masque is more real than "reality" itself. It is the truth (to misquote Pratchett slightly) of an image in a mirror but without the mirror.

Yet, appropriately enough, we have only really skimmed the surface of Pratchett's interest in surfaces. To say that he is obsessed is no exaggeration when one considers just how often his novels visit and revisit the subject. Think of his recent obsession with Moist von Lipwig, a character who knows everything about the essence of forgery (making "the glass look so much more like a diamond than the diamond does")[74] and who applies these rules to himself—no postmaster/bank governor/railroad comptroller ever looked *more* like a postmaster/bank governor/railroad comptroller than Moist. Or take his obsession with Lord Vetinari's preoccupation with surface performance, a mania that lends him wit of which Groucho Marx would be proud ("'You needn't look surprised.' / 'I don't intend to. I am surprised'").[75] Or think of his obsession with dwarf performativity and what it means to perform as a dwarf (Carrot is a dwarf although he is "six feet three inches in his stockinged feet,"[76] while Pepe is a kind of blank space on which the traces of dwarfishness are performed so that he is "sort of a dwarf."[77] Masques, veils, performance, and disguises; masks and masquerading; acting, playing, and play-acting: there is "a kind of magic in masks."[78] They are real—more real than reality itself; they might not be *true*, but that has nothing to do with it.

Notes

1. Surely this *is* a form of theater – if not, why is Manchester United's soccer stadium semi-informally known as 'The Theater of Dreams'?

2. T. Pratchett (2002) *Lords and Ladies* (New York: HarperTorch), p. 233.
3. T. Pratchett (2003) *Small Gods* (New York: HarperTorch), p. 24.
4. T. Pratchett (2004) *Monstrous Regiment* (London: Corgi), p. 310.
5. T. Pratchett (2000) *Maskerade* (New York: Harper Torch), p. 161.
6. Ibid., p. 103.
7. Pratchett, *Lords and Ladies*, p. 35.
8. T. Pratchett (2010) *I Shall Wear Midnight* (London: Doubleday), p. 16.
9. Pratchett, *Lords and Ladies*, p. 93.
10. T. Pratchett (1999) *Carpe Jugulum* (London: Corgi), p. 76.
11. T. Pratchett (2005) *Going Postal* (London: Corgi), p. 171.
12. Pratchett, *Lords and Ladies*, p. 152.
13. So, for instance, Granny will allow those who visit her to believe that she knew in some unearthly way that they were coming when she actually just always keeps an eye on the path that leads up to her cottage.
14. Pratchett, *Maskerade*, p. 29.
15. Pratchett, *Lords and Ladies*, p. 91.
16. Pratchett, *Carpe Jugulum*, pp. 39–40.
17. Much to the annoyance of Sam Vimes: "'Mr. Vimes,' said Mrs. Winkings, 've cannot help but notice that you still haf not employed any of our members in the Vatch. . .' / Say 'Watch', why don't you? Vimes thought. I know you can. Let the twenty-third letter of the alphabet enter your life" (T. Pratchett (2006) *Thud!* (London: Corgi), p. 22).
18. T. Pratchett (2005) *Going Postal* (London: Corgi), p. 327.
19. T. Pratchett (2002) *Moving Pictures* (New York: HarperTorch), p. 286.
20. J. Loxley (2007) *Performativity* (Abingdon: Routledge), p. 154.
21. V. Turner (1987) *The Anthropology of Performance* (New York: PAJ Publications), p. 81.
22. This, at least, used to be the case in the United Kingdom.
23. At least, this was the case in the university I attended in the early 1990s.
24. In my house, Uncle Reg does not feel any meal is complete until he has made at least three lewd jokes (one for the entrée, one for the main, and one for the dessert).
25. E. Goffman (1959) *The Presentation of Self in Everyday Life* (New York: Doubleday), p. 72.
26. Pratchett, *Carpe Jugulum*, p. 86.
27. In fairness, Vimes knows this, at least subconsciously, as we discover that, when wearing the hat, "he avoided meeting his own gaze in the mirror" (T. Pratchett (2008) *Men at Arms* (New York: Harper), p. 236).

28. "Fresh clothes had been laid out for him. Tonight there was something dashing in red and yellow . . . / . . . about now he'd be patrolling Treacle Mine Road / and a hat. It even had a feather in it" (ibid.).

29. Pratchett, *Monstrous Regiment*, p. 342.

30. Ibid., p. 61.

31. T. Pratchett (1998) *Jingo* (London: Corgi), pp. 118–19.

32. Pratchett, *Maskerade*, p. 256.

33. Pratchett, *Going Postal*, p. 137.

34. T. Pratchett (2013) *Raising Steam* (London: Doubleday), p. 280.

35. Pratchett, *Moving Pictures*, p. 255.

36. Ibid., p. 264.

37. Pratchett, *I Shall Wear Midnight*, p. 121.

38. S. Žižek (2006a) *How to Read Lacan* (New York: Norton), p. 113.

39. Pratchett, *Monstrous Regiment*, p. 346.

40. Ibid., p. 306.

41. What could be more Shakespearean than dressing up? As we are reminded towards the end of *Monstrous Regiment*, it was all "much ado, in fact, about nothing" (ibid., p. 441).

42. Žižek, *How to Read Lacan*, pp. 113, 115.

43. J. Riviere (1986) "Womanliness as Masquerade" in *Formations of Fantasy*, edited V. Burgin, J. Donald, and C. Kaplan (London: Routledge), p. 38.

44. S. Heath (1986) "Joan Riviere and the Masquerade" in *Formations of Fantasy*, op. cit., p. 48.

45. It must be pointed out that, on other occasions, Pratchett would *not* seem to agree. Although he appears to be in harmony with Lacan's phallocentric ideas in *Monstrous Regiment*, in other novels he seems much more in harmony with Judith Butler's notion that *all* gender is a performance, not just womanliness. This is a point taken up below in our discussion of Pratchett's presentation of the dwarf female, Cheery Littlebottom.

46. Originally appearing as a footnote in *Das Kapital*, Marx's insight makes frequent appearances in the work of Slavoj Žižek. See, for example, S. Žižek (1997) *The Plague of Fantasies* (London and New York: Verso), p. 100.

47. T. Pratchett (2009) *Unseen Academicals* (London: Doubleday), p. 333.

48. Pratchett, *Thud!*, p. 73. Vimes's thoughts echo the philosopher Herbert Marcus's famous slogan: "There Is a Policeman Inside All Our Heads."

49. Pratchett, *Carpe Jugulum*, p. 41.

50. T. Pratchett (2000) The *Fifth Elephant* (London: Corgi), p. 395.

51. S. Žižek (2013) *Demanding the Impossible* (Cambridge: Polity Press), p. 118.
52. Ibid., p. 117.
53. Pratchett, *Men at Arms*, p. 370.
54. T. Pratchett (2001) *Wyrd Sisters* (New York: HarperTorch), p. 224.
55. Pratchett, *Carpe Jugulum*, p. 246.
56. "Otherness" or "alterity" arises in philosophy in the examination of relations between the self and the Other person, or, as in this case, in the encounter between different cultures ("ours" and "theirs"). Many philosophers/theorists since the 1970s have expressed the idea that it is precisely the negative construction of Others that founds and sustains *our own* personal/national identity (I am/we are "civilized" exactly because I am/we are not "barbaric" like the Other(s)).
57. E. Said (2003) *Orientalism* (London: Penguin), p. 229.
58. Ibid., p. 230.
59. What could be funnier than, for instance, a vampire trying to condition himself to enjoy garlic using the Coué method?
60. The fussy little vampire Otto Chriek, for example, who is about as far from being a dark, blood-sucking creature of the night as it is possible to be. We note in passing that Otto wears an obvious vampire disguise (he looks like a "music hall vampire") (Pratchett, *Thud!*, p. 18) to create the impression that he is a *fake* vampire in order that people will not be afraid of him.
61. Feminists on Discworld do not burn their bras but rather (if they are dwarfs, at least) melt down their breastplates so that they can be remolded.
62. Pratchett, The *Fifth Elephant*, p. 374.
63. J. Butler (1990) *Gender Trouble: Feminism and the Subversion of Identity* (London and New York: Routledge), p. 25.
64. J. Butler (1993) *Bodies that Matter: On the Discursive Limits of Sex* (London New York: Routledge), p. 8.
65. Butler. *Bodies that Matter*, p. 210.
66. For a more extensive look at this point, see Chapter 5 of A. Rayment (2014) *Fantasy, Politics, Postmodernity: Pratchett, Pullman, Miéville and Stories of the Eye* (Amsterdam: Rodopi).
67. The careful reader will note that I have claimed that Pratchett makes contradictory presentations in regard to gender. Earlier I claim that Pratchett presents, in line with Rivierian/Lacanian theory, that *womanliness* is a performance and yet, in the sections above, I claim that Pratchett presents *all gender* as a performance. How can both be right? The answer, of course, is that they cannot, but there is no reason why they have to be. This is literature – Pratchett is under

no obligation to be consistent or to attempt to reconcile the two irreconcilable philosophical viewpoints. The fact is that in some places Pratchett resonates with Butler (gender seems non-biological on Discworld), yet, in others, he resonates more with Riviere and Lacan (there is an unremitting focus on women performing their gender). Let us be content with saying that this is an example of the extraordinary multi-resonances that are possible in non-existent fantasy spaces – paradoxically, both lines of thought seem plausible on Discworld!

68. Pratchett, *Men at Arms*, p. 265.
69. Ibid.
70. Pratchett, *Maskerade*, p. 327.
71. Pratchett, *Men at Arms*, pp. 266–7.
72. S. Žižek (2006b) "Is this Digital Democracy, or a New Tyranny of Cyberspace?" at www.theguardian.com/commentisfree/2006/dec/30/comment.media.
73. Pratchett, *Maskerade*, p. 332.
74. Pratchett, *Going Postal*, p. 270.
75. Pratchett, *Unseen Academicals*, p. 228.
76. Pratchett, *Thud!*, p. 71.
77. Pratchett, *Unseen Academicals*, p. 317.
78. Pratchett, *Maskerade*, p. 332.

Bibliography

Butler, J. (1990) *Gender Trouble: Feminism and the Subversion of Identity* (London and New York: Routledge).

_____ (1993) *Bodies that Matter: On the Discursive Limits of Sex* (London and New York: Routledge).

Goffman, E. (1959) *The Presentation of Self in Everyday Life* (New York: Doubleday).

Heath, S. (1986) "Joan Riviere and the Masquerade" in *Formations of Fantasy*, edited V. Burgin, J. Donald, and C. Kaplan (London: Routledge), pp. 46–59.

Loxley, J. (2007) *Performativity* (London: Routledge).

Pratchett, T. (1998) *Jingo* (London: Corgi).

_____ (1999) *Carpe Jugulum* (London: Corgi).

_____ (2000) *Maskerade* (New York: HarperTorch).

_____ (2000) *The Fifth Elephant* (London: Corgi).

_____ (2001) *Wyrd Sisters* (New York: HarperTorch).

_____ (2002) *Lords and Ladies* (New York: HarperTorch).

_____ (2002) *Moving Pictures* (New York: HarperTorch).

_____ (2003) *Small Gods* (New York: HarperTorch).

_____ (2004) *Monstrous Regiment* (London: Corgi).

_____ (2005) *Going Postal* (London: Corgi).

_____ (2006) *Thud!* (London: Corgi).

_____ (2008) *Men at Arms* (New York: Harper).

_____ (2009) *Unseen Academicals* (London: Doubleday).

_____ (2010) *I Shall Wear Midnight* (London: Doubleday).

_____ (2013) *Raising Steam* (London: Doubleday).

Rayment, A. (2014) *Fantasy, Politics, Postmodernity: Pratchett, Pullman, Miéville and Stories of the Eye* (Amsterdam: Rodopi).

Riviere, J. (1986) "Womanliness as Masquerade" in *Formations of Fantasy*, edited V. Burgin, J. Donald, and C. Kaplan (London: Routledge), pp. 35–44.

Said, E. (2003) *Orientalism* (London: Penguin).

Turner, V. (1987) *The Anthropology of Performance* (New York: PAJ Publications).

Žižek, S. (1997) *The Plague of Fantasies* (London and New York: Verso).

_____ (2006a) *How to Read Lacan* (New York: Norton).

_____ (2006b) "Is this Digital Democracy, or a New Tyranny of Cyberspace?" at www.theguardian.com/commentisfree/2006/dec/30/comment.media.

_____ (2013) *Demanding the Impossible* (Cambridge: Polity Press).

4 "Knowing Things that Other People Don't Know Is a Form of Magic": Lessons in Headology and Critical Thinking from the Lancre Witch

Tuomas W. Manninen

Bertrand Russell famously claimed: "The point of philosophy is to start with something so simple as not to seem worth stating, and to end with something so paradoxical that no one will believe it."[1] Following Russell's lead, allow me to start this philosophical essay about the Discworld with the following truism: while magic is prevalent in Discworld, it is not so in Roundworld. As for the paradoxical part which we (hopefully) reach at the end: there *is* magic in the Roundworld—and we can learn important lessons applicable for the Roundworld by closely scrutinizing (some) instances of magic in the Discworld.

Lest this sound like a flat-out contradiction, allow me to assure the reader that this is not so. As it turns out, both the beginning and the end of this chapter can be true; it all just depends on how magic is defined. To make the initial truism more accurate, consider this revision: There is more magic (or, more forms of it) in the Discworld than there is in the Roundworld. Still, the forms of magic that exist both in the Discworld and in the Roundworld are often called by different names. And this is why our journey here will begin with an investigation into the nature of magic.

But before that, consider the following words of caution. After all, as many inhabitants of the Disc are willing to testify, mucking about with magic is risky.[2] Even if magic in the Roundworld turns out to be different in some respects from the Discworld variant, due caution should still be exercised. Thus, the following will be a cautionary tale of sorts. We will look at one particular version of Discworld magic, the one practiced (or, perfected—since she doesn't need much practice) by Granny Weatherwax: headology. After considering the nature of magic in general, we will move on to find the Roundworld counterpart to headology—which turns out to be critical thinking. Nevertheless, the following pages *will not* amount to a 'how-to' manual for using critical thinking in the manner that Granny uses headology. That is, the goal of this chapter is not to chart the path for using headology—or critical thinking, for that matter. Instead, the following is mostly written for (and from) the perspective of an end-user of critical thinking, in an attempt to show where the common pitfalls lie, and how best to avoid them. With that said, now read on.

The Varieties of Magic

Let us start with magic in the Discworld. Here's one way of defining magic on the Disc, borrowed (quite shamelessly) from the *Discworld Companion*:

> All three [of the Lancre witches: Granny Weatherwax, Nanny Ogg, and Magrat Garlick] of course fulfill . . . the usual daily functions expected of a rural witch: midwifery, the laying out of the dead (and sitting up with them at night, possibly playing cards with the more unusual cases) and folk medicine. Their approach to this last again used to represent three aspects of witchcraft: Magrat: would give patients a specific remedy which careful observations over the years had suggested is most efficacious for that complaint; Nanny Ogg: will give patients a stiff drink and tell them to stay in bed if they want to; Granny Weatherwax: will give them the first bottle of

coloured water that comes to hand and tell them it can't possibly fail. Her success rate is notable.[3]

In this description of the Lancre coven, we see three different witches' approaches to healing—as well as which of these three appears to be the most successful: Granny Weatherwax's. We could analyze this in Roundworld terms (such as "subject-expectancy effect" or "self-fulfilling prophecy" and suchlike). Still, this would depart from the intended scope of this chapter. After all, this phenomenon is not limited just to healing, which is a fact of which Granny Weatherwax is keenly aware, and of which she makes good use:

> Granny Weatherwax's personal power is built on a considerable practical knowledge of psychology ("headology"), an iron will, an unshakeable conviction that she is right and some genuine psychic powers, which she distrusts.[4]

So, instead of focusing the investigation here on psychic powers (which seemingly don't, after all, exist in the Roundworld), we will take a close look at headology (some versions of which seemingly *do*, even if under different labels). Moreover, as Granny Weatherwax explains to Esk in the following exchange from *Equal Rites*, magic does take many forms:

GW: Do you think I used magic [in extracting the queen bee from the midst of a beehive]?
Esk: No, I think you just know a lot about bees.
GW: Exactly correct. That's one form of magic, of course.
Esk: What, just knowing things?
GW: Knowing things that other people *don't know*.[5]

Now we are dealing with knowledge, which is a territory that philosophers have claimed for themselves for—oh—forever. So, instead of treating headology as (just) practical psychology, we will model it after critical thinking.

What Is Critical Thinking?

Looking at popular culture/media, it appears that critical thinking is all the rage, given how frequently its benefits are exhorted, and how frequently calls for teaching it are heard. This leaves the impression that everyone knows what they are talking about when they refer to critical thinking. Still, looking for actual instances of critical thinking in the wild typically yields results that are similar to trying to see a (living) specimen of the ambiguous puzuma on the Disc. Just as the Disc's natural philosophers have concluded that the ambiguous puzuma is "flat and dead" in its general appearance based on the fact that this is how it is most commonly encountered, the examples of critical thinking as they appear in popular culture/media likely suggest the many and various failures of critical thinking.[6]

As with many cases, we can make progress by trying to define critical thinking as what it is not; this is how many textbook authors spend their introduction in books titled *Approach to Critical Thinking* or some such. The basic common understanding of critical thinking is that it is *critical*: it's critical of views held by others, or critical in the sense of being antagonistic. And so on, and so forth. Yet, if one actually consults any of the textbooks, we get a different picture, according to which:

> Critical thinking is not just being critical in the negative sense.
> Critical thinking is not just passing judgment on the views of others.
> Critical thinking is not just antagonistic.
> Critical thinking is not just destructive.[7]

Nevertheless, the former are the prevalent ways in which people understand critical thinking, and they are not entirely mistaken. We can say that these attempts at defining critical thinking succeed in capturing *some* aspects of it, or that they form *a part* of what it is, but they do not capture its nature in totality.[8] To further illustrate this, let us turn back to magic in the Discworld.

As avid readers of Pratchett's *Discworld* books are aware, there are many distinct definitions for magic. First, there is the wizards' explanation (or explanations):

> Older wizards talk about candles, circles, planets, stars, bananas, chants, runes, and the importance of having at least four good meals every day. Younger wizards, particularly the pale ones who spend most of their time in the High Energy Magic building, chatter at length about fluxes in the morphic nature of the universe, the essentially impermanent quality of even the most apparently rigid time–space framework, the implausibility of reality, and so on: what this means is that they have got hold of something hot and are gabbling physics as they go along.[9]

And then there are the witches' explanations of the same, again depending on the age of the witch offering the explanation:

> Older witches hardly put words to it at all, but may suspect in their hearts that the universe really doesn't know what the hell is going on and consists of a zillion trillion billion possibilities, and could become any of them if a trained mind rigid with quantum certainty was inserted in the crack and *twisted*; that, if you really had to make someone's hat explode, all you needed to do was *twist* into that universe where a large number of hat molecules all decide at the same time to bounce off in different directions. Younger witches, on the other hand, talk about it all the time, and believe it involves crystals, mystic forces, and dancing about without yer drawers on.[10]

So if you were to ask, 'What is magic?,' the answer you receive would depend on to whom you posed the question; more pointedly, Mustrum Ridcully has one answer as to what magic is, while Ponder Stibbons has another, not entirely congruent, answer. Likewise, Granny Weatherwax would answer the question differently than someone like Perdita Nitt or Diamanda Tockley. As Pratchett remarks here, "everybody may be right, all at the same time. That's the thing about quantum."[11] Although philosophers typically eschew the notion of "quantum," a similar point can be made about the concept "critical thinking."[12] We will return to this point later on, but for now we will take a close look at the partial definitions of critical thinking.

Returning to the Roundworld, we can say that in addition to the popular understanding of critical thinking, there is the academicians' (especially philosophers') understanding of it. Consider the following:

> Critical thinking [is] the systematic evaluation or formulation of beliefs, or arguments, by rational standards.[13]

As concise as this definition is, it is also hopelessly abstract when compared to the popular definitions of critical thinking. We could say that the popular understanding is only partial and, further, that it (among many other concepts as understood by the general populace) rests on white knowledge.

Critical Thinking and White Knowledge

A significant part of critical thinking involves the analysis of arguments in order to distinguish the good ones from the bad ones. But even if it provides us with the tools for discerning good arguments from bad, there is a further concern: the tools provided by critical thinking are somewhat limited in their use. After all, one cannot just wield these tools and expect to get correct results without starting with something.

When we justify claims by giving arguments for them, we take some claims as *premises* and use them to argue for the truth of *conclusions*. Obviously, if *every* claim had to be justified by some preceding argument, we would have no place to begin and our reasoning would never get underway. Hence, we must have some starting points, some claims that are not based on prior arguments.[14]

To illustrate this, consider the following scene from *Maskerade*. Jarge Weaver, "a man who'd twice failed to become Village Idiot through being overqualified" and a chronic back pain sufferer, visits Granny Weatherwax for a remedy. As Jarge's luck would have it, Granny has prepared a potion for him: "a mixture of rare herbs and suchlike . . . including sucrose and akwa."[15] Jarge drinks the potion, receives instructions from Granny, and, upon walking out of the door, has his back surreptitiously adjusted by Granny, who "inexplicably" trips over his cane, places her knee on a spot in his back, and *twists*. As the end result, by the time he reaches home, he is carrying his walking sticks.

From Jarge Weaver's perspective, he reasons along the following lines:

Witches make good potions.
Granny Weatherwax is a witch.
Granny Weatherwax makes good potions.
If I take a good potion, it will cure my backache.
If I take a potion made by Granny Weatherwax, it will cure my backache.

Still, even if we reconstructed Jarge's reasoning along the above lines, we would find very limited use for this analysis. For one, it is unlikely that Jarge himself engaged in such an analysis. For another, this reconstruction of his reasoning process would only show us that it was *valid*. In other words, if he had reasoned from true premises, he would have reached the (true) conclusion. As it turned out, he didn't. But his reasoning was not premised on *entirely* false statements. Rather, his reasoning was premised on statements that were in the ballpark of truth, in a manner of speaking. To put the point slightly differently, Jarge Weaver's knowledge was "white knowledge."

"White knowledge" is a term coined by Terry Pratchett, and although he doesn't explicitly (or at all) define it, it operates on two levels in his *Discworld* novels. On one level, it involves an allusion to some popular cultural item that a reader has picked up without making an attempt; just like white noise fills the background of any moment without a conscious effort of listening, white knowledge fills the epistemic background with no conscious effort to acquire it. Pratchett elucidates this in an interview: "If I put a reference in a book I try to pick one that a generally well-read (well-viewed, well-listened) person has a sporting chance of picking up; I call this 'white knowledge,' the sort of stuff that fills up your brain without you really knowing where it came from."[16]

The allusions work because most people have enough awareness of pop culture that they can get the joke. It would be too extensive to list all the Discworld/Roundworld instances of this, but here's one:[17] In *Truth*, the protagonists discover that the late Mr. Tulip is carrying a wallet with an inscription "Not a very nice person at all." Those readers who have seen (or know of) Quentin Tarantino's *Pulp Fiction* recognize this as a riff of the character Jules Winnfield, played by Samuel L. Jackson, whose wallet bears the inscription "Bad M**********r."

The second level on which white knowledge operates can be seen in the actions of the characters. And, as we will see, this level of white knowledge is crucial for critical thinking. To begin with our analysis, consider the populace of Lancre, who have acquired a certain conception of witches. They know, for instance, that witches are—in general—old, that they've "always been daft," and that they make good potions from "rare herbs and suchlike . . . including akwa and sucrose" that take away the pain. Instead of fighting against these preconceptions, or attempting to disabuse her customers of them, Granny Weatherwax indulges them for their benefit as well as for her own reputation. Granny gives her customer suffering from chronic back pain a bottle of sugar water, tells him to sleep on a board from a 20-year-old pine ("so's the knots in me back end up in the pine?"), and surreptitiously performs a spinal adjustment with a carefully placed knee, while maintaining her reputation—of being a daft, yet skilled, potion-maker.[18]

The failure in Jarge Weaver's reasoning process has very little to do with the process itself. Instead, it has a whole lot to do with the premises with which he operated. And this is the reason why critical thinking needs to involve more than just the analysis of arguments; the analysis needs to extend to the beliefs that are used as source material (or premises) for the arguments. If critical thinking was comprised of just analyzing arguments, we'd find ourselves in trouble. That is to say, if we demanded that every belief we have must follow from a valid argument (or a strong argument), we would find ourselves stuck. Hence, there are some beliefs we need to take in as sources (or premises) for our arguments. As it turns out, we need a starting place for the arguments—there need to be some beliefs from which we argue—some reasonable beliefs.[19]

Sometimes, the premises of our argument are beliefs that are assumed just for the sake of the argument. Other times, we accept certain statements as premises because they are self-evidently true (for example, "Either I left my manuscript in the Place Where the Sun Does Not Shine, or I did not leave my manuscript in the Place Where the Sun Does Not Shine"[20]), or because our experience has shown the statements to be true (for example, "I can tell by the faint scent of apples that this drink is Scumble"), or because those statements are made by someone we take to be an authority figure (which is why Commander Vimes signed the note "Under the protection of the Watch" he left at Mr. Goriff's store in Sergeant Detritus's name).[21]

Once we have our premises, we are able to use them in an argument to draw further conclusions. And *if* the arguments that we use are valid (or strong), *then* we could expect that the conclusions we reach are *true*. But this is so only if the premises themselves are true—which is something we don't often check. Furthermore, even if we happen to get lucky with the truth of untested statements, we are also prone to overlook the *scope* of the statement. A statement which is true in a limited number of cases can turn out false when applied in an atypical situation, as we will see.

To go back to our example of Jarge Weaver, we could reconstruct his reasoning process further, along the following lines:

> After I drank the potion made by Granny Weatherwax, my back ache went away.
>
> Granny Weatherwax tripped over my cane, and hit my back with her knee, but that is because she is an old witch and she is getting clumsy.
>
> Therefore, my back ache went away because I drank the potion made out of rare herbs, like sucrose and akwa.[22]

At no point did Jarge pause to consider that the potion (made out of rare herbs like akwa and sucrose) had nothing to do with the fact that his back pain went away—and that it had most everything to do with the fact that Granny had performed a spinal adjustment on him; as Granny herself put it "It wasn't the medicine that did the trick, though. It was, in a way, the spoon."[23] His belief "Witches make good potions" was probably accurate—if it were applied properly. But as was the case, it was misapplied to a witch who didn't bother with cooking potions.

In the situation described above, Jarge Weaver's reasoning provides us with a textbook example of less-than-critical thinking. Still, one might think—as Jarge certainly seems to do—that there was no harm in what took place. He was given a remedy to a problem that he had—so what if that was done under false pretenses? The problem here is that while Granny Weatherwax is a good witch (though not a nice one), Jarge might have ended up in a world of hurt had she not been. In short: just because Granny did not take advantage of Jarge's plight, this doesn't mean that anyone else would have been as kind. At this point, consider the following case. Suppose that Jarge Weaver lived in Ankh-Morpork instead of Lancre, but that he still suffered from chronic, debilitating back pain. Further, suppose that in seeking remedies he came across a salesman who offered him a tonic designed to take away the pain that was made of rare herbs (like akwa and sucrose)—and who assured him that at the price he was selling the tonic, he was cutting his own throat. Alternatively, suppose that Jarge (with his chronic back-ache) lived in the city of Genua and sought remedies from the local fairy godmother, one known as Lilith de Tempscire. In short, operating with white knowledge beliefs is not necessarily bound to lead one into a disaster. In some cases, it doesn't—while in others it certainly could; on the whole, it offers roughly the same assurance of prosperous longevity as does flipping a coin. Hence, it seems advisable that Jarge moves beyond his white knowledge beliefs and obtains more accurate ones.

In the case of Jarge Weaver in his encounter with Granny Weatherwax, we see an instance where operating with white knowledge turns out to be advantageous to him. But as was duly noted above, the reliance on white knowledge can be precipitous to one's well-being. From Granny Weatherwax's perspective, when people rely on white knowledge beliefs, this makes her craft all the more easier. After all, her alternative would have been to convince Jarge that he needs massage therapy rather than sugar water for his back—and people tend to be fairly reluctant to accept new beliefs. But from Jarge's perspective it would be prudent to do so; it would be prudent to scrutinize some of the beliefs he has and, in doing so, guard himself against some of the dangers.

In what follows, I will consider three common cases in which people operate with white knowledge. Although these cases occur on the Disc, it would be really straightforward to find analogous situations in the Roundworld. As an upshot of considering these cases, we will come to see how prevalent white knowledge is, and how susceptible we are to relying on white knowledge beliefs. As for practical applications of the cases, we will see about ways in which the common pitfalls can be avoided.

Case Study: Bad Examples (of Witches, Dwarves, and so on)

Let us consider Jarge Weaver's encounter with Granny Weatherwax again. At some point prior to his visit, Jarge had acquired the belief that witches could provide him with remedies to his ailments. Although we may not be able to pinpoint when he acquired this belief, it is safe to say that it is due to his past experiences. That is, he may have witnessed a case where a witch was able to cure someone's ailments (or he may have heard of such a case). But where would he have obtained the idea that if *he* were to visit a witch, his ailments could be cured, too? One answer could be found in the works of John Locke who, in his classic *An Essay Concerning Human Understanding*, argues for empiricism, or the view that there are no innate ideas. Instead, all the ideas we have, whether about the appearance of the color octarine, or the taste of scumble, or what witches are like, ultimately come to us from experience: for us to have the idea of what octarine looks like, we must have seen it; for us to have the idea of what scumble tastes like (and what it does to the human body), we must have tasted it; for us to know what witches are like, and what they do, we must have encountered a witch, and so on. But despite having these ideas (of octarine, scumble, and witches), we have not seen *every* item that is colored octarine, nor have we tasted *all* batches of scumble,[24] nor have we encountered *every* witch that there is. Instead, we have a more limited exposure to these things, and on that basis we have formulated the *general ideas* of octarine, scumble, and witches. As Locke himself puts it:

> If every particular idea that we take in should have a distinct name, names must be endless. To prevent this, the mind makes the particular ideas received from particular objects to become general; which is done by considering them as they are in the mind such appearances, separate from all other existences, and the circumstances of real existence, as time,

place, or any other concomitant ideas. This is called ABSTRACTION, whereby ideas taken from particular beings become general representatives of all of the same kind; and their names general names, applicable to whatever exists conformable to such abstract ideas.[25]

So, we come to have the general ideas that we have (of octarine, scumble, witches, and whatever else) by forming an abstract idea from the particular experiences we have had. Subsequently, we apply this general idea to whatever conforms to it. But here's the worry: what if our experiences of scumble are not representative after all? Or what if the witches that we have encountered are somewhat atypical of all witches? For a concrete case, suppose you formulate the general idea of "dwarf" after encountering just one dwarf. If you had encountered Gunilla Goodmountain, chances are that your idea of "dwarf" is representative of other dwarves. But if you had encountered Carrot Ironfoundersson, and used that encounter as the basis of your idea of "dwarf," you would be mostly mistaken.[26]

To put the point more formally, if the general idea of "dwarf" is formulated in the above manner, this amounts to the informal fallacy of *hasty generalization*: the sample size used in making the generalization is inadequate; moreover, the sample is quite atypical of dwarves on the whole.[27] Here we have one instance in which white knowledge is formed: the belief is accurate only in a very limited number of cases, but if it gets employed as a general idea, it can fall miserably short. At most, on the basis of our limited encounters, we could say that *some* dwarves are short-tempered, or that *some* octarine-colored items are sort of fluorescent greenish-yellow-purple, or that *some* people who call dwarves "short-tempered" will not live to tell the tale, and so on. But we frequently underestimate or misconstrue the full range of variation and think that *all* dwarves, or octarine-colored objects, or what-have-yous, must meet the same criteria. This mistake would be easy to correct, provided that we paid attention to the specifics. That is, if only.

Case Study: Elves, Vampires, and Vampyres

Happily, not all of our general ideas result from non-representative examples or from hasty generalizations. Somewhat more unhappily, many of them do not stand the test of time. This point is vividly illustrated both in *Lords and Ladies* and in *Carpe Jugulum*. In both of these cases, the current generation of Lancrians and Escrowians, respectively, is reliant on hand-me-downs, when it comes to epistemological matters. That is, the current generation has never encountered either the elves or the vampires. As a result, they only know that there should be a horseshoe hung up above one's door or that garlic is useful for—um—spicing up the dishes, supposedly.

To review these examples in order, take the elves—sorry: "The Fair Folk. The Gentry. The Shining Ones. The Star People. *You know.*"[28] It has been a while since Lancrians have had encounters with them, and when the Lords and Ladies return after Diamanda crosses the barrier at the Dancers, bringing them in, no one really remembers what they are like, aside from Granny Weatherwax and Nanny Ogg, that is. As a result, many Lancrians are in for a nasty surprise when they encounter the Lords and Ladies for themselves. The knowledge of the Lords and Ladies that present-day Lancrians have has been passed down from past generations, and although the past generations lived to see the Lords and Ladies in person, the hand-me-down knowledge is somewhat worse for the wear. As Granny Weatherwax explains to King Verence II, who protests that the tales about elves are just folklore:

GW: Of course it's folklore, you stupid man!
Verence: I do happen to be king, you know.
GW: You stupid king, your majesty. I mean it doesn't mean it's not true! Maybe it gets a little muddled over the years, folks forget details, they forget *why* they do things. Like the horseshoe thing.
Verence: I know my granny had one over the door.

GW: There you are. Nothing to do with its shape. But if you lives in an old cottage and you're poor, it's probably the nearest bit of iron with holes in it that you can find [to keep the elves away, as they can't stand iron].[29]

In short, the knowledge (in this case "Elves cannot stand iron, so you should have some iron to protect yourself from elves") is passed down the generations. However, just as with concrete hand-me-downs, the epistemic ones suffer from this transmission.[30] Clearly there is a reason to have a horseshoe hanging over one's door, but if you don't know the original reason, or if no one bothered to tell you, you are likely to come up with one of your own—like "It's a good luck talisman!" The original reason for having a horseshoe has been watered down, or, given how we are discussing *white knowledge*, let's say it has been whitewashed; the practice or tradition remains, but has been repurposed.[31] Of course, it is full well possible to reach the original reason behind the practices. Alas, this would require more effort than most are willing to put in.

The events in *Carpe Jugulum* follow a similar pattern. On the Disc, there have been vampires for ages, and past generations have dealt with them (and, given their undead nature, often with the same ones, many times over). The past generations of Lancrians, and especially Escrowians, whose village is in closer proximity to the Don'tgonearthe Castle, have developed approaches that worked on vampires in the past, ranging from splashing them with holy water to decapitating them, and all points in-between. Still, as the immediate threat of vampires was removed, often in very incisive ways, the need to keep those skills, not to mention the stakes, sharp was mitigated. The predictable result of such an approach was that every time vampires re-emerged, the populace—be it Lancrian or Escrowian—had to reinvent the proper response, provided that someone within that populace had been stupid enough to revive the vampires in the first place. Of course, Count de Magpyr (the younger) counted on this to happen—which is why he opted not to play by the original rules. Instead of just reviving the vampires, he reinvents them as vampyres, who don't shun away from the garlic stakes, or holy water, or even holy symbols, at least not initially. Still, while he manages to cause problems for Escrowians and Lancrians alike, these are largely due to the fact that everyone had forgotten the lessons of the past. Or, more precisely, what they had received by way of lessons about vampires had been diluted, down to a paler shade of white. The comment made by Piotr (whose grandmother had encountered the *Old* Count de Magpyr) during the final showdown is instructive: "He [the Old Count] only ever came round every few years and anyway *if you remembered about the garlic he wasn't a problem.* He didn't expect us to like him."[32] This shows the twofold nature of the problem. First, even vampires can adapt, and become vampyres, as shown throughout the events in *Carpe Jugulum*. Second, and going back to the events in the novel, most people are bound to forget about garlic and what it is for, especially if they do not encounter vampires on a regular basis. Here, the mindset of the past generations could be summed up as follows:

> Being exposed to garlic (or lemon) is typically fatal to vampires.
>
> Thus, if vampires were ever to return, we should have some garlic (and lemon) around, so that we could fight them.

But given how there had been no vampires around for years (or generations even), the olden beliefs had become diluted. Sure, it's important to still have garlic and lemon around—they make for a tasty garnish! Given human nature, we are unhappy to do things (like keep garlic, lemons, or horseshoes accessible) without a reason. Unfortunately, we are all too happy to invent reasons if we don't know the original one. Sometimes, this process works through pure luck—but this poses the problem that sometimes it might not. And there is, admittedly, something unsettling about having one's prospects for survival depend on a game of chance.

If we were to leave the elves, vampires, and vampyres of the Disc aside, and turn our attention to the affairs of the Roundworld for a moment, we can easily find numerous examples of traditions that have become diluted—or that have lost their original purpose due to changing times—without the tradition being ended. This phenomenon can also be found in intellectual debates as well, given how there are some debates that seem to be perpetual in nature. This has not gone without notice from Roundworld philosophers. In fact, John Stuart Mill, in his book *On Liberty*, argued that, in order to ensure liberty of thought, one must not censor opposing viewpoints. Although Mill hardly envisioned that his claim could be applied in dealings with elves or vampires, his point still stands: if we deliberately suppress viewpoints that are different from ours, we run the risk of losing a proper understanding of our own view. Mill argued that in many debates, such as those in natural philosophy, and even more so in those "subjects infinitely more complicated [like] morals, religion, politics, social relations, and the business of life . . . three-fourths of the arguments for every disputed opinion consist in dispelling the appearances which favor some opinion different from it."[33] The problem here is: what if the differing opinions are mere strawmen of the actual different opinions? What if, instead of responding to the actual objections from opponents whose views have been lost due to censorship, the defensive response is directed at a caricature? Mill answers these questions in the following:

> He who knows only his own side of the case, knows little of that. His reasons may be good, and no one may have been able to refute them. But if he is equally unable to refute the reasons on the opposite side; if he does not so much as know what they are, he has no ground for preferring either opinion. The rational position for him would be suspension of

judgment, and unless he contents himself with that, he is either led by authority, or adopts, like the generality of the world, the side to which he feels most inclination. Nor is it enough that he should hear the arguments of adversaries from his own teachers, presented as they state them, and accompanied by what they offer as refutations. That is not the way to do justice to the arguments, or bring them into real contact with his own mind. He must be able to hear them from persons who actually believe them; who defend them in earnest, and do their very utmost for them. He must know them in their most plausible and persuasive form; he must feel the whole force of the difficulty which the true view of the subject has to encounter and dispose of; else he will never really possess himself of the portion of truth which meets and removes that difficulty.[34]

And finally:

So essential is this discipline to a real understanding of moral and human subjects, that if opponents of all important truths do not exist, it is indispensable to imagine them, and supply them with the strongest arguments which the most skillful devil's advocate can conjure up.[35]

Let us return to the Disc for a brief moment. The Lancrians lost track of the real reason behind the practice of keeping iron handy, because there were no elves around for a while, and they ended up inventing a new reason for the practice. Back in the Roundworld, we see this in various debates in the sciences, in politics, philosophy, and numerous other fields. No one takes the olden positions seriously anymore, because those views have no defenders left for them. Over time, we can no longer recall the reasons why someone might have held such a view—so we become contented with the idea that we know better nowadays. But in doing so, we lose the significance of those views. This point is well illustrated in the discussion between Lord Vetinari and Hughnon Ridcully, the High Priest of Blind Io:

> A thousand years ago we thought the world was a bowl. Five hundred years ago we knew it was a globe. Today we know it is flat and round and carried through space on the back of a turtle. Don't you wonder what shape it will turn out to be tomorrow?[36]

In light of this example, we can rely on our present-day knowledge and dismiss our (white knowledge about) past beliefs as embarrassing mistakes of our past, when people didn't know any better. Or, we can expend efforts to find out about the reasons behind these beliefs. Sadly, it seems that the former approach will prevail—and we are all the worse off for that. Again, it is not guaranteed that our white knowledge of the past will leave us worse off; sometimes, we may zero in on the truth. But again, this uncertainty does not offer much by way of guaranteeing good consequences.

Case Study: On (not) Trusting what You Read

As noted above, many of the beliefs we have result not from personal experience, but from receiving them from authoritative sources. Or, to be more precise, we could say that many of those beliefs come from sources that we *deem* to be authoritative. For instance, Jarge Weaver did not challenge Granny Weatherwax's advice because he took her to be an authoritative figure when it comes to helpful potions. Here, it should be noted that Granny Weatherwax's general demeanor does a lot to help her command of authority. Although not everyone on the Disc grants this authority to witches or wizards, many grant such an authority to printed words, as is readily illustrated in *The Truth*. The lodgers gathered around the breakfast table at Mrs. Eucrasia Arcanum's Lodging House for Respectable Working Men steadfastly held that 56 people were hurt in a brawl for the simple reason that "it says here fifty-six people were hurt in a brawl."[37] Moreover, Lord Vetinari reached a similar conclusion: "Well, well . . . I see fifty-six people were hurt in a tavern brawl . . . It must be true, Drumknott, it's in the paper."[38]

These examples illustrate that unwavering reliance on printed word(s) can lead to incorrect conclusions. Nevertheless, such reliance seems to be all too common; for the purposes of this essay, we can identify this as—yet—another source of white knowledge. And this is something of which most of us are guilty. Just think about it: when we read the headline from our pre-ferred news outlet, do we really care enough to cross-reference it with other outlets to see how they reported it? Or do we even bother to look in the details of the report? Here, it appears that an uncritical reliance on just one news outlet may bias your out-look. For instance, imagine an average Ankh-Morporkian, who received his or her news not from *The Ankh-Morpork Times* but from its competitor, the *Ankh-Morpork Inquirer*.

When it comes to relying on printed words, it appears that Granny Weatherwax is ahead of the curve here. Although she doesn't trust the printed word all that much (read: at all), she is capable of discerning what those words say.[39] And ditto for numbers, as evidenced by her exchange with Agnes (or Perdita) when they peruse the ledgers of the Ankh-Morpork Opera House:

> She [Granny Weatherwax] riffled through the bits of torn envelope and scribbled notes that seemed to be the Opera House's equivalent of proper accounts. It was a mess. In fact, it was more than a mess. It was far too much of a mess to be a real mess, because a real mess has occasional bits of coher-ence, bits of what might be called random order. Rather, it was the kind of erratic mess that suggested that someone had set out to be messy. Take the account books. They were full of tiny rows and columns, but someone hadn't thought it worthwhile to invest in lined paper and had handwriting that wandered a bit. There were forty rows on the left-hand

side but only thirty-six by the time they reached the other side of the page. It was hard to spot because of the way your eyes watered.

Agnes: What are you doing?
GW: Amazin'. Some things is entered twice! And I reckon there's a page here where someone's added the month and taken away the time of day!
Agnes: I thought you didn't like books.
GW: I don't. They can look you right in the face and still lie. How many fiddle players are there in the band?
Agnes: I think there are nine violinists in the orchestra.
GW: Well, there's a thing. Seems that twelve of 'em are drawing wages, but three of 'em is over the page, so you mightn't notice. Unless you've got a good memory, that is.[40]

This episode at the Ankh-Morpork Opera House is quite comparable to some events in the Roundworld. More truthfully, this episode is comparable to *a whole lot of* events in the Roundworld. Moreover, the lesson we can draw from the night at the Ankh-Morpork Opera House episode—that it can pay off to pay attention to the details—is equally applicable here. Concrete examples of this phenomenon are so plentiful in the Roundworld that, instead of focusing on just one of them, we will focus on the general pattern, elucidated in the following hypothetical—and archetypical—scenario.

Suppose that a newspaper runs the headline "Survey Shows that the Number of Incoming Students at Unseen University Is not as High as the UU Administration Claims it to Be." Now, depending on your views about UU, you could draw your conclusions about the worth of UU (or the lack thereof) just from seeing this headline. That is, you could draw your conclusions *without* ever looking at the *details* of the claim. Suppose that it turns out (in this extremely hypothetical case) that the headline *is* accurate—that there *is* a discrepancy between the findings of the survey and the claims reported by UU. Now, suppose further that the reason for this discrepancy was that *the actual number of incoming students was higher than what the UU administration claimed it to be*![41] The headline would still be true—on a technicality, given that it merely stated that the reported number was not *as high* as the actual number was. Even if the actual number was *higher than* the one reported, the headline would be true—albeit misleading (but who cares about that?). Now, if you had put in the effort of reading the article, you might have learned about such seemingly pesky details. Still, if you just went with the headline—as many Ankh-Morporkians (and Roundworldians alike) are wont to do—you would be left with a *technically* true belief that was still misleading. But that's just how it goes.

In sum, the potential number of actual Roundworld situations comparable to the hypothetical example just outlined is virtually unlimited. Given all this, it would seem that it is prudent for most everyone to follow Granny Weatherwax's suggestions and not trust anything that is written down, at least not without checking things out. Alas, doing such fact-checking would be quite burdensome.[42] At this point, we also see the allure of *white knowledge*: we seem to come to "know" things while expending minimal effort—or none at all—to vet it for accuracy. As long as we make do with this, why should we expend any further resources to get to the bottom of things? Put differently, if our *white knowledge* beliefs are good enough for everyday living—why bother?

What is Magic? (Redux)

To answer the above question, let us return to the topic from earlier on in this chapter—that of defining the nature of "magic." As was noted, each of the considered definitions of "magic" for the Disc—and, analogously, each definition considered for *critical thinking* for the Roundworld—was a partial one: the proposed definition captured *some* aspect of magic, or *some* aspect of critical thinking, but not all of them. To generalize this point: we go astray when we do this—when we think that a partial definition is the same as the complete definition. At the same time, the partial definition has its uses. This point is well put by Ludwig Wittgenstein:

> Consider, for example, the activities that we call "games." I mean board-games, card-games, ball-games, athletic games, and so on. What is common to them all?—Don't say: "They must have something in common, or they would not be called 'games'"—but *look and see* whether there is anything common to all.—For if you look at them, you won't see something that is common to *all*, but similarities, affinities, and a whole series of them at that. To repeat: don't think, but look!—Look, for example, at board-games, with their various affinities. Now pass to card-games; here you may find correspondences with the first group, but many common features drop out, and others appear. When we pass next to ball-games, much that is common is retained, but much is lost . . . And the upshot of these considerations is: we see a complicated network of similarities overlapping and criss-crossing: similarities in the large and in the small.
>
> I can think of no better expression to characterize these similarities than "family resemblances"; for the various resemblances between members of a family—build, features, colour of eyes, gait, temperament, and so on and so forth— overlap and crisscross in the same way.—And I shall say: "games" form a family.[43]

The problem we encounter when defining "games" is the same problem we encounter in defining "magic" or "critical thinking"—or any concept, for that matter. For ordinary purposes, whatever those may be, our initial definition may be adequate for the task, and we resist the effort of expending further energy. Still, this hardly changes the fact that the initial definition for which we have settled may be a partial one; it may have resulted from unrepresentative samples, or from beliefs that we have inherited without fully scrutinizing their origins, or from something we have read, or—you get the point. In short, the type of definition we begin with (and all-too-frequently end up with) comes to us nearly effortlessly; in a word, it is white knowledge. It comes to us with ease, or with no effort—and we are just too comfortable with the status quo and don't want to expend any more effort.

Bringing It All Back to Roundworld

A nagging question remains: what's so bad about relying on white knowledge? To return to Jarge Weaver's case, he did receive a remedy for his back pains—even if it took a different form than what he was expecting, or even what he thought he received. But here's a simple consideration that shows (or one that *should* show) the dangers inherent in relying just on the (effortlessly acquired) white knowledge: Jarge received a cure for his back pains because he went to see a *good* witch. But, as noted above, suppose that Jarge lived in Genua, and went to see the local witch, who in this case would be Lilith de Tempscire— or Lily Weatherwax, Genua's own fairy godmother—for a remedy. Operating with just white knowledge, Jarge got lucky—but his imaginary counterpart in Genua might not have gotten so lucky. And this point can be well generalized: if you operate with white knowledge, without a whit of critical thinking, you might get lucky—or you might not. The operative question here is—much like the one posed to the mob that had gathered around Lady Ramkin's house in *Guards! Guards!* who ended up staring down the barrel, er, throat, of Lord Mountjoy Quickfang Winterfort IV, wielded by then-Captain-of-the-Night-Watch, Samuel Vimes—"*Am I feeling lucky?*"

In conclusion, we (as the Jarge Weavers of the Roundworld) *might* get by in our everyday living when we rely on white knowledge: "knowledge" that we passively receive without putting any effort into acquiring, or "knowledge" that we never really scrutinize. The important point to keep in mind is that we *might not* get by with our everyday living; we might, though, get by with our everyday *dying*. We wish that maybe—just maybe—we will get lucky; *maybe* the person asking us whether or not we feel lucky has an empty swamp dragon, after all. At the same time, *maybe* the swamp dragon they are pointing at us is not empty, but it is about to burp . . . but just maybe. *Are you feeling lucky?*

Notes

1. B. Russell, "The Philosophy of Logical Atomism" (1956 [1918]), in *Logic and Knowledge*, ed. R.C. Marsh (London: Allen & Unwin), p. 193.
2. The Librarian might have something pertinent to add to this—even if it amounted just to 'Oook!' Similarly, so might Casanunda (who turned out to be a fast learner), as well as the bandit chieftain in *Lords and Ladies* (who didn't).
3. T. Pratchett and S. Briggs (2012) *Turtle Recall: The Discworld Companion . . . So Far* (London: Victor Gollancz), p. 189.
4. Pratchett and Briggs *Turtle Recall*, p. 188.
5. T. Pratchett (1987) *Equal Rites* (New York: HarperCollins), p. 38.
6. Pratchett and Briggs, *Turtle Recall*, p. 232.
7. P. Tittle (2011) *Critical Thinking: An Appeal to Reason* (New York: Routledge), p. 6.
8. These considerations are offered in Tittle, *Critical Thinking*, pp. 6–8; L. Vaughn (2013) *The Power of Critical Thinking: Effective Reasoning About Ordinary and Extraordinary Claims*, 4th edn (New York: Oxford University Press), ch. 1, *passim*; as well as many other textbooks on the topic.
9. T. Pratchett (1992) *Lords and Ladies* (New York: HarperCollins), p. 95.
10. Ibid., p. 107.
11. Ibid.
12. More accurately, *some* philosophers eschew the notion of quantum, while others seemingly embrace it. The latter type usually write papers concerning topics like the theoretical status of quantum mechanics, or whether quantum particles are individual objects, or if quantum theory could prove helpful in understanding consciousness. You know, the usual ones.
13. Vaughn, *The Power of Critical Thinking*, p. 4.

14. D.A. Conway and R. Munson (1997) *The Elements of Reasoning*, 2nd edn (New York: Wadsworth), p. 148.

15. T. Pratchett (1995) *Maskerade* (New York: HarperCollins), p. 18.

16. L. Breebart (editor) (2008) "Words from the Master" in *The Annotated Pratchett File, v. 9.0*, at www.lspace.org/books/apf/words-from-the-master.html (accessed 19 August 2012).

17. Besides, the *Annotated Pratchett File, v. 9.0* already does a tremendous job at this. See Breebart, "Words from the Master".

18. Pratchett, *Maskerade*, pp. 18–19.

19. This point is more thoroughly discussed, for example, in Conway and Munson, *The Elements of Reasoning*, pp. 148ff. and in many other textbooks on critical thinking.

20. Located near Slice, in Lancre; Pratchett and Briggs, *Turtle Recall*, p. 264.

21. T. Pratchett (1997) *Jingo* (New York: HarperCollins), p. 133. These types of examples are discussed in greater detail in Conway and Munson, *The Elements of Reasoning*, pp. 149–51.

22. Pratchett, *Maskerade*, p. 20.

23. Ibid., p. 18.

24. Which is, quite likely, for the best.

25. J. Locke (1997 [1689]) *An Essay Concerning Human Understanding* (New York: Penguin), Book II, ch. XI, §9, p. 155.

26. After all, Carrot is happy to tell you that he is a dwarf; what he might leave out is the fact that he is a dwarf by adoption. He was a human foundling raised by dwarf upbringing—but his human genetics raised him to six feet six inches.

27. For further discussion on enumerative induction—and all the various pitfalls associated with it—see, for instance, Vaughn, *The Power of Critical Thinking*, pp. 277–89.

28. Pratchett, *Lords and Ladies*, p. 47.

29. Ibid., p. 117. As for Granny Weatherwax's point—that just because something is folklore, it doesn't mean that it isn't true, at least in part—this theme is explored in great detail in T. Pratchett and J. Simpson (2008) *The Folklore of Discworld* (London: Doubleday); see especially the chapter on "Witches."

30. Just think of the game "Telephone" or "Chinese Whispers" and how the original message morphs as it is passed down from one player to the next.

31. Besides, what would be the alternative—giving up the tradition because no one knows the origins anymore? As a counterpoint, consider Archchancellor Bowell's Remembrance (at Unseen University), which is the place for the ritual of "one small currant bun and one copper penny to be placed on a high stone shelf on one wall every

second Wednesday"—although "no one now knows why." Still, "if you left off traditions because you didn't know why they started you'd be no better than a foreigner." T. Pratchett (1996) *Hogfather* (New York: HarperCollins), p. 139.

32. T. Pratchett (1998) *Carpe Jugulum* (New York: HarperCollins), pp. 356–7; my emphasis.

33. J.S. Mill (1989 [1859]) *On Liberty and other writings* (New York: Cambridge University Press), p. 38.

34. Ibid., pp. 38–9.

35. Ibid., p. 39.

36. T. Pratchett (2000) *The Truth* (New York: HarperCollins), p. 33.

37. Ibid., p. 71.

38. Ibid., p. 70. Never mind the fact that the headline in question in *The Ankh-Morpork Times* was *supposed* to read "5/6 hurt in a tavern brawl"—it's just a slash, right?

39. "Granny Weatherwax was grudgingly literate but keenly numerate. She assumed that anything written down was probably a lie, and that applied to numbers too. Numbers were used only by people who wanted to put one over on you." Pratchett, *Maskerade*, p. 40.

40. Ibid., pp. 300–1.

41. Maybe this was due to the (unreported) fact that the Bursar was fresh out of dried frog pills when he was making the estimates. Or for any other reason, for that matter; the point still stands.

42. Coincidentally, this is the reason why the *Almanac* published by Mr. Goatberger is so successful: if you claim that there will be "astounding rains of curry in Klatch" in May, who amongst your intended audience is going to know that "you don't get curry that early?" Pratchett, *Maskerade*, pp. 8, 187.

43. L. Wittgenstein (1999 [1958]) *Philosophical Investigations*, trans. G.E.M. Anscombe, 3rd edn (Malden, MA: Wiley/Blackwell), §66–7, pp. 31–2.

Bibliography

Breebart, L. (editor) (2008) "Discworld Annotations" in *The Annotated Pratchett File, v. 9.0*, at www.lspace.org/books/apf/introduction.html (accessed 10 April 2014).

_____ (editor) (2008) "Words from the Master" in *The Annotated Pratchett File, v. 9.0*, at www.lspace.org/books/apf/words-from-the-master.html (accessed 19 August 2012).

Conway, D.A. and R. Munson (1997) *The Elements of Reasoning*, 2nd edn (New York: Wadsworth).

Locke, J. (1997 [1689]) *An Essay Concerning Human Understanding* (New York: Penguin).

Mill, J.S. (1989 [1859]) *On Liberty and Other Writings* (New York: Cambridge University Press).

Pratchett, T. (1987) *Equal Rites* (New York: HarperCollins).

_____ (1991) *Witches Abroad* (New York: HarperCollins).

_____ (1992) *Lords and Ladies* (New York: HarperCollins).

_____ (1995) *Maskerade* (New York: HarperCollins).

_____ (1996) *Hogfather* (New York: HarperCollins).

_____ (1997) *Jingo* (New York: HarperCollins).

_____ (1998) *Carpe Jugulum* (New York: HarperCollins).

_____ (2000) *The Truth* (New York: HarperCollins).

Pratchett, T. and S. Briggs (2012) *Turtle Recall: The Discworld Companion . . . So Far* (London: Victor Gollancz).

Pratchett T. and J. Simpson (2008) *The Folklore of Discworld* (London: Doubleday).

Russell, B. (1918 [1956]) "The Philosophy of Logical Atomism" in *Logic and Knowledge*, ed. R. C. Marsh (London: Allen & Unwin).

Tittle, P. (2011) *Critical Thinking: An Appeal to Reason* (New York: Routledge).

Vaughn, L. (2013) *The Power of Critical Thinking: Effective Reasoning About Ordinary and Extraordinary Claims*, 4th edn (New York: Oxford University Press).

Wittgenstein, L. (1999 [1958]) *Philosophical Investigations*, trans. G. E. M. Anscombe, 3rd edn (Malden, MA: Wiley/Blackwell).

Part II Social and Political Philosophy

5 Capitalism, Socialism, and Democracy on the Discworld

Kevin Guilfoy

Pratchett does not push a political ideology, but he has a clear inclination. He is libertarian-friendly, maybe even libertarian-curious. The largest finest city on the disc, Ankh-Morpork, is a place of freedom and opportunity, free markets, limited government, diversity, ingenuity, and prosperity. These are the city's strengths. In Pratchett's fantasy, dwarves, trolls, golems, and goblins can literally come out from under a rock and make a life for themselves. Whether Pratchett himself would agree with this sentiment, most citizens of Ankh-Morpork believe that every person should be free to engage in any kind of mutually agreed upon activity they wish. For purposes of making money, they are grudgingly willing to count just about everyone as a person. This gives hope to men like Cut-Me-Own-Throat Dibbler. They hope that with a little bit of freedom and a little bit of charm they can get rich dealing with these "people." Samuel Vimes is always there to enforce the impartial rule of law. However, from the purveyors of fine meat-like sausage to Moist von Lipwig and Harry King, it is hard to tell a criminal from a captain of industry. The vibrant life of the city revolves around the impossible character of Lord Havelock Vetinari. He is clearly inspired by Machiavelli's Prince, but there is more to Vetinari. He has near perfect knowledge of the workings of his city. He knows the minds of the citizens. He is skilled at pulling all the levers of power. But Pratchett's libertarian proclivities shape Vetinari in the mold of Adam Smith and F. A. Hayek. The

Tyrant of Ankh-Morpork may be Machiavelli's Prince, but he is ruling Smith and Hayek's world. Vetinari knows the limits of his knowledge and does not act merely to preserve his own power. He stands above the fray, occasionally guiding, but rarely dictating. Vetinari recognizes the social, political, and economic forces described by Smith and Hayek. As they would recommend, he lets these forces play out as they will.

On Roundworld, libertarianism is a bit of a fantasy as well. There are no libertarian states, but there are many "just so" stories. Like pure communism, a pure system of freedom and markets has never really been tried, but the true believers know their system would work if just given the chance. Discworld is no different. The river Ankh is toxic sludge, yet there are no water shortages or public-health consequences. There are poor people, but social and economic injustice occurs in Klatch and the Agatean Empire, maybe a bit in Djelibeybi, but not in Ankh. On Pratchett's Discworld there is the firm faith that an individual ingenuity and spirit will overcome these problems. This commercial spirit is fixed in the nature of the disc's inhabitants. It defines who they are.

Let Others Boast of Martial Dash

> For we have boldly fought with cash
> We own all your helmets, we own all your shoes
> We own all your generals—touch us and you'll lose.
> (Ankh-Morpork National Anthem)[1]

How did the commercial spirit of Ankh-Morpork evolve? As in another famous telling, the disc's story starts with an apple. In *Interesting Times* an aging Cohen the Barbarian assembles the hoard for one final conquest. They are going to conquer and become the civilized rulers of the Agatean Empire. The first step in the civilizing process is clean underwear. The second is an attempt to buy an apple. He wrestles mightily with the concept, but eventually successfully purchases an apple. He then beats up the shopkeeper and steals everything else in the shop. There is more Thomas Hobbes than Adam Smith in Cohen the Barbarian. Hobbes and Smith think people are motivated by self-interest, even greed, but they disagree on exactly what this means. For Hobbes our self-interest drives us to seek power. In a passage worthy of Pratchett, Thomas Hobbes argues that, in our natural state, all people are physically, mentally, and therefore morally equal. While equality sounds nice, it is in fact the reason we steal and kill. "From this equality of ability, ariseth equality of hope in the attaining of our ends. And therefore if any two men desire the same thing . . . they become enemies; and in the way to their end . . . endeavor to destroy one another."[2] Cohen certainly exemplifies this principle of equal hope and respect. Others have what he wants, and so need to be killed; or they want what he has, and so need to be killed. He respects everyone, as a threat to his interests. Cohen eventually faces the same problem we all face in Hobbes's state of nature. At some point we want some security to enjoy what we have. Cohen seizes control of the Agatean Empire and seems primed to run the state as Hobbes's Leviathan: imposing a few simple rules and brutally enforcing compliance. Dispatches have not come in to judge the success of this endeavor.

Adam Smith also argues that by nature people are self-interested even selfish, but this selfish impulse spurs us to a uniquely human activity, trade. Dogs will fight and kill each other over a bone. However, "no one ever saw a dog make a fair and deliberate exchange of one bone for another with another dog. Nobody ever saw an animal, by its gestures and natural cries, signify to another this is mine, that is yours, I am willing to give you this for that."[3] For Smith, self-interest drives us to satisfy our desires through trade. The butcher, the brewer, and the baker are not moved by good will to produce goods that others want. Each believes that if he produces something others want, he can trade for goods he wants. Trade does not come easily to Cohen. But this capacity to specialize and trade comes naturally to Cut-Me-Own-Throat

Dibbler and countless others. Just like on Roundworld, there is more Adam Smith than Thomas Hobbes on the disc.

Smith announces this fight with Hobbes in the very first sentence of his *Theory of Moral Sentiments*: "However selfish man may be supposed, there are evidently some principles in his nature, which interest him in the fortune of others, and render their happiness necessary to him, though they derive nothing from it except the pleasure of seeing it."[4] The primary principle is sympathy. But sympathy isn't niceness or altruism. Sympathy is what allows the evolution of the social rules in Mrs. Cake's boarding house. At Mrs. Cake's, the differently-living have worked out a system of rules and norms based on the two elements of sympathy: a "fellow feeling" and a similar emotional response. Each individual can identify and perceive the other tenants' need for privacy and discretion. They have a "fellow-feeling" with the emotions the other tenants are experiencing. This is our modern notion of empathy, but it is only half of Smith's notion of sympathy. If another person exhibits a response to his emotions that we might exhibit ourselves, then we feel a sympathetic affinity with them. They will also come to feel the same sympathetic affinity with us. We share our moods, emotional responses, and judgments. Sympathy is not altruistic because we expect much in return. We enjoy and seek out people who reflect our emotive responses. We are simply more comfortable and at ease around those who intuitively share our feelings and judgments. Sympathy is also not purely self-interested because we feel a genuine interest and concern for the good of others, at least the others we have sympathy with.

This principle of sympathy guides the formation of social order as society progresses through Smith's four stages of human civilization: hunter, shepherd, agricultural, and commercial. As they enter the Century of the Fruitbat, Ankh-Morporkians are evolving from an agricultural to a commercial civilization. There is little evidence of the Discworld's progress through the first three stages. But there is also limited evidence of the Roundworld developing the way Smith describes. It is, nonetheless, an interesting theory.[5] In the first three stages the economic activity of the people is focused on the production of food. Groups are small and individuals are interdependent. Smith imagines that a powerful landlord in an agricultural society may want to consume the entire produce of his land; but he cannot.

> The rich only select from the heap what is most precious and agreeable. They consume little more than the poor, and in spite of their natural selfishness and rapacity . . . they divide with the poor the produce of all their improvements. They are led by an invisible hand to make nearly the same distribution of the necessaries of life, which would have been made, had the earth been divided into equal portions among all its inhabitants.[6]

The mutual sympathy between rich and poor does not make greed go away. Rather it gives rise to the "nearly equal" distribution of the community's produce. This is the myth of the noble feudal lord, perhaps best represented by King Verence II of Lancre. On Roundworld it is also best exemplified in fiction.

Problems arise in the transition from agricultural to commercial society. An agricultural society produces food. It does not mass-produce luxury goods, and it lacks a financial sector that allows the creation of capital. In Smith's agricultural society the invisible hand can guide us to a just distribution of goods. The wealth that needs to be distributed cannot be hoarded, so it is easier to feel sympathy for the poor and feel good about sharing. In a commercial society this changes. Here capital can be accumulated and hoarded without limit. There are social changes as well. With industrialization people leave the agricultural occupations and flock to cities. This migration breaks down the social bonds of reciprocal sympathy that held together the old social order. Ankh-Morpork is particularly susceptible to this. The social tension between troll and dwarf, between human native and other immigrant, between worker and Golem, all show how our networks of mutual sympathy are limited. We form sub-communities within the larger community. Sympathy is strongest for those we are close to. It is severely taxed for those we are not.

Smith is aware of the problems that arise as a society becomes affluent and diverse, but he is optimistic. Again, his hope is the invisible hand. Each person acting in sympathy and self-interest satisfies his or her own desires and this complex self-interested interaction produces socially good results. No party in an economic transaction "intends to promote the public interest, nor knows how much he is promoting it . . . yet in this, as in many other cases, he is led by an invisible hand to promote an end which was no part of his intention."[7] The public interest, or common good, is not merely the sum of individual goods. Smith uses the phrase "invisible hand" only three times.[8] The metaphor is not explanatory. It merely expresses Smith's belief that the common good is produced as the unplanned result of individual economic transactions.

Right alongside the optimistic Smith is the realistic Smith: the Smith that recognizes that wealth and power will do anything to preserve themselves. Wealth in an affluent commercial society is held in a form that can be accumulated without limit. The rich no longer take the best and leave enough for everyone else; now they take a disproportionate share. This distribution of goods creates resentment:

> For one very rich man there must be at least five hundred poor, and the affluence of the few supposes the indigence of the many. The affluence of the rich excites the indignation of the poor, who are often both driven by want, and prompted by envy, to invade his possessions. [The rich man is] at all times surrounded by unknown enemies, whom, though he never provoked, he can never appease . . . Civil government . . . is in reality instituted for the defense of the rich against the poor, or of those who have some property against those who have none at all.[9]

So while the invisible hand could guide us in mutual sympathy to a just distribution of goods, the rich and powerful have more sympathy with each other. Ankh-Morpork has a well-entrenched aristocracy with the power to use the law as protection against the less sympathetic poor who might want their stuff. Watch-Commander Samuel Vimes frequently reflects on the etymology of the word "privilege," as he continually offends against this sense of "private law."

There are some basic laws needed for the free market to function. The law must define property rights, establish rules for finance, and create a legal system that recognizes and enforces transfer of property and adjudicates disputes. There are many theories as to how property is created and how laws originate. On the Discworld the predominant theory seems to be some version of Vetinari's maxim *quia ego sic dico*. The rich and powerful pass laws "because I say so." The guild system crowds out innovation: the printing press is prohibited by the guilds. The banking system serves as a piggy bank for the wealthy. The legal system was literally created by a 300-year-old zombie. The result is that Harry King, the entrepreneur who can turn a golden river into a river of gold, was not admitted into any guild and cannot get financing to grow his business. King's operation is down-river and technically outside the city's legal jurisdiction. In the literal sense of the term, Harry King is an outlaw. The Aristocracy of Ankh-Morpork acquired their property and position generations ago in the earlier stages of social development. They have created a system of laws that defines and protects their wealth and capital, their property, from the threat of redistribution to the poor. The realistic Smith saw this. Government is created by the rich to serve one purpose: "till there be property there can be no government, the very end of which is to secure wealth, and to defend the rich from the poor."[10]

Lord Havelock Vetinari has inherited this government. He must deal with much of what Smith observed in 18th-century England. The wealthy aristocrats of the agricultural stage of civilization have accumulated great wealth and created the institutions to protect it. The city is transitioning into an ethnically diverse, fully commercial state. The new captains of industry, Harry King and Moist Von Lipwig, are in conflict with the entrenched aristocracy of Lord Rust and William de Worde Sr. Of course there are always the poor. The bonds of common sympathy are taxed to their limits. In Smith's smaller communities the bonds of mutual sympathy give rise to a common value system. We choose to associate with people who feel and react as we do. We even modify our own sentiments to solidify the bonds in the group we have chosen. The government and the invisible hand can guide people to the agreed upon common good. In the transition to commercial society those bonds break down. The rich coalesce around one set of shared values; the poor around another; immigrant, religious, and ethnic groups around still others. With proper laws, institutions, and regulations, Smith believes that competition would also produce the common good in a wealthy society, but he had no empirical example to work from. On the disc several hundred years of evolving social forces can drive the plot of a single novel. The social forces at play in Smith's 18th-century England exist on the disc alongside the social forces of the 20th and 21st centuries.

This is where F. A. Hayek steps in. Hayek directly confronted the issues that arise as a society becomes more economically developed, larger, and diverse. Hayek recognizes this development as destructive, but he also sees hope: "only after people are free from the ties of custom and ordinary activities can the spontaneous order of freedom arise."[11] When Pratchett satirizes the social forces of the 20th and 21st century he is satirizing Hayek's world. In many ways Vetinari rules the city exactly as Hayek would recommend.

The Post of Tyrant Has Been Somewhat Redefined by the Incumbent, Lord Vetinari, as the Only Form of Democracy that Works

As society has grown there is less we agree upon: "the rules of which our common moral code consists have progressively become fewer and more general in character."[12] Within the larger community, smaller groups will develop more coherent systems of shared values along Smithian lines. The values of these smaller groups are incommensurable and irreducibly in conflict. Thus there is no complete ethical code that would unify and prioritize the value judgments of these various factions: "not only do we not possess such an all-inclusive scale of values: it would be impossible for any mind to comprehend the infinite variety of different needs of different people which compete for the available resources and to attach a definite weight to each."[13] Hayek expands the marginal theory of economic value to moral values. A universal system of moral values would have to be based on the degree to which each individual values each good in each choice situation relative to every other good open to that individual at that moment.

This leads Hayek to two conclusions. First, in a diverse society there is no common good. Individual interactions will not be guided by an invisible hand to produce public benefit, because in a diverse society there is no agreement about what is beneficial:

Common action is thus limited to the fields where people agree on common ends. Very frequently these common ends will not be ultimate ends to the individuals, but means which different persons can use for different purposes. In fact, people are most likely to agree on common action where the common end is not an ultimate end to them, but a means capable of serving a great variety of purposes.[14]

There can only be agreement about common means to multiple different ends. Related to this claim is Hayek's feeling that we should not fetishize laissez-faire capitalism or democracy. Unfettered, one threatens the tyranny of the powerful, the other the tyranny of the majority. Thus the second conclusion is that a ruler must occasionally interfere in the market "like a gardener who tends a plant in order to create conditions most favorable to its growth."[15] Violations of the rights and freedoms of citizens are justified in order to produce a functioning free market. Vetinari rules according to these two principles.

In *The Truth*, William de Worde Sr. leads a coup. He organizes the aristocracy and the guilds to have Vetinari kidnapped and replaced. These people had been disproportionately benefited by the laws created in the old regime and Vetinari is no longer running the state for their benefit. Of course they criticize him for having no mission, vision, or plan. His kidnappers pay him the highest compliment Hayek could give a politician:

Mr. Tulip: "From what I understand he doesn't do a —ing thing."

Mr. Pin: "Yeah, one of the hardest things to do properly in politics."[16]

Of course Vetinari doesn't have a vision of the common good. There is no common good.

The aristocrats' chosen successor to Vetinari, Lord Scrope, has vision. Scrope promises to usher in a new era, to put the city back on the path to responsible citizenship. He promises a return to the values that made the city great. The coup follows the pattern Hayek lays out to explain the failings of democracy and the potential rise of fascism. Vetinari is creating the framework for competition rather than advancing the interests or values of one faction. He does not really have a constituency to rally behind him. No particular group is having its version of the good implemented by Vetinari, so everyone is mildly disgruntled. Where it is impossible for a whole community to coalesce around a positive version of the common good, a large group of disaffected can coalesce around a negative agenda. Quite simply, Hayek argues that the dim will accept a simplistic explanation that blames their disgruntlement on a scapegoat. People cannot agree on a common good, but they can choose a common enemy: "the contrast between the 'we' and the 'they,' the common fight against those outside the group, seems to be an essential ingredient in any creed which will solidly knit together a group for common action."[17] Naturally, the main item on Scrope's agenda is the expulsion of non-human immigrants. Vetinari himself pronounces the final Hayekian judgment on the common good: "pulling together is the aim of despotism and tyranny. Free men pull in all kinds of directions."[18]

Closely related to these arguments about the common good is Hayek's rejection of economic planning. Vetinari has an impossibly detailed knowledge of the events in his city. He has amazingly accurate knowledge of people's motivations and desires. He wishes sometimes that he were wrong: he would relish the new experience. Vetinari should be a master planner. He should be able to pull all the strings and make everything work as he wishes. It would seem he could predict the needs of his citizens with near perfect accuracy and plan for all of them to be supplied quickly and efficiently. But like Hayek, Vetinari knows that this is impossible.

There seems to be a great deal of unnecessary suffering and inefficient allocation of resources in an unplanned economy, where the free market allocates resources based on price. Price is determined by individual desire for resources. So, the person to whom the resource is most important is willing to pay the most for it, and so gets it. The problem is that the price system is reactive. If there is a single item, and ten people want it, the one item will go to the highest bidder. In Hayek's world this satisfies the momentary marginal desires of consumers and sends a signal to producers that there is a market for their product. If the product can be manufactured for $15 but is selling for $100, other producers will enter the market. Eventually the market reaches an equilibrium price. The selling price will be such that the item can be profitably produced and there are enough consumers at that price to purchase the items. The phenomenon is always most easily observed with products like bread and gasoline after a natural disaster. Therein lays the impulse to plan. When people are willing to spend $100 for a gallon of gas, someone will find a way to supply that demand, but a lot of people will go without gas and a lot of people will go broke. In more ordinary circumstances, people can afford $3 per gallon for gas but not $4. If we can predict a demand spike or supply shortage we could plan production and allocate resources to maintain the $3 per gallon price. If this planning could be done successfully it would prevent a great deal of needless suffering.

In Ankh-Morpork the task of planning falls to Hubert Turvey and the glooper. Vetinari describes the glooper as "the future of economical planning." But Moist notes that Vetinari "looked if not worried, at least unaccustomedly puzzled" by the prospect of an economic plan.[19] Hubert could simulate an increase in demand for dwarfish chain-mail hand bags. The glooper would show which industries would experience a shortage of iron, and which industries would have a surplus of leather. The planner who knew the degree to which people will increase demand for dwarfish handbags could arrange for increased production of iron and decreased production of leather. The planner is proactive where the price system is reactive. Planning eliminates the fluctuations and scarcities that are required to send signals in the price system. Vetinari is not a fan of Hubert.

In the middle of the 20th century, planners like Oskar Lange developed the theory of market socialism: with enough data about the choices people have made in a free market, the state can implement a more efficient process to produce market results. If the plan works, individuals can be more efficiently provided with what they would have chosen in the free market. The Fabian Society in England argued that "if by conscious forward planning (people) can escape present frustrations, they will rightly be judged to be more truly free."[20] The amount of data required is immense. Organizing this data into a form that can be used accurately to predict future wants is an exceptionally difficult task. Lange was doubtful through the 1940s, but by the 1960s he thought that a computer could be designed to process the information from all the relevant economic interactions. He would not have called his computer the glooper, but it does the job. Vetinari, with Hubert's help, seems to have complete mastery of all the relevant information. However, he is wise enough to know better: 'you cannot plan the future, only presumptuous fools plan. The wise man steers."[21] That is exactly what Hayek would want him to do.

Hayek argued that the knowledge required for economic planning is dispersed throughout the whole of society and changes at every given moment. Lange's theory rests on a false understanding of the nature of social science:

> Today it is almost heresy to suggest that scientific knowledge is not the sum of all knowledge. But a little reflection will show that there is beyond question a body of very important but unorganized knowledge which cannot possibly be called scientific in the sense of knowledge of general rules: the knowledge of the particular circumstances of time and place. It is with respect to this that practically every individual has some advantage over all others because he possesses unique information of which beneficial use might be made, but of which use can be made only if the decisions depending on it are left to him or are made with his active cooperation.[22]

In each economic transaction people act on knowledge that is unique to the particular situation—the marginal costs of that choice compared to all other choices at that moment. The very act of aggregating the data removes the necessary information of the particular circumstances. It is not possible to formulate general rules that would reflect knowledge that is particular to an individual at a time and place. The knowledge exists, but it is irreducibly subjective: it can only be known by the individual at the moment of choice. In the natural sciences it is reasonable to think that there are objective properties of the objects studied. The very objects involved in the study of economics are defined subjectively:

> That the objects of economic activity cannot be defined in objective terms but only with reference to a human

purpose goes without saying. Neither a "commodity" or an "economic good," nor "food" or "money," can be defined in physical terms but only in terms of views people hold about things.[23]

The social and economic order that the social scientist observes and describes is the spontaneous result of the inchoate and often contradictory beliefs, desires, and opinions people have at a given moment. The patterns are not created by objective qualities of the items involved. The patterns, if there are any, arise as an unintended consequence of each individual's conscious actions. The social sciences, unlike the natural sciences, cannot make generalizations that allow for precise predictions of future events. Economics can describe what choices people have made in the past, but the data about the beliefs and desires and shifting values of the agent are subjective, unique, and only knowable by an individual at the moment of choice. There is no objective data on which an economist could base a general rule that would allow an accurate prediction of future beliefs, desires, and values. Planning to satisfy someone's desires before he is in a position to choose is impossible.[24] Any attempt to do so removes the freedom of the individual to make his own free choice at the moment. The Fabians are wrong: we would be less, not more, free.

Vetinari recognizes that the social and economic system is the unintended, spontaneous result of millions of individual interactions. It was not planned itself. It responds in inherently unpredictable ways to new events. Vetinari also understands his role in the city: "I did not become ruler of Ankh-Morpork by understanding the city. The city is depressingly easy to understand. I have remained ruler by getting the city to understand *me*."[25] Hayek argues for the paramount importance of the state to create a framework in which competition and the price system can coordinate human efforts. This system will not necessarily arise automatically. What arises automatically is Smith's system of law that preserves power. Vetinari, instead, provides stability and opportunity. The citizens of Ankh-Morpork understand this:

> The functioning of competition not only requires adequate organization of certain institutions like money, markets, and channels of information—some of which can never be adequately provided by private enterprise—but it depends above all on the existence of an appropriate legal system, a legal system designed both to preserve competition and to make it operate as beneficially as possible.[26]

When Vetinari interferes in the market and infringes the rights and freedoms of the citizens of Ankh-Morpork, it is along Hayekian lines. Vetinari steers the market. He revitalizes the post office and nationalizes, or steals, the clacks (he describes his actions both ways). He did not do this for the common good. He acted because communication is essential as a means to multiple different conceptions of the good. Vetinari acts similarly in other sectors of the economy. He creates the rules and structures that expand the opportunity for individual market interactions. In *Making Money*, he overhauls the financial system, because the gold standard inhibits investment and growth. His "undertaking" seems to be a modern transportation system. He has opened Ankh's borders to immigration. In *Jingo* he surrenders to the Klatchian Empire, giving up territory for favorable trading agreements. These are all quite unpopular decisions. An elected official could not hold office for long with this list of affronts to the public mood. As tyrant, though, his goal is not his own aggrandizement. He is creating an environment where individuals can pursue their own private goods. Hayek famously, and controversially, endorsed Chilean dictator Augusto Pinochet. In hindsight this was certainly unwise. Vetinari, on the other hand, is a dictator that could be endorsed by the great defender of liberty.

Whole New Theories of Money Were Growing here like Mushrooms, in the Dark and Based on Bullshit

Vetinari's reshaping of the financial system is his most intrusive attempt to shape the market. His goal is clear: he needs finance for the "undertaking." Speculation is that this undertaking is a sewer system, a subway system, or, on the American model, both. Either would provide a benefit to the citizens by facilitating growth and development. Either will require massive amounts of money that does not exist: finance. Unfortunately, Ankh-Morpork's financial sector lacks fortune. A traditional thinker might believe the problem is a lack of gold; not Vetinari. The problem is that people falsely believe that gold is wealth, and they falsely believe that gold is money.

When Moist is appointed to the Royal Bank of Ankh-Morpork the city is on the Gold Bullion Standard. The Royal Bank holds gold in reserve and circulates currency. The bank agrees to exchange that currency for a fixed quantity of gold on demand. A one dollar coin is not itself one dollar's worth of gold but it can be exchanged for one dollar's worth of actual gold at the bank. People believe the wealth of a city is the gold that the city holds. Currency is a token way of exchanging small portions of that wealth for goods and services. It all makes sense, but on Discworld, and on Roundworld, as the society evolves and technology, innovation, and urbanization increase productivity and economic growth, the gold standard is an idea whose time has gone.

Moist von Lipwig, like Adam Smith, recognizes these errors. Gold is useless on its own. A large pile of gold is only as valuable as those desirable things it can be exchanged for. If there are no necessary or desirable objects produced, then the gold is just shiny. The magic is gone. The real wealth of a nation is the productive capacity of the population. Moist's task is to turn this into money.

The problem with the gold standard is that it impedes economic growth by limiting the money supply and restricting credit. In a strict sense this is a mathematical truism. If the wealth of a nation is the quantity of gold, this wealth does not increase without more gold. An increase in productivity produces more goods not more gold. When innovation results in more goods being produced, then the same money is chasing more things. The same quantity of money chasing more goods lowers the nominal price of goods. This nominally lowers wages, profits, and changes the assessment of one's future purchasing abilities. Rapid productivity increases cause rapid deflation. Deflation puts the brakes on entrepreneurs, stopping productivity increases. Nominal deflation is sometimes dismissed, but the psychological effects, what Keynes called animal spirits, or confidence, affects people's actions across the whole economy. Moreover, as the economy is growing, more people want to borrow money to invest but there is not more gold to back those loans. Entrepreneurs cannot get financing. This is the situation Vetinari finds himself in. He recognizes that finance is the key to growth and development. He interferes in the free market at the most fundamental level by forcing Moist von Lipwig to overhaul the financial sector in order to create credit for his own undertaking as well as for private entrepreneurial projects.

This is where Moist works magic. Moist describes himself as "a natural born criminal, habitual liar, fraudster, and totally untrustworthy perverted genius." These are the skills he needs if he is going to create money out of nothing. Vetinari replies: "I pride myself on being able to pick the right man."[27] So, how does Moist create money? The first step is to print it. But this is only how circulating currency is made. This is not really creating money. A bank creates money by lending. When a bank has one million dollars in currency because it has in fact printed it, it lends this currency out. This debt becomes the bank's asset. When you borrow one million dollars from the bank you don't carry that cash around with you. You deposit it in the bank for safe keeping. The bank now has another one million dollars in assets to lend. Each time the bank makes a loan they create more money. Under the gold standard the bank's currency is backed by the gold in the vault. Banks may issue more currency than they have gold reserves, but not too much. Mr. Bent claims that the Royal Bank circulates four times as much currency as they hold gold: a 25 per cent reserve ratio. Without gold, there is no asset in the bank that backs your bills and coins. As there is nothing backing the currency the reserve ratios on Roundworld approach zero. There is a whiff of smoke and a hint of mirror in all this. Some have called this system of banking "embezzlement and counterfeiting." "It should be clear that modern fractional reserve banking is a shell game, a Ponzi scheme, a fraud."[28] Vetinari needs a confidence trickster to sell the financial system to the people. It is a confidence trick.

So what is the asset that backs the paper money? It is the city. Entrepreneurs borrow money to invest in productive enterprise. This productive enterprise is now the commodity that backs the currency. With a zero reserve requirement, credit can be expanded indefinitely. One way or another, the banks can produce enough money. However, Moist has one thing bankers on Roundworld don't: 4,000 golems. Moist bases the currency on golems rather than gold, but it is not clear how this works. The golems are buried; they are neither a commodity like gold nor productive like the city. Presumably they could be called upon to do work if needed to keep the engines of commerce moving. But really they seem to be just a metaphor. They represent the pent up creative and productive power of the city. The 4,000 Umnian golems are an anthropomorphic personification of the wealth embodied in the productive capacity of the city. The financial system works ultimately because the city is productive and people have faith in the legal structures. In Ankh-Morpork this means faith in the city and in Vetinari.

"It could have been good, sergeant," said Reg, looking up. "It really could. A city where a man can breathe free." "Wheeze free, Reg," said Vimes, sitting down next to him. "This is Ankh-Morpork."

Ankh-Morpork is not a perfect city. Pratchett writes fantasy not utopian fiction. Like Smith and Hayek, he is a sane and reasonable observer of society. However, Smith and Hayek are, in many ways, more attuned to the social costs of a libertarian society than Pratchett. The complete lack of environmental regulation allows Sam Vimes to joke about the city's air quality. But, no one gets lung cancer. No one suffers a disabling illness from breathing this amusingly chemical air. No one dies penniless on the street because they cannot afford treatment. Pratchett writes about the obvious social costs involved in this libertarian vision, but no one ever seems to be harmed by it too badly. On Discworld the social costs are just not that bad. This could be fantasy or just wishful thinking; either way it is a flaw in the political and economic vision.

When Moist von Lipwig is appointed to the Royal Bank, there are no laws governing the financial sector. The gold standard had worked by trust and convention. The limit of how much each bank will lend out is not set legally; it is set by the competitive forces of the market. Risk too much and your bank fails. There was no fixed exchange rate for gold, and no central bank. The system had failed because of the short-sighted stupidity of the bankers. The social cost of the failure for the people of Ankh-Morpork was slow economic growth. In Roundworld this failure would create genuine poverty from lack of opportunity. The system is saved by a charming, sometime-criminal. Moist removes Ankh from the gold standard, takes deposits from the poor and working classes, introduces fiat currency, paper money, and fractional reserve banking to the masses. There are still no laws governing the financial sector. One wonders what Mr. Slant does. When Moist is done, the new financial system works by trust and convention. The working classes trust that their deposits will be there. The merchants on Tenth Egg Street accept paper money because it is convenient and Moist is a good salesman. The patrician had put Moist in charge, but the government had done nothing. On Roundworld we needed deposit insurance and laws forcing people to use fiat money. The Royal Bank of Ankh seems to have been unaffected by Roundworld's financial crisis. Perhaps the fantasy is that it cannot occur here, or the wishful thinking is that the wealth created will be worth it.

There is no social safety net in Ankh's libertarian fantasy. Sam Vimes personally and anonymously takes care of police widows and orphans. High risk professions, like the alchemists guild, have a mutual insurance scheme for survivors' benefits. They take care of themselves. Every indication in the stories suggests that this private charity is sufficient. There are those on Roundworld who share the same fantasy.

Ankh-Morpork is teeming with poor people. They are a resourceful, hearty, and self-reliant lot. Harry King worked his own way up from the muck and provides an opportunity for goblins and gnomes to work. As they are not human, their working conditions are a point of anthropological interest, not human rights violations. This belief is held in many corners of the Roundworld. The beggars have organized a guild to defend their interests. Below the beggars are Foul-ole Ron and his crowd. Even they work or barter productively for what little they want. Sam Vimes may muse about poverty as he marries the richest heiress in Ankh-Morpork, but his thoughts are about how hard he has worked. He is frequently angered by the condescension of the aristocracy, but rarely by the injustice of the socio-economic order. The closest he comes is musing that the rich spend less money on shoes because they can afford to buy quality shoes that don't wear out. The ethos is summed up by William de Worde Jr. who explains that the world is divided into two kinds of people. It is not a question of whether your glass is half-full or half-empty. Instead, the world is divided into people who demand that their glass be filled, "and at the other end of the bar the world is full of the other type of person, who has a broken glass, or a glass that has been carelessly knocked over (usually by one of the people calling for a larger glass), or who had no glass at all, because he was at the back of the crowd and had failed to catch the barman's eye."[29] In Pratchett's world William de Worde considers himself one of the glassless. The son of one of the oldest and most powerful aristocrats is one of the rare characters to find his "poverty" unjust. Nonetheless, his poverty is his fault. He once had a perfectly fine glass. He just failed to catch the barman's eye. De Worde is not protesting injustice, he is whining. Once he pulls himself together he succeeds.

Poverty in Ankh-Morpork is a challenge, a difficulty to overcome. Poverty and lack of social status are never barriers to achievement. Ankh-Morpork is full of people who succeed through their own work and ingenuity: Trevor Likely is a plucky, streetwise young man who finds success. Mr. Nutt the orc is a despised minority who develops a special skill and earns his place in the city. Eskarina Smith becomes the Discworld's only female wizard when her talent wins the grudging recognition of the Unseen University patriarchy. And the golems strive for freedom from slavery behind their slogan "by our own hand or none."[30] It seems sometimes as if no one in Ankh has limited opportunities. There is no recognition that one's freedom can be limited by economic and social circumstances. To paraphrase Socrates in the *Meno*, we shall be better, braver, and, less helpless if we believe we succeed or fail by our own effort. This may be the most significant part of the libertarian fantasy in the Discworld novels.

The lack of concern for poverty and the absolute faith in the power of the individual to succeed or fail on his or her own follows from the commitment to economic freedom. Milton Friedman has argued that freedom to own and trade property, without restriction, is a primary value regardless of the effects, good or bad, that result from the exchange. Economic freedom gives people the incentive to take control of their own lives and disperses wealth and hence power throughout society. Economic freedom is an end in itself, and a necessary condition for all other political freedoms.[31] Vetinari embraces this philosophy and explains the rest of the idea as well as Friedman has. "I believe in freedom," he says to Moist. "Not many people do, although they will, of course, protest otherwise. And no practical definition of freedom would be complete without the freedom to take the consequences. Indeed it is the freedom on which all others are based."[32] Again, following Hayek, Vetinari is not one to fetishize freedom. Reacher Gilt writes an editorial criticizing Vetinari's restrictions on economic freedom. Vetinari notes that laws against murder restrict the murderer's freedom and that "freedom may be man's natural state but so is sitting in a tree eating your dinner while it is still wriggling."[33] The freedom accorded the citizens of Ankh-Morpork is not complete, but it is extensive. In good libertarian fashion, when liberties are restricted it is not to save people from suffering the consequences of their own actions, and it is not to help people who should be helping themselves.

The Agatean Empire is at the opposite end of the freedom spectrum. The Empire, a thinly veiled satire of communist China, is not Pratchett's most subtle skewering of politics and culture. Rincewind describes their differences. In Ankh-Morpork, he claims, people are "free to starve or get robbed by the thieves' guild."[34] But in Ankh-Morpork he does not have to bow to anyone. The citizens of the empire regret lacking the more dubious freedoms of Ankh-Morpork, they also lack economic and political freedom. They have a dubious form of security, but they are not flourishing happy human beings. Pratchett's contrast between Ankh-Morpork and the Agatean Empire reflects Hayek's account of the virtues that citizens must have to flourish in a free society and those virtues needed to survive in a collectivist society. The virtues of "independence, self-reliance, the willingness to bear risks, the readiness to back one's own conviction against a majority, and the willingness to voluntary cooperation with one's neighbors—are essentially [the virtues] on which the workings of an individualist society rests."[35] These virtues are clearly exemplified by the citizens of Ankh-Morpork, provided one does not take too broad a reading of "cooperation." Hayek would claim that the collectivist state of the Agatean Empire "has nothing in their place. Insofar as it has already destroyed [these virtues] it has left a void filled by nothing other than the demand for obedience and the compulsion of the individual to do what is collectively decided to be good."[36] Hayek believes that the virtues of an economically free society are essential for our flourishing as human beings. He was primarily an economist, not a philosopher, so never spells this out in exactly these terms. On the Discworld Pratchett does.

Rincewind's adventures in the Agatean Empire show that the citizens have had all the virtues necessary for human flourishing beaten out of them. With the notable exception of Two-Flower and Disembowel-Meself-Honourably Dibhala, the citizens lack initiative, independence, and the entrepreneurial spirit that is so praised in Ankh-Morpork. The citizens of the empire labor endlessly and live on pig's ear stew. They do not enjoy the benefits of their labor, because "some other bugger is taking the rest of the pig."[37] As Hayek describes it, this is what collectivism does. In eliminating the freedom to engage in trade and commerce and to experience the consequences, good and bad, a collectivist state removes even the capacity for individual thought. Much of the plot in *Interesting Times* involves Rincewind being shocked and amazed by the passive and dehumanized citizens of the empire. They are shackled by something "worse than chains." Guards do not have to watch prisoners: the prisoners would never run. The citizens simply do not see what they are not supposed to see. There is a similar phenomenon in Djelibeybi. There, criminals turn themselves in to the police and stay in prison awaiting execution because they fear the gods. Whatever else you can say about them, the gods of the Discworld are real. Even if the high priest Dios is playing fast and loose with the faith, the citizens of Djelibeybi are making a choice about what they value. In the empire the citizens simply obey. They have "whips in their soul."[38]

The depiction of the Agatean Empire is not subtle social commentary, but in its blunt way it reveals Pratchett's political and economic inclinations. If, as Adam Smith argues, the tendency to specialize and trade is a uniquely human activity, then economic freedom is essential to human flourishing. The Hayekian virtues that people must form in an economically free society are the capacities we need in order to reach our potential as human beings. These virtues of "independence of mind or strength of character are rarely found among those who cannot be confident that they will make their way by their own effort."[39] These virtues are not found in the empire.

There is elegance and simplicity to this Smith and Hayek-inspired libertarian vision. In Ankh-Morpork Pratchett has created a city of charming and hardworking, if venal and acquisitive, people. But there is more than a little wishful thinking, maybe even fantasy, in this vision. On Roundworld there are trade-offs of human happiness and wellbeing. Market freedom has a benefit but also a social cost. Pratchett pokes fun at the absurdities of this system, but he gives the tragedies and costs brief mention. Pratchett, just as Smith and Hayek do, always comes back to the defense of freedom and liberty. For all three the benefits are worth the costs.

Notes

1. T. Pratchett (2009) *Unseen Academicals* (New York: HarperCollins). The full text is undeveloped, as most people mumble the words waiting for the soccer game or pitched battle to begin. A performance of the anthem by the BBC Scottish Symphony Orchestra with soprano Clare Rutter is available at www.youtube.com/watch?v=EAqCbOJc6RU.
2. T. Hobbes (1994) *Leviathan*, edited E. Curley (Indianapolis: Hackett), § XIII.

3. A. Smith (1982) *Theory of Moral Sentiments*, edited A.L. Macfie and D.D. Raphael (Indianapolis: Liberty Press), I, II, 2.
4. Ibid., I, I, 1, 5
5. C. Smith (2006) "Adam Smith on Progress and Knowledge" in *New Voices on Adam Smith*, edited L. Montes and E. Schliesser (London and New York: Routledge), p. 293.
6. *Smith, Theory of Moral Sentiments*, IV, 1, 10.
7. A. Smith (1976) *An Inquiry into the Nature and Causes of the Wealth of Nations*, edited R.H. Campbell and A.S. Skinner (Indianapolis: Liberty Press), IV, II, 9.
8. The use not quoted here is in a work on the history of astronomy.
9. Smith, *An Inquiry*, V, I, ii, 2.
10. A. Smith (1982) *Lectures on Jurisprudence*, edited R.L. Meek and D.D. Raphael (Indianapolis: Liberty Press), § V.
11. F.A. Hayek (2007) *The Road to Serfdom: Text and Documents—The Definitive Edition* in *The Collected Works of F. A. Hayek, vol. 2*, edited B. Caldwell (Chicago: University of Chicago Press), p. 69.
12. Ibid., p. 101.
13. Ibid., p. 102.
14. Ibid.
15. Ibid., p. 71.
16. T. Pratchett (2000) *The Truth* (New York: HarperCollins), p. 43.
17. Hayek, *The Road to Serfdom*, p. 161.
18. Pratchett, *The Truth*, p. 340.
19. T. Pratchett (2007) *Making Money* (New York: HarperCollins), p. 31. There is a Roundworld counterpart to the glooper. William Phillips of the London School of Economics (LSE), the man who gave us the Phillips Curve, designed and perfected a hydraulic analogue computer. Phillips's computer was called variously MONIAC (Monetary National Income Analogue Computer), Financephalograph, or, when people were not feeling silly, the Phillips Hydraulic Computer. "The prototype was an odd assortment of tanks, pipes, sluices and valves, with water pumped around the machine by a motor cannibalized from the windscreen wiper of a Lancaster bomber. Bits of filed-down Perspex and fishing line were used to channel the coloured dyes that mimicked the flow of income round the economy into consumer spending, taxes, investment and exports" (www.sciencemuseum. org.uk/objects/computing_and_data_processing/1995-210.aspx).

    The Phillips computer could show the impact of increased or decreased government spending, investment rates, etc. Compared to the glooper it was a very blunt instrument. The MONIAC could only be calibrated to an accuracy of 2 per cent. MONIACs were purchased by the Harvard Business School, the Ford Motor Company, and the Central bank of Guatemala, among others. One was used in teaching at the LSE until 1992 (www.theguardian.com/business/2008/may/08/bankofenglandgovernor.economics).

20. I. Sieff (1932) *Freedom and Planning* (London: British Library of Political and Economic Science; Political and Economic Planning Archive) PEP A "Committee and Miscellaneous Papers,"/7 "Meetings" / Folder 3.
21. Pratchett, *Making Money*, p. 261.
22. F.A. Hayek (1945) "The Uses of Knowledge in Society," *American Economic Review* XXXV(4), p. 521.
23. F.A. Hayek (2010) "The Subjective Character of the Data in the Social Sciences" in *Studies on the Abuse and Decline of Reason: Text and Documents* (*The Collected Works of F. A. Hayek, Volume 13*), edited B. Caldwell (Chicago: University of Chicago Press), p. 94.
24. It might be objected here that businesses plan all the time. In a free market, businesses do not plan they hope. A business does not have the ability to organize the entire economy of the state to produce its product. The business believes, based on past actions, that consumers will purchase its product, so it produces it and hopes consumers choose it. For the contrary view, the classic source is J.K. Galbraith (1967) *The New Industrial State* (Boston: Houghton Mifflin); a brief modern rebuttal of Hayek's point is H.J. Chang (2010) *23 Things They Don't Tell You About Capitalism* (New York: Bloomsbury Press).
25. Pratchett, *Making Money*, p. 73.
26. Hayek, *The Road to Serfdom*, p. 87.
27. Pratchett, *Going Postal*, p. 15.
28. M. Rothbard (2002) *The Mystery of Banking*, 2nd edn (Alabama: Ludwig von Misses Institute), p. 97.
29. Pratchett, *The Truth*, p. 21.
30. Pratchett, *Going Postal*, p. 18.
31. M. Friedman (2002) *Capitalism and Freedom* (Chicago: University of Chicago Press), p. 8.
32. Pratchett, *Going Postal*, p. 15.
33. Ibid., p. 77.
34. T. Pratchett (1994) *Interesting Times* (New York: HarperCollins), p. 108.
35. Hayek, *The Road to Serfdom*, p. 217.
36. Ibid.
37. Pratchett, *Interesting Times*, p. 75.
38. Ibid., p. 215.
39. Hayek, *The Road to Serfdom*, p. 147.

Bibliography

Chang, H.J. (2010) *23 Things They Don't Tell You About Capitalism* (New York: Bloomsbury Press).

Friedman, M. (2002) *Capitalism and Freedom* (Chicago: University of Chicago Press).

Galbraith, J. (1967) *The New Industrial State* (Boston: Houghton Mifflin).

Hayek, F.A. (1945) "The Uses of Knowledge in Society," *American Economic Review* XXXV(4), pp. 519–30.

_____ (2007) *The Road to Serfdom: Text and Documents—The Definitive Edition* (*The Collected Works of F. A. Hayek, Volume 2*), edited B. Caldwell (Chicago: University of Chicago Press).

_____ (2010) "The Subjective Character of the Data in the Social Sciences' in *Studies on the Abuse and Decline of Reason: Text and Documents* (*The Collected Works of F. A. Hayek Volume 13*), edited B. Caldwell (Chicago: University of Chicago Press).

Hobbes, T. (1994) *Leviathan* in *Leviathan, with Selected Variants from the Latin Edition of 1668*, edited E. Curley (Indianapolis: Hackett).

Lange, O. (1936) "On the Economic Theory of Socialism, Part One," *Review of Economic Studies* 4(1), pp. 53–71.

_____ (1937) "On the Economic Theory of Socialism, Part Two," *Review of Economic Studies* 4(2), pp. 123–42.

_____ (1967) "The Computer and the Market' in *Socialism, Capitalism and Economic Growth*, edited C.H. Feinstein (Cambridge: Cambridge University Press).

Pratchett, T. (1990) *Moving Pictures* (New York: HarperCollins).

_____ (1994) *Interesting Times* (New York: HarperCollins).

_____ (2000) *The Truth* (New York: HarperCollins).

_____ (2009) *Unseen Academicals* (New York: HarperCollins).

Rothbard, M. (2002) *The Mystery of Banking*, 2nd edn (Alabama: Ludwig von Mises Institute).

Sieff, I. (1932) *Freedom and Planning* (London: British Library of Political and Economic Science; Political and Economic Planning Archive) PEP A "Committee and Miscellaneous Papers" /7 "Meetings" / Folder 3.

Smith, A. (1976) *An Inquiry into the Nature and Causes of the Wealth of Nations*, edited R.H. Campbell and A.S. Skinner (Indianapolis: Liberty Press).

_____ (1982) *Lectures on Jurisprudence*, edited R.L. Meek and D.D. Raphael (Indianapolis: Liberty Press).

_____ (1982) *Theory of Moral Sentiments*, edited A.L. Macfie and D.D. Raphael (Indianapolis: Liberty Press).

Smith, C. (2006) "Adam Smith on Progress and Knowledge" in *New Voices on Adam Smith*, edited L. Montes and E. Schliesser (London and New York: Routledge).

6 Plato, the Witch, and the Cave: Granny Weatherwax and the Moral Problem of Paternalism

Dietrich Schotte

The witches of Discworld are famous for their use of "headology," the Discworld equivalent of Roundworld's folk psychology.[1] If asked for help by the common people (a group which from the witches' perspective generally includes anyone but themselves), most witches avoid the attempt to explain the true nature of things. Instead, they leave the common people's beliefs and prejudices unharmed and often tell them "a story" which encapsulates said beliefs and, by making use of them, directs the questioners towards their good. Of course, the witches act this way even towards those who did not ask for help, they "generally get . . . into the business of minding everyone's business for them because there'd be no telling what business people'd get up to without a witch around."[2]

Among the many readers superbly entertained by the many episodes in which especially Granny Weatherwax fools people to make them do what *she* thinks is good for them, those who have children are likely also to envy Granny's brilliant wit and her outstanding sophistication. And this for a simple reason: we treat our children like Granny treats the common people, only we're not a quarter as good as she is. However, her wit and cunning cover up a serious problem that lurks behind headology: that it involves treating full-grown, normally intelligent and sane *adults* like children. Differently put, headology is inherently paternalistic.

Being challenged by Tiffany Aching that she should better tell people "the truth" to enable them to (correctly) judge for themselves, Granny in a stiff upper lip sort of way points out the dilemma that paternalism poses: "Look at it this way. Tomorrow, your job is to change the world into a better place. Today, my job is to see that everyone gets there."[3] Sometimes the only alternatives you have are treating adults like children or refraining from doing this and letting them run into their peril. This, Granny tells Tiffany, is what being a witch is all about: "It's making the choices that have to be made. The hard choices."[4]

To show that it is indeed a dilemma, I will proceed as follows. First, I will give a definition of paternalism as a sort of "beneficial lying." Then I will present arguments for and against paternalism, followed by a discussion of the crucial and certainly not undisputed premise of every paternalistic argument or action: that the person or people so treated are otherwise unable to see or achieve their good when not "guided" by others who have more expertise.

The main goal of this chapter is to show that paternalism is a problematic, but also an indispensable, approach, even in liberal politics—while the basic assumption of most anti-paternalistic arguments (if not to say resentments), that the right to autonomy or self-sovereignty is absolute, is anything but self-evident.

Plato, or the Essence of Paternalism

As mentioned, paternalism means (roughly speaking) treating normally intelligent and sane adults like children; hence its name, derived from the Latin *pater*, for father. As such, paternalism has at least two key aspects, namely that the respective paternalistic actions (a) are directed at the addressee's well-being and that they (b) override the addressee's own decisions in these matters, stating that his or her decision or judgment is wrong and that the agent's judgment is superior.[5] The means used are therefore, largely but not exclusively, means of deception or force. It is for this reason that the essence of paternalism is perhaps best encompassed by Plato's notion of "beneficial lies."[6]

Let's flesh this out a bit. Consider the following examples:

(a) You witness a traveler attempting to cross a bridge that you know to be badly broken. Assuming that she wants to reach the other side but does not want to fall to her death, you run to her and, using force, stop her from stepping onto the bridge.[7] Remember that Granny usually slaps Tiffany (and others) to stop their mind from wandering off.

(b) Your partner is suicidal which is why you decide to hide your sleeping pills to prevent him or her from using them to kill him or herself.[8] Nanny Ogg, on the other hand, uses her grandson Pewsey to stop Granny from going on with a duel that she is very likely to lose.[9]

(c) A doctor has been told that the son of her patient died in a car accident. Since the doctor knows that the patient is currently trying to defeat cancer and will hardly be helped to do so if informed of her son's death, when asked by her patient why her son failed to pay her his weekly visit, the doctor decides not to tell her patient about his death—although she beforehand accepted her patient's plea never to lie to her. Consider how Granny tricks Magrat into her marriage to Verence—by sending a letter with instructions to him behind her back.[10]

(d) As many philosophers from Plato onwards have argued, most people fail to recognize that the morally right thing is always the best thing to do (and the best for them) and instead follow their immediate desires, which sadly tend to lead them to fraud, theft, and murder. Since the police can't be everywhere, the best way to make people behave morally is to make them believe in an afterlife, in which the good get rewarded and the bad punished. The premise of this argument is that no such afterlife exists. As Spinoza put it: "if we did not possess this testimony of Scripture, we would have to consider the salvation of almost all men to be in doubt."[11] This is why, as Leo Strauss[12] argued, every true philosopher acknowledges his or her "social duty" not openly to attack the (from her point of view false) beliefs and faiths of the common people.

Taking for granted that all four examples undoubtedly are cases of paternalism, the agent's motive in all four cases is to secure the addressee's well-being. It need not, of course, be the only motive;[13] Nanny certainly wants to stop Granny from hurting (or killing) herself in the duel, but most likely she also wants to avoid losing Granny. These examples also have in common the fact that the addressee's own judgments or decisions are regarded as irrelevant;[14] they are ignored (a, b, c) or substituted by the agent's (d).

Still, there are important differences between the four cases. As the examples (b), (c), and (d) show, paternalism may (as in the first example) include *forcing* the addressee to her own good, though it need not rely on means of force:[15] if the doctor lies to her patient, or if Granny writes to Verence in what she considers to be Magrat's interest, no force is involved. While in (c) and (d) the agents lie to or deceive the addressees, examples (a) and (b) show that this also is not a necessary aspect of paternalism: slapping Tiffany to stop her from losing her focus includes neither deceiving nor lying to her and as long as you simply hide your sleeping pills from your partner, you also do neither of these (you do so, of course, when your partner asks you for them and you say that you don't know where you put them).

Gerald Dworkin[16] has, therefore, made a distinction between "hard" and "soft" paternalism.[17] While both hard and soft paternalism direct the addressee's actions toward what the agent thinks is best for him or her, only hard paternalism overruns the addressee's *explicit* interests and preferences, usually by means of force or threat. Soft paternalism, on the other hand, "redirects" the addressee's judgment such that it becomes supplanted by the agent's. Compare for example Nanny's sending in Pewsey with Magrat's suggestion that she could *order* Granny to stop the duel.

In addition to (b) and (d), another example could be what Richard Thaler and Cass Sunstein[18] call "Nudges": while the addressees' are left to decide on their own, the circumstances of their decisions are biased so as to make them choose not what they would under normal circumstances, but rather what the agent thinks is best for them. Differently put: "Got to use headology. Got to make 'em send 'emselves."[19] Consider the high level of taxation on goods the government thinks are bad for its citizens' health, for example tobacco of various sorts: the idea is to stop the citizens' smoking, not by making it illegal (which would mean to *force* them to stop), but by making it so expensive that they *decide themselves* not to smoke (because of the money this saves them). One could say that Miss Treason "nudges" people by her "Boffo," the "art of expectations"—she plays the role of the "wicked old witch," including the stories about her demon in the cellar or her clockwork-heart, and thus ensures that the people are afraid of her and so follow her counsel.[20] These everyday measures may be "soft," but they certainly are paternalistic, since for example those people's decision to prefer to smoke is supplanted by the government's judgment that not to smoke is better for them. In *Wintersmith*, Tiffany is nudged by Granny in a similar way into helping Anagramma.

Example (b) moreover shows that, other than Bernard Gert and Charles Culver[21] have argued, paternalism may, but need not, involve a violation of the addressee's rights—none of Granny's rights is violated when Nanny sends in Pewsey, as Granny violates none of Magrat's rights when she writes the letter to Verence.[22] And by taxing tobacco, the government also does not violate any of your rights—it simply makes smoking more expensive for you. We might, however, introduce another distinction, that between "weak" and "strong" paternalism.

While strong paternalism relies solely on the agent's judgment about the addressee's best interest, weak paternalism is directed at what the addressee him or herself wants, only disregarding the addressee's judgment concerning what means are best to reach it. Therefore, Nanny's sending in Pewsey is strong paternalism. In contrast, consider example (c): the patient *wants* to succeed in fighting her cancer—but she falsely thinks that being always told the truth is the best means, or at least not a hindrance, in achieving this. For this reason, the doctor acknowledges her patient's interest (getting cured), but ignores her request (being told the truth) because she judges this to be a hindrance, indeed an obstacle, to the cure of the patient from cancer. This is, by the way, exactly what Granny Weatherwax does: the villagers come to her asking for aid from their various illnesses and maladies, and she cures them by giving them some "jollop" and "telling them a story" or, differently put, by lying to them—because she holds their own judgments to be unreliable. However, she helps them achieve what they are *explicitly* asking for: a cure.

To conclude, paternalism comes in various forms (soft, hard, weak, strong), but its essence is that (a) it is always directed at its addressee's well-being and that the means employed to reach this in effect is always (b) to substitute the agent's judgment about what this well-being consists in or how it is best achieved for the addressee's own judgment.

It is, however, important to acknowledge that the notion "well-being" is all but definitely settled: it might just be the addressee's being alive (examples (a) and (b)), it might be the addressee's peace of mind or psychological stability (example (c)), but it may also include the addressee's leading what is (by the person acting paternalistically) deemed a morally good form of life (example (d)).

Aristotle argued that even to sacrifice oneself in the name of friendship or patriotism, if need be, is better than to stay alive as a coward or traitor, which is to fail to attain the moral life;[23] an argument that has—in the form of a plea for what we might call the "ideal of moral integrity"—recently been taken up by Philippa Foot.[24] Making someone sacrifice him or herself for his or her fatherland (either by force or by deception, for example by indoctrination) is therefore according to Aristotle nothing else than helping this person become a good citizen and, in effect, a good man (or, rather anti-Aristotelian, a good woman). In other words: it means helping the person achieve "his or her best." Obviously, the broader this notion of well-being is understood, the harder paternalism is to justify.

The Witch, or Paternalism—for and against

Now, while we might feel uncomfortable treating sane and intelligent adults like children, since we don't like to be treated this way ourselves, it seems equally clear that doing so is not per se wrong. For why should it be considered wrong when we stop a drunken friend from doing something he or she would never do if sober? Or to stop a stranger who is going to cross a bridge we know to be badly broken, to use Mill's example? In both cases we substitute our judgment for that of another person whom we *generally* or at least in principle hold to be able to judge for him or herself. But, the argument runs, the concrete situation they are in permits us to interfere with their decisions and respective actions. Granny *knows* that Magrat wants to marry Verence—but she also knows that Magrat, being a "wet hen," will certainly screw it up. Also, Nanny *knows* that Granny does not want to get killed in a duel with a younger witch (if only because that is what prevents her from stopping the elves). In the same way we know that our friend, were he or she sober, would not jump from the roof of his or her house.

Just consider Granny's situation: were she not to tell people the "stories" Tiffany loathes so much, she would accept the people remaining ill, or maybe even dying. Since Granny's case is one of weak paternalism, this would include accepting that certain people miss (or lose) what they explicitly want and need—while *knowing* that she was able to help them, if only by means of paternalism. So, in such cases the interference with the addressee's liberty seems justified, it even seems to be obligatory, for non-interference would mean to stand by and watch another person inflicting unwanted harm upon him or herself.[25] However, the case is less obvious with example (c). True, the patient wants to get cured and, equally true, the grief about her son's death might jeopardize this. But does that allow us not only to ignore her explicit interest, but also to violate an agreement made before—namely, *always* to tell her the truth, if asked for? And for what reason does Granny think that she might as easily interfere with Magrat's life, practically pairing her off?

The most famous anti-paternalist argument, stated by John Stuart Mill in his *On Liberty*, answers this question decidedly in the negative: "the only purpose for which power can be rightfully exercised over any member of a civilized community, against his will, is to prevent harm to others. His own good, either physical or moral, is not a sufficient warrant."[26]

In other words, *none* of the four examples is a case of justified paternalism (if, following Mill, there can be any such thing), since the addressee's "own good" can *under no circumstances* count as a "warrant" to interfere with his or her actions or choices. The person attempting to cross the bridge will presumably hurt herself, as will Granny when she keeps dueling— but that does not justify anyone in interfering with said actions; one may, of course, start to reason with them, persuade them, etc.[27] As Mill states, "over himself, over his own body and mind, the individual is sovereign."[28] This might stop the person in example (a) from crossing the bridge, but the rest are lost, as are Granny's patients (and she herself).

The obvious problem with Mill's "harm principle" is that it is not case-sensitive. Given examples (a) to (c), it seems implausible to reject outwardly any possibility of justifying the respective agent's actions. What if in case (a) there is no time to start a discussion with the person attempting to cross the bridge—what if seizing her is the only option left to stop her from falling to her death? She might well argue that suicide was indeed what she had in mind, like your partner in case (b). But does the explicit wish to kill oneself seal any option to interfere justly with a present attempt to do so? It may or may not, given the concrete circumstances under which this attempt is made. What if the suicidal person is delirious, drugged, or disoriented? What if she attempts suicide because she thinks her partner is dead—when, in fact, she is misinformed and he is alive and well? Granny for example would never answer any plea or argument to stop (which is why Nanny sends in Pewsey and rejects Magrat's offer to "command" Granny to stop the duel), because she is too proud and too overtly self-confident, which is why she fails to see that she *will* lose. In these cases, interference might well be justified. Mill's note, that his principle refers "only to human beings in the maturity of their faculties,"[29] is hardly of any help here—since Granny Weatherwax's and Miss Treason's patients have such mature faculties.

There is, of course, a reason why Mill's harm principle is not case-sensitive, since the example relevant to his argument is (d). The most famous phrase from his *On Liberty* is perhaps his label for the attempt to extend widely accepted values and rules to *every* member of a given society: he calls this the "tyranny of the majority."[30] Mill is primarily concerned with the political consequences of *generally* allowing interference with another person's behavior when the only reason is the latter's "good." These political consequences are, in Mill's view, that minorities are forced, by social pressure or even by threat of punishment, to take over the majority's habits, opinions, and ways of life—and that this could then be justified with regard to "the well-being" of the minorities. With well-known phrases like "would they see clearly, they would themselves agree that they need to," majorities could use the legitimation of paternalist interference as a license to enforce their own way of life. Just consider how Lily, Granny's sister, treats the inhabitants of Genua;[31] and how Vetinari, the Patrician of Ankh-Morpork, does not act very differently, but is only more attractively portrayed. Undoubtedly, social pressure put onto minorities by the majority did exist in Mill's time as it does now, regardless of how high or low the general opinion of paternalism is. It is, however, also hard to doubt that this social pressure would be intensified were paternalism in general considered to be morally neutral or even positive. But this begs the question as to why it should be considered *generally* wrong to interfere with a person's "self-sovereignty."

It is a built-in presumption of our liberal Western societies that to govern one's own life oneself is an absolute right, a right that should by no means be violated.[32] Still, as Mill's harm principle shows, it cannot be an *absolute* right, since we consider it rightfully violated when its owner violates another's rights; it stops, so to speak, at the "welfare of others."[33] For example, it is a serious violation of any elf's right to self-sovereignty if a witch stops him from raping or killing a peasant by violently hitting him on the head with a poker—but this violation is justified, given that the elf violates the peasant's right and that the punch is the only means available to stop him. At best, we might consider the right to self-sovereignty a prima facie absolute right, granted and secured, if its owner cannot be proven to have violated any of his neighbor's rights. Yet why should self-sovereignty have even this status?

Mill presents two arguments to justify this nearly absolute right to self-sovereignty, both still largely present in contemporary discussions of paternalism. The first, and relatively weak, argument points to the aforementioned large-scale consequences which the denial of this right would have: while there might be cases in which the consequences of paternalistic interference are better than the consequences of anti-paternalistic non-interference, the consequences of allowing paternalistic interference in general, or so Mill claims,[34] are disastrous. Not only will this help establish a "tyranny of the majority," it will moreover stop any valuable progress in the respective society.[35]

This argument, which Mill explicitly adopts from Wilhelm von Humboldt,[36] is not overtly convincing. The large-scale consequences are not as easily anticipated as Mill suggests, which is why, to substantiate his argument, he draws on a comparison between the free, liberal, and prospering Western societies of his day and contemporary illiberal societies which show no comparable signs of scientific and economic progress;[37] hence, the consequences of rejecting the individual's right to self-sovereignty are that the respective societies "become stationary."[38]

The linkage between liberal political regimes and scientific and economic progress, however, is not as easily established as Mill suggests. Economic growth and scientific revolutions, which secured Western societies the predominant position they had in Mill's day, happened largely under less free regimes. Nowadays, the People's Republic of China among others grows economically without establishing anything that we could call a liberal regime. And on Discworld Ankh-Morpork flourishes no less than Ephebe, neither of which are, strictly speaking, liberal regimes. The problem with Mill's first argument is, in short, that he, like other liberals, mistakes political liberty for economic liberty (the liberty freely to speculate, to buy and sell, etc.)—and only the latter is important for economic growth. And since this is also largely dependent on discoveries in the sciences, but not the humanities, political liberty is, again, anything but a necessary condition for economic and political success, as Mill's first argument claims.

Something similar could be said concerning the following argument of Arneson: "Disastrous life plans can set an instructive example for others as well as life plans that turn out favorably. Even in extreme cases where individuals voluntarily choose catastrophe for themselves, interventions will weaken the general atmosphere of freedom that we know is as difficult to maintain as it is necessary to human flourishing."[39]

It is wholly unclear, and not overtly convincing, to argue that the death of a drug addict is "an instructive example" that prevents others from trying crystal meth. Likewise, it is wholly unconvincing that laws prohibiting, or at least regulating, the sale and consumption of drugs should in any way "weaken the general atmosphere of freedom." Germany may be a less liberal country than the USA, but this is definitely not due to the fact that in Germany the denial of the Holocaust is illegal. Put with a hint of sarcasm, Arneson's argument asks us to sacrifice the individual on the altar of individuality.

This makes the second argument even more important, and it has some persuasive force and prima facie plausibility. Like many modern defenders of the right to self-sovereignty, Mill claims that only the individual himself can judge (a) what his interests are and (b) what, therefore, best suits them: a "human creature of ripe years . . . is the person most interested in his own well-being," and this person "has means of knowledge immeasurably surpassing those that can be possessed by anyone else."[40]

Indeed, why should anyone but I be able to judge what my interests, my preferences, and my problems are? This, then, seems to be an argument for a strong presumption against paternalism, because everyone considering his or her judgment superior to someone else's will necessarily mistake his or her preferences or interests for those of the addressee of his or her actions; the paternalist may well be acting in the firm belief that he or she is laboring toward nothing but the addressee's good or even what is best, but such an outcome, if it indeed occurs, will only be by coincidence. Most likely, the paternalist will force upon the other person a way of life that *he or she* thinks is best.

Remember that the witches of Discworld even have a word for this—"cackling":

> "Cackling," to a witch, didn't just mean nasty laughter. It meant your mind drifting away from its anchor. It meant you losing your grip . . . It meant you thinking that the fact you knew more than anyone else in your village made you better than them. It meant thinking that right and wrong were negotiable.[41]

"Cackling" is a prima facie argument in favor of anti-paternalism even if we reject Mill's "harm principle": when we start treating adults like children in certain situations, we run the risk of *always* treating them like children—because every paternalist action rests on the premise that we know better. And once this has been accepted, why should we suppose that there are only a few situations where this is the case? This is why among the basic rules of witchcraft there is the following: "*Never cackle.*"[42] As Granny remarks to Tiffany, witches should do everything to "remember" that they are "human,"[43] e.g. visit other witches.

The Cave, or why Strict Anti-Paternalism Fails

Famously, in his *Republic*, Plato establishes an analogy between the normal situation of the common people and the situation of people who are bound in a cave with their back to its entrance. They can see nothing but shadows of the real things that are going to and fro at the cave's entrance.[44] They mistake the shadows of things for the things themselves, and thus they generally judge on the basis of false "opinions." This is, or so Plato suggests, the normal situation of all those that are not philosophers: having no knowledge of the true nature of things, the common people lead their lives on the basis of, not necessarily false, but at least inadequate opinions and beliefs. Therefore, to really achieve their good, they have to be guided by those who do know the true nature of things—because these people are of course more competent to judge which action is good and which is bad, which consequences are likely to follow a given action, etc. But since the common people, being unable to know the true nature of things, will not be open to arguments drawn from this true nature, their "guides" have to trick them—using "beneficial lies". The analogy to Granny's relationship with the people of Lancre is, to my mind, obvious! One could even say that Miss Treason's "Boffo," the "art of expectations," is somewhat of a boiled-down version of Plato's argument. As Hilta Goatfounder puts it in *Equal Rites*: "Can't stand the dark and fug myself," only to add that "the customers expect it. You know how it is."[45]

Roughly put, Plato's argument runs as follows. The assumption of Mill is wrong—we *know* that a lot of people live as if they were inhabitants of the cave, that is, for different reasons they are not able to judge what is best for themselves. Instead, they base their judgments on false or inadequate opinions, like the patients of Miss Level who believe in fairies and goblins, or like Granny who too firmly believes in herself.

To appreciate fully Plato's argument, we need to distinguish at least three reasons that prevent people from being able to judge for themselves or, so to speak, three different "caves":

(a) People may be unable to judge for themselves either because their judgment is blurred by drugs, violent passions, etc., or because they generally lack the cognitive capacities necessary to do so.
(b) People may be unable to judge the consequences of their actions because they lack the expert knowledge necessary to do so. The best examples are large public projects, such as restructuring a big city or establishing a complex system of public health care or a system of guilds in a major metropolis of Discworld.
(c) People may be in a state that prevents them from freely weighing and judging their own interests, not because they are mentally disabled, but because they are indoctrinated, uneducated, or for some other reason. If, for example, you live in a very traditional and socially closed community or under a totalitarian regime, the means necessary to develop your own judgment are very likely to be systematically blocked; and even more likely, certain beliefs and opinions are taught as sacrosanct, holy, or otherwise not to be doubted. Remember Omnia!

Case (a) is not very problematic. Taking Mill's argument again as the classic anti-paternalist position, we see that he acknowledges the justification of paternalistic interference in such cases. Recall that it is only to "human beings in the maturity of their faculties" that his principle refers. Mentally disabled persons are clearly not "in the maturity of their faculties," and persons deluded in a concrete situation by their violent passions or by drugs can legitimately be considered exceptions from the general rule. Cases (b) and (c), however, are different.

Cases of type (b) are less rare than we might assume. Just consider example (c): the patient wants to succeed in fighting cancer but she, for whatever reason, falsely believes being always told the truth will help, or will at least not hinder her reaching this goal. Even if the illness and its consequences are usually less lethal, we all know that we tend to trust our own judgment way too much—instead of trusting the doctor's judgment. In the example, being an expert in the medical treatment of cancer, the doctor knows that the psychological stability of the patient is a crucial factor in the healing process.

Other examples are large public building projects, such as wind turbines—citizens often judge these and similar projects with regard to the short-term consequences ("I don't want this in MY landscape!") or with regard to the hardly, if at all relevant, question "Which political party is the driving force behind this?" From an outsider's point of view, such projects, taking into account their long-term consequences (less nuclear energy, thus less threats to public health), are usually judged positively; from the directly affected citizens' point of view, they are, however, often judged negatively, for reasons such as those mentioned. Were Mill right, the citizens' would be the better, more competent, judges (or, to move back to the first example, the patients should be considered more competent than their doctors).

Before Ankh-Morpork had its guilds, thieves and assassins in particular thought themselves better off, and still do even after the guilds have been established. However, as Vetinari is well aware, not only the citizens but also the guild members profit from the regulated and legalized theft and murder (well, *some* citizens do not, but that's life).

Jeremy Blumenthal has presented *empirical* evidence that "experts" are not only more competent (which comes as no surprise), but also more neutral and hence, with regard to *all* relevant aspects, better judges.[46] In other words: the sneaking suspicion, implicit for example in the motto ("Who watches the watchmen?"), that so-called experts are, like others, only acting and judging in favor of their own interests, lacks evidence. While at least in Europe it has of late become more and more fashionable to devalue political decisions made on the basis of advice from experts (especially in fields like environmental or immigration policy), this empirical evidence brought forward by Blumenthal strongly suggests that Europe's citizens would in many cases be better off were they to follow their government's judgments. So, given that most competently made decisions require special expertise, Mill's *strict* anti-paternalism is certainly wrong.

The direst problem, and probably the best case *for* anti-paternalist positions, however, is presented by the third "cave." In the first and also in the second cave, it is rather obvious that the potential addressees of paternalist actions are indeed not the best judges regarding the relevant matters. But the third cave is different: the people inhabiting it are neither deluded nor without expertise; they are, while certainly "in the maturity of their faculties," said not to be able to judge what their true interests are. As Edmund Burke put it in his *Reflections on the Revolution in France*: "The will of the many, and their interest, must very often differ." And he adds: "and great will be the difference when they make an evil choice."[47] The argument from conservative and leftist thinkers alike runs as follows. The largest part of the citizen body is for a simple reason *generally* not the best advocate of its own interests—because these people lack the competence to see what really is in their interest (because they are indoctrinated, alienated, or, well, just plain stupid). But is there any evidence to sustain this argument, apart from those already mentioned cases where the problem is that expertise is needed?

There certainly is. Even Mill recognized that outside the Europe and North America of his time, many societies were in "those backward states . . . in which the race itself may be considered as in its nonage."[48] If we strip his argument of its colonial and arrogant overtones, we have to admit that he has a point. As Martha Nussbaum[49] has repeatedly pointed out, many relativist attempts to defend non-Western "traditional and authentic ways of life" are in one important way flawed: to be able to defend a certain way of life as worthy of protection from "cultural imperialism," one has to prove that it is *freely chosen*, that means to prove that those living it *could have done otherwise*—since only then is there present an expression of their own beliefs, opinions, and choices, and not simply a consequence of indoctrination or force. One irksome feature of most "traditional" societies, however, is that traditional rules, manners, and role models (especially those for women: mother, housekeeper, and, basically, the husband's slave) are often shielded by some sort of taboo. In a society that features only *one* way of life and that (as is very likely) leaves no room for critical discussions about it, let alone whether its members are encouraged to question it, there is virtually no possibility for arguing that members actually *choose* this way of life—because to be able to choose *this* way of life means also to be able to discard it and choose *another one* instead. But as long as a person or group of persons lacks the required capacities (mental and political), we have to assume that they are *not* the best advocates of their interests, because there is no reason to assume that they have the chance to judge what these are.[50] Remember that Granny's patients are wholly ignorant of the true cause of their illness and that they will never be able to see the benefits of hygiene, etc.

Just consider the examples of ethnic or social minorities in our societies and of those "traditional" African cultures that to this day perform the heinous and abominable practice of female genital mutilation. In the latter example, women that have been brought up in such a culture often neither question the rightfulness of their own "circumcision," nor do they stop the respective practice—because "that is how it is done." Similarly, traditional female role models are often established not only by male, but also by female members of a society, who, being brought up this way, defend such role models as "natural" or "willed by God." In a free society, where alternative role models are available and can with equal right be chosen, we may have reason to respect such choices. After all, as Constable Dorfl finds out in *Feet of Clay*, "You say to people 'Throw off your chains' and they make new chains for themselves," this being "a major human activity," as Vimes remarks.[51] However, in a traditional or otherwise closed society, no such presumption is reasonable—and the argument that external interference with these societies is a case of unjustified paternalism (or "cultural imperialism") is unconvincing. In this case, the strict anti-paternalist would sacrifice the individual certainly not on the altar of individualism, but on the altar of misunderstood charity instead.[52]

However, as mentioned before, even such a stout-hearted anti-paternalist as Mill agrees to this, at least in part. It is, therefore, the example of minorities to which we have to turn to see why strict ("Millian") anti-paternalism is, even in liberal democracies, not an option.[53]

The Witch again, or the Moral Dilemma of Paternalism

Now, why should minorities be examples of case (c)? Especially in liberal democracies, where every citizen's civil rights, including the right to vote and to speak freely, are guaranteed? Following Mill, one should think that it is *anti*-paternalism, and not paternalism, that secures minority rights.

As with the liberal policies that follow it, Mill's argument rests on a powerful, yet contestable and unconvincing, assumption: that civil rights by themselves guarantee that (a) each citizen is able to choose and live his or her own way of life and moreover that (b) every citizen's interests are protected. None of this is, however, given solely by the enforcement of civil rights. Thus, organizations like the "Golem Trust" are a legal, anti-paternalist, and sufficient way to ensure that the voice of the minority is heard, while the "Campaign for Equal Heights" is just "patronizing."[54]

Of course, the rights to life and personal safety can be guaranteed by legal prohibition of unwanted interference. But what about the many other, legitimate interests a citizen or group of citizens may have? As long as this group is a minority, civil rights protect their basic interests (to life, etc.), but they do not protect them from being overpowered, especially not in a democracy. In itself, this of course presents no "presumption of paternalism," but this changes once we take into account the fact that minorities in democratic societies often are such for reasons of ethnic or social factors (it's quite similar on Discworld, if you look at the dwarfs and trolls and golems in Ankh-Morpork). As a group distinguishable from other groups, minorities often are formed by their members; the fan-groups in the various popular sports spring to mind. But they are equally often formed by others, most notably by the majority who construct a group out of those people who share a feature that members of the majority do not possess: usually a skin-color, an ethnic or religious background, or a certain social status. It is this mechanism which brings groups like "blacks" or "the poor" into existence, which then, of course, after a given period of time start to act *as the group* they have been said to be (the case is more complex with religiously defined minorities, of course). In both cases, and other than for most members of a majority, the access by individuals to the institutions relevant for propagating their interests is restricted, these being dominated and ruled by members of the majority ("and we're not letting THOSE people in to spoil OUR schools, golf courses, etc."). The most important group of institutions considered here being those constituting the educational system, especially its higher levels. Thus, the argument that "the poor" lack education for reason of being poor is less an analysis of social facts, but more like a self-fulfilling prophesy.

More important, we face a similar problem like that of the closed societies discussed above: the interests of minorities are very likely to be pictured as insignificant, or even dangerous, by members of the majority. And these opinions do not stay private (whatever that's supposed to mean). Since members of the majority will inevitably also provide the majority amongst the representatives of the media, the educational system, the political parties, etc., their opinion will also appear to members of the respective minority as correct rather than as what it is: an individual interest, and as such of the same importance as other interests. In such a situation, Burke and his conservative heirs are indeed correct when they argue (or, more likely, would be *if* they argued) that these people most certainly do know their will, but do *not* know their interests.[55] And the fact that the majority's biased opinions quiver through the whole set of public institutions makes this even worse. The "Campaign for Equal Heights" may be "patronizing," but it may also be an indispensable instrument to secure dwarfs' interests in being heard in public in Ankh-Morpork. If their behavior in public seems to be simply annoying to you, then remember that up to the present day this is the favorite reaction of conservatives to the call for gender equality.

The problem is, however, as (again) Granny remarks, that treating a minority or another group paternalistically may well result *not* in their being able to acknowledge their real interests, but simply in the supplanting of the rule of tradition by the rule of the majority: "I can't go meddling . . . Fundamental rule of magic, is that. You can't go round ruling people with spells, because you'd have to use more and more spells all the time."[56] But then there are times when "meddling" is the only alternative left, as Nanny tells Magrat:

"So, what you're saying," said Magrat, icily, "is that this 'not meddling' thing is like taking a vow not to swim. You'll absolutely never break it unless of course you happen to find yourself in the water?"

"Better than drowning," said Nanny.[57]

This is why paternalism poses a dilemma, since we have two equally problematic alternatives: we can either (a) respect the individual's or the people's right to lead their lives according to their own decisions, even if their outcomes are disastrous; or we can (b) supplant our own judgment about the individual's or people's interest for theirs, thereby on the one hand treating them like children and on the other hand running the risk of mistaking for their interest what is in fact ours.

Only "weak" paternalism like Granny's is relatively safe (but still, I suppose, not absolutely safe). But as the examples discussed above show, her case does not present the most pressing problems to which paternalism provides the solution.

Concluding Remarks

What establishes the appeal, and even the indispensability of paternalism, is the fact that in our wealthy, peaceful, and liberal Western democracies many people, and for various reasons, are unable to identify what contributes to their well-being. If we follow Mill, we will have to leave these "wretched" individuals to their fate. Much like Tiffany suggests to Granny, we might benevolently teach them the true nature of things, and then go our way, leaving them to their "self-sovereignty." After a while the truth will probably cast out most of the superstition and the false, indoctrinated self-perceptions. But given the historical evidence we have, this will take a few generations, if it happens at all.

If, however, we follow Granny, we will make ourselves the advocates of the interests of minorities, for, if we really care for our neighbors, we have to adopt her maxim: "Tomorrow, your job is to change the world into a better place. Today, my job is to see that everyone gets there." Remember the comparable maxim of Granny Aching: *"Speak up for those who don't have voices."*[58]

Notes

1. T. Pratchett (1987) *Equal Rites* (London: Corgi Books): "Listen," said Granny. "If you give someone a bottle of red jollop for their wind it may work, right, but if you want it to work for sure then you let their mind *make* it work for them. Tell 'em it's moonbeams bottled in fairy wine or something. Mumble over it a bit" (p. 62).
2. T. Pratchett (1993) *Lords and Ladies* (London: Corgi Books), p. 22.
3. T. Pratchett (2005) *A Hat Full of Sky* (London: Corgi Books), pp. 258–9.
4. Ibid., p. 313.
5. S. Clarke (2002) "A Definition of Paternalism," *Critical Review of International Social and Political Philosophy* 5, p. 89.
6. Plato (1963) *The Republic of Plato*, two vols, edited J. Adam (Cambridge: Cambridge University Press), p. 414b.
7. See J.S. Mill (1991) *On Liberty* in *On Liberty in Focus*, edited J. Gray and G.W. Smith (London and New York: Routledge), p. 110.
8. See G. Dworkin (1988) *The Theory and Practice of Autonomy* (Cambridge: Cambridge University Press), p. 122.
9. Pratchett, *A Hat Full of Sky*, pp. 101–3.
10. Pratchett, *Lords and Ladies*, pp. 355–6.
11. B. Spinoza (2007) *Theological-Political Treatise*, edited Jonathan Israel (Cambridge: Cambridge University Press), p. 194.
12. L. Strauss (1988) *Persecution and the Art of Writing* (Chicago: Chicago University Press), p. 183.
13. K. Grill (2007) "The Normative Core of Paternalism," *Res Publica* 13, pp. 441–2; Clarke, "A Definition of Paternalism," p. 82.
14. S.V. Shiffrin (2000) "Paternalism, Unconscionability Doctrine, and Accommodation," *Philosophy & Public Affairs* 29, pp. 213, 222. The example is from T. Pratchett, *A Hat Full of Sky*, p. 123.
15. Clarke, "A Definition of Paternalism," pp. 84–5.
16. Dworkin, *The Theory and Practice of Autonomy*, p. 124.
17. See C. Coons and M. Weber (2013) "Introduction: Paternalism— Issues and Trends," in *Paternalism: Theory and Practice*, edited C. Coons and M. Weber (Cambridge: Cambridge University Press), p. 2.
18. R.H. Thaler and C.R. Sunstein (2009) *Nudge: Improving Decisions about Health, Wealth and Happiness* (Harmondsworth: Penguin).
19. T. Pratchett (1992) *Witches Abroad* (London: Corgi Books), p. 16.
20. T. Pratchett (2006) *Wintersmith* (London: Doubleday), pp. 87, 140–1.

21. B. Gert and C.M. Culver (1979) "The Justification of Paternalism," *Ethics* 89, pp. 199–200.

22. Clarke, "A Definition of Paternalism," pp. 86–7; Dworkin, *The Theory and Practice of Autonomy*, p. 122.

23. Aristotle (2002) *Nicomachean Ethics*, edited S. Broadie and C.J. Rowe (Oxford: Oxford University Press), § 1169a.

24. P. Foot (2001) *Natural Goodness* (Oxford: Clarendon Press), pp. 96–7.

25. R. Carter (1977) "Justifying Paternalism," *Canadian Journal of Philosophy* 7, pp. 136–9; R.J. Arneson (1980) "Mill versus Paternalism," *Ethics* 90, p. 488.

26. Mill, *On Liberty*, p. 30.

27. Ibid., pp. 30–1.

28. Ibid., p. 31.

29. Ibid.; cf. p. 91.

30. Ibid., p. 26.

31. Pratchett, *Witches Abroad*, p. 240.

32. Arneson, "Mill versus Paternalism," pp. 477–8, 480.

33. D. Scoccia (2013) "The Right to Autonomy and the Justification of Hard Paternalism," in *Paternalism: Theory and Practice*, op. cit., pp. 74–93.

34. Mill, *On Liberty*, pp. 81–9.

35. P. Wall (2013) "Moral environmentalism" in *Paternalism: Theory and Practice*, op. cit., pp. 93–115.

36. The argument is that the necessary condition of social development is "individuality" or, more precisely, the ability of the members of a society to develop their individuality (Mill, *On Liberty*, pp. 73–4).

37. Ibid., p. 31.

38. Ibid., p. 87.

39. Arneson, "Mill versus Paternalism," p. 481.

40. Mill, *On Liberty*, p. 91.

41. Pratchett, *Wintersmith*, p. 29.

42. Ibid., p. 57.

43. Ibid., p. 341.

44. Plato (1963) *The Republic of Plato*, 2 vols, edited J. Adam (Cambridge: Cambridge University Press), 514a–515c.

45. Pratchett, *Equal Rites*, p. 98.

46. J.A. Blumenthal (2012) "Expert paternalism," *Florida Law Review* 64, pp. 721–58.

47. E. Burke (2004) *Reflections on the Revolution in France* (Harmondsworth: Penguin), p. 141.

48. Mill, *On Liberty*, p. 31.

49. M. Nussbaum (2007) *Frontiers of Justice: Disability, Nationality, Species Membership* (Cambridge: Belknap Press).

50. Blumenthal, "Expert paternalism," pp. 739–42.
51. T. Pratchett (2000) *Feet of Clay* (New York: HarperTorch), p. 349.
52. And neither can the ways of life of such closed societies be called "authentic," since this (at least to my mind) presupposes that the respective way of life is, again, freely chosen.
53. I skip the discussion of the above mentioned "nudges." They can reasonably be called paternalistic, in that they deliberately seek to influence, even to bias, citizens' judgments; but at least they leave the final decision up to the citizens. It will be very expensive, but you *do* have the option to smoke!
54. T. Pratchett (2004) *Going Postal* (London: Doubleday), p. 64.
55. It is a chilling fact, *but it is a fact*, that those suppressed by an institution, the "wretched of the earth," often take over the normative standards of their suppressors. Recall that it is women who fight *for* female circumcision. Another depressing example is Catholic priests who, after having been indoctrinated by the Catholic Church, see their own homosexual desires as a "sin," or as a serious "illness," or as a "divine punishment."
56. T. Pratchett (1989) *Wyrd Sisters* (London: Corgi Books), p. 103.
57. Pratchett, *Lords and Ladies*, p. 251.
58. T. Pratchett (2004) *The Wee Free Men* (London: Corgi), p. 43.

Bibliography

Aristotle (2002) *Nicomachean Ethics*, edited S. Broadie and C.J. Rowe (Oxford: Oxford University Press).

Arneson, R.J. (1980) "Mill versus Paternalism," *Ethics* 90, pp. 470–89.

Blumenthal, J.A. (2012) "Expert Paternalism," *Florida Law Review* 64, pp. 721–58.

_____ (2013) "A Psychological Defense of Paternalism," in *Paternalism: Theory and Practice*, edited C. Coons and M. Weber (Cambridge: Cambridge University Press), pp. 197–216.

Burke, E. (2004) *Reflections on the Revolution in France*, ed. C.C. O' Brien (Harmondsworth: Penguin).

Carter, R. (1977) "Justifying Paternalism," *Canadian Journal of Philosophy* 7, pp. 133–46.

Clarke, S. (2002) "A Definition of Paternalism," *Critical Review of International Social and Political Philosophy* 5, pp. 81–91.

Coons, C. and M. Weber (2013) "Introduction: Paternalism—Issues and Trends," in *Paternalism: Theory and Practice*, op. cit., pp. 1–25.

Dworkin, G. (1988) *The Theory and Practice of Autonomy* (Cambridge: Cambridge University Press).

Foot, P. (2001) *Natural Goodness* (Oxford: Clarendon Press).

Gert, B. and C.M. Culver (1979) "The Justification of Paternalism," *Ethics* 89, pp. 199–210.

Grill, K. (2007) "The Normative Core of Paternalism," *Res Publica* 13, pp. 441–58.

Mill, J.S. (1991) *On Liberty*, in *J.S. Mill: On Liberty in Focus*, edited J. Gray and G.W. Smith (London and New York: Routledge), pp. 23-131.

Nussbaum, M. (2007) *Frontiers of Justice: Disability, Nationality, Species Membership* (Cambridge: Belknap Press).

Plato (1963) *The Republic of Plato*, 2 vols, edited J. Adam (Cambridge: Cambridge University Press).

Pratchett, T. (1987) *Equal Rites* (London: Corgi Books).

_____ (1989) *Wyrd Sisters* (London: Corgi Books).

_____ (1992) *Witches Abroad* (London: Corgi Books).

_____ (1993) *Lords and Ladies* (London: Corgi Books).

_____ (2000) *Feet of Clay* (New York: HarperTorch).

_____ (2004) *The Wee Free Men* (London: Corgi Books).

_____ (2004) *Going Postal* (London: Doubleday).

_____ (2005) *A Hat Full of Sky* (London: Corgi Books).

_____ (2006) *Wintersmith* (London: Doubleday).

Rebonato, R. (2012) *Taking Liberties: A Critical Examination of Libertarian Paternalism* (New York: Palgrave Macmillan).

Scoccia, D. (2013) "The Right to Autonomy and the Justification of Hard Paternalism," in *Paternalism: Theory and Practice*, op. cit., pp. 74–93.

Shiffrin, S.V. (2000) "Paternalism, Unconscionability Doctrine, and Accommodation," *Philosophy & Public Affairs* 29, pp. 205–51.

Spinoza (2007) *Theological-Political Treatise*, edited J. Israel (Cambridge: Cambridge University Press).

Strauss, L. (1988) *Persecution and the Art of Writing* (Chicago: Chicago University Press).

Thaler, R.H. and C.R. Sunstein (2009) *Nudge: Improving Decisions about Health, Wealth and Happiness* (Harmondsworth: Penguin).

Wall, P. (2013) "Moral Environmentalism" in *Paternalism: Theory and Practice*, op. cit., pp. 93–115.

7 Equality and Difference: Just because the Disc Is Flat, Doesn't Make It a Level Playing Field for All

Ben Saunders

Ankh-Morpork, the "Big Wahoonie," naturally attracts those seeking fame, fortune, and adventure, whether from the plains of Sto Lat or the mountains of Lancre. Unsurprisingly, then, it is a particularly cosmopolitan city, home to various cultures, races, and species. This diversity presents special challenges when it comes to matters of equality. What, for instance, should we say to a young girl from the Ramtops who comes to the Unseen University because she wants to be a wizard?[1] Or how should the Ankh-Morpork City Watch ensure equality between its various new recruits?

There is, of course, one simple conception of equality, so simple that even a troll can understand it: treat everyone exactly the same. Let us call this "simple equality" or "equality as sameness." According to simple equality, people are treated equally when they are treated identically. This notion of equality is blind to differences of sex, race, or species.[2] This difference-blindness can itself be a significant achievement, since it suggests an absence of overt discrimination. No one should be treated differently from others, simply because he is, for instance, a dwarf, a zombie, or for that matter a she.

However, while absence of discrimination is a significant achievement in itself, the trouble with simple equality is that it's too simple. "Equal treatment" is not always appropriate, and can actually be unequal in effect, when there are relevant differences between the persons in question. Sometimes people need to be treated differently in order to be treated as equals.

If the Boot Fits . . .

Suppose that Sergeant Colon is issuing boots to new recruits in the Watch. Clearly, it would violate equality if he gave some recruits $10 cardboard-soled boots (the sort that let Sam Vimes feel the cobbles beneath his feet) and others good quality, $50 leather boots.[3] One demand of equality is that everyone be given boots of the same quality.

However, equality does *not* require that everyone be given exactly identical boots, because these may be of different value to different recruits.[4] A size seven and a half, for instance, would fit Sam Vimes.[5] But it would be misguided of Colon to issue everybody size seven and a half boots in the name equality. Such boots would be too small for a troll, but too large for the average dwarf and, in either case, useless to them. It's hardly equal to give Vimes a useful pair of boots and his dwarf and troll colleagues useless boots. This suggests that we need a more sophisticated understanding of equality.

A contrarian individual, of which there are many in Ankh-Morpork, might argue with this. They may insist that simple equality, or equality as sameness, is clearly treating everyone equally and that it is not their fault that this equal treatment suits some more than others. Why, they might ask, should dwarfs or trolls receive different—or "special"—treatment? But note that the minorities in question are not demanding that they receive *different* treatment, but only that they are treated in ways that satisfy their needs. They may be perfectly happy for all others to receive the same treatment that they do.

Suppose the dwarf in question has size four feet. In this case, what he[6] wants is some size four boots. If accused of seeking special treatment, he could reply that he would be content for everyone to be given size four boots, so that simple equality is preserved. (Of course, he might reply more forcefully, such as with a big axe. But we'll assume, for present purposes, that this particular dwarf is amenable to reasoned dialogue on the subject.) His objection, then, is not to sameness of treatment as such, but to the fact that universally issued seven and a half boots don't fit his needs. When we consider the alternative of issuing everyone with size four boots, we can see his point.

Adopting a standard designed to suit the needs of some group, and then applying it even-handedly to other groups with different needs, is likely to disadvantage members of the latter groups. The point here is that though simple equality treats everyone identically, without regard to differences, this is hardly equal if the treatment imposed uniformly on everyone is more suited to some than others. If all boots are designed for humans, then giving these same boots to dwarfs does not really treat those dwarfs with equal concern and respect, any more than giving humans dwarf-sized boots would. Either human-sized boots for all or dwarf-sized boots for all is consistent with equality as sameness, but neither seems an adequate response to the different needs of the individuals in question.

Neither the dwarfs nor the humans demand *better* boots than other recruits, but they all want boots that fit their feet. If we give everyone human-sized boots, then the dwarfs will resent the fact that the treatment applied uniformly to everyone better suits human needs than their own needs. Likewise, giving everyone dwarf-sized boots will give the humans cause for complaint. In either case, those who get ill-fitting boots will envy not what the others get (boots that would be no better fit for them), but the fact that what others get better fits those others' feet. They want something similarly fitting for themselves.

It is important to recognize not only that equality may be consistent with different treatment of different cases, but also that sameness of treatment (or simple equality) may be unequal, in the morally important sense, where the same treatment suits some better than others. We need a notion of equality that is compatible with different treatment for those with different needs. If Colon wants to treat his new recruits equally, then he should give each of them a pair of boots that fit their feet.[7] This is a rule that can be applied even-handedly to everyone, without giving anyone cause to complain. Let us call this "sophisticated equality."

Equality of Well-being

How should we understand the demands of sophisticated equality? One possibility would be to say that people should have the same quality of life or well-being. Thus, a dwarf and a human should each be given whatever is necessary to make them as well-off as each other. Perhaps one's needs or wants are more expensive to satisfy than the other's, but they shouldn't be penalized for this.

There is something attractive to this view in that it focuses on what fundamentally matters to us—our well-being—rather than fetishizing material goods which are, after all, only a means to well-being. Nonetheless, striving to equalize well-being is likely to have some perverse consequences.

Some people can be content with quite modest resources. For instance, even when briefly elevated to the ranks of Ankh-Morpork's nobility, Nobby still enjoys pints of Winkle's Old Peculiar beer and pig knuckle sandwiches.[8] Perhaps, given longer to acclimatize to his newfound status, his tastes might have become more refined, but probably not. If we're concerned with equalizing well-being then those, like Nobby, who don't need much to satisfy them, won't get much. That they are happy with their humble lot is taken to mean that they are not the most needy members of society, whereas someone like Vimes—who is rich but miserable—may have a much greater claim on us for assistance.

That equality of well-being may require us to help the rich might already seem embarrassing, but matters are even worse when we consider matters of individual responsibility. Consider someone who, unlike Nobby, does cultivate more expensive tastes. Let's call him Louis.[9]

Suppose that Louis was originally happy with a diet based on inexpensive "meat," of the sort peddled by Cut My Own Throat Dibbler and similar enterprising vendors. Perhaps he was even prepared to eat rat without ketchup! But now imagine that, one day, Louis tries ketchup on his rat and, having tasted this, feels that he cannot go back to eat rat without ketchup. What used to make him happy (rat without ketchup) no longer does so.

If our aim is to equalize levels of well-being, then Louis now needs to be given rat with ketchup in order to have the same level of well-being as before, and thus the same as everyone else. But, given that rat with ketchup costs almost twice as much as rat without ketchup, it now costs much more to provide Louis with a meal that gives him the same level of satisfaction as before.[10] If Louis were to develop more refined tastes still—perhaps demanding meat from a named animal other than rat, for instance—then the costs of keeping him happily fed might spiral astronomically.

The costs of feeding Louis aren't an issue, of course, if they are borne by Louis himself. If he wants to spend his own money on satisfying his more refined palate, it's nobody else's business. The problem comes, however, when some other authority seeks to ensure equality of well-being between the likes of Nobby, whose tastes are cheap, and Louis, whose tastes are more expensive.

Suppose, for instance, that Colon is placed in charge of the Watch's canteen and charged with feeding all recruits equally. Is it really fair to spend a far greater portion of the catering budget on Louis than Nobby, just because Louis has deliberately cultivated more expensive tastes?

The problem is not that Louis will be better off than Nobby as a result, for we're assuming that each will be equally happy with the meals provided for him. Nonetheless, it costs more to make Louis this happy than it does to bring Nobby to the same level of well-being. Many think that there is something

161

unfair about spending more on Louis than Nobby, even in order to raise him to the same level of well-being. According to these critics, Louis ought to bear responsibility for the cost of his own expensive tastes.

According to an alternative conception of equality—"equality of resources"—what Colon should do is spend an equal share of his budget on feeding Louis and Nobby. This needn't mean providing them with the same food; it's still possible to provide each with food tailored to their preferences, but it would be wrong to spend more on Louis than on Nobby, simply because it costs more to satisfy him. On this view, individuals should bear responsibility for the costs of their preferences and have no right to expect others to subsidize them.

Clamshells and Coconuts

Equality of resources is easily applied when it comes to spending a budget on different individuals or groups, but it can also be applied more generally if we imagine individuals purchasing the resources they want in a hypothetical marketplace. Imagine that Rincewind, Granny Weatherwax, the Librarian, and Wee Mad Arthur were—improbably—washed up together on an uninhabited island.[11] They might reasonably claim ownership of everything on the island, but doing so simply by dividing the island into four identical bundles (simple equality) would run in to the problems already demonstrated, even if practicable.

An alternative way for them to divide the island's resources equally would be for them to sell, or auction, the resources off amongst themselves. That is, they might use some plentiful but worthless tokens—such as clamshells or, if the island is in the Aurient, gold—as a currency to "bid" for those resources they want. If each of them starts the auction with an equal number of these clamshells, say one hundred, then each of them should end with a bundle of resources with the same market worth as each other.

After the auction, no one should have reason to envy anyone else's bundle, because each will have a bundle worth one hundred clamshells. If Rincewind wanted something the Librarian was bidding on more than the Librarian then he should have been able to outbid the latter for it. That he chose not to suggests that he preferred to spend those clamshells on some other resources that he values more. Given equal bidding power (clamshells), giving resources to the highest bidder should mean allocating them efficiently (that is, to who wants them most).

If everyone had the same preferences, then the result of the auction would be simple equality (an equal division of everything on the island), but this is unlikely. Most likely, people will have different preferences over the available resources. The hypothetical auction allows each to get as much as possible of what he or she wants, compatible with all others having a share of equal market worth.

Let's say that there are eight coconuts and 16 bananas on the island (ignoring for now everything else). One way to divide these fruits equally would be to give everyone two coconuts and four bananas. But what if neither Granny Weatherwax nor the Librarian like coconuts? They might want to swap their coconuts for more bananas. Assume that Rincewind is unwilling to swap, because he is happy with what he currently has, but Wee Mad Arthur will trade his bananas for coconuts (he likes coconuts because he can use them for shelter after eating the insides).

One possibility is that Arthur is willing to trade his bananas for coconuts on a one-for-one basis. In that case, after exchanges, it might be that Arthur has six coconuts and no bananas (having given each of Granny Weatherwax and the Librarian two bananas in exchange for two of their coconuts), while Granny and the Librarian each have six bananas and no coconuts. Here, though not everyone has the same fruits, it is still the case that everyone has six fruits in total. Moreover, there is no inequality, despite the difference between their respective bundles, because no one prefers another's bundle to their own. Once again, we see that equality is compatible with difference.

But what if Arthur hadn't been so keen to give up all of his bananas? He might want more coconuts, but not at the cost of all of his bananas. Moreover, since he is the only one "selling" bananas, while both Granny Weatherwax and the Librarian want those bananas, he might be able to drive a better bargain. Perhaps he will swap one of his bananas for *two* coconuts, no fewer.

Suppose that Granny balks at this and decides to keep what she has, but that the Librarian is willing to trade even on these terms (he really likes bananas). The upshot is that the Librarian ends up with no coconuts and five bananas, while Wee Mad Arthur has four coconuts and three bananas. In this case, the result of trading is that our islanders no longer have the same number of fruits. Does this mean that the outcome is now unequal? Not necessarily.

There's no reason to assume that all fruits are of the same value and ought to be exchanged on a one-for-one basis. After all, this would hardly be intuitively plausible if the fruits in question were a grape and a watermelon. If Wee Mad Arthur will only sell one banana for two coconuts, and the Librarian is willing to pay two coconuts for one banana, then the obvious conclusion to draw is that a banana is *worth* two coconuts, since this is the exchange rate that develops in a free market.

On this view, the appropriate way to value resources is according to what others in that society would give up in order to have them. If Arthur would prefer two coconuts to the banana that he currently possesses, then he ought to swap with the Librarian (which is presumably what he will do, in a free market). If he won't swap, then he must value his banana more than two coconuts and thus more than the Librarian is willing (or able) to pay for it.

It may seem surprising to suggest that a market, or auction, can serve equality, because those of us living in capitalist market economies on Roundworld are familiar with significant inequalities between rich and poor. The claim is not that markets magically *create* equality though, but only that they can serve as a means to efficient allocation of resources, while preserving initial (in)equality.

If people enter a market unequally situated, then this inequality will remain (and, perhaps, grow). What's crucial, in this example, is that all parties start out with equal numbers of clamshells with which to purchase other resources. The claim is that we should therefore consider the end point of the auction to be equal also since, though those involved may choose to buy different bundles of resources, the resources that they buy will be equal in value, as measured by their clamshells. Thus, markets can be harnessed to serve equality, provided that participants enjoy equality of purchasing power from the start.

Hi-po-fetty-kal Inn-sewer-ants

Equality of resources has the advantage that it does not subsidize expensive *tastes*, but it risks burdening those who have expensive *needs* through no fault of their own. Louis is responsible for having cultivated his refined tastes, but another individual may have more expensive dietary needs through no fault of his or her own. In fact, in a world where dwarfs eat rats, gargoyles eat pigeons, and zombies and golems don't apparently need to eat at all, it may be that humans qualify as having expensive dietary needs!

Giving everyone an equal share of external resources is all very well, but if people differ in what we might call their "internal" resources—if some, for example, are stronger or smarter than others—then these talented individuals will have better prospects with the same external resources than those less well-endowed naturally.

Ronald Dworkin proposes that people's shares of resources should be sensitive to their responsible choices, but not to their initial endowments, whether social (such as inherited wealth) or natural (such as inherited genes). His proposed solution is that the hypothetical auction be supplemented with a hypothetical insurance scheme, thereby making all matters of luck the outcome of a chosen gamble. Thankfully, being merely hypothetical, this system is less open to abuse than the "inn-sewer-ants" that Twoflower introduced to Ankh-Morpork.[12]

Insurance allows individuals to protect themselves from risks, such as being handicapped by an industrial accident or an argument with a troll. Dworkin's idea is that, provided that all have the opportunity to insure themselves, the costs of such accidents are legitimate because they reflect those choices.[13] If someone chooses not to purchase insurance, and then has an accident, they must bear the costs of their decision, since they had their share of resources but chose to purchase other things than insurance. There's no reason why other members of society ought to pick up the tab for such imprudence, since that would be unfair on those who had already paid for their own insurance.

The problem with this is that individuals cannot actually insure against all misfortunes; specifically, one cannot purchase insurance to cover the risk of being born handicapped in some way. Dworkin's proposal is that we look at what coverage people purchase on average and then modify the initial auction as if people had purchased such coverage, assuming that this is what they would have done given the chance.

Supposing the average individual would have purchased insurance against being born deaf, we reduce the bundle of all those who are not born deaf by a number of clamshells equal to their insurance premium, and then use this to provide a payout for those who are (through no fault of their own) born deaf. Thus, the deaf get a larger bundle of external resources to compensate for their disability, but this corrects for an unchosen inequality and reflects the insurance decisions people would have made (given the chance).

Fiscal Relativity: It's What You Can Do with It that Counts

A resource auction is intended to ensure that everyone has a bundle of resources of equal value, measured by what others are willing to pay for it. Resource equality, however, overlooks the fact that the same good might be worth more to one person than another—or what might be called fiscal relativity.[14] A given resource might be worth more to one person than another, because one is able to do more with it.

A loaf of bread, for instance, might feed a normal human for a day, but for Wee Mad Arthur it can feed him for a week and provide him with shelter once it's hollowed out. Or, to take another example, a wizard's staff may be no more than a fancy walking stick to one person, but is far more useful in the hands of a trained wizard. If these resources are valued according to the average price that people are willing to pay for them, then some will be able to buy resources that are far more useful to them than what others can afford.

The Roundworld economist Amartya Sen argues that it's silly to focus on resources, rather than what people can do with them, and instead proposes what he calls the "capability approach"— that is, we instead focus on what things people are capable of doing with their resources.[15] For instance, someone responsible for distributing rations should ensure that everyone gets enough food to satisfy their nutritional requirements. Thus, Wee Mad Arthur will be given less food than a full-sized human, but both will have enough to satisfy their needs.

Unlike equality of well-being, the capabilities approach does *not* insist that people's needs or preferences be equally met, since it focuses on what people are *able* to do, rather than what they actually do. It is possible that some people's needs are unmet as a result of their own choices. A religious devotee, such as Constable Visit, might be hungry because he or she is fasting. Nonetheless, he or she retains the *capability* to be well-nourished, since a capability refers to what one is *able* to do, whether or not one does it. Thus, the capability approach holds individuals responsible for the choices that they make with their resources, but not for the fact that they may—through no fault of their own—need more resources than others to achieve the same level of functioning.

Consider the things a watchman needs to be able to do in order to do his or her job. He or she must be able to patrol the streets and be able to apprehend petty criminals, such as unlicensed thieves. Presumably this requires that he or she be adequately nourished which, as already noted, may necessitate different kinds and amounts of food according to his or her personal requirements (metabolism, and so on). To be able to patrol the streets in comfort, he or she will generally need sturdy boots, again suited to his or her feet. While some may choose not to wear their standard issue boots—preferring to patrol barefoot, for instance—they ought nonetheless to have the capability to walk in comfort, while those unable to walk will need some other means of conveyance that enables them to patrol, like Arnold Sideways's wheelbarrow.[16] He or she must also be able to navigate the streets, even at night. A dwarf, used to underground tunnels, might be able to see perfectly in the dark, while Angua might be guided by her sense of smell, but others will need a torch or lantern to enjoy the same capability. Finally, he or she will need to be capable of apprehending criminals if necessary. A troll may not need weapons to do this, but others may require a sword, axe, or bow, all of which are different means of bestowing them with the same basic capability.

As we can see from even this brief example, some people will need more resources than others in order to enjoy the same capabilities. Angua, for example, is perfectly capable of doing her job in wolf form without any extra equipment, whereas someone else, like Arnold Sideways, might need not only the usual equipment but special provision in order to enjoy the same capabilities.

These differences wouldn't all be corrected by Dworkin's hypothetical insurance market, since most people probably

wouldn't insure against the costs of not being a werewolf or of
suffering a particularly rare disability. Thus, despite the ingenuity of Dworkin's auction and insurance model, it fails to ensure
that people really would be equal in what matters, namely the
things that they can do.

Someone concerned with equality should, according to
Sen, focus on ensuring that people enjoy equal capabilities,
in particular prioritizing certain "basic" capabilities such as
being well-nourished, moving around, and generally being a
functioning member of society.

What Do You Do with a Six-Foot-Plus Dwarf?

Unlike simple equality, the approach I have defended is sensitive to different needs of different people; in other words, it recognizes that treating people as equals may require treating them
differently, rather than uniformly. However, this approach does
have something in common with equality as sameness, namely
its blindness to group difference. Note that so far no reference
has been made to whether someone is a human, dwarf, troll,
zombie, or any other species. Sophisticated equality is responsive to individuals' needs or capabilities, which may be a result
of their species, but it is not sensitive to species membership as
such.

Consider a circumstance in which height is an advantage.
Here, most dwarfs may need extra help to compensate for
being short; that is, to give them the same capabilities that a
taller person enjoys naturally. But a four-foot dwarf is no more
needy than a four-foot human (like Nobby) just because he is
a dwarf, while a six-foot six-inch dwarf (like Carrot[17]) suffers
no disadvantage at all for being a dwarf. It is height that we
should be responsive to, rather than species. To help *all* dwarfs,
including Carrot, simply because *most* dwarfs are short would
be over-inclusive, while refusing to help a four-foot human
because he or she is not a dwarf—though no better off than
one—would be under-inclusive.

This approach to equality differs from a group-based approach, as exemplified by the Silicon Anti-Defamation League[18] or the Community Co-ordinator of Equal Heights for Dwarfs.[19] Group-based approaches often seek special treatment, such as exemptions, for members of a particular group, such as dwarfs. The Community Co-ordinator of Equal Heights for Dwarfs, for instance, demands that dwarfs in the watch be allowed to carry an axe rather than the traditional sword.

Does equality require accommodation of such demands? Not necessarily. Though equality may allow or even require differential treatment, it does not follow that we ought to differentiate based on group membership as such. In fact, I shall argue that equality is better served by focusing on individuals, rather than groups.

I argued, above, that equality may be consistent with, and sometimes even requires, differential treatment of different individuals. If dwarfs have smaller feet, for instance, then they will need smaller boots. But that equality *sometimes* requires differential treatment does not mean that differential treatment is always appropriate. Equality as sameness may be too simple an understanding of equality for a diverse society like Ankh-Morpork, but that doesn't mean that it's wholly without merit.

Applying different rules or standards to different people is always potentially unequal and thus it stands in need of justification. Pointing to the different needs or circumstances of the individuals concerned *may* justify this differential treatment, but not all differences justify differential treatment.

It's not clear that dwarfs should be entitled to carry different weapons, simply because they prefer axes to swords. After all, if the purpose of either a sword or an axe is to grant its wielder the capability to wound an adversary, then a dwarf with a sword likely has much the same capability for wounding as a dwarf with an axe. The dwarf doesn't *need* an axe to address some disadvantage in capabilities, since a sword is just as good for its purpose. Moreover, allowing dwarfs to carry axes, while insisting that all other watchmen must use swords, creates a potentially unjustified inequality between dwarfs and others. Why should they have different weapons, if they are no different in needs or capabilities?

At this point, we might reasonably ask why it should be the case that watchmen are required to carry swords rather than axes in the first place. Perhaps this is simply an unjust prejudice that, though it can be applied even-handedly to all, ought to be abolished. Why not say that each watchman should carry a sword or an axe (his or her choice)? This would allow dwarfs to retain their traditional axes, but note that it would not do so by singling out dwarfs: it would also allow other watchmen the option to carry an axe rather than a sword if they so wished. If there are no good reasons to insist that watchmen carry swords rather than axes, then there is no reason to require this of any of them, dwarf or not.

On the other hand, perhaps there are good reasons why axes are forbidden to watchmen. Maybe it's because a watchman with an axe serves as a symbolic reminder of "Old Stoneface" Vimes's regicide.[20] Perhaps, in light of this history, it's reasonable to suggest that no watchman should ever again walk the streets of Ankh-Morpork with an axe. I don't commit myself either way on this point but, *if* this is a sufficient justification for banning watchmen with axes, it applies equally to dwarfs.

In short, either there are good reasons to mandate that watchmen use swords rather than axes or there aren't. If there aren't, then there's no reason to restrict any of them, dwarf or not, while if there are then these reasons are reasons to restrict everyone, including the dwarfs. In neither case is there any good reason to exempt dwarfs from the general policy that applies to everyone else.

A policy that allows anyone to carry an axe if they so wish might be better than one that requires all to carry swords, but to allow axes only for dwarfs amounts to granting dwarfs an unjustified privilege on the basis of their species, which is contrary to equality. It's hard to imagine good reasons for requiring all watchmen except dwarfs to carry swords rather than axes, while exempting dwarfs, and only dwarfs, from this requirement.[21]

Focusing on group membership risks creating inequalities between individuals, if some are granted a privilege just because they are dwarfs (or whatever). If short people are disadvantaged in a particular circumstance, then we should provide assistance for all short people, even those who are not dwarfs, while there is no need to help tall people, even if they are dwarfs, like the six-foot six-inch dwarf-by-adoption Carrot. Thus, we ought to focus on the needs or capabilities of individuals, rather than taking group membership as a proxy.

The Tyranny of Groups

Focusing on group membership is supposed to protect minority groups from being dominated by the majority culture. A further problem with this though is that it may allow the majority of a given minority to oppress a minority group within that minority. For instance, giving dwarfs special "group rights" serves to reinforce certain standards of dwarfishness that a dwarf leader[22] (typically male) may use to oppress female dwarfs who do not wish to conform to typical dwarfish standards. Suppose dwarfs are allowed to depart from usual uniform regulations in the Watch, in order to allow traditional dwarf dress. This traditional dress may mandate trousers instead of a skirt, allowed to other female Watchmen, which would restrict female dwarfs like Cheery (or Cheri) Littlebottom.[23]

Some suggest that there is no problem with groups restricting their own members, provided that group membership is voluntary, that is, that these groups recognize a right to exit.[24] The thought is that if female dwarfs feel oppressed by traditional dwarfish norms, they can simply renounce their dwarfishness and no longer be subject to whatever rules apply to dwarfs, beneficial or burdensome.

However, this is perhaps too quick. There's nothing simple about renouncing part of one's identity; it's not clear that a female dwarf can cease to be a dwarf (what else would she become?) and, even if she could, it's still not clear why she should be required to make such a sacrifice. Perhaps she values and identifies with her dwarfish heritage, except insofar as she finds it unduly masculine. She might, for instance, enjoy singing songs about gold and want to carry her traditional axe, yet at the same time want to wear skirts and make-up because she is also a woman as well as a dwarf. In other words, she doesn't want to have to choose between these two identities and there's no obvious reason why she should have to.

Again, someone might say that, in seeking to combine both dwarfishness and femininity, she's seeking what amounts to special treatment, but this isn't so. Male dwarfs have no problem being both dwarfs and men, so why should female dwarfs not be able to combine species and gender identities? The problem, once again, seems to stem from a misguided application of simple equality, which assumes that all dwarfs have to be treated the same, in this case, by male standards.

What our female dwarf wants is not better treatment, but merely treatment in accordance with her gender (and species) identity. She would be perfectly happy, let's assume, to have all dwarfs treated as female. So, some dwarfs want to be male and others female. Applying the same gender standards to all of them will therefore frustrate some, so the solution is to recognize that being a dwarf is in fact compatible with being either male or female.

A group-based approach to equality will have to accommodate those with multiple group identities, such as those who are both dwarf and female (and, perhaps, share in other identities too). The best way to achieve this, I have suggested, is not to focus on these group identities at all, but rather to focus on individuals and their needs.

Suppose, once again, that Colon is issuing uniforms to new recruits to the Watch. If one recruit is shorter than average (dwarf or not) then they will need a smaller uniform to fit them. If one recruit wants a skirt, rather than trousers, then this should be allowed, provided it is compatible with them performing their function. If it just so happens that this results in a dwarf in a skirt, that's fine so long as it's what she—or he—wants.

The fact that different individuals will receive different uniforms, suited to their needs and preferences, does not show any inequality between them, because all have been outfitted in accordance with their own needs and preferences. No recruit has any reason to prefer what another recruit received to what he or she received.[25]

Conclusion

Simple equality works fine in a homogeneous society but, where people are different, treating everyone the same can amount to treating those whose needs or preferences are well-catered for better than others. In a diverse community, such as Ankh-Morpork, treating people as equals requires sensitivity to relevant differences between them.

Where people are already differently situated, treating each of them the same will preserve, and perhaps increase, inequalities between them. A more sophisticated theory of equality needs to consider in what respects people should be equal. If we think people should enjoy equal levels of well-being, then some may need more resources to be spent on them than others. On the other hand, if we think that each person is entitled to an equal share of resources, we will have to accept that some may make better use of those resources than others.

Differences between people are often bound up with particular group identities, such as species or gender. Though some argue that members of particular groups ought to receive special treatment as such, this risks creating more arbitrary inequalities, since not all members of a particular group need to share a given disadvantage (for instance, some dwarfs are tall), while there may be disadvantaged individuals who are not members of that group (some humans are no taller than the average dwarf).

A sophisticated understanding of equality requires us to be sensitive to differences between individuals, but not to attend to groups as such. Unfortunately, such equality may be too sophisticated for the Sergeant Colons of the world, not to mention much harder to implement in practice than simple equality. Nonetheless, since simple equality is plainly inadequate in a diverse society, we need to rethink our understanding of equality.

Notes

1. This, of course, is the plot of *Equal Rites*.
2. According to T. Pratchett (1992) *Witches Abroad* (London: Corgi), p. 167: "Racism was not a problem on the Discworld, because—what with trolls and dwarfs and so on—speciesism was more interesting. Black and white lived in perfect harmony and ganged up on green."
3. Prices from T. Pratchett (1994) *Men at Arms* (London: Corgi), p. 35.
4. This example and the discussion here draw upon D. Rae (1981) "Two Contradictory Ideas of (Political) Equality," *Ethics* 91, pp. 451–6.
5. See T. Pratchett (1997) *Feet of Clay* (London: Corgi), p. 148.
6. I come to the issue of female dwarfs later.
7. Assuming, that is, that they have two feet. Similar considerations suggest that those with more or fewer feet should receive more or fewer boots, as appropriate to their needs. The implications of the Luggage joining the Watch don't bear thinking about.
8. Pratchett, *Feet of Clay*, pp. 276–7, 281–2.
9. This example comes from R.M. Dworkin (2000) *Sovereign Virtue: The Theory and Practice of Equality* (Cambridge, MA and London: Harvard University Press), pp. 48–59.
10. At least, in one of Ankh-Morpork's dwarfish eateries, rat with ketchup costs 7p, compared to 4p for rat without. See Pratchett, *Men at Arms*, p. 157.
11. The following discussion draws on Dworkin, *Sovereign Virtue*, ch. 2.
12. See T. Pratchett (1985) *The Colour of Magic* (London: Corgi), pp. 55, 80, 87.
13. Dworkin, *Sovereign Virtue*, pp. 73–83.
14. Pratchett, *Feet of Clay*, pp. 249–50.
15. Sen has written much on this topic, but for an accessible introduction see his 1979 Tanner Lectures "Equality of What?" at http://tanner-lectures.utah.edu/_documents/a-to-z/s/sen80.pdf (accessed 14 May 2014).

16. T. Pratchett (1995) *Soul Music* (London: Corgi), p. 271.
17. T. Pratchett (1990) *Guards! Guards!* (London: Corgi), p. 35.
18. Pratchett, *Feet of Clay*, p. 35.
19. Ibid., p. 156.
20. That "Old Stoneface" used an axe is implied in T. Pratchett (1998) *Jingo* (London: Corgi), p. 372.
21. This argument is from Brian Barry (2001) *Culture & Equality: An Egalitarian Critique of Multiculturalism* (Cambridge: Polity Press), ch. 2.
22. That is, mine supervisor (*dezka-knik*). See Pratchett, *Guards! Guards!*, p. 37.
23. Pratchett, *Feet of Clay*, p. 246.
24. For instance, C. Kukathas (1992) "Are there Any Cultural Rights?," *Political Theory* 20, pp. 105–39.
25. This "envy test" comes from Dworkin, *Sovereign Virtue*, p. 67.

Bibliography

Barry, B. (2001) *Culture & Equality: An Egalitarian Critique of Multiculturalism* (Cambridge: Polity Press).

Dworkin, R.M. (2000) *Sovereign Virtue: The Theory and Practice of Equality* (Cambridge, MA and London: Harvard University Press).

Kukathas, C. (1992) "Are there Any Cultural Rights?" *Political Theory* XX.

Pratchett, T. (1985) *The Colour of Magic* (London: Corgi).

_____ (1987) *Equal Rites* (London: Corgi).

_____ (1990) *Guards! Guards!* (London: Corgi).

_____ (1992) *Witches Abroad* (London: Corgi).

_____ (1994) *Men at Arms* (London: Corgi).

_____ (1995) *Soul Music* (London: Corgi).

_____ (1997) *Feet of Clay* (London: Corgi).

_____ (1998) *Jingo* (London: Corgi).

Rae, D. (1981) "Two Contradictory Ideas of (Political) Equality," *Ethics* 91.

Part III Ethics and the Good Life

8 Millennium Hand and Shrimp: On the Importance of Being in the Right Trouser Leg of Time

Susanne E. Foster

In the world of Terry Pratchett, there lies a second-hand set of dimensions in which Great A'Tuin swims slowly through the interstellar gulf. The Discworld rests atop four giant elephants on his back.[1] Given the strange nature of the Discworld, it is not surprising that space–time in this dimension should have a bewildering set of properties. Here, time can ooze in bags[2] or be wound and unwound from spools.[3] Space–time can be distorted into L-Space by the power of books.[4] And as events unfold on the Discworld, a multitude of other parallel realities unfold so close to it that the inhabitants may find themselves intentionally or accidentally traveling between them.[5] Individuals from the Discworld can also find themselves in other dimensions.[6] Time can be shattered and then reassembled into something that approximates the original sequence.[7] And being insufficiently tethered to space–time leads to various psychic abilities like seeing into the future and the ability to commune with the dead.[8] Others with but loose connections to space–time become confused or at least unintelligible to those who are better anchored.[9] Finally, those who exist outside of time—in eternity—have an entirely different set of difficulties to deal with.

It is more surprising that in Pratchett's world even dear old Briton exists in a space–time continuum playful enough to pixellate the unwary. Over the course of three novels, Johnny Maxwell learns that bag ladies may carry extra time in their carts, the dead hang around graveyards, aliens in video games are persons too, and alternate timelines are all too easy to stumble into.[10]

But, the most interesting feature of Pratchett's conception of space–time is the moral lessons his characters draw from their encounters with it. Various philosophical and religious systems have speculated about the effects that time travel, alternate realities, and eternal existence would have on choice and on the possibility of happiness. Aristotle postulated that the best existence is one in which perfection is achieved and change ceases. Christianity offers that changeless eternity as a reward to those who love God. An everlasting but changing existence, on the other hand, has met with mixed opinion. In philosophy and in popular culture, the possibility that things may have gone right elsewhere may be taken as comfort by individuals facing tragedy.[11] Others argue that infinite possibility would paralyze an agent or render choice meaningless.[12]

But mortals in Pratchett's world tend not to be beguiled or paralyzed by eternity or alternate realities. Many mortals reject eternity when offered it. Those that embrace it find that their personalities become arrested by "living" in it. And characters as disparate as Granny Weatherwax and Johnny Maxwell conclude that the existence of other realities where they may have made different choices is neither comfort nor reason not to bother acting here and now. It is critically important to find oneself in the right trouser leg of time—the one in which one can be content with both one's strengths and one's weaknesses because here one is true to oneself.

In this chapter, I will examine Pratchett's ethical views by exploring different characters' experiences of space–time and how they develop in light of their experiences. Pratchett considers character, not the internalization of objective rules governing action, as the basis of moral insight into right choice and into what will bring the agent true happiness. Thus, the struggles and developments of his characters can best be understood in terms of a virtue ethics.

I will utilize an Aristotelian virtue ethics to illuminate some key features of Pratchett's ethics. Like Aristotle, Pratchett characterizes moral development as a product of external influence, reflection, and accumulation of choices.[13] It makes no small difference where and when one is raised nor what one has made of oneself in the past. But, unlike Aristotle, who believed that human happiness was rooted in human nature, Pratchett's conception of virtue and human flourishing rests on a less universal basis. As a result, Pratchett does not provide one rather narrowly defined best way to be. Happiness on the Discworld is as varied as the characters who inhabit it. Pratchett also differs from Aristotle in rejecting the attainment of an unchanging perfection. According to Pratchett, happiness is only found in continuing to work toward one's goals, and never in resting content with what one has accomplished. Though the nature of virtue and moral choice can be characterized in broadly Aristotelian terms, the conception of human flourishing offered by Pratchett cannot. And because it more closely fits human experience, his conception is superior to that offered by Aristotle.

Life Is a Trick, and You Get One Chance to Learn It

Central to any virtue ethics are the questions: What is the best life? How does one attain it? According to Aristotle, the process of ethical development is rooted in the individual's nature. As rational animals, humans are drawn toward the same ends as other living beings—consuming nutrients, growing, reproducing, and experiencing the world. Through these activities, animals attain what being they can—participation in the ongoing existence of the species form. But, though they share activities with other living things, the human pursuit of these activities is informed by reason.[14] Eating, which in animals is a means to nutrition and enjoyment, becomes socially rich. Humans eat to celebrate. They fast to mourn. They share food to build community at family dinners, at weddings, and at religious ceremonies. And, it is the role reason plays in the activities humans share with other animals that transform them into *human activities*, a part of a flourishing human life, rather than leaving them as mere prerequisites for the possibility of flourishing.[15] The rational part of human nature gives humans an end beyond those they share with other animals. Humans structure and reflect on their activities. They come to understand their own nature and the world in which they live. Ultimately, they can come to understand the principles of reality and being—that is, God. For Aristotle, the fact that the human mind can engage in contemplation of God is evidence that mind is immaterial, and so not subject to the forces of change that govern matter. When a human thinks, his or her activity is a complete actuality—unchanging and therefore eternal. Being in some measure like God's activity, this form of human flourishing is happiness. The only happy life, then, is directed toward the attainment of an understanding of human nature, the world, and God. The practical life is happy insofar as one comes to understand human nature and actualize that nature in the world.

Though human nature directs the agent toward fulfillment, and though reason enriches the activities through which one is fulfilled, one's upbringing and circumstances can distort the individual's ethical perception and interfere with the possibility of attaining happiness. Hunger can make food seem more important than it is. Repeated injury can lead to excessive fear. To lead a good life, a truly happy life, the individual must cultivate both the correct reaction to his or her environment, feeling fear only at those things that are truly fearful and wanting only as much food as is conducive to physical health. And, he or she must form the correct understanding of what is good for human beings. The former traits constitute the virtues of character, the latter practical wisdom.

According to Aristotle, a virtue of character comprises both the right psychological response to the environment (cognitive and emotive) and also the right physical response (action).[16] Because of her practical wisdom, the virtuous agent recognizes the importance of the morally salient features of her environment and their relationship to the good.[17] And, she is moved by sensual desire or fear or anger or some other affect to do the right thing, sleeping when she is tired, buckling her seat belt, voting against unjust laws and the like. Over time, she creates a life for herself that is filled with good things, friends to whom she is loyal, a family that she loves, financial security resulting from her excellent stewardship of her resources, a career that allows her to exercise her physical and intellectual skills, hobbies that express her creativity and make the world a better place. It is not surprising that others notice her success, ask her advice, admire her, and wish they were more like her. Though her life will be unique because of her particular circumstances, there is a set of virtues that she will possess and a set of choices that will typify her life. That is, her perfection as a human being, her happiness, rests not in what is particular to herself but in her conformity to an ideal—a sameness of human excellence. She will realize that the highest human calling is the acquisition and contemplation of truth, and that the life devoted to leadership and maintenance of the community is also a good human life. The other lives she might choose, those aimed at filling a lack or at attaining pleasure, are not really happy.

The Aristotelian account of happiness, choice, and character development then is that an agent begins with some awareness of the good, generated by his nature, which is then molded by his society, his prior choices and his reflection on what he wants from life. For Aristotle happiness is found in a well-defined life because the account of happiness more or less mirrors the objective truth about what constitutes happiness, the attainment of actuality through contemplation, and, to a lesser extent, the exercise of reason in practical life.

"But First, Mistress Weatherwax—We Will Exchange Cards"

While Aristotle presents an outline of the best life—and even a second best life that anyone fortunate enough to have the ability should pursue—Pratchett's account of the best character and life is as varied as the individuals that populate his books. This is, in part, because Aristotle uses an objective perspective from which to judge the goodness of a life—the fulfillment of a nature that is common to all human beings—whereas Pratchett believes a life is best judged from an internal perspective and should be consonant with the *individual's* nature. Sam Vimes is committed to integrity, service to the community, and loving relationships with his wife and son.[18] The Patrician seems to gain satisfaction from keeping the city running well and possibly from his relationships first with Wuffles and later with Mr. Fusspot.[19] Rob Anybody, on the other hand, adheres to the Nac Mac Feegle belief that this world, filled with drinking and fighting, must be heaven. When he is chosen to be the father of his tribe, he takes on a deep commitment to doing what is best for them, but he is still convinced that drinking and fighting is integral to that good.[20] Cohen the barbarian wants only "Hot water, good dentrishtry, and shoft lavatory paper."[21] Mr. Nutt finds happiness in the realization that he and his kind are not irredeemably evil. Indeed, orcs are no worse than human beings.[22] Mightily Oats discovers his own life's quest when Granny Weatherwax helps him expand his religious vision.[23]

But would Aristotle be right that Cohen is satisfied with good teeth because of his prior lack, and Rob Anybody's vision of happiness is the result of his lacking the intelligence, education, and reflection that would fit him to a better life? Pratchett's answer seems to be "No." Each of these characters has chosen a life that is the fulfillment of *his nature—his happiness*. Evidence for this is presented in many of his books; and there are two particularly clear examples. In *Lords and Ladies*, the trouser legs of time twist together and Granny Weatherwax has the opportunity to experience a very different life that she might have lived. And, in *Johnny and the Bomb*, multiple trips into the past give Johnny the opportunity to change his life, if he wanted to. As a result of these circumstances, Granny and Johnny find themselves uniquely qualified to judge their choices and the lives they lived.

A pivotal moment in Granny Weatherwax's life was the day she met the elf queen, the same day she decided to run away from her suitor Mustrum Ridcully. Rejecting the queen's help and asserting that one day she would be a witch, she then ran into the woods and away from Ridcully. He gave up the chase, and the two drifted apart. Mustrum became a wizard and eventually Archchancellor of Unseen University, and Esmerelda, true to her word, became an extremely powerful witch. As is typical of a witch,[24] she had no family, and though she was respected, she was not generally liked. She possessed no material wealth. Most of what she owned (her keepsakes) fit in a small wooden box. Indeed she lived in a witch's cottage:

> not exactly built, but put together over the years as the areas of repair join up, like a sock made entirely of dams. The chimney twists like a corkscrew. The roof is thatch so old that small but flourishing trees are growing in it, the floors are switchbacks, it creaks at night like a tea clipper in a gale. If at least two walls aren't shored up with balks of timber then it's not a true witch's cottage at all, but merely the home of some daft old bat who reads tea leaves and talks to her cat.[25]

She had power and wisdom; and she frequently displayed both. But, as is again typical of a witch, her power was power to serve her community[26] and to help those in need. In *Lords and Ladies*, for example, she challenged Diamanda, a young would-be-witch, whose activities were causing substantial troubles, to a contest. Diamanda suggests that they each try to out stare the sun, but when Pewsey, Nanny Ogg's grandson, stepped into the circle of power around the two witches and screamed, Granny stopped her staring and walked over to help the child. The young witches declare Diamanda the winner, but Nanny responds:

> "This is not a contest about power, you stupid girls, it is a contest about witchcraft, do you not even begin to know what being a witch IS?"

"Is a witch someone who would look round when she heard a child scream?"

"And the townspeople said, Yess!"[27]

Her role as healer in her community also provides a couple of important insights into her character and values. In *Maskerade*, Granny, called to help with a difficult delivery, bargained with Death to trade the cow for the life of a child. Death allowed her to challenge him to a game of poker—double (her and the infant) or nothing (the cow)—and she agreed to risk her own life in a bid to save the infant. What constitutes the character of Esmerelda Weatherwax is evident in the exchange. Death, respecting Granny's courage and determination, read his hand of four aces as a hand of four ones against her four queens to allow her to win, but not before he revealed that he understood her thoroughly. After Granny dealt the cards and before they turned them over, Death insisted that Granny change hands with him.[28]

Granny's courage, then, is supplemented by a willingness to use her talents to ensure the right outcome. Some means might well be justified by an important end. Five novels later, she attends another delivery. In this case, the mother had been kicked by the family cow earlier in the day, and the damage to the mother and child was extensive. Granny's craft was enough to save one, if she sacrificed the other; when Death appeared, she asked which he had come for. "ON THE VERY EDGE YOU WILL ALWAYS FIND SOME UNCERTAINTY." Granny chose to save the mother, and when the midwife objected that the father should have been allowed to choose, Granny answered, "You don't like him? You think he's a bad man? . . . Then what's he done to me, that I should hurt him so?"

Granny is powerful, but much of her power lies in her insight and her willingness to do what needs to be done. She will cheat when necessary. She places little value on having a "good" reputation. The virtues she possesses are, in a sense, distorted because of her unusual position in society and because she serves her less-than-perfect community. Her courage, for example, is the courage to make *hard* choices, choices that are morally compromised, like the choice to let one life go to save another.[29] Her distorted perspective and her odd virtues give her a peculiarly astute comprehension of the moral landscape and allow her to accomplish so much good. The life isolated from society, characterized by a witch's poverty, and given over to doing what she believed was "right" was her life.

In the alternate timeline Granny experiences in *Lords and Ladies*, she chose to allow Mustrum to catch her. The two then married and had children and eventually grandchildren. As memories from the alternate Esmerelda crept into Granny's mind, so too did the beliefs and feelings from that other life, her love for Mustrum, her joy over her family, the time to reflect on a life well-lived. Lost between the two lives, Granny was convinced she was going crazy. When, at last she discovered that an alternate time line had been melding with the Discworld, she was in a unique position to judge the two lives she might have lived. The alternate life, one with a husband, a home, and children is more conventional and it manifested the virtues that Aristotle's account of the good life would favor. And the Esmerelda of that time line clearly was happy. Indeed, Mustrum, who has also had a glimpse of that other life, expresses a sentimental joy that at least they had been together somewhere. But, Granny rejected Mustrum's sentiment outright:[30]

"Do you think," said Ridcully, "that ... somewhere ... it all went right?"

"Yes. Here!"

Softening at his disappointment, Granny admitted that it had gone right when they married as well.[31]

However, Granny's own choice was clear. The life she had chosen, the life she told the elf queen she would have, is *her* life. She is the girl who ran away, the witch so powerful that she bargains with Death. Contrary to what Aristotle might judge, she was evidently satisfied, and even happy. Furthermore, those in her practice agree that she is an excellent witch. Those in her community agree that witches are good. And, as is evident in *Lords and Ladies*, Granny prefers her life to one that resembles Aristotle's conception of a good life.

Like Granny, Johnny Maxwell had a life one would find strange to envy. He wasn't financially well off. His mother worked a lot. They lived with his grandfather, a dour man who spent most of his time watching television. He had a few rather odd friends, and he seemed prone to depression and beset with worries for one as young as he was.[32] But, like Granny, he displayed a remarkable sensitivity to the moral landscape. In *Only You Can Save Mankind*, his sympathy with alien invaders in a video game allowed him to avert a war and save the aliens from destruction. In *Johnny and the Dead*, he noticed the dead hanging around the local graveyard and helped them free themselves from their past and move on to new adventures. Johnny even hid a radio in the graveyard so that the one ghost, who was too broken to let go of his "sins," would have the comfort of listening. Finally, in *Johnny and the Bomb*, he was assigned an essay on a local World War II bombing, which started to haunt him. His grandfather would not answer questions about the war, telling him to shut up about it.[33] He also found himself daydreaming about finding a time machine, so that he might go back and put everything right in his life. But, when he attempted to help a bag lady, Mrs. Tachyon, he and several friends did find themselves traveling back and forth in time from the present to 21 May 1941, the night of the bombing. Various changes to the timeline (including leaving one of their number, Wobbler, back in 1941) result in various changes to the present. However, on the last trip, Johnny and his friends arrived where Johnny's grandfather, Tom, had been stationed as a young man. When the planes were spotted, the telephone at the station wouldn't work, and Tom's motorcycle wouldn't start. So Tom ran to sound the alarm, the children running with him. As fast as they ran, there wasn't enough time. Tom couldn't get to the siren before the planes were in range: "The bike wouldn't start! The phone wouldn't work! There was a storm! I tried to get down here in time! How could it have been my fault?" Now, when it actually mattered, Johnny found himself able to manipulate time. He grabbed Tom and the others, and they ran across the field together, arriving seven minutes earlier than they had left—in time to sound the alarm. Back home again, Johnny asked his grandfather about the bombing, and an importantly different man pulled out his medal and told the story of how he had sounded the alarm, though there couldn't have been enough time.[34] The clock at the station must have been fast.

Given the time machine he had dreamed of having and the opportunity to change his own life, Johnny used his gift to save 19 people and fix the external circumstance that had haunted his grandfather. External circumstances can mar a life. In the original timeline, his grandfather was broken by the physical impossibility of saving those caught in the bombing. But, aside from catastrophe, external circumstances do not touch character and are, thus, relatively unimportant. When Johnny's friend Wobbler was left in 1941, he used his knowledge of the future to make a fortune, but neither his special knowledge of the future nor his wealth altered his personality. It is not surprising, then, that for all the limited circumstances of his own life, Johnny made no attempt to alter the past in his own favor or fix his own "mistakes." In the end, he was content with himself.

It is worth noting the strong similarities between Pratchett's ethics and the account of ethics present in the early works of Alasdair MacIntyre. Like most contemporary virtue ethicists, MacIntyre has abandoned the belief that one can discover an objective account of happiness based on an understanding of human nature. Rather, happiness is cast in terms of a coherent narrative woven together out of the projects and social roles of the individual. Virtues, then, are practice (project/social role) specific. They comprise the psychological and physical responses that facilitate the attainment of those goods at which a particular practice aims. And the only objective judgment that can be made about a particular practice or life is whether it is coherent—logically consistent.

It is clear that Pratchett would agree that those attitudes and habits that facilitate the agent's projects are his or her virtues. And he relies heavily on narrative coherence and satisfaction with one's ends and projects in judging the goodness of a life. But, unlike MacIntyre, Pratchett still accepts objective criteria beyond logical consistency for judging the goodness of a life. It is clear that the "heroes" of his books perceive morally salient features in their world. Their projects and perspectives reveal parts of a complex moral landscape rather than constituting the basis of the moral landscape.[35]

Have You Been Naughty?

Even on Pratchett's rather expansive view of happiness, that what constitutes the best life is determined subjectively, by the person choosing the life, there are a few objective limits. Behaviors are wrong when they are rooted in a failure to recognize other persons as more than mere objects.

> "And sin, young man, is when you treat people like things. Including yourself. That's what sin is."
>
> "It's a lot more complicated than that—"
>
> "No. It ain't. When people say things are a lot more complicated than that, they means they're getting worried that they won't like the truth. People as things, that's where it starts."
>
> "Oh, I'm sure there are worse crimes—"
>
> "But they starts with thinking about people as things ..."[36]

And for Pratchett, not treating others as things is not merely a limit on one's pursuit of one's projects. Kant separates the necessity of treating others as ends-in-themselves from the satisfaction or happiness of the agent. He argues that any attempt to fulfill one's own desires must be carried out in ways that do not violate the personhood of others. However, actions done out of respect for the moral law are considered to be better than those done from any sort of attachment to others.[37] But Pratchett's view is more like that of J.S. Mill.[38] Pratchett seems to think that an attachment to others and, in particular, a fellow feeling with persons generally is a precondition of being happy. To consider someone or something as an object of moral concern, an agent must find a way to see into the perspective of that other. In his "Lecture on Ethics," Wittgenstein calls this a common language rooted in a shared way of living.[39] Martin Buber called it an I–Thou relationship,[40] and Sartre refers to the acceptance of the other as free from our determination as authenticity.[41]

Some Discworld characters are clearly wrong about the best life because they disregard the personhood of everyone else. Consider Mr. Teatime, who it is intimated killed his parents. His technical skills as an assassin are so developed that he can even sneak up on the head of the guild, Lord Downey.[42] And his devotion to his profession is so great that he spends time plotting how to assassinate even anthropomorphic personifications. He is remorseless and this, as much as his brutality, makes him a despicable character. Even though Mr. Teatime is content with his character, Pratchett and his audience judge him to have chosen an unworthy life. The same is true of the villain Carcer Dun.[43] Carcer enjoys a high degree of success in his projects, and he displays no desire that he should have turned out differently than he did, but he is simply wrong to think his life is good.

Other Discworld characters go wrong because they discount groups of persons: the sexists and the "speciesists."[44] In *Monstrous Regiment* Pratchett gives an account of the problem of sexism. In order to find her brother, a young girl named Polly dressed as a man and joined a group of soldiers recruited by Sergeant Jackrum. As the book progresses, each of the other soldiers is revealed to be a woman. When, toward the end of the book, the whole regiment is brought up on charges for their deception, Jack reveals that (s)he—and a significant number of the generals at the hearing—are also women.[45] This final revelation confirms the ludicrous nature of the rule barring women from service. Another case can be found in *Equal Rites*, where Drum Billet, intending to pass his wand to the eighth son of an eighth son, accidentally hands it to the eighth child (a daughter) of an eighth son, Eskarina Smith. Though long tradition was against her (there had never been a female wizard), she did well at Unseen University, and eventually became powerful enough to walk through time and even give it orders.[46]

Themes surrounding interspecies relationships and speciesism are even more prevalent in Pratchett's work. In various novels, a new species seeks to integrate into the culture of Ankh-Morpork. There is initial resistance (usually on both sides); but in the end, the group finds itself accepted and accepting, aside from a small minority on either side. Those that will not accept the integration and those that engage in active discrimination are condemned. This is true of the conservative dwarfs of Ankh-Morpork who killed a dwarf and left him to die in the tunnels beneath the city,[47] and it is true of Stratford and his group, who kidnap and enslave goblins, abandoning them to die when they can no longer work. In the latter instance of speciesism, the difference between goblins and others is so great that their way of life seems incomprehensible. The goblins are considered not merely as different but as disgusting. Through association with the goblin community, Vimes, Nobby, and Colin gain a familiarity with the goblins and begin to form some understanding and appreciation of their strange customs. The problem of motivating a broader group to recognize the goblins as fellow persons is solved by Lady Sybil who holds a recital for a young goblin musical protégé, Tears of the Mushroom. The soulful beauty of the goblin's playing bridges the gap between her and the audience, creating the possibility of understanding. In both these cases of speciesism, the crimes are so grave that the

Summoning Dark, a semi-sentient demonic entity, manifests and helps Vimes to avenge them.[48] For Pratchett, then, differences in ability and fitness to particular jobs is individual, not determined by species or gender. And individuals ought not to be alienated on the basis of species differences.

As the story of the Tears of the Mushroom shows, overcoming our tendency to view others differently from ourselves as "things" we must come to view them as importantly "like us." Furthermore, to live in a community there must be rules and expectations. Rules requiring conformity to social norms, along with the ethical importance of emphasizing the critical similarities between individuals, can lead to an overlooking of important differences and can all too easily become a move toward assimilation. If the best life is particular to the individual, then the emphasis on being "like me," may blind the individual to important elements in the other's identity. And, sharing rules and expectations can cut off an individual's ability to manifest critical parts of the other's identity and frustrate his or her ability to pursue a happy life. As each species immigrates to Ankh-Morpork it tends to lose differences both superficial and seemingly essential to its identity. Dwarfs begin dwelling above ground. Female dwarfs begin wearing make-up and dresses. Vampires even give up drinking blood.

The social differences between self and other that comprise the material of both ethics and politics is delicate and difficult. And if I were to criticize Pratchett on any point, it would be the easy manner in which seemingly important differences are sometimes overcome or overlooked.

I Ain't Dead Yet

Another profound difference between an Aristotelian and a Pratchettean view is whether the attainment of perfection and changelessness or the process of continued change constitutes happiness and human flourishing. The drive toward the goal of changeless goodness is rooted in Aristotelian metaphysics. In searching for that which is most real, Aristotle concludes that that which is so in the primary sense is also most complete and best. Hence, being is better than becoming. Eternal, change-less existence, is better than everlasting change. All things are drawn toward being. That is, they move toward perfection.[49] The heavenly bodies travel in circular motion, a movement that is everlasting and therefore is the most perfect motion. Living things actualize their own natures and reproduce, thus partici-pating in the eternality of their species. In human beings, there is the possibility for direct participation in the immaterial and therefore changeless actuality—thought. Turned toward life and well-being, reason is practical, and its perfection is prac-tical wisdom. Its object being a part of the material world, there is still movement, the application of knowledge of the human good to activity here and now. Directed upward toward metaphysics, it is theoretical and its perfection is wisdom. Since both the faculty of thought and its object are immate-rial, its actuality is complete, and therefore changeless.[50] If it could hold its entire object before itself, and if it were not tied to a body with needs of its own, the activity of thought would not need to be discursive in object or in time. And, it is this timeless comprehension of God, changing only insofar as the human intellect cannot hold the whole of the divine nature before itself at once, that constitutes the classic conception of beatitude, heaven. Notice that, for Aristotle, the active intellect, being immaterial and complete, would be indistinguisha-ble from any other active intellect. It is not clear in his works whether there is more than one such intellect, or whether, like light, the active intellect illumines all objects of thought and makes them intelligible to each human mind, as a single sun illumines all visual objects, making them visible to all eyes reached by the light.[51]

But, for Pratchett, eternal, unchanging existence is the antithesis of a good or happy life. This is true both because to be a person is to be unique and also because life is the process of change. There are beings in the Discworld novels which are changeless because they are undistinguished by differences, the Auditors of Reality. These beings are immaterial and have no opinions or ideas of their own to distinguish them from one another. Should one develop an opinion or idea distinct from the group, it ceases to be an Auditor, and excepting Myria LeJean, ceases to be. They loathe the living because they are unpredictable and difficult to track and audit. So, in *Thief of Time*, the Auditors plotted to end time and so life, even sending one of their number, now Myria LeJean, into the corporeal world to further their designs. The key flaw in their plan was that corporeality immediately exposed the now human auditor to sensations and desires and emotions. What develops in Myria is not merely an idea but an entire personality. As an individual, and differentiated, Myria switched sides, helping to defeat the auditors; though, having lost her nature (she is renamed Unity), she chooses to die. However, being, now a person, her death is followed by an afterlife, and Death collects her soul, sending it on its way.[52]

The changelessness of Windle Poons was of a very different sort. At 130, he was the oldest wizard at Unseen University. He did little but remember the good old days, when things were better. Nothing was interesting anymore. He had no projects, and he seemed to be hanging around waiting to die. Much to his chagrin, his death came just as Death was deposed. Windle went nowhere, so he decided to go somewhere. Through a series of adventures, he befriended the Fresh Start Club, a support group for the undead and helped each member find a place in the world, a way forward. Content with his recent accomplishments, he met Death on a bridge, commenting to him how good his afterlife had been. Death responded that those post mortem days had, in fact, been Windle's life.[53]

There is a powerful drive among the living on the Discworld to stay alive and among the non-living to continue in existence. Alberto Malich, a powerful wizard from Unseen University—reasoning that if the rite of AshkEnte summons Death then, recited backward, it would banish

Death—attempted to extend his life indefinitely. But, instead of banishing Death, the reversed spell drew *him to Death*. Though Alberto did not achieve the goal of avoiding Death, being transported to Death's realm took him out of time and so his existence was extended indefinitely. As a denizen of a timeless realm, Alberto continued to exist for over 2,000 years, and it is clear that he did prefer his existence with Death to death. But there is a difference between continuing on and existing unchanged. In all his time in Death's realm, Alberto's being was arrested. He spent his existence as Death's cook, acquiring no new talents or knowledge. He created nothing new of lasting value.[54] That is, Alberto's life in Death's domain was much like the old age of Windle Poons. Though some may cling to it, such an existence does not seem enviable. Death's adopted daughter, Ysabell, allowed to age to 16 in Discworld before being transported to Death's realm where she never aged, begged Mort to free her from the boredom of her endless and changeless existence (imagine for a moment being 16 forever). And Mort, Death's new apprentice, was only too happy to oblige. He risked his own existence, fighting Death for their freedom. In the end Death relented, turned Mort's empty hourglass over, and procured time from the god's and a future for the couple. At Ysabell's and Mort's wedding Death remarked:

> IT'S A SMALL THING. YOU *COULD* HAVE HAD ETERNITY.
> "I know," said Mort. "I've been very lucky."[55]

And when, at last, the couple die in an accident, their daughter—Death's granddaughter, Susan Sto Helit—complained to Death that he did not save them:

> She thought: but he could have done *something*. Couldn't he?
> YES. I COULD HAVE DONE SOMETHING ... AND NOW UNDERSTAND THIS: YOUR PARENTS KNEW THAT THINGS MUST HAPPEN. EVERYTHING

MUST HAPPEN SOMEWHERE. DO YOU NOT THINK I SPOKE TO THEM OF THIS? BUT I CANNOT GIVE LIFE. I CAN ONLY GRANT AN EXTENSION. CHANGELESSNESS. ONLY HUMANS CAN GIVE LIFE. AND THEY WANTED TO BE HUMAN, NOT IMMORTAL.[56]

Time and possibility are precious. With the gift of a few extra minutes that Johnny was able to give his grandfather, he changed the latter's self-image from failure to hero. Pratchett's commitment to development as a necessary element in a happy existence extends even to the afterlife. The ghosts in Johnny Maxwell's graveyard are morose and fearful. They have had their journey arrested and must be freed to continue. The souls that Death harvested were often confused about where they should go, but Death is clear that they should GO. Those that do not move on seem to suffer for it—from the king's ghost in *Wyrd Sisters*[57] to Vorbis when he cowers at the beginning of the journey in *Small Gods*.[58]

In the Discworld, even Death wanted life—experience and meaningful interactions with others. Early in the series, he took Mort in as an apprentice so that he might take a holiday in Ankh-Morpork and find out what it is to be alive. And, when in *Reaper Man*, Death's nemesis, the Auditors, managed to have Death fired, he was finally given what he never had before—time. He took his small life-timer and went to work on a farm as Bill Door. Interestingly, though Miss Flitworth, the owner of the farm, was alive, her life, like Windle's, had been arrested. Her projects and aspirations were frozen when her fiancé didn't return from a trip. Toward the end of the novel, the new Death came to take Bill's life. And, it was only because Miss Flitworth gave Bill the precious gift of a few of her own moments that he won the battle. One of the most profound scenes in the Discworld novels presents Death, kneeling before Azrael, begging for the time to return Miss Flitworth's gift of life. When Azrael agreed, Death placed the best of the World before her and ultimately returned her to the space–time where her true love died so that she might go forward with him. Living is changing. To remain unaltered, to be eternal, is to be trapped in time like an insect trapped in amber.

"It Is Said Your Life Flashes before Your Eyes just before You Die. That Is True, It's Called Life"

The world Pratchett has created is, like our world, broken and morally complex. His characters must thread their way through that world, responding to the moral landscape. The best of his characters are able to recognize both the complexity and the brokenness. They respond imaginatively to the challenges it presents. Granny has no doubt that she has decided to save one life at the expense of another. But, the alternative was to let both die. Furthermore, Pratchett seems to believe that there are better and worse answers as well as objective limits on choices. While he rejects what may seem easy and nice, Pratchett calls his readers to embrace a world in which others call upon our sympathetic imagination, recognizing that different is not wrong and should not be greeted with fear. Indeed, there are points when he is so eager to include everyone in the moral and social community that he overlooks the ways in which seeing the other as "like me" and limiting behaviors that would violate the social good may leave individuals unsupported in their differences and force some to give up elements that seem to be essential to their identities.

In addition to his conviction that each must fashion a life of his or her own choosing, and that a person's moral compass must include a care for the individuals and groups around him or her, Pratchett presents a conception of ethics that champions persistent development over one aimed at the attainment of perfection. Pratchett's characters can never rest content with themselves. Even the dead must progress. The failure to be oneself or to cease developing is death in the worst possible sense.

Susanne E. Foster

Notes

1. T. Pratchett (1983) *The Color of Magic* (London: Corgi Books), p. 11.
2. T. Pratchett (1996) *Johnny and the Bomb* (London: Corgi Books), pp. 71–2.
3. T. Pratchett (2001) *Thief of Time* (London: Corgi Books), p. 145.
4. T. Pratchett (1989) *Guards! Guards!* (London: Corgi Books), p. 13.
5. T. Pratchett (1992) *Lords and Ladies* (London: Corgi Books), pp. 148–55.
6. T. Pratchett (1990) *Eric* (New York, NY: HarperCollins), pp. 26ff.
7. Pratchett, *Thief of Time*, pp. 146–50.
8. T. Pratchett (1991) *Reaper Man* (London: Corgi Books), pp. 104–7.
9. T. Pratchett (1993) *Men at Arms* (London: Corgi Books), pp. 311–12; T. Pratchett (2000) *The Truth* (London: Corgi Books), pp. 23–4. There are a number of hypotheses about why Mrs. Tachyon shares the phrase "Millennium hand and shrimp" with Ron—including the possibility that she picked it up from him while traveling through space–time. My own thesis is of a dual nature. First, the chief goddess in Pratchett's pantheon impressed upon the Creator the narrative force of the phrase. Second Foul Old Ron, like Mrs. Tachyon and Mrs. Cake, is insufficiently tethered to space–time. The latter part of this explanation has the virtue of explaining why it should be that both Mrs. Tachyon and Ron are persistently unintelligible to those with a more linear existence.
10. T. Pratchett (1992) *Only You Can Save Mankind* (New York, NY: HarperCollins); T. Pratchett (1993) *Johnny and the Dead* (London: Corgi Books); Pratchett, *Johnny.*
11. J.H. Wyman, J. Pinkner, A. Goldsman, and J. Singer (2010) "Peter," *Fringe* Season 2.
12. V. Frankl (1980) *The Doctor and the Soul* (New York, NY: Vintage), pp. 65–6; F. Nietzsche (1882) *The Gay Science*, translated W. Kaufmann (New York, NY: Random House), aphorism 341.
13. Consider, for example, that long after he became king, Verence was unable to give up the life-long habits he developed as a professional fool. See Pratchett, *Lords and Ladies*, p. 377.
14. Aristotle (1984) *Nicomachean Ethics*, in *The Complete Works of Aristotle*, vol. 2, edited J. Barnes, Bollingen Series LXXI (Princeton, NJ: Princeton University Press), 1.7 [1097b21–1098a17].
15. Ibid., 1.13 [1102a5–1103a10].
16. Ibid., 3.5 [1114b26–30].
17. Ibid., 6.8 [1142a23–30].
18. T. Pratchett (2002) *Night Watch* (London: Corgi Books), pp. 128–51; T. Pratchett (2005) *Thud!* (London: Corgi Books), pp. 150–60.

19. Pratchett, *The Truth*, pp. 51–2; T. Pratchett (2007) *Making Money* (London: Corgi Books), pp. 399ff.
20. T. Pratchett (2003) *The Wee Free Men* (London: Corgi Books), pp. 89–91; T. Pratchett (2004) *A Hat Full of Sky* (London: Corgi Books), pp. 10, 39–48.
21. T. Pratchett (1986) *The Light Fantastic* (London: Corgi Books), p. 50.
22. T. Pratchett (2009) *Unseen Academicals* (London: Corgi Books), pp. 516, 528–35.
23. T. Pratchett (1998) *Carpe Jugulum* (London: Corgi Books), pp. 336–9, 394–6.
24. One notable exception to this rule is, of course, Nanny Ogg. See Pratchett, *Lords and Ladies*, pp. 28–9.
25. Ibid., p. 166.
26. Here, too, there is a notable exception: Granny's sister, Lily. See T. Pratchett (1991) *Witches Abroad* (London: Corgi Books), p. 349.
27. Pratchett, *Lords and Ladies*, p. 109.
28. T. Pratchett (1995) *Maskarade* (London: Corgi Books), pp. 99–102.
29. Pratchett, *Carpe Jugulum*, p. 37.
30. Pratchett, *Lords and Ladies*, pp. 230–9.
31. Ibid., p. 395.
32. Pratchett, *Johnny and the Bomb*, pp. 16–17, 66.
33. Ibid., p. 77.
34. There are multiple instances in Pratchett's books where he explores the effect of multiple possibilities and the efficacy of choice. The evolution of his awareness of the interaction between external circumstance and choice is evident in his reworking of *The Carpet People*. In the original story, the Thunorg, a race powerful because of their long study of the Carpet, intervene in the final battle, creating a music that averted Frey; see T. Pratchett (1971) *The Carpet People* (Buckinghamshire: Colin Smythe), pp. 185–6. But in the reworking of the story, the Thurnorg named Culaina has the power to sort through the various possible outcomes of an action, and she aids the book's hero, Snibril, and his fellows to beat those that want to enslave the people of the Carpet by tipping the future toward one particular outcome in which they win; see T. Pratchett (1992) *The Carpet People* (New York, NY: Houghton Mifflin Harcourt), pp. 248–9.
35. For an excellent summary of MacIntyre's account of narrative, practice, and virtue, see J. Horton and S. Mendus (editors) (1994) *After Virtue: Critical Perspectives on the Work of Alasdair MacIntyre* (Notre Dame, IN: Notre Dame University Press), pp. 8–14.
36. Pratchett, *Carpe Jugulum*, p. 303.
37. I. Kant (1981) *Grounding for the Metaphysics of Morals*, translated J.W. Ellington (Indianapolis: Hackett Publishing Co.), pp. 19–38.

38. J.S. Mill (1861) *Utilitarianism* (Indianapolis: Hackett Publishing Co.), p. 13.
39. L. Wittgenstein (1965) "A Lecture on Ethics," *Philosophical Review* 74, pp. 3–12.
40. M. Buber (1923) *I and Thou*, translated W. Kaufmann (New York, NY: Simon and Schuster).
41. J.-P. Sartre (1946) "Existentialism is a Humanism" in *Existentialism from Dostoevsky to Sartre*, translated W. Kaufmann (New York, NY: Meridian), pp. 345–69.
42. T. Pratchett (1996) *Hogfather* (London: Corgi Books), p. 29.
43. Pratchett, *Night Watch*, pp. 20–1.
44.   In the Discworld, "speciesism" refers to the practice of discriminating against other rational species, e.g. vampires, dwarfs, or orks.
45. T. Pratchett (2003) *Monstrous Regiment* (London: Corgi Books), pp. 402–32.
46. T. Pratchett (1987) *Equal Rites* (London: Corgi Books).
47. T. Pratchett (2005) *Thud!* (London: Corgi Books), p. 18.
48. Ibid., pp. 410–17, 460–1; T. Pratchett (2011) *Snuff* (London: Corgi Books), pp. 371–6.
49. Aristotle (1984) *Metaphysics*, in *The Complete Works of Aristotle*, vol. 2, edited J. Barnes (Princeton, NJ: Princeton University Press), 12.7 [1072a19–1073a13].
50. An excellent account of the difference between the practical and theoretical use of reason can be found in Boethius of Dacia's (1987) *On the Supreme Good*, in *On the Soul*, translated J.F. Wippel (Toronto, Canada: Pontifical Institute of Medieval Studies).
51. Aristotle (1984) *On the Soul*, in *The Complete Works of Aristotle*, vol. 1, edited J. Barnes (Princeton, NJ: Princeton University Press) 3.5 [430a10–25].
52. Pratchett, *Thief of Time*, pp. 347ff.
53. Pratchett, *Reaper Man*, pp. 346–8.
54. See, for example, Pratchett, *Hogfather*.
55. T. Pratchett (1987) *Mort* (London: Corgi Books), p. 316.
56. T. Pratchett (1994) *Soul Music* (London: Corgi Books), pp. 353, 423.
57. T. Pratchett (1987) *Wyrd Sisters* (London: Corgi Books), pp. 14–19ff.
58. T. Pratchett (1987) *Small Gods* (London: Corgi Books), pp. 370–1, 397.

Bibliography

Aristotle (1984) *Metaphysics*, in *The Complete Works of Aristotle*, vol. 2, edited J. Barnes (Princeton: Princeton University Press).

_____ (1984) *Nicomachean Ethics*, in *The Complete Works of Aristotle*, vol. 2, edited J. Barnes (Princeton: Princeton University Press).

_____ (1984) *On the Soul*, in *The Complete Works of Aristotle*, vol. 1, edited J. Barnes (Princeton: Princeton University Press).

Boethius of Dacia (1987) *On the Supreme Good*, in *On the Soul*, translated J.F. Wippel (Toronto: Pontifical Institute of Medieval Studies).

Buber, M. (1923) *I and Thou*, translated W. Kaufmann (New York, NY: Simon and Schuster).

Frankl, V. (1980) *The Doctor and the Soul* (New York, NY: Random House).

Horton, J. and S. Mendus (editors) (1994) *After Virtue: Critical Perspectives on the Work of Alasdair MacIntyre* (Notre Dame, IN: Notre Dame University Press).

Kant, I. (1981) *Grounding for the Metaphysics of Morals*, translated J.W. Ellington (Indianapolis: Hackett Publishing Company).

Mill, J.S. (1861) *Utilitarianism* (Indianapolis: Hackett Publishing Co.).

Nietzsche, F. (1882) *The Gay Science*, translated W. Kaufmann Vintage (New York, NY: Random House).

Pratchett, T. (1971) *The Carpet People* (Buckinghamshire: Colin Smythe).

_____ (1983) *The Color of Magic* (London: Corgi Books).

_____ (1986) *The Light Fantastic* (London: Corgi Books).

_____ (1987) *Equal Rites* (London: Corgi Books).

_____ (1987) *Mort* (London: Corgi Books).

_____ (1987) *Small Gods* (London: Corgi Books).

_____ (1987) *Wyrd Sisters* (London: Corgi Books).

_____ (1989) *Guards! Guards!* (London: Corgi Books).

_____ (1990) *Eric* (New York, NY: HarperCollins Publishers).

_____ (1991) *Reaper Man* (London: Corgi Books).

_____ (1991) *Witches Abroad* (London: Corgi Books).

_____ (1992) *The Carpet People* (New York, NY: Houghton Mifflin Harcourt).

_____ (1992) *Lords and Ladies* (London: Corgi Books).

_____ (1992) *Only You Can Save Mankind* (New York, NY: HarperCollins).

_____ (1993) *Johnny and the Dead* (London: Corgi Books).

_____ (1993) *Men at Arms* (London: Corgi Books).

_____ (1994) *Soul Music* (London: Corgi Books).

_____ (1995) *Maskarade* (London: Corgi Books).

_____ (1996) *Hogfather* (London: Corgi Books).

_____ (1996) *Johnny and the Bomb* (London: Corgi Books).

_____ (1998) *Carpe Jugulum* (London: Corgi Books).

_____ (2000) *The Truth* (London: Corgi Books).

_____ (2001) *Thief of Time* (London: Corgi Books).

_____ (2002) *Night Watch* (London: Corgi Books).

_____ (2003) *Monstrous Regiment* (London: Corgi Books).
_____ (2003) *The Wee Free Men* (London: Corgi Books).
_____ (2004) *A Hat Full of Sky* (London: Corgi Books).
_____ (2005) *Thud!* (London: Corgi Books).
_____ (2007) *Making Money* (London: Corgi Books).
_____ (2009) *Unseen Academicals* (London: Corgi Books).
_____ (2011) *Snuff* (London: Corgi Books).
Sartre, J.-P. (1946) "Existentialism is a Humanism" in *Existentialism from Dostoevsky to Sartre*, translated W. Kaufmann (New York, NY: Meridian).
Wittgenstein, L. (1965) "A Lecture on Ethics," *Philosophical Review* 74.

9 Categorically not Cackling: The Will, Moral Fictions, and Witchcraft

Jennifer Jill Fellows

The witches of Lancre—Nanny Ogg, Granny Weatherwax, and a rotating cast of maidens—occupy a unique position in Pratchett's Discworld. Caught between the magical and the mundane, the witches occupy the center: a center which never moves, despite the forces of nature, magic, and social pressure that pass through it. Through this immobile center, the witches serve an integral role in developing and anchoring morality in Lancre and on the Chalk. They are the moral compasses of their respective communities. They have conviction; they simply know what is right, regardless of what others think at the time. However, though each witch must have complete conviction in her own sense of right and wrong, no witch completely trusts any other witch's convictions. Only in this manner can cackling be avoided. And it must be avoided, at all costs.

In the Discworld stories centered on the witches, Pratchett develops a sophisticated and persuasive picture of morality. His moral system can be seen as offering a direct response to Nietzsche's attempt to overcome nihilism. In providing a solution to Nietzsche's problem, Pratchett's witches offer a very Kantian model of morality. Since Nietzsche's problem with nihilism arose through a direct rejection of Kant's transcendental foundations for morality, one might wonder how a return to a Kantian moral system can possibly offer a viable solution to Nietzsche's problem. What is surprising is that the model illustrated by Pratchett's witches is not only a viable one for

Nietzsche's problem, but also fills in a gap in Kant's own moral system. In effect, Pratchett's witches illustrate that moral reasoning is best done alone, but not in isolation.

Crooked Wood

In his *Grounding for the Metaphysics of Morality* the German philosopher Immanuel Kant offers just what the title might lead one to expect: an explanation of what grounds our moral claims. Kant, as a moral absolutist, argues that morality holds over all rational beings at all times. In giving this argument, Kant offers one universal moral rule that should apply to all people, everywhere, regardless of context, circumstance, or individual character. He called this rule "the categorical imperative." One formulation of the imperative is this:

> So act in regard to every rational being (yourself and others) that he may at the same time count in your maxim as an end in himself.[1]

To be "an end in himself" is to be a being who is intrinsically valuable, and deserves to be shown respect as a result of a recognition of his or her dignity, regardless of whether or not the being in question is of instrumental value to you. In effect, Kant tells us that we must act in ways that recognize the intrinsic value of other rational beings, and not just consider them as things that provide us with valuable services, or help us attain our own desires.

The witches of Lancre and the Chalk, at first glance, appear very Kantian. Kant's absolute moral rule bears a striking resemblance to Granny Weatherwax's assertion to the Priest of Om in *Carpe Jugulum*. When a family of vampires moves into Lancre intent on domesticating the locals as cattle for their own needs, Granny Weatherwax claims that this treatment of the people of Lancre is sinful. It is not sinful because the vampires plan to kill people. It is not sinful because of any particular outcome of the action. It is sinful because the action itself—raising people as cattle to feed vampires—reduces the people of Lancre to things that serve the vampires' purpose. It reduces their value to that of an instrumental value, instead of recognizing them as ends in themselves. Or, as Granny eloquently puts it: "Sin is when you treat people like things, including yourself."[2] In effect, one might claim that Granny Weatherwax is a Kantian (or Kant is a Weatherwaxian). The main thrust of the idea, of course, is older than Kant or Discworld; it is that morality begins when one treats people *as* people, recognizing their humanity.

In providing a foundation for this absolute moral rule, Kant argues that morality arises from one's will. He further claims that a free will and a moral will are the same thing. When one chooses morality, one chooses freedom. This is in contrast to other philosophical theories that have viewed morality as constraining our will. While other theories stress the ways in which moral laws constrain us (*don't* lie, *don't* cheat, *don't* steal) Kant argues that when we live morally, we are living by our *own* laws. We cannot be said to be constrained, then, for there is nothing external constraining us.

> Man was viewed as bound to laws by his duty; but it was not seen that man is subject only to his own, yet universal, legislation and that he is bound only to act in accordance with his own will, which is, however, a will purposed by nature to legislate universal laws . . . I want, therefore, to call my principle the principle of the autonomy of the will, in contrast with every other principle, which I accordingly count under heteronomy.[3]

Kant's claim is that our will legislates universal laws. Nonetheless, we are free when we follow this will precisely because we are doing what we *choose* to do. We are following *our will*. No one made the choice for us. No one is forcing or constraining our will. We will freely. And we freely will to be moral. Morality, according to Kant, is enacted in freedom. This is juxtaposed against what Kant calls the "heteronomy of the will" where our will is not freely directing our actions. Our will is not free when we follow our desires, or give in to our emotions. In these cases, we are not in control, and are thus not free. It is only with will power that we freely act.

Freedom is, for Kant, the only thing that is intrinsically valuable. While I might value money because of what I can buy with it, my own freedom I simply value having (though I may *also* value what I can *do* with it). But, as long as we are acting based on our desires or inclinations, we aren't acting freely. Paul Guyer, in discussing Kant's moral philosophy, explains the situation in the following way:

> We often make excuses for our behavior by claiming that our inclinations are irresistible, but, Kant is claiming that we do not really believe this, we know that we could resist a momentary gratification, no matter how desirable, if our life were at stake, and in fact we know that we can always choose to do what is right, even at the greatest cost to ourselves.[4]

Thus, according to Kant, though we may make excuses by claiming to have been overpowered by desires or inclinations, we are actually *always* able to follow reason. Reason, in turn, will lead us to accept the categorical imperative as an absolute moral law.

Reason leads to the categorical imperative because freedom is an intrinsic value and, in willing my own freedom, I must also will the freedom of every other rational being, or risk being inconsistent and thus violating reason. Or, as Guyer puts it, "to treat others as ends and not merely as means is to treat them as entitled to *choose their own particular ends*."[5] So, insofar as one accepts freedom as the highest good, one must treat others as ends in themselves because to not do so is to restrict their freedoms, and thus to not accept freedom as the highest good. The struggle is, of course, that insofar as one loves oneself, one often does not want to make the hard choice of resisting one's desires. Even more, one does not want to acknowledge one's own responsibility in the promotion of the free will of others. For Kant, morality is difficult. It is always a struggle between what we *want* to do and what we know we *ought* to do.

The witches of Discworld face this struggle head on, and no one can claim to be a witch without successfully winning this battle against herself. In commenting on the power Granny Weatherwax holds, the vampires in *Carpe Jugulum* state that "the Weatherwax women have always had one foot in shadow. It's in the blood. And most of their power comes from denying it."[6] Granny Weatherwax's power comes from self-denial, from not giving in to what she *wants* to do, and instead holding fast to what she *ought* to do.

The Tiffany Aching chronicles—the four-book series that follow the training and education of a young witch—reinforce this message. In *Wintersmith*, the third of the four books, Tiffany accidentally supplants the Summer Lady in the dark Morris dance. As a consequence, she draws the unwanted attention of the Summer Lady's counterpart, the Wintersmith. We find Tiffany Aching at the end of the tale battling a harsh winter storm that has seized the Chalk in its grasp, despite the fact that it is now spring. The turning of the seasons has been upset by Tiffany's accidental involvement in the dark Morris. The Wintersmith still has a hold on the Chalk, and the Summer Lady cannot return. This unexpected cold snap is threatening the lives of the lambs, as well as any humans unfortunate enough to have been caught out of doors. Tiffany begins her battle against the storm with the following statement: "This I choose to do. If there is a price, this I choose to pay. If it is my death, then I choose to die. Where this takes me, there I choose to go. I choose. This I choose to do."[7] Here, Tiffany chooses to take responsibility for her actions and to face the Wintersmith in order to save the sheep and usher in spring. Though she originally acted in ignorance when dancing the dark Morris, she takes responsibility and does what she ought, instead of running away as she wants to. But, she did not always have this attitude.

In the early chapters of *Wintersmith*, Tiffany refuses to take responsibility for her actions. After accidentally disrupting the turning of the seasons, she argues that this wasn't her fault because she didn't know that she was not meant to interfere with the dance. She protests that she didn't mean for anything to happen, but was simply following a desire to dance. Her mentor at the time, a witch by the name of Miss Treason, replies: "Then what did you mean? Will you tell me? . . . To mean is to think. Did you think at all?"[8] Still Tiffany insists that this was all an accident, and she should not be held responsible. Miss Treason replies: "Once again, you didn't mean it. A witch takes responsibility! Have you learned nothing, child?"[9] In effect, *a witch must always mean it*. She is a free agent. Tiffany chose to act, whether she meant to or not. And the consequences of those choices are her responsibility.

Tiffany learns that she must always *mean it*. She must always *think*. She must always act from a will that is governed by reason. To do otherwise is to threaten the freedom of those around her, as the Wintersmith's storm so vividly illustrates. Tiffany's protestations that she cannot be held responsible are met with disbelief. Miss Treason, like Kant, dismisses Tiffany's assertion that she was caught up in the passion of the dance and acted without thinking. The option of acting from a place of reason was available and Tiffany freely chose to restrict her own freedom by following her passions instead. Thus, she is responsible for the devastation her actions caused.

Tiffany's transformation from a child shirking responsibility to a witch acting from a place of reason is a puzzling one. Guyer claims that, for Kant, human beings will "always have to choose between morality and self-love."[10] When we are constantly being pulled by the forces of self-love, the difficulty becomes one of explaining how a moral system ever takes hold in the first place. How do we as a society encourage each other to choose morality over self-love?

In a short article entitled "Idea for a Universal History from a Cosmopolitan Perspective" Kant details the challenges facing the human race in its perpetual struggle between morality and self-love. He argues that our innate self-love, and in particular our wish to see ourselves succeed in relation to others, is necessary for the flourishing of the human race. He calls this need we have not only to associate with others, but also to compete against the very people we associate with an "unsocial sociability":

> This unsocial sociability is obviously a part of human nature. Human beings have an inclination to *associate* with one another because in such a connection they feel themselves to be more human, that is to say, more in a position to develop their natural predispositions. But they also have a strong tendency to *isolate* themselves, because they encounter in themselves the unsociable trait that predisposes them to want to direct everything only to their own ends and hence to expect to encounter resistance everywhere, just as they themselves tend to resist others . . . It is this resistance that awakens all human powers and causes human beings to overcome their tendency to idleness and, driven by lust for honor, power, or property, to establish a position for themselves among their fellows, who they can neither *endure* nor *do without*.[11]

In effect, humanity flourishes because we are all striving to be better than our neighbors whom we feel compelled to socialize with, even though we don't like them very much. It is our proximity to these others that encourages us to strive to be better, smarter, and as free and autonomous as possible.

Any reader of the Discworld novels centered on the witches will realize quickly that this principle definitely seems to hold for them. While witches in general dislike one another, it is rare to find a Pratchett story in which only one witch is mentioned. Any story about one of them invariably involves others who stare over that witch's shoulder, observing and judging her actions and her decisions. When Tiffany Aching faces the hollow man in the last book in the series, *I Shall Wear Midnight*, she does so in the presence of other witches. Their presence drives Tiffany to do better and gives her a firm conviction to illustrate that she can act without help. She doesn't want to fail. But, more importantly, she doesn't want to fail *in front of them*:

> "Blast it," Granny Weatherwax said. "You are a witch, a good witch. But some of us think that it might be best if we *insisted* on helping you."
> "No," said Tiffany. "My steading. My mess. My problem."
> "No matter what?" said Granny.
> "Definitely!"[12]

The presence of the other witches drives Tiffany to succeed, and, as Tiffany knows, it provides a safeguard should she fail. Should she fail, they will take over. They will protect the community, but they will also conclude that she cannot handle things on her own. Her need to prove herself empowers her to express her autonomy to its fullest extent. Thus, the witches perfectly exemplify Kant's unsocial sociability.

Though Kant has illustrated how nature has created an environment in which our very proximity to others forces us to choose mindfully, and to do everything in our power to assert our own autonomy and freedom, he is still left with a puzzle because humans are still human. Kant acknowledges this problem and suggests a solution, but it is a solution he leaves incomplete:

> And even though he [the human] as a rational creature, desires a law that sets limits of the freedom of all, his selfish animal inclinations will lead him to treat himself as an exception whenever he can. For this reason he needs a master who will break his individual will and compel him to obey a will that is universally valid. But, such a master is just as much an animal in need of a master.[13]

While we desire maximum freedom for its own sake, we must recognize a limit to this freedom. That is, my own freedom must not come at the expense of your freedom. Thus, if we are perfectly rational, humanity will recognize that we need to have limits on *all* of our freedoms in order to ensure maximum freedom for all. Unfortunately, we are not perfectly rational and our self-love will compel us to find ways to justify the choices we make that extend our own freedoms at the expense of others. Kant argues that it is because of this inclination to self-love that we need to be governed by an authority figure who will punish us in cases where we give in to self-love. Unfortunately, anyone granted the power of authority over us will also be human and subject to his or her own self-love. Hence, this puzzle manifests:

> The supreme authority must be just *in itself* but also *a human being*. This task is thus the most difficult of all. Indeed, its perfect solution is impossible: nothing entirely straight can be fashioned from the crooked wood of which humankind is made.[14]

Kant is right: there is no clear way to solve this because any supreme authority will be human, and will be driven by self-love. As a result, Kant claims, in a larger work (*The Critique of Practical Reason*), that we must assume the truth of God and the immortality of the soul in order to believe in morality. As Guyer notes,

> Kant's argument is then, first, that it is rational to pursue a goal only if we have good reason to believe that this goal can be realized; that the goal imposed by morality is not always realizable *in the natural* world . . . because of the wayward inclination of others and even ourselves; so we must therefore postulate an as it were unnatural world, beyond the temporal frame of ordinary existence and ruled by a wise, benevolent and powerful God, in which the ideal result of morality will be actual.[15]

For Kant, the postulation of God and the immortality of the soul is necessary in order to solve the problem of human self-love. While here on earth we might be tempted to give in to self-love in ways that harm others, and avoid taking responsibility for that harm, in the next world God will ensure that all humans are perfectly moral and reap the benefits of their moral behavior.

Here it seems evident that Pratchett's witches are not perfectly Kantian. They do not believe in any particular god, and they do not have any firm belief in an afterlife. While they are on speaking terms with Death, they do not know—nor form any beliefs about—what happens after death. In fact, the general population of Lancre and the Chalk are characterized as having no strong religious convictions: "Religion, apart from its use as a sort of cosmic registrar, had never caught on in Lancre."[16] They, unlike Kant, do not find it necessary to postulate either the existence of God (or gods) or a belief in an afterlife. So, one must speculate that, if the witches are able to hold fast to their moral convictions, they do *not* do so by postulating the existence of a wise and benevolent God. How they *do* do so requires some further exploration.

From Faith to Fiction

The German philosopher Friedrich Nietzsche's investigations into morality begin from a position of rejecting the Kantian postulation of God. As Walter Kaufmann puts it, Nietzsche's central concern is that "we have destroyed our own faith in God. There remains only the void. We are falling. Our dignity is gone. Our values are lost. Who is to say what is up and what is down?"[17] We are falling into the void, staring into the abyss, and the existence of our own dignity and intrinsic worth are not found, nor do we discern a benevolent being safeguarding morality. Kaufmann points out that "Nietzsche himself has characterized the situation in which his philosophic thinking started by giving it the name of nihilism."[18] Nietzsche's goal is to overcome nihilism while still facing it as a truth. In sum, Nietzsche's problem with Kant's moral system is that Kant never questioned *that* morality existed. Assuming that there must exist a universal moral code, Kant set out to discover *how* this code operated. And, in the end "Kant *invented* the transcendent world to leave a place for moral freedoms."[19]

Nietzsche viewed Kant's postulation of God, the immortality of the soul, and the possibility of human freedom as dishonest. These postulations were methods of avoiding the truth of nihilism. According to Nietzsche, "to overcome nihilism, we must first of all recognize it."[20] Thus, our first task should not be to invent things that must be true in order to avoid nihilism, but rather to admit that nihilism itself is true. But, once we do this, once we "look long into the abyss,"[21] we find ourselves falling into a void. Without God to provide a firm anchor for our belief in morality, morality itself looks like a falsehood. Without God, how are we to "overcome nihilism" as Nietzsche says we must?

In *Beyond Good and Evil* Nietzsche speaks at great length about the need for a type of person he calls a *new philosopher*, an individual strong enough to recognize the truth of nihilism without falling into despair, and creative enough to use their own will to reshape the world around them. He argues that humanity must strive "toward *new philosophers*: there is no choice; toward spirits strong and original enough to provide the stimuli for opposite valuations and to revalue and invert 'eternal values.'"[22] The new philosophers are people who recognize that values are not eternal (hence the scare quotes around the words "eternal values") and that we ourselves can change and reinvent morality. New philosophers will be able to ask seriously the following questions: Is a belief in morality (specifically in Kant's type of morality) necessary? And if so, why?

Nietzsche argued that, though morality may not truly exist in our world, *it might still be necessary that morality exist.* In Nietzsche's words, it might be necessary to "comprehend that such [Kantian moral] judgments must be *believed* to be true, for the sake of the preservation of creatures like ourselves; though they might, of course, be *false* judgments for all that!"[23] The new philosophers will have the difficult task of (1) recognizing which judgments are necessary and which are not, and (2) recognizing that something can be necessary and yet not true. If morality is necessary, but does not truly exist, it will be the new philosopher's task to create and legislate morality. This will *not* result in true moral claims. Rather, when morality is created (as opposed to found) Nietzsche labels this a creation of "fictions": "Though the intellect is an instrument, its figments should be frankly labeled as fictions. Utility, however great, is no argument for truth."[24] New philosophers must have a strong enough will to face the truth, even the disturbing truth of nihilism. In legislating moral laws, new philosophers must never make the Kantian mistake of labeling morality as a necessary truth. It is not truth. It is a useful falsehood, or, as Nietzsche puts it, a fiction.[25] Thus, Nietzsche's real debate with Kant, as Kaufmann sees it, is that Kant did not recognize his postulating as the creation of a fiction, but instead viewed it as the discovery of a fact.[26]

The usefulness of fictions is something the inhabitants of Pratchett's Discworld know quite well. In *Hogfather*, Susan, Death's granddaughter, must save the Hogfather (a Santa-like character) so that the New Year will begin again. At the end of the tale, Susan asks Death what would have happened if she had not saved the Hogfather. Death replies:

THE SUN WOULD NOT HAVE RISEN.
    "Really? Then what would have happened, pray?"
    A MERE BALL OF FLAMING GAS WOULD HAVE ILLUMINATED THE WORLD.[27]

This response is unsatisfactory to Susan, who pushes him on this point, asking why it should matter whether a flaming ball of gas, or the sun, rises. Death responds that:

HUMANS NEED FANTASY TO BE HUMAN . . . YOU HAVE TO START OUT LEARNING TO BELIEVE THE *LITTLE* LIES.
    "So we can believe the big ones?"

YES. JUSTICE, MERCY, DUTY, THAT SORT OF THING . . .
TAKE THE UNIVERSE AND GRIND IT DOWN TO THE FINEST POWDER AND
SIEVE IT THROUGH THE FINEST SIEVE AND THEN *SHOW* ME ONE ATOM OF
JUSTICE, ONE MOLECULE OF MERCY AND YET— Death waved a hand.
AND YET YOU ACT AS IF THERE IS SOME IDEAL ORDER IN THE WORLD, AS
IF THERE IS SOME . . . SOME *RIGHTNESS* IN THE UNIVERSE BY WHICH IT
MAY BE JUDGED.

"Yes, but people have *got* to believe that, or what's the
point—"

MY POINT EXACTLY.[28]

In Discworld, stories and lies come together to create something
necessary and meaningful. The myth of the Hogfather matters
because it is a training ground upon which to practice creating
our own moral fictions. It is a training ground upon which to
learn that beliefs have power, regardless of whether or not they
are, conventionally speaking, true.

The idea that the will can create meaningful fictions, and even
more concretely that the will can create *moral* fictions, is one
that Nietzsche seems committed to. Arguing that the Western,
largely Christian-based, morality is a morality that is weakening
humanity and making us sick, Nietzsche stresses the need to recognize that morality is not absolute and that it can (and should)
be evaluated. However, once we recognize and acknowledge that
there is no eternal foundation for our moral truths, it is a quick
jump to the conclusion that there is no *real* morality at all and no
basis from which to evaluate our current morality. But Nietzsche
did not advocate that we give in to nihilism. Instead, he wanted
us to recognize that morality is not simply given to us; we create it.
In this act of creation, we can overcome nihilism. We can use
nihilism as a tool to drive our creative abilities. As Nadeem
Hussain puts it, Nietzsche's new philosophers are to "pretend to
value something by regarding it as valuable in itself while knowing
that in fact it is not valuable in itself."[29] The new philosophers
are to engage in a sort of make-believe, where they create

fictions about morality and bind their will to these fictions, while simultaneously recognizing them *as fiction*.

For Nietzsche, what is necessary is to recognize the role of our will in the shaping of reality. What we believe, and how we act, affects the world around us. As long as we believe in an all-powerful God who legislates moral truths, we will be confined by those beliefs in ways that may not be fruitful for our survival or flourishing as a species. Conversely, if we fear the reality of nihilism, that fear itself will manifest as a will to nihilism. We will, in effect, live in a world of nihilism. It is only our will that can save us from the confines of absolutism and the emptiness of nihilism. The will, then, is the key to morality. Though Nietzsche has a fundamental disagreement with Kant in regards to the status of moral laws—Nietzsche holding that they are useful fictions, and Kant holding that they are absolute truths—he nevertheless agrees with Kant that the will is of vital importance when it comes to creating and cultivating a moral world.

If Nietzsche is right then there are no absolute moral laws, no God, but simply a void, an abyss, nihilism. Nonetheless, the creative act of inventing necessary moral codes can turn these codes into a reality. Though moral codes may not have existed independently of the human creative act, the new philosophers who legislate moral laws are shaping reality to their ends. Thus, fictions are not simply falsehoods: they are falsehoods with the power to alter reality. This is no less true of our own world than it is of Discworld.

After defeating the Hiver in *A Hat Full of Sky* (the second book in the Tiffany Aching series) Tiffany sits with Granny Weatherwax, and asks her if what transpired was real. Weatherwax responds: "And the answer is: If it wasn't real, it wasn't *fake*."[30] This is an important distinction. That morality, like the myth of the Hogfather, is not real does not mean that morality is fake. It is created. And it has power over the witches as long (and only as long) as they continue to create it.

But this puts both the witches and the new philosophers in a difficult situation. A self-invented morality may have the potential to become quite self-serving. Individuals, like the witches, who recognize the role of the will in shaping morality, might be viewed with a little bit of trepidation. After all, what's to stop them from willfully twisting morality to serve their own ends?

Indeed, one thing to be critical of in Nietzsche's own moral system is that he appears to urge individuals to twist morality to serve their own ends. The importance of individual flourishing is more valuable, for Nietzsche, than collective thriving. Nietzsche often compares humans who fail to recognize the potential of their own will to shape morality to a sickly, stupid herd: "Morality in Europe today is a herd animal morality."[31] Those who accept and follow morality without acknowledging the fictive aspects of it are described as "good-natured, easy to deceive, a little stupid perhaps."[32]

The problem here is that Nietzsche, like Kant, is relying on a human will to uphold moral laws. But, humans can easily be directed by self-love. Kant tries to curb this tendency with reference to God and immortality. Nietzsche cannot fall back on either of these, having committed himself to recognizing and acknowledging the truth of nihilism. The new philosophers seem to have far too much opportunity to exercise the possibility of tyranny, and it seems that Nietzsche viewed this as a necessary danger to face in order to promote individual flourishing.

Categorically not Cackling

Kant has a problem: he cannot explain how morality can be brought about in this world by flawed, self-loving humans. Nietzsche has a problem: he cannot explain how the new philosophers are to hold moral fictions and simultaneously recognize them as fictions without falling into despair. On the one hand, if we agree with Kant, we need a way to anchor morality that will not be open to exploitation by those in a position of power to do the anchoring. On the other hand, if we agree with Nietzsche, we cannot appeal to a divine authority to do the anchoring, as that is a dishonest avoidance of the truth of nihilism. In one decisive move, Pratchett's witches provide the solution to both of these philosophical puzzles. They do anchor morality for their respective communities, but they do not do so by postulating a divine being. Instead, they are able to hold fast to moral laws, holding their respective steading to account, without becoming tyrants or falling into the void.

Witches do reinvent moral truths. They live on the "edge," making the decisions that no one else wants to make. Even Discworld's law enforcement recognizes this. In *I Shall Wear Midnight*, when Tiffany moves to the big city, she encounters a situation in which what is legal, and what is right, conflict. And the Night Watch turns a blind eye, allowing the witches to do what needs to be done, even though it violates the law of the land:

> People need witches; they need the unofficial people who understand the difference between right and wrong, and when right is wrong and when wrong is right. The world needs the people who work around the edges.[33]

Being able to work around the edges of right and wrong is exactly the skill Nietzsche's new philosophers possess. It is also exactly what makes them dangerous.

In contrast to the good-natured, stupid masses who accept morality as given, and do not participate in creating moral fictions, Nietzsche describes the new philosophers as dangerous because they can reshape morality. They are isolated and alone, individuals above the collective: "High and independent spirituality, the will to stand alone, even a powerful reason are experienced [by the collective] as dangers."[34] The collective are fearful of individuals who stand out, who are extraordinary in some way. They fear that these individuals will not play by the moral rules that everyone else accepts. And, indeed, the witches do not always play by the rules.

Tiffany Aching's grandmother, an unacknowledged witch, illustrates why it is sometimes needful to bend the rules. When the baron of the Chalk's dog kills a sheep, the law of the land says the dog must be put to death. The baron does not want this to happen, as he loves his dog. But he knows that, if he circumvents the law for his dog, it will show an unacceptable level of favoritism and he may lose the trust of his subjects. Torn between morality and self-love, he, like the members of the Night Watch, turns to a witch (Granny Aching), who finds a solution that exists between right and wrong. She allows the dog to live, but only after subjecting it to a brutal conditioning to ensure that it will never approach a sheep again, much less kill one. After saving his dog's life, Granny Aching gives a cautionary message to the Baron:

> "For you, at a word, the law was brake," said Granny Aching. "Will ye mind that, ye who sit in judgement. Will yer remember this day? Ye'll have cause to."[35]

The message from the witches seems to be that moral laws must *appear* to be absolute. But they cannot, in practice, really *be* absolute. Life is complicated and messy. And morality must take note of this messiness. If, as Kant says, humanity is crooked, then sometimes morality must bend. Thus, recognizing the truth of nihilism, and the nature of moral laws as fictions, gives the witches room to respect the flexibility. Like Nietzsche's new philosophers the witches are creating and re-creating morality as needed. This makes them a powerful influence in Lancre and on the Chalk, and naturally makes others wary of them. It gives them, like the new philosophers, a dangerous sense of superiority.

The threat of the attitude of superiority is one that is taken quite seriously among Pratchett's witches. But, unlike Nietzsche, they do not view their superiority as something to celebrate, but rather as something to be wary of. The witches of Lancre make the hard decisions that others turn a blind eye to. This gives the witches a real power. But the power is not *only* the power to do good. And every witch knows this. Behind all the talk of responsibility that runs through every Discworld story featuring the witches is the recognition that the power wielded by them is dangerous: dangerous to others, and dangerous to the witch herself. Power can lead to cackling.

For Pratchett's witches, the word "cackling" captures the worst characteristics that are possible for a witch to have. In *A Hat Full of Sky* Tiffany learns that a witch must guard against cackling, which means that she must guard against a feeling of superiority as a result of her power:

> It was too easy to slip into careless little cruelties because you had power and other people hadn't, too easy to think other people didn't matter much, too easy to think that ideas like right and wrong didn't apply to *you*. At the end of *that* road was you dribbling and cackling to yourself all alone in a gingerbread house, growing warts on your nose.[36]

The fear seems to be that a witch who recognizes the malleability of morality may eventually cease to be the anchor of moral fictions and instead will manipulate them (or outright ignore them) to serve her own purpose. She would then no longer be engaged in make-believing, but rather in lying. But a witch who does this, can no longer serve as an anchor. So, she can no longer function as a witch.

Cackling, then, must be avoided if a witch is to serve her role as the moral anchor of her community. This puts the witches in a tricky position. They create the moral fictions. But they must believe in these fictions *as fact*. To acknowledge them openly as fiction, risks cackling. After all, if it's a fiction, then why should a witch be bound by the same laws as everyone else? Thus cackling, and the avoidance of cackling, is serious business.

There are two main ways the witches are able to avoid the slide into cackling. The first, most basic, and most important way is by relying on other witches. This is paradoxical, as the tales of the witches drive home again and again the fierce independence of each witch. Other than Nanny Ogg, none of the witches have been married while working as witches. They all live alone except in the rare cases in which they take on an apprentice. None would dream of interfering in the domain of another witch unless asked. And there is an unspoken rule that no witch should ask for help. Each witch anchors morality for her own village, or steading, alone. Nonetheless, this fierce independence notwithstanding, each witch knows she is being watched carefully by the others and that this careful watching is necessary in order to ward against cackling:

> So witches had to keep one another normal, or at least what was normal for witches. It didn't take very much: a tea party, a singsong, a stroll in the woods, and somehow everything balanced up, and they could look at adverts for gingerbread cottages in the builder's brochure without putting a deposit on one.[37]

Social engagements are never just for fun. They are times to check up on each other. The witches prevent a slide into nihilism by reinforcing that, while each witch works alone, each is also part of a collective. They are not individuals against the collective. They are individuals in their own steading, but they nonetheless belong to a dispersed community; the community of other witches. Their individuality allows them to bend morality and create new moral fictions. The collective they belong to ensures that this dangerous power is never abused and that they hold fast to the most important fiction: to never begin to treat people as things.

Thus, the witches conform exactly to Kant's "unsocial sociability" discussed above. They are exceedingly unsociable:

> Witches were a bit like cats. They didn't much like one another's company, but they *did* like to know what all the witches *were*, just in case they needed them. And what you

might need them for was to tell you, as a friend, that you were beginning to cackle.[38]

The very fact that they are not very social, but are fierce individuals, prevents them from forging a collective identity and elevating themselves above others. They cannot act to secure special privileges for witches, or decree that certain moral laws do not hold over witches, because they do not view themselves as a collective, much less act in the best interests of that collective. Thus, Pratchett's witches demonstrate a way to create a solution to Kant's problem of how to anchor morality in *this* world *without* recourse to the next. As such, they also solve Nietzsche's problem of how to overcome nihilism. They create moral fictions as individuals. The fictions are maintained as a collective. This prevents any witch from falling into the void, or becoming lost in the abyss.

But, while checking up on each other is a line of defense against cackling, it is not the only way the witches avoid cackling. They also avoid the temptation to abuse their dangerous power by remaining in constant contact with the communities they serve. The witches not only anchor morality, but also provide a sort of social safety net for their communities. They take care of those who cannot care for themselves. This is a worthy and noble role to fulfill in any society, and is one our own society praises. But the witches don't do it for the betterment of the people, or for praise. They do it for themselves. As Granny Weatherwax reminds Tiffany in *A Hat Full of Sky*:

"That's why we do all the tramping around and doctorin' and stuff," said Mistress Weatherwax. "Well and because it makes people a bit better, of course. But doing it moves you into your centre, so's you don't wobble. It anchors you. Keeps you human, stops you cackling."[39]

The work that the witches do—cutting toe-nails, giving baths, cleaning rooms, delivering food, and sitting up with the dead—is not only work that desperately needs doing; it is also work that is *grounding*. It reminds the doer of what and who they are working *for*. Just as the witches anchor morality for the people, the people anchor the humanity of the witches. It is worth noting that this is the opposite of Nietzsche's desires for the new philosophers. The new philosophers were to be likened to the *Übermensch*, the "overman," a man who overcomes man.[40] In a sense, the new philosophers would not be human anymore. They would be *more than* human. The witches actively resist this move.

The witches take care of the people in their lives, not (or not only) because they need their help, but also because the witches *need* to take care. Taking care shows respect. It acknowledges and reinforces the belief in intrinsic human dignity. And in acknowledging the humanity of others, the witches demonstrate their own humanity. Pratchett's witches achieve the extraordinary feat of anchoring morality and affirming human dignity without recourse to the divine, and with a steady awareness that both morality and dignity are fictions.

Conclusion

In order to prevent the cackling, witches check up on each other. A witch's convictions and decisions must be checked against the thoughts and opinions of other witches. But she must also be firm. This is the delicate balance in Pratchett's development of morality among the witches: they must firmly believe that what they are doing is right. Often the obstacles they face can *only* be overcome if an individual witch is able to hold fast to her beliefs. But they must be self-aware enough to recognize that these beliefs themselves are fictions, and thus can be bent as needed. This requires careful balance. At the intersection of story and reality, fact and fiction, and balanced between individual action and collective decision, the witches are able to hold firm to a Kantian-like duty while creating Nietzschean-like fictions.

Though they fight monsters in every story they appear in, the witches cannot be transformed into monsters, no matter how many monsters they face. Each witch watches the others for signs of cackling. Collectively, the witches provide support for each individual witch's action and decision. Thus, they stand together and give their best glare into the abyss, acknowledging it as truth, and making up moral fictions in spite of it. And the abyss does not look back.

Notes

1. I. Kant (1993) *Grounding for the Metaphysics of Morals; On a Supposed Right to Lie because of Philanthropic Concerns*, translated James W. Ellington (Indianapolis: Hackett Publishing Company), p. 36.
2. T. Pratchett (1998) *Carpe Jugulum* (London: Victor Gollancz), p. 210.
3. Kant, *Grounding*, p. 39.
4. P. Guyer (2006) *Kant* (New York: Routledge), pp. 224–5.
5. Guyer, *Kant*, p. 199.
6. Pratchett, *Carpe Jugulum*, p. 16.
7. T. Pratchett (2006) *Wintersmith* (New York: HarperTempest), p. 11.
8. Ibid., p. 56.
9. Ibid., p. 60.
10. Guyer, *Kant*, p. 229.
11. I. Kant (2006) "Idea for a Universal History from a Cosmopolitan Perspective," in *Towards a Perpetual Peace and Other Writings in Politics, Peace and History*, translated D.L. Colclasure, edited P. Kleingeld (New Haven: Yale University Press), pp. 6–7.
12. T. Pratchett (2010) *I Shall Wear Midnight* (New York: Harper), p. 110.
13. Kant, "Idea for a Universal History," p. 9.
14. Ibid.
15. Guyer, *Kant*, p. 232.
16. Pratchett, *Carpe Jugulum*, p. 76.
17. W. Kaufmann (1974) *Nietzsche: Philosopher, Psychologist, Antichrist* (Princeton: Princeton University Press), p. 97.
18. Ibid., p. 96.
19. Ibid., p. 106, my *emphasis*.
20. Ibid., p. 110.
21. F. Nietzsche (1966) *Beyond Good and Evil: Prelude to a Philosophy of the Future*, translated Walter Kaufmann (New York: Random House), p. 89.
22. Ibid., p. 107.

23. Ibid., p. 19.
24. Kaufmann, *Nietzsche*, pp. 356–7.
25. See also the *Stanford Encyclopedia of Philosophy*'s entry on "Fictionalism" for a discussion of Nietzsche as an historical precursor to modern fictionalism.
26. Kaufmann, *Nietzsche*, p. 205.
27. T. Pratchett, *Hogfather* (London: Victor Gollancz), p. 269.
28. Ibid., p. 270.
29. N. Hussain (2007) "Honest Illusions," in *Nietzsche and Morality*, edited B. Leiter and N. Sinhababu (Oxford: Clarendon Press), p. 170.
30. T. Pratchett (2004) *A Hat Full of Sky* (New York: HarperCollins), p. 268.
31. Nietzsche, *Prelude*, p. 115.
32. Ibid., p. 207.
33. Pratchett, *I Shall Wear Midnight*, p. 168.
34. F. Nietzsche (2000) *Beyond Good and Evil*, reprinted in *Basic Writing of Nietzsche*, translated W. Kaufmann (New York: The Modern Library), pp. 303–4.
35. T. Pratchett (2003) *The Wee Free Men* (New York: HarperCollins), p. 77.
36. Pratchett, *Hat Full of Sky*, pp. 8–9.
37. Pratchett, *I Shall Wear Midnight*, p. 53
38. Pratchett, *Hat Full of Sky*, p. 8.
39. Ibid., p. 198.
40. F. Nietzsche (2000) *The Genealogy of Morals*, reprinted in *Basic Writing of Nietzsche*, translated W. Kaufmann (New York: The Modern Library), pp. 531–2.

Bibliography

Guyer, P. (2006) *Kant* (Routledge: New York).

Hussain, N. (2007) "Honest Illusions," in *Nietzsche and Morality*, edited B. Leiter and N. Sinhababu (Clarendon Press: Oxford).

Kant, I. (1993) *Grounding for the Metaphysics of Morals; On a Supposed Right to Lie because of Philanthropic Concerns*, translated J.W. Ellington (Indianapolis: Hackett Publishing Company).

——— (2006) "Idea for a Universal History from a Cosmopolitan Perspective," in *Towards a Perpetual Peace and Other Writings in Politics, Peace and History*, translated D.L. Colclasure, edited P. Kleingeld (New Haven: Yale University Press), pp. 3–16.

Kaufmann, W. (1974) *Nietzsche: Philosopher, Psychologist, Antichrist* (Princeton: Princeton University Press).

Nietzsche, F. (1966) *Beyond Good and Evil: Prelude to a Philosophy of the Future*, translated W. Kaufmann (New York: Random House).

———— (2000) *Beyond Good and Evil*, reprinted in *Basic Writing of Nietzsche*, translated W. Kaufmann (New York: The Modern Library).

_____ (2000) *The Genealogy of Morals*, reprinted in *Basic Writing of Nietzsche*, op. cit.

Pratchett, T. (1996) *Hogfather* (London: Victor Gollancz).

_____ (1998) *Carpe Jugulum* (London: Victor Gollancz).

_____ (2003) *The Wee Free Men* (New York: HarperCollins).

_____ (2004) *A Hat Full of Sky* (New York: HarperCollins).

_____ (2010) *I Shall Wear Midnight* (New York: Harper).

_____ (2011) *Wintersmith* (New York: HarperTempest).

10 The Care of the Reaper Man: Death, the Auditors, and the Importance of Individuality

Erica L. Neely

In Terry Pratchett's Discworld novels, there is an ongoing battle between Death and a group of beings known as the Auditors. These beings strive to maintain order in the universe and dislike humanity and all its inherent messiness. Death, on the other hand, is rather fascinated by humans and sees value in the individuality humans exhibit. This causes tension between him and the Auditors, which comes to a head in three novels wherein the Auditors attempt to impose their view of order upon the Discworld: *Reaper Man*, *Hogfather*, and *Thief of Time*.

In each of these novels Death thwarts the Auditors by acting in concert with humans. His motives for this stem from an odd allegiance to the importance of individuality and care. Humans have different desires and beliefs; they are not all the same. While this may distress the Auditors, it is fundamental to the nature of humans—we are individuals and must be treated as such. To ignore this and attempt to deal with humans purely collectively is to be unjust.

This illustrates a more general tension between the individual and the collective. While humans are driven to form communities, we also wish to maintain our individuality; there is thus a question as to how to balance commitments to the group with commitments to the individual. One place this tension emerges is in ethical theorizing. While traditionally there is a push towards universalization in ethics, recently many have come to believe that our ethical thinking must recognize the embodied and individual nature of humans; we cannot impartially treat humans as essentially all the same. This position is echoed by Death in his battle with the Auditors; he knows that humans are inherently individual and this cannot be stifled without destroying humanity.

While there are many examples of this tension between individual and collective in the works of Terry Pratchett, I will focus specifically on the conflict between Death and the Auditors. Not only is Death the unexpected champion of humanity and individuality, he also is explicitly committed to the importance of care. This has unexpected ramifications, not least of which is that it enables Death to create justice on the Discworld; his care for humanity is the catalyst for justice.

Individuality and Community

Humans are driven to form communities for a number of reasons. Both David Hume (1711–76) and Jean-Jacques Rousseau (1712–78) discuss this drive to form communities, as well as the problems generated by such behavior. Hume notes that one of our motivations for forming communities is that humans are not well-suited to survive as individuals in the wild. Animals such as bears have tough skin, sharp teeth, and claws to defend themselves. Against them, humans are relatively weak. When we join together, however, we are able to overcome our physically weaker state by harnessing the power of our intellect and combining our forces.[1] This is one motivation for creating communities of people: survival.

There are further compelling reasons for joining communities. Rousseau largely agrees with Hume as to the survival value of communities, but he adds a twist. Even if humans could exist outside of communities, in perfect isolation from each other, he believes that this would be undesirable, as "the earth would be covered with men amongst whom there would be almost no communication," and he sees this as undesirable.[2] Communication is taken to be a kind of good, connecting us to other people and forming a whole that is greater than the individual parts.

This idea that there is value in connecting with others, or belonging to a greater whole, is reflected at many levels of human interaction. People form families, social organizations, churches, universities, businesses, and even nations; we see value in joining with others to achieve some kind of purpose, ranging from simple enjoyment to the pursuit of knowledge, commerce, or social order. This is reflected on the Discworld as well, both with the Unseen University bringing together groups of wizards and with a variety of guilds serving various professions. We are, in general, better off when we are not trying to do everything by ourselves.

However, while we are pushed in the direction of forming communities, a conflict arises with our desire for individuality. In some ways, a community functions more smoothly when its members share certain values and ideals; a relatively homogeneous community is more likely to reach consensus about what it is trying to accomplish and methods for achieving those goals. This creates a certain pressure to conform and an incentive for avoiding too much individuality among a group's members.

Yet, of course, there is value to individuality as well, both for individual members and the community. Humans tend to value autonomy, namely, having the capacity to control one's own life and make one's own decisions; these are seen as important expressions of individual freedom. Most people recognize that our autonomy is not absolute, for it can be limited by other factors. Colloquially, the right to swing my fist ends at your nose; my autonomy does not extend so far that it allows me to harm others simply as an expression of my own freedom. Yet, the ability to swing my arms through the air as I walk, or choose my career path, or decorate my house as I see fit are all expressions of my personality, and most of us would be loath to give all such rights up completely. If I cannot make certain choices in my life, there is a sense in which it is not *my* life at all.

Furthermore, it is not simply individuals who value autonomy. A community that praises conformity too much runs the risk of stagnation. Individuality allows for creativity that allows for growth in the community. Thus while a community of clones would, in some sense, be very easy to predict and govern, it would also likely be rather dull. We need a balance of traits in order to have a vibrant community that is also cohesive enough to function.

This need for balance is one of the hardest aspects of belonging to a community. Individual members of a community will undoubtedly need to make certain sacrifices for that community. Yet there are limits to what should be required. Rousseau argues, for instance, that members should be willing to give up whatever the society asks; and at the same time the society should not ask for more than it needs.[3] The key question, then, is how to make this work. How can we be just to individuals while still acknowledging the needs of the community?

This debate is echoed in political philosophy in the disagreement between two competing schools of thought: liberalism and communitarianism. The tradition of political liberalism is perhaps best typified by John Rawls (1921–2002). Rawls developed a theory of justice which portrayed individuals as rationally choosing to pursue certain goals and developing their own conception of what is good; each person autonomously decides what the good life is for him or herself and how best to pursue it. In order to form society, the best course is to adopt rules that would be acceptable to a group of ideally rational people with no knowledge of their own status in that society. These people are often referred to as choosing from behind a "veil of ignorance," and the idea is that they would create a society which is fair to all, since they do not know what their position in that society would be.[4]

Communitarians such as Michael Sandel criticize this idea, in part for the weight Rawls places on individuals and individual liberty. First, our goals are frequently not formed independently of social ties: we are influenced by the desires of our families, the messages from society about what is possible for us in our position, and so on. We do not simply sit down in isolation and decide what we wish to accomplish in our lives. Second, the liberal tradition contains a certain unreflective acceptance of individuals' desires and rights that is perhaps not best for the community. The ideally rational people in Rawls's society will likely adopt rules that preserve their freedom. Yet we may ask whether preserving our freedom is necessarily the best way to form a community; perhaps not all of our desires and wishes *should* be protected and preserved. Perhaps the individual should give way to the community.[5]

Just as philosophers argue over the relative importance of individuals and communities, this conflict also arises in a number of places in the Discworld books. Lord Vetinari, the Patrician of Ankh-Morpork, is a clear example of a man who is trying to figure out how to rule a diverse population. His choice is to be a benevolent dictator who tries to give people at least the illusion of choice; this was illustrated when Vetinari freed Moist von Lipwig and gave him a choice about whether he would like to run the post office or simply leave. Of course, leaving would result in dropping into a pit and dying horribly, but Moist still had some choice in the matter.[6] Ultimately, Vetinari seems to realize that, while he is a dictator, it is not wise to rule with too heavy a hand: not only is this likely to lead to his removal,[7] but the population itself needs more careful attention. Thus he is described as tending Ankh-Morpork "as one tends a topiary bush, encouraging a growth here, pruning an errant twig there. It was said that he would tolerate absolutely anything apart from anything that threatened the city."[8] Vetinari, therefore, has recognized that the good of the city depends on the freedom of its members—interfering too much with individuals is apt to cause problems for the group as a whole.

Sam Vimes is an example of a man struggling with a conflict between individuality and conformity to expectations on a number of different fronts. Starting out as a regular guardsman in Ankh-Morpork, he was mostly ignored by much of society. However, his promotion to Commander of the Watch brought him into contact with more of the political aspect of his job: he had to balance his desires to remain an ordinary working man with the need for dressing the expected part and being diplomatic.[9] This was further exacerbated by his marriage to Lady Sybil, since he became a member of a much higher social class than he was used to; this also carried certain expectations with it that clashed strongly with his own sense of individuality.[10]

The Auditors also exemplify this struggle as they engage in a number of schemes to impose conformity on the Discworld and its inhabitants, frequently coming into conflict with Death in their pursuit of structure and order. As beings that revere order above all else, the messiness inherent in living beings, particularly humans, is displeasing to them. In many ways they are the perfect embodiment of this conflict, since they strongly represent the forces of conformity in the face of humanity's strong desire for individuality. I will thus focus on this conflict between the Auditors and Death, who becomes humanity's unexpected champion. This will illustrate the tension between individuality and conformity, both on the Discworld and more generally. In order to do so, however, it will help to investigate both Death and the Auditors in somewhat greater detail first.

Belief and the Personification of Death

On the Discworld, belief has creative power: if enough people believe in something, it comes into being. While people may think that an object exists, which is then believed in, this is not the case in Pratchett's universe—belief precedes the object.[11] This is not entirely unlike our own world, such as when inventors have an idea and then work to create it; the difference with the Discworld is a matter of scope. In addition to mundane objects, belief can also create more fantastical creatures. Monsters are created and sustained by children's beliefs.[12] Gods are a reflection of human beliefs and desires; they do the sorts of things we wish we could do, such as smite our enemies.[13] Furthermore, various personifications of human concepts are also created by belief.

Death features in many Discworld books and takes the shape he does because of the beliefs of humanity. Note that belief does not create death—that existed long before humans and is simply a "prolonged absence of life."[14] Rather belief creates the personality and the shape; it creates Death, not death. As noted in *Hogfather*:

> The shape of Death was the shape people had created for him, over the centuries. Why bony? Because bones were associated with death. He'd got a scythe because agricultural people could spot a decent metaphor. And he lived in a sombre land because the human imagination would be rather stretched to let him live somewhere nice with flowers.[15]

Being created by human imagination is not the same as being human, of course. Nevertheless, by being amongst humans Death picks up aspects of humanity. He is a kind of imitator of humanity. His house thus contains a bedroom, despite the fact that he does not sleep.[16] Why? Because human houses contain bedrooms. Similarly, he has silver backed hairbrushes by his bed, despite the fact that he has a skull for a head (and thus no use for such brushes.) Why? Again, because this is what humans keep in their bedrooms.[17]

One might wonder why Death tries to mimic humans. The answer to this rests with a recurring theme throughout Pratchett's work: one's shape influences one's being. When belief creates a being, it creates the broad outlines. So humans imagine Death as a bony figure with a scythe, but the details get filled in over time as he exists; so being imagined as human-oid results in him picking up certain aspects of humanity. According to Death, "IT CAN BE NO OTHER WAY, EVEN OUR VERY

BODY SHAPE FORCES UPON OUR MINDS A CERTAIN WAY OF OBSERVING THE UNIVERSE. WE PICK UP HUMAN TRAITS."[18] Perhaps this is why Death is fascinated by humans: they created him and influence his very being.

The Auditors and their Obsession with Order

The Auditors are a group of gray, collective beings that watch over the universe and ensure it operates in accordance with its laws; they "see to it that gravity operates and that time stays separate from space."[19] They are not life-forms exactly—indeed, Pratchett specifies at one point that they are "nonlife-forms," and also that they hate life.[20] The reason for this hatred is complex and stems from their obsession with order and conformity.

The good thing about an atom of hydrogen, for the Auditors, is that it is the same as any other atom of hydrogen—it has a regularity to it. The same is true of physical laws: if you repeatedly drop something of a particular mass under identical conditions, the law of gravity should ensure the same result every time. These are the kinds of laws the Auditors find reassuring because they are regular and predictable.

Life, however, is not regular.[21] It cannot be predicted or quantified in the way physical objects can. Humans are particularly bad because they have personalities, which the Auditors regard as highly inefficient. Indeed, the Auditors are so wedded to collectivity that if any of them display personality, they are destroyed; personality and individuality are seen as leading to discord.[22] The universe would be far more efficient, they believe, without being hindered by the messiness that humans bring.[23]

This represents, in an extreme form, the view of collectivity discussed previously: that a group (in this case the universe) would run more efficiently without too much individuality from its parts (in this case living beings). Their desire for order and, particularly, the erasure of human messiness leads the Auditors into several creative schemes. They cannot simply destroy life or humanity directly, since this would violate the Rules.[24] However, they employ a number of indirect tactics to attempt to impose more order on the world, frequently by involving a human. Their direct participation is not necessarily required because, as Death's granddaughter Susan observes, with humans "at last there was a species that could be *persuaded* to shoot itself in the foot."[25] The Auditors can set the wheels in motion while being confident that their human confederates will carry out the plan. Until, that is, Death and his various allies interfere.

The Auditors' first, and least ambitious, scheme arises in *Reaper Man*, when they decide that Death is inefficient because he has a personality. They do not think that such a thing is necessary in order to do his job well; as such, they petition the god Azrael to force Death's retirement and replacement. They intend to create a new Death, one that lacks personality (and, presumably, sympathy for humanity). When Death is forced to retire, he takes on the guise of a farmhand and helps a woman named Miss Flitworth with her crops. He encounters a machine, the Combination Harvester, which threatens to render him obsolete as a farmhand; this is akin to how the new Death has attempted to render him obsolete in his previous job. In both cases he fights back against the anti-individualistic threat they pose: the harvester reaps many crops at once with a kind of impersonal behavior, much like the new Death. Indeed, the final stand of the Auditors in *Reaper Man* is to harness the power of the Combination Harvester to fight Death. Unfortunately for them, Death has removed a key bolt from the machine, and this attempt ultimately fails.

The Auditors devise a second scheme for ridding the world of humanity in *Hogfather* by hiring assassins to kill the Hogfather, who is the Discworld's version of Santa Claus. They do this in order to disrupt belief in the Hogfather— after all, as Death observes, "IT IS THE THINGS YOU BELIEVE WHICH MAKE YOU HUMAN."[26] If the Hogfather no longer exists, then they assume that people will stop believing in him; more than that, those people will have their belief disrupted, since he no longer can fill the role people expect him to play. Because of this, it will cause a strong shift in belief. It is already the case that many children do not believe but rather simply pretend to believe.[27] The assassination and attendant absence of the Hogfather will push people over the edge, however, into active disbelief. Death helps thwart this scheme, partially by filling the role of the Hogfather to buy time; he goes through the motions of all the things the Hogfather is supposed to do in order to help stabilize the populace's belief. However, he also points Susan in the right direction to get her to help; together this is sufficient to retain belief in the Hogfather, so the Auditors' plan fails.

The third plan the Auditors attempt has an ingenious idea at the root of it. If the problem with humans—and life in general—is its messiness, and that humans can change in unexpected ways, then all we need to do is stop the ability to change. As such, in *Thief of Time*, the Auditors plot to stop time. If they succeed, then it will not matter that humans have so much potential chaos and disorder in them; humans will never be able to use that potential because they will be frozen in a particular moment. There will, in essence, be no future—just an eternal orderly present.[28] Once again, Death is involved in thwarting the Auditors by recruiting aid from Susan; he needs her help partially because he has an obligation to ride out for the end of the world, and partially because there are places humans can go that he cannot.[29] Between Susan and the History Monks—whose job it is to ensure that tomorrow occurs—the Auditors are thwarted in their plan to build a clock that will trap time.

In all three of these cases, the Auditors are defeated by humans acting in concert with Death. While in *Reaper Man* there is a direct fight between Death and the Auditors' Death, the only reason why Death is able to have this fight is due to a human: Miss Flitworth gives Death some of her time once his runs out. In *Hogfather* the roles are somewhat reversed,

237

because now it is Death who is buying time for others to act. He takes on the role of the Hogfather in order to keep belief alive, but this is not sufficient: someone still has to find the assassin and stop him, which is what Susan does. Death's role in *Thief of Time* is less prominent, as he works much more in the background than in the previous two fights. He is obligated to ride out for the end of the world, limiting his ability to interfere directly; he has duties to attend to. However, he notices the Auditors' schemes and again alerts Susan. While for much of the book Susan is less directly involved in stopping the Auditors than in *Hogfather*, she ultimately joins forces with Lobsang Ludd and Lady LeJean in order to defeat the Auditors.

The Value of the Individual

One might wonder why Death gets involved in these disputes at all. With the exception of *Reaper Man*, where the Auditors specifically target him for replacement, he does not seem to be directly affected by most of their schemes. It is true that he would lack function in a world without life, hence perhaps one could suppose that he seeks to thwart the Auditors in *Thief of Time* in order to preserve his importance. However, the same could have been said of War, Pestilence, and Famine—none of them has purpose in a world without life. Yet they were not even moved to ride out for the end of the world; so what is different about Death?

Well, it is not any natural, innate difference. Death acknowledges that "To THE REAPER MAN, ALL STALKS START OFF AS ... JUST STALKS," thus naturally humans all look the same to him. However, he continues to state that he has started to notice the differences among them.[30] Not only that, but he also values the individuality humans possess. Ironically, the attempt by the Auditors to replace Death likely hastens this development; it is in *Reaper Man* that he seems to gain the most appreciation for humans and their value. Clearly this is not the only influencing factor, since Death showed flashes of personality before the

Auditors interfered—indeed, that is *why* they interfered—but when Susan asks him why he gets involved in *Hogfather* he replies "I THINK IT'S SOMETHING TO DO WITH HARVESTS . . . YES. THAT'S RIGHT. AND BECAUSE HUMANS ARE SO INTERESTING THAT THEY HAVE EVEN INVENTED DULLNESS."[31]

Not everyone shares Death's view of humans, of course, since the Auditors spend a great deal of time trying to get rid of humanity. Their perfect world is ordered and changeless, not messy with life.[32] They do not attach importance to humanity, seeing humans as simply an imperfection; in *Hogfather* they even state that they have "a duty to rid the universe of sloppy thinking," which is a nice justification for trying to exterminate humanity.[33] Yet clearly Death sees a value in humans, messiness and all, which the Auditors miss, or else he would not be so intent on stopping them.

One of the key aspects of humanity, according to Death, is that the things we believe are what make us human.[34] This has both an individual and a collective component. Individually, people vary in what they believe. Unlike rocks or hydrogen atoms, humans are not all alike: you cannot simply substitute one for another. Part of this stems from a multiplicity of beliefs and experiences. While my beliefs may overlap with the beliefs of others, they are unlikely to be identical: we are each in part defined by what we believe.

This may well be part of what the Auditors object to, since they value conformity. A group with diverse beliefs has a harder time reaching consensus and acting than a group with uniform beliefs; similarly, that group is more difficult to rule or administrate. If you know what a person believes, you can make some predictions about how he or she will react to a given situation. However, if you do not know his or her beliefs—or if you are faced with a great many people who hold conflicting beliefs—then the person or group becomes unpredictable. The Auditors do not like unpredictability.

The overlap between our beliefs also has power, however. Recall that collectively belief in Death or the Hogfather has formative force on the Discworld. Humans create the tooth fairy, the Hogfather, Death, and similar entities by the power of their belief. Certainly the concepts existed beforehand, but the personalities are created by our collective beliefs.[35] Events then reinforce or destroy those beliefs, which is what Death worried about when the Hogfather was missing; if too many people stopped believing in the Hogfather, there would be bad consequences.

The true problem for Death was not that one particular entity would no longer be believed in; the problem is that he sees this sort of belief as necessary for humans. Susan is initially dismissive of this claim, thinking that Death means that humans need "*fantasies* to make life bearable."[36] However, his point is larger. He argues instead that humans need fantasy in order to be human. And while belief in tooth fairies or the Hogfather may seem trivial, humans have to start out believing in them in order to believe the bigger lies of justice, mercy, duty, and so on. Susan objects that believing in justice, for instance, is not the same as believing in the tooth fairy, which leads to the following exchange:

YOU THINK SO? THEN TAKE THE UNIVERSE AND GRIND IT DOWN TO THE FINEST POWDER AND SIEVE IT THROUGH THE FINEST SIEVE AND THEN *SHOW* ME ONE ATOM OF JUSTICE, ONE MOLECULE OF MERCY. AND YET— Death waved a hand. AND YET YOU ACT AS IF THERE IS SOME IDEAL ORDER IN THE WORLD, AS IF THERE IS SOME . . . SOME *RIGHTNESS* IN THE UNIVERSE BY WHICH IT MAY BE JUDGED.

"Yes, but people have *got* to believe that, or what's the *point*–"

MY POINT EXACTLY.[37]

Death's point, then, is that humans must believe in these abstract concepts in order to find meaning in their lives. It was to preserve this belief in the point of life that he impersonated the Hogfather. Without belief in the Hogfather, the sun would not rise—it would only be a ball of gas.[38]

The reason for Death's involvement in these disputes, therefore, is to protect humanity from the forces of conformity that the Auditors represent. In order to be human, we must retain our ability for unique beliefs and ideas—if we were all the same, as the Auditors desire, we would in some sense cease to be human.[39] Yet there is another facet to the conflict between Death and the Auditors, which also focuses on how to treat humanity.

Death as the Embodiment of Care

One of the key aspects of the dispute between Death and the Auditors centers on the importance of care. Death has a horrified reaction to the Combination Harvester when he encounters it in *Reaper Man*. Largely this is because he saw importance in treating each human as an individual, not simply as a member of a group. Cutting many blades of grass at once strikes him as wrong; the correct thing to do is to cut one blade at a time.[40] Similarly, humans must also be reaped individually, not seen simply as a mass to be taken care of. In this way we acknowledge the individuality of each person, something that the Auditors do not do.

This emphasis on individuality is central to the ethics of care. Ethical theories, in general, strive to answer questions such as how we should live our lives or what sort of people we should be. A major debate in ethics is over universalization: do we need an ethical theory to apply to everyone (or everyone in similar situations)? On the face of it, this seems plausible. Frequently we assume that being just or treating people equally is required for ethical behavior; if this is the case, then surely we are being capricious if we allow an action for one person but forbid a similar action for a different person.

There is concern, however, raised by ethicists of care that this does not do justice to lived human experience, because actual, particular relationships are at the heart of our lives. Virginia

Held notes that, for the ethics of care, the central focus is on the "compelling moral salience of attending to and meeting the needs of the particular others for whom we take responsibility."[41] The theory calls into question the idea that we are always seeking impartiality or universal rules. For instance, it seems reasonable to assert that it is ethical to prefer our family or friends on certain occasions.

Fundamentally, the ethics of care sees a problem in too much abstraction. Nel Noddings argues that:

> As we convert what we have received from the other into a problem, something to be solved, we move away from the other. We clean up his reality, strip it of complex and bothersome qualities, in order to think it. The other's reality becomes data, stuff to be analyzed, studied, interpreted. All this is to be expected and is entirely appropriate, provided that we see the essential turning points and move back to the concrete and the personal . . . If I do not turn away from my abstractions, I lose the one cared-for. Indeed, I lose myself as one-caring, for I now care about a problem instead of a person.[42]

For Noddings, this is a problem that arises in many contexts, including in situations where we are most committed to providing care, such as schools. She argues that there is a problem when we treat people only as members of a group rather than individuals, claiming that "to be treated as 'types' instead of individuals, to have strategies exercised on us, objectifies us. We become 'cases' instead of persons."[43] The strategy of generalizing similar cases, or of treating individuals merely as a representative of a kind of problem, is morally problematic for Noddings; doing so strips the person of their humanity. This is, of course, exactly what the Auditors strive for: they do not wish to deal with individuals, but simply with categories. Humans are problematic for them precisely because of this insistence on individuality.

However, ethicists of care emphasize the need to recognize and respect this individuality. Noddings sees care as concerning a kind of engrossment, wherein you are intimately concerned with the welfare and well-being of another person.[44] Specifically, "to act as one-caring, then, is to act with special regard for the particular person in a concrete situation."[45] She believes that, fundamentally, care is tied to a specific person—one cannot care about humanity in general, but simply for specific humans. More specifically, she equates the idea that someone should care for everyone to maintaining "an internal state of readiness to try to care for whoever crosses our path."[46] However, this is far less concrete than the sort of caring she is concerned with; she sees this as "a verbal commitment to the possibility of caring"[47] rather than anything actualized.

Not all ethicists of care agree on our inability to care for large groups of people. Held, for one, argues that it is possible to have a kind of care for people in general.[48] This is due to the fact that she sees care as emphasizing the intertwined nature of the person caring and the person being cared-for. Since it is presumably possible to acknowledge that our own interests are bound up with those of people around the globe, it should be possible to have care for people we have not met. While remaining neutral on whether this is possible for the average human in our world, it seems clear that it is possible for Death if he chooses—he has a unique ability to interact with everyone individually (even if only for a short period of time at the end of their lives). He thus has the ability to acknowledge each individual's life.

Furthermore, he argues that this acknowledgement is important, as demonstrated by his appeal to Azrael in *Reaper Man*:

LORD, WE KNOW THERE IS NO GOOD ORDER EXCEPT THAT WHICH WE CREATE . . .

THERE IS NO HOPE BUT US. THERE IS NO MERCY BUT US. THERE IS NO JUSTICE. THERE IS JUST US . . .

ALL THINGS THAT ARE, ARE OURS. BUT WE MUST CARE. FOR IF WE DO NOT CARE, WE DO NOT EXIST. IF WE DO NOT EXIST, THEN THERE IS NOTHING BUT BLIND OBLIVION.

AND EVEN OBLIVION MUST END SOME DAY. LORD, WILL YOU GRANT ME JUST A LITTLE TIME? FOR THE PROPER BALANCE OF THINGS. TO RETURN WHAT WAS GIVEN. FOR THE SAKE OF PRISONERS AND THE FLIGHT OF BIRDS . . .

LORD, WHAT CAN THE HARVEST HOPE FOR, IF NOT FOR THE CARE OF THE REAPER MAN?[49]

The world requires order, perhaps. But humanity requires more than that—it requires an acknowledgment of its fundamentally messy and individualistic nature. This is what Death understands and the Auditors do not: that beyond rules and order, in the face of a seemingly unjust universe, humans can still seek care. And, as strange as it seems, Death cares for humanity. We may all fall to his scythe, but our passing does not go unremarked or uncared for.

Moreover, this care creates a kind of justice. Death argues that there is no justice in the universe; there are simply forces such as himself and Azrael. In this sense he is denying any metaphysical force of justice—it is simply a matter of people's actions. I submit that Death himself creates justice through care. Held argues that care is ethically prior to justice in the following sense:

> Though justice is surely among the most important moral values, much of life has gone on without it, and much of that life has had moderately good aspects. There has, for instance, been little justice within the family in almost all societies but much care; so we know we can have care without justice. Without care, however, there would be no persons to respect and no families to improve.[50]

It is not clear that Death always had care; more likely it developed over time as his fascination with humans continued. I believe that the most important step for Death occurred as a result of the Auditors' scheming in *Reaper Man*. Because Death was forced to become mortal, he began to feel viscerally the importance of specific people rather than only experiencing them in an abstract sense. This develops over time in his relationship to Miss Flitworth, but it comes to a head when a little girl is caught in a fire. While he may believe, as Death, that everyone has a time to die and one should not interfere with that time, he realizes that his human persona, Bill Door, sees this view as rubbish.[51] He has moved from an abstract, detached view of humanity—where it really does not matter much whether one specific individual lives or dies—to forming personalized relationships with people. This is at the heart of care.

While it could be possible for Death to care without also creating justice, his actions demonstrate a commitment to justice as well. Held argues that an ethic of justice "focuses on questions of fairness, equality, individual rights, abstract principles, and the consistent application of them."[52] These are traits that Death exhibits. For instance, he sees himself as bound by certain rules; one reason why he needs Susan's help in *Thief of Time* is because there are places he cannot go.[53] Similarly, he notes in *Hogfather* that Death cannot save the little match girl from dying, but the Hogfather can; there are rules about permitted behavior, which Death adheres to.[54] Furthermore, he sees himself as bound by these rules even when the Auditors break them by trying to assassinate the Hogfather.[55]

The motivating force behind Death's actions is his commitment to individuality and to reaping one soul at a time; this is a commitment to both justice and care. It is because he sees the need to care for each person that he treats them justly. While the Auditors might seem in some sense more committed to justice because of their emphasis on abstract principles and order, they end up being less dedicated precisely because they do not care; they seek to rule humanity, not to care for them.[56] Whereas Death acts to preserve belief in justice, and thus the possibility of justice, the Auditors act unjustly in their attempts to eliminate the essential messiness of humanity. The side of Death is the side of justice.

On the Discworld, as in our world, there is conflict between the individual and the collective. On one side, we have Death, who champions humanity by demonstrating that each person must be reaped individually; we must show care to them by treating them as individuals. On the other side, we have the Auditors, who attempt to classify the universe and value the collective over the individual. Ultimately, Death's actions in their various skirmishes demonstrate that the only way to do justice to the group is by fairly treating the individual; to care for the individual in the way he does is to enable justice to occur. While Death may claim that "THERE IS NO JUSTICE. THERE IS JUST US,"[57] his care is the catalyst for justice to occur.

Notes

1 . D. Hume (1978 [1740]) *A Treatise of Human Nature*, 2nd edn, edited L.A. Selby-Bigge and P.H. Nidditch (Oxford: Clarendon Press), pp. 484–6.
2. J.-J. Rousseau (1997 [1762]) *The Social Contract and Other Later Political Writings*, edited and translated V. Gourevitch (Cambridge: Cambridge University Press), p. 154.
3. Ibid., p. 61.
4. J. Rawls (1971) *A Theory of Justice* (Cambridge, MA: Harvard University Press).
5. M. Sandel (1998 [1981]) *Liberalism and the Limits of Justice*, 2nd edn (Cambridge: Cambridge University Press).
6. T. Pratchett (2005) *Going Postal* (New York: HarperTorch), p. 15.
7. Ibid., p. 69.
8. T. Pratchett (1990) *Guards! Guards!* (London: Corgi), reprinted 1995, p. 78.
9. For instance, there is an allusion in *Jingo* to Vimes's tendency to prefer the hands-on portions of his job to the ceremonial or diplomatic parts; see T. Pratchett (1998) *Jingo* (London: Corgi), p. 71.
10. T. Pratchett (2003) *Night Watch* (New York: HarperTorch), p. 5.
11. T. Pratchett (1992) *Reaper Man* (London: Corgi), p. 104.
12. T. Pratchett (1997) *Hogfather* (London: Corgi), pp. 37–8.
13. Pratchett, *Reaper Man*, p. 104.
14. Ibid.
15. Pratchett, *Hogfather*, p. 276.

16. Ibid., p. 122.
17. Ibid., p. 285.
18. T. Pratchett (2002) *Thief of Time* (New York: HarperTorch), p. 86. As Death speaks purely in capital letters, I have quoted him as such.
19. Ibid., p. 6.
20. Ibid., p. 7.
21. Pratchett, *Hogfather*, p. 408.
22. Pratchett, *Reaper Man*, p. 7.
23. Pratchett, *Hogfather*, p. 365.
24. Pratchett, *Thief of Time*, p. 85.
25. Ibid.
26. Pratchett, *Hogfather*, p. 409.
27. Ibid., p. 74.
28. Pratchett, *Thief of Time*, pp. 81–2.
29. Ibid., p. 85.
30. Pratchett, *Reaper Man*, p. 167.
31. Pratchett, *Hogfather*, p. 433.
32. Pratchett, *Thief of Time*, p. 301.
33. Pratchett, *Hogfather*, p. 119.
34. Ibid., p. 409.
35. Pratchett, *Reaper Man*, p. 104.
36. Pratchett, *Hogfather*, p. 422.
37. Ibid., pp. 422–3.
38. Ibid., p. 422.
39. The converse likely also holds true, as the Auditors discovered in *Thief of Time*—to become human is to have individual thoughts and, in some sense, to cease to be an Auditor.
40. Pratchett, *Reaper Man*, p. 91.
41. V. Held (2006) *The Ethics of Care: Personal, Political, and Global* (New York: Oxford University Press), p. 10.
42. N. Noddings (2003) *Caring: A Feminine Approach to Ethics and Moral Education*, 2nd edn (Berkeley and Los Angeles: University of California Press), p. 36.
43. Ibid., p. 66.
44. Ibid., p. 17.
45. Ibid., p. 24.
46. Ibid., p. 18.
47. Ibid.
48. Held, *Ethics of Care*, p. 157.
49. Pratchett, *Reaper Man*, p. 264.
50. Held, *Ethics of Care*, pp. 71–2.
51. Pratchett, *Reaper Man*, pp. 137–8.
52. Held, *Ethics of Care*, p. 15.

53. Pratchett, *Thief of Time*, p. 85.
54. Pratchett, *Hogfather*, p. 218.
55. Ibid., pp. 111–12.
56. Pratchett, *Reaper Man*, p. 230.
57. Ibid., p. 264.

Bibliography

Held, V. (2006) *The Ethics of Care: Personal, Political, and Global* (New York: Oxford University Press).

Hume, D. (1978 [1740]) *A Treatise of Human Nature*, 2nd edn, edited L.A. Selby-Bigge and P.H. Nidditch (Oxford: Clarendon Press).

Noddings, N. (2003) *Caring: A Feminine Approach to Ethics and Moral Education*, 2nd edn (Berkeley and Los Angeles: University of California Press).

Pratchett, T. (1989) *Guards! Guards!* (London: Corgi), reprinted 1995.

_____ (1991) *Reaper Man* (London: Corgi).

_____ (1994) *Soul Music* (London: Corgi).

_____ (1996) *Hogfather* (London: Corgi).

_____ (1997) *Jingo* (London: Corgi).

_____ (2001) *Thief of Time* (New York: HarperTorch).

_____ (2002) *Night Watch* (New York: HarperTorch).

_____ (2004) *Going Postal* (New York: HarperTorch).

Rawls, J. (1971) *A Theory of Justice* (Cambridge: Harvard University Press).

Rousseau, J.-J. (1997 [1762]) *The Social Contract and Other Later Political Writings*, edited and translated V. Gourevitch (Cambridge: Cambridge University Press).

Sandel, M. (1998 [1981]) *Liberalism and the Limits of Justice*, 2nd edn (Cambridge: Cambridge University Press).

11 "YES, SUSAN, THERE IS A HOGFATHER": *Hogfather* and the Existentialism of Søren Kierkegaard

J. Keeping

Ask someone untutored in philosophical discourse to name a movement or school of thought in philosophy and the answer you would most likely receive, if you receive any answer at all, is "existentialism" or "existential philosophy." But although many people have heard of existentialism, few (even among those schooled in philosophy) would be able to tell you what the word means or what it refers to. In this chapter, we're going to explore this most misunderstood of philosophical terms by means of an interpretation of my favorite Discworld novel, *Hogfather*. When we're done, you'll have an idea of what existentialism is, why it's important, and how one of our favorite authors just might be an existentialist.

Hogfather is all about Hogswatchnight, the midwinter festival which on Roundworld goes by the name of Christmas. The spirit of Hogswatchnight (or simply "Hogswatch") is represented by the Hogfather, who like Death is an *anthropomorphic personification*, and who we can think of as the Disc's equivalent of Father Christmas—or as we call him on the less fashionable side of the Atlantic, Santa Claus.[1] It is the night before Hogswatch, and all the little boys and girls in Ankh-Morpork have hung up their stockings in breathless (not to mention sleepless) anticipation of the Hogfather's arrival. Pork pies and sherry have been left out in the traditional manner. But this Hogswatch is different. The metaphysical beings known as the Auditors of Reality, who are responsible for the administration of the laws of nature (if you traveled faster than the speed of light, they would likely give you a speeding ticket),[2] have set out to destroy the Hogfather. You see, the Auditors—who manifest in the form of small gray hooded robes with invisible occupants—believe that the universe should be run as tidily as possible and see humans as a bunch of organic molecules that have forgotten their place. Death enlists his (mostly human) granddaughter Susan Sto Helit to thwart them, and hijinks ensue.

Why do the Auditors care so much about the Hogfather? Well, according to Death, the Hogfather symbolizes something vitally important to human beings, a trait that the Auditors would very much prefer we did not possess. Death attempts to explain in a conversation with Susan:

"All right," said Susan. "I'm not stupid. You're saying humans need ... *fantasies* to make life bearable."

REALLY? AS IF IT WAS SOME KIND OF PINK PILL? NO. HUMANS NEED FANTASY TO BE HUMAN. TO BE THE PLACE WHERE THE FALLING ANGEL MEETS THE RISING APE.

"Tooth fairies? Hogfathers? Little—"

YES. AS PRACTICE. YOU HAVE TO START OUT LEARNING TO BELIEVE THE *LITTLE* LIES.

"So we can believe the big ones?"

YES. JUSTICE. MERCY. DUTY. THAT SORT OF THING.

"They're not the same at all!"

YOU THINK SO? THEN TAKE THE UNIVERSE AND GRIND IT DOWN TO THE FINEST POWDER AND SIEVE IT THROUGH THE FINEST SIEVE AND THEN *SHOW* ME ONE ATOM OF JUSTICE, ONE MOLECULE OF MERCY. AND YET— Death waved a hand. AND YET YOU ACT AS IF THERE IS SOME IDEAL ORDER IN THE WORLD, AS IF THERE IS SOME ... SOME *RIGHTNESS* IN THE UNIVERSE BY WHICH IT MAY BE JUDGED.

"Yes, but people have got to believe that, or what's the *point*—"

MY POINT EXACTLY.[3]

The notion that humans need fantasies to make life bearable can be found in the work of the famed German philosopher Friedrich Nietzsche (1844–1900), who argued that "we possess art, lest we perish of the truth."[4] But Death is apparently proposing something more sophisticated than this. He describes humans as "the place where the falling angel meets the rising ape." And when prompted to explain this, he asserts that humans need to believe that there is some ideal order in the world or there's no point in going on. As explanations go, this is not entirely satisfying. To begin with, it isn't quite clear how this differs from what Susan says, that humans need fantasies in order to make life bearable. Also, how do we get from believing in tooth fairies and Hogfathers to big philosophical abstractions like duty and justice? And what in Io's name does it have to do with rising apes and falling angels? (Perhaps we should ask the Librarian?)

Eternal Apes and Temporal Angels

We can find the answers to these questions in the philosophical movement known as "existentialism." Now, existentialism just happens to be the most misused and ill-understood term in the history of philosophy. There are a number of reasons for this. The first is that the authors commonly associated with the term are somewhat disparate in space and time. Unlike, say, logical positivism, existentialism was not a discrete philosophical movement involving authors sharing similar views engaged in dialogue with one another. Or rather, there was such a movement, prominent members of which included Martin Heidegger (1889–1976), Jean-Paul Sartre (1905–80), and Simone de Beauvoir (1908–86), but the authors who influenced them such as Friedrich Nietzsche and Søren Kierkegaard (1813–55) are commonly labelled existentialists as well, even though they did not ascribe this label to themselves because *it didn't exist yet*.[5] The second reason is that the ideas expressed by these authors are quite subtle and complex, and liable to being misunderstood or even unintentionally parodied. Given an uncertain range of authors, some of whom call themselves existentialists and some of whom do not, who possess distinct though overlapping views, and all of which are difficult to understand, one wonders whether it is possible to give a coherent explication of existential philosophy at all. For this reason, I am going to focus mainly upon the views of a single author, who is generally credited with originating existential philosophy, and who heavily influenced the later authors who popularized the term. This is the Danish philosopher and theologian Søren Kierkegaard.

Curiously, although existential thought is commonly associated with atheism, its origins lie in the reflections of a deeply religious man on how to be a good Christian. Even though Kierkegaard lived in 19th-century Denmark, the problems he sought to address are easily recognizable to us today. He was very conscious of the disjunct between the standard of religious commitment demanded by the Bible and the religious practice of those he saw around him. Christians and others in the monotheistic tradition are presented with the story of Abraham as their prototype of faith—Abraham, who was called upon by God to sacrifice his only legitimate son and heir as a sign of his faith. The typical modern-day Christian, by contrast, sacrifices a bit of his or her time on bored Sunday mornings and perhaps a tithe of his or her income. No doubt some do much more than this, taking vows of poverty and chastity, but this is not the norm and no one believes that such vows are *required* of us to be good Christians. The vast majority of us believe that faith asks no more than attesting to certain beliefs and engaging in certain rituals.[6]

At this point you may be imagining Kierkegaard as some Omnian preacher railing against the moral decline of society. But this would be a mischaracterization. Instead, he was acutely aware of how empty and unfulfilling life often was for most modern day Europeans and saw their apathetic attitude to religion as a major factor. Among the impoverished, life was a struggle and faith no doubt offered some consolation in that. But among the bourgeoisie—who were, after all, Kierkegaard's audience—life appeared to offer little beyond social status and distractions such as gossip and fashion. Religious observance in particular had devolved into social conformity. But in Kierkegaard's view, the purpose of religion was to *give meaning to existence*.[7] It was supposed to lend passion and focus to one's life. It was supposed to prescribe a way of life and offer at least some assurance of finding personal fulfillment in that way of life. Again, this is not to suggest that there are not today, as in Kierkegaard's day, individuals who do find personal fulfillment in their religion—Christian evangelicals for example—but this was not and is not the norm. Furthermore, Kierkegaard's idea of what the religious life consists in differs greatly from that of the evangelicals. For him, the religious life is about bridging the temporal and the eternal sides of our existence.

The temporal and the eternal are terms Kierkegaard takes over from theological discourse, but he gives them his own existential twist, and it's here that the parallels between his philosophy and that expressed in *Hogfather* start to become apparent.[8] The eternal refers to God, angels, and other divine matters. They are called "eternal" because such things are not subject to time: they do not age, wear out, or pass away. They exist, according to the Christian theological tradition—which was heavily influenced by Plato (424–348 BC) and his followers and Aristotle (384–322 BC) and his followers—outside of time. Also belonging to the eternal sphere are other things that transcend space and time: the laws of mathematics and logic, for example. The temporal, by contrast, refers to things that *are* subject to time: the flawed, finite, ephemeral stuff of the material world. Humans, while clearly situated within the temporal, also contain a spark of the eternal, and this is why Death describes us as "the place where the falling angel meets the rising ape." Although we are finite, although we age and die, although we have all these icky bodily needs and secretions, we nevertheless are capable of transcending the temporal through our reason, our imagination, and our moral consciousness. This distinction, as I said, is not original to Kierkegaard, but recurs throughout the history of Western thought. We can find it, in fact, all the way back in Plato's theory of the Forms, which posited a perfect, eternal world of which everything in the material world was a poor copy, accessible through reason rather than the senses. It is there in Aristotle's definition of man as the "rational animal" (rational = eternal; animal = temporal). And it is there in Descartes's (1596–1650) distinction between soul and body, which we still take for granted today (although we have replaced the word "soul" with the word "mind").

But we do not need to buy into any of these philosophical positions to see what Kierkegaard is driving at. It can hardly be denied that we are each one of us born into a particular time and place, which significantly constrain the options for thinking and acting that are available to us. Moreover, we are each one of us born with a particular body, with a unique set of aptitudes, inclinations, imperfections, and limitations. This is the temporal side of our existence: the embodied, the particular, and the personal. But it is equally undeniable that we are not entirely bounded by our bodies and context. Through our powers of reflection and imagination we can contemplate distant places and times.

Vimes can think back to his childhood in Cockbill Street, and although he is not there in a physical way which allows him to influence events, he does enjoy a kind of access to it which transcends time in a limited but also remarkable way. Our powers of reasoning also appear to transcend time and space. If the Ephebean philosopher Didactylos were to demonstrate to us the Pythagorean Theorem (for any right triangle the square of the hypotenuse is equal to the sums of the squares of the other two sides), he would no doubt claim credit for it himself, but more importantly for our purposes, we would then understand it to be true not only for *this* right triangle, but *any right triangle whatsoever*. In the moral sphere, our ability to imagine consequences and ponder alternatives grants us a power of *choice* that appears to be the sole province of human beings (on Roundworld, anyway). When confronted with an antelope, a jaguar doesn't wonder if the antelope has children or fret over whether it should be a vegetarian, because it *can't*. But we can, and consequently we have the power to transcend our animal nature. We can weigh our own interests against those of others, we can contemplate our place in the larger scheme of things, we can aspire to be *more than we are*. Because this set of capacities allows us to transcend the real and the present toward the possible and the universal, it has come to be called the eternal side of our existence.[9]

I think you can see where I'm going with this. When Death describes humanity as "the place where the falling angel meets the rising ape," his image is remarkably similar to Kierkegaard's, with the angel representing the eternal and the ape standing for the temporal. This is the human condition, to be neither fully divine nor fully bestial. Historically, the philosophical tradition (and through a kind of intellectual trickle-down, science and popular thought) has almost exclusively preferred the angel to the ape. This is because of the almost magical power of the eternal side of our existence, through reason and imagination, to escape the particular and access the universal. It seems self-evident that universal truth (logic, mathematics, the laws of physics) is more important than particular truth (Granny Weatherwax's incredible aptitude for magic, Lord Vetinari's antipathy toward mimes), and that the group (nation, species, football team) should have priority over the individual. Kierkegaard, however, was one of the first thinkers to suggest that the eternal and the temporal might *both* be valuable and indeed *necessary* for us to be fully human.[10] Why did he think this? A full answer to this question would necessitate a foray into Hegel's philosophy (1770–1831) for which the reader might never forgive me.[11] So let it suffice to say that, insofar as the eternal trades in the universal and general (*all* triangles, *all* rational beings, and so on), it effaces the specific details of any given concrete situation. But life is *always* and *only* lived in concrete, specific situations. Hence what Western philosophy overlooks is precisely *existence*. The inapplicability of philosophy to everyday life is infamous and not entirely undeserved. To be able to step out of one's own perspective and examine one's situation objectively is extremely valuable. But it does not free us of the necessity to *choose*, and our choice cannot rest solely upon universal principles, but upon the concrete, messy, confusing details of our own particular life and situation.

In a similar way, the failure of contemporary Christianity to impact our existence in a positive way is owed to the fact that it has become abstract and removed from the concerns of everyday life. It's worth noting that Kierkegaard's Denmark possessed, as it does today, a national religion—the Church of Denmark—and that all Danish citizens were members of this church merely by virtue of being Danish. It therefore constitutes a striking example of the "one size fits all" model of religion, which fails to address us in our individuality. It is not enough for a religion to promulgate *a* meaning of existence; for it to matter to *us* we must take the active step of making it *our* meaning, of incorporating it into our lives. But this is only possible if it resonates with our loves and fears, our anxieties and aspirations. Another way of putting this is to say that there is no such thing as an impersonal relationship with God. We can only relate to God personally, as individuals. And like any personal relationship, its character is going to be informed by our unique personality and situation. An institutionalized religion can facilitate this by exposing us to the stories, songs, and other emotionally resonant products of its faith, and also by offering role models. But more often, the institution instead takes the place of the personal relationship and the possibility of building one never occurs to us.

Thus, religion can only serve its function of giving meaning to existence by being faithful to *both* the temporal and eternal aspects of our being. To abide in the temporal is to lead an animal existence, to be ruled by the inclinations of the moment, to be born and to die with nothing but a succession of moments in between. For a life to be meaningful, it must possess a coherence, a design, it must add up to something. For preference, this something (let us call it a "project," borrowing a term from subsequent existential authors) should not perish when we die, but merge with the greater flow of time. This could be in the form of something that outlasts us, such as a book or other creative work, or through participation in some larger project or ideal, such as social justice. Indeed, it could be something as commonplace as raising a family. There is a difference, however, between merely performing the concrete actions involved in raising a family and taking it on as one's fundamental project.[12] The latter entails a decisive commitment and a restructuring of one's hierarchy of goals such that everything we do—going to work, brushing our teeth, walking the dog—is directly or indirectly in service to the fundamental project of raising a family. In so doing, we express the eternal (the overarching goal or principle) in the temporal (everyday life). But it works only if our commitment is not merely theoretical, but also deeply personal. And thus it must accord with our likes and dislikes, our strengths and weaknesses.

So far, so good. But did I not say that it is specifically *religion* which is supposed to bridge the temporal and eternal and thereby give meaning to existence? How does religion fit into the picture I just described? The answer to this question is complex and points to the differences between Kierkegaard and the later thinkers associated with the existential movement.

Wistful Lying

Let us consider: everything in one's life receives its meaning from the fundamental project. But where, then, does the fundamental project get its meaning? It cannot be for the sake of anything else, because then whatever it would be for the sake of takes on the status of a fundamental project. And so we would not have answered the question, but only postponed it. If we are to avoid an infinite regress, we must at some point *stop asking for justification*, and so run up against the limits of reason.

This brings us to the issue of *faith*. When asked by Archchancellor Ridcully to explain why the Auditors wish to get rid of the Hogfather, Death responds:

> THEY WANT YOU TO BE ... LESS ... DAMN, I'VE FORGOTTEN THE WORD. UNTRUTHFUL? THE HOGFATHER IS A SYMBOL OF THIS ... Death snapped his fingers, causing echoes to bounce off the walls, and added, WISTFUL LYING?[13]

Obviously, the human trait that Death struggles to name here is the same as what he describes to Susan as believing in things that aren't real (like Justice, or the Hogfather). This sounds very similar to what we commonly call faith. Pratchett avoids using the *word* faith in the novel, perhaps to avoid offending religious believers who think very much that the object of their faith is real. But that's part of the point, isn't it? To have faith means to believe in something that cannot be rationally demonstrated, that may even be at odds with what *can* be rationally demonstrated. Kierkegaard would say that from an objective standpoint, the object of your faith is not real. It cannot be made evident either by our senses or by our reason; it evinces itself only in the form of a *feeling*. But a feeling is something irreducibly subjective. So the difference between faith and Death's "wistful lying" appears to be merely one of *perspective*: to the faithful, the object of their faith appears real, but to an outside observer it appears unreal.

Looking at it in these terms actually helps us to grasp Kierkegaard's unique notion of faith. Faith is conventionally understood as a kind of unjustified belief. To believe in God, supposedly, is no different from believing in the Eiffel Tower, except that there is ample physical evidence for the existence of the Eiffel Tower, and consequently a near-consensus about its reality. For Kierkegaard, by contrast, faith is not so much a *belief* as an *act*—it is a decisive break with reason, an affirmation of a value higher than reason.[14] This is why it is sometimes called a "leap" of faith: like leaping off a precipice, it is to give up the solid ground of reason, to affirm the priority of existence over reason. It is to take a *risk*, because the alternative is to remain trapped on a precipice. This is why for him the *content* of one's faith matters less than the *quality* of it. He writes:

> If one who lives in the midst of Christendom goes up to the house of God, the house of the true God, with the true conception of God in his knowledge, and prays, but in a false spirit; and one who lives in an idolatrous community prays with the entire passion of the infinite, although his eyes rest upon the image of an idol: where is there more truth? The one prays in truth to God though he worships an idol; the other prays falsely to the true God, and hence worships in fact an idol.[15]

The point here seems to be that one's life receives its value through a relation to God, and this relation depends upon the wholeheartedness of one's commitment rather than the truth or falsity of one's specific beliefs.

It was this "existentialized" version of faith that was taken up by subsequent existential thinkers such as Sartre. Wishing for various reasons to distance themselves from religious discourse, they avoided the language of faith, but the content of the insight changed little. What they recognized was that Kierkegaard's question of how to be a sincere Christian was only a case of the larger problem of how to live a meaningful and fulfilling life. If our life is to be more than a matter of satisfying appetites and impulses, if it is to be a distinctively human life, then it must be a life lived in the service of some goal or ideal— what I called earlier, following Sartre, the "fundamental project." But an honest appraisal of our existential position reveals that nothing compels us to choose one goal over another. This is not to say that nothing *motivates* us—some lives are going to be more suited to our tastes or talents, and many will not be open to us at all. Such motives, however, are the consequence of our unique, personal situation, and do not affect the question of what makes the goal itself more worthy than count-less other goals. Any criterion that we could name would have to be weighed alongside other criteria, leaving us in a similar dilemma. Sartre's contention is that the only thing that can possibly make our chosen project worthy is the fact that we have chosen it. We give it its value by making it the guiding principle of our life. The demand for outside justification misses the point, because the putative justification can only func-tion as a justification if we have already tacitly or deliberately affirmed it. To illustrate this, Sartre tells the story of a student of his who was faced with the choice of going off to fight in the war—and in so doing avenge his brother who was killed by the opposing side—or staying at home to care for his wid-owed mother.[16] If he consults the advice of a priest, this advice can only sway his decision if he has already expressly or tacitly chosen to affirm the Christian perspective out of which the priest speaks. If he goes to his philosophy teacher instead, this entails affirming the priority of reason over faith. The point is that nothing frees him from the position of having to choose. This is what Sartre means when he says we are "condemned to be free."[17]

How Else can They Become?

What does this tell us? It tells us that faith is, in Kierkegaard's words, the "paradox of life and existence."[18] We can escape the leap of faith only on the condition that we *never choose*, that we never commit ourselves unreservedly to a project or an ideal. Instead, we engage in roles and relationships only "for now," without investment, exchanging them for others when they no longer suit our inclinations. To do more than this means to affirm expressly or tacitly the unconditioned value of the principle of our action, to believe in either justice or mercy, duty or truth, despite the fact that their existence can never be demonstrated. It is to act in faith, whether we acknowledge this or not.

What does all this have to do with the Hogfather? Well, remember that Death describes believing in fantasies like the Hogfather and the Soul Cake Duck as "practice" for believing in abstractions like justice and mercy. Now, believing in justice and mercy is different from believing in the Eiffel Tower. It is more accurately described as *affirming* them. We are, therefore, dealing with something very much like Kierkegaard's existential version of faith.

What makes the Hogfather and the Soul Cake Duck and so on suitable to the role that Death ascribes them is that they are a particular *kind* of fantasy. Specifically, they are all animistic, they are all, as Death would put it, anthropomorphic personifications of abstract things. Mercy and justice are rather complex concepts for children to absorb, so we start them off on relatable figures like animals and men in red coats. A fat man in a red coat is easier to believe in than an abstraction such as justice, which you can't even visualize, let alone see. But it's a *bit* like believing in justice. The Hogfather is, after all, the spirit of Hogswatch in human(ish) form. That's halfway to believing in the spirit of Hogswatch as an abstraction. All you have to do is take away the fat man.

A good way to think of the way ideals like justice and mercy exist is by analogy with money. I have a comfortable amount of money in the bank, but that money isn't *made* out of anything. It's not like my money consists in a particular stack of bills. And if I want to buy something with it, nothing physical has to change hands: all I have to do is swipe a plastic card. So what is money, then? Well, it's a kind of fantasy. We all agree that these numbers on a computer somewhere represent value, and as long as everyone plays along, the system works pretty well. What about paper money, you ask? Isn't that a real thing made out of real atoms, rather than a fantasy? Well, while paper money is indeed made out of paper, and therefore atoms, *money* is not made out of paper. It would be more appropriate to say that the paper *represents* money. By itself, the paper is worthless, as the collapse of currencies such as that of the Icelandic krona in 2008 demonstrates. All that makes these pieces of paper worth anything is our *agreement* to behave as if they do. Money is a shared fantasy. And yet it often seems to be the most real thing in our lives.

Similarly, mercy and justice are real insofar as we act as if they are real. The universe may not punish the guilty, but we can, and the world is a better place if we do (for us, anyway). And just as it's a helpful shorthand to think of the little pieces of paper as actually possessing value, rather than merely acting as tokens in a system of exchange, it is sometimes beneficial to think of justice as a real thing (as Justice) rather than a set of rules that humans agree to behave in accordance with. "YOU NEED TO BELIEVE IN THINGS THAT AREN'T TRUE," asserts Death. "HOW ELSE CAN THEY *BECOME?*"[19]

So why do the Auditors target the Hogfather in particular? One answer is that, since he is associated with the most powerful holiday, he is the most important symbol. Perhaps the Auditors hope that with the demise of the Hogfather, there will be a kind of domino effect, and belief in the other anthropomorphic personifications will wane. But there's a more interesting answer. The Hogfather is the spirit of Hogswatch. And what is the spirit of Hogswatch? For this we have only to consider the Hogswatch carol, 'Wouldn't It Be Nice if Everyone Was Nice?' Or perhaps you prefer the Roundworld version of the slogan: 'Peace on earth and goodwill toward men.' The spirit of Hogswatch is kindness, compassion, generosity, and community. It is a moral vision. It is the belief in an ideal order in things, if only for one day a year. It's also worth noting that the Hogfather gives presents only to *good* little boys and girls. (Bad ones get a bag of bloody bones, at least in theory.) In other words, he rewards the righteous and punishes the guilty. He behaves justly. We can therefore see believing in the Hogfather as practice for believing in the ideal of justice specifically. As Susan could probably tell you, nothing motivates a small child to comprehend abstractions faster than greed.

And so we have arrived at the conclusion of our Hogswatch tale. It's been a pretty heady discussion, so a review might be helpful at this point. In *Hogfather*, Terry Pratchett presents us with a particular view of the human condition. This view greatly resembles the philosophical perspective known as "existentialism," in particular certain ideas expressed by its founder, Søren Kierkegaard. To be human, according to this view, is to live a contradiction: to be an animal, with all that that entails, while at the same time being able to transcend our animal nature through our powers of reason and imagination. Animal existence is a mere succession of moments that do not add up to anything, and therefore unsatisfying to beings with an eye on the eternal. But reason and imagination are empty, because they do not by themselves provide either motivation or passion. The key, then, is to get them to work together, to use our reason and imagination to give our lives a coherent structure—a meaning if you will—which both draws upon our animal passions for motivation while training them to work in harmony. Accomplishing this requires living "for" something: an ideal or goal that is larger than ourselves that acts as the guiding principle for this coherent structure. Because there can be no rational justification for our choice of one life-goal over another (since any such justification would have to be in terms of a more fundamental goal or ideal, which would stand equally in need of justification, and so on), affirming the worthiness of our goal requires an act of *faith*. We develop the ability to place our faith in ideals by first learning, in childhood, to believe in personifications of ideals such as the Hogfather. Belief in the Hogfather and his ilk thus plays, according to Pratchett at least, a vital role in fulfilling our potential as human beings.

Notes

1. As I've learned on the basis of a little cursory Internet research (i.e. Wikipedia), Santa Claus and Father Christmas, although the names are used interchangeably today, are based on two different myths about two different historical characters. I'm going to waive the distinction, however, by appealing to the ancient philosophical doctrine of *qui curis* or "who cares?"

2. T. Pratchett and S. Briggs (1997) *The Discworld Companion* (London: Gollancz), p. 49.

3. T. Pratchett (1996) *Hogfather* (London: Gollancz), pp. 422–3.

4. F. Nietzsche (1968) *The Will to Power*, translated W. Kaufmann and R.J. Hollingdale (New York: Random House), p. 435.

5. And let's not forget the fiction authors who are often lumped together with them as well, such as Fyodor Dostoyevsky (1821–81) and Albert Camus (1913–60), and the writers who were influenced by *them*.

6. For this see S. Kierkegaard (1985) *Fear and Trembling*, translated A. Hannay (New York: Penguin).

7. In existential discourse, the word "existence" is more or less equivalent to "the human condition." Existentialists are concerned with what it means to be human, and in particular the challenges we face in striving to live up to our potential as human beings. It was because of their frequent use of this term that they became dubbed the "existentialists."

8. See S. Kierkegaard (1941) *The Sickness Unto Death*, translated W. Lowrie (Princeton: Princeton University Press).

9. A brief note on terminology: Kierkegaard employs a fascinating rhetorical strategy he calls "indirect communication." This means that rather than stating his views directly and systematically, he tries to lead the reader to derive them on his or her own, in a way that more resembles literary (fiction) writing than philosophical writing. Consequently, he presents his thoughts over the course of many different books, written in distinctive styles and voices. He even employed pseudonyms such as Johannes Climacus and Constantin Constantius to represent different viewpoints, although he made no actual attempt to conceal his authorship. Because he wrote in different styles, voices, and contexts, his terminology is not consistent across his different works. So although for clarity's sake I will continue to speak of "temporal/eternal," he employs other pairs of expressions to refer to (more or less) the same distinction. These include "particular/universal," "finite/infinite," and "subjective/objective." I say "more or less" because each pair of concepts

approaches the problem from a different perspective and thereby emphasizes different aspects. The reader may find that one or another of the pairs of terms resonates better with him or her in a particular context, and so it might be best to keep all of them in mind when reading this chapter.

10. Another example (not from the existential tradition) is from the Scottish thinker David Hume (1711–76), who famously asserted that "reason is, and ought only to be the slave of the passions"; see D. Hume (2003) *A Treatise of Human Nature* (New York: Dover), p. 295.
11. Hegal's work can be regarded as the pinnacle of systematic philosophy, purporting to explain the whole of history in terms of the dialectic of reason. It can equally be regarded (as it was by Kierkegaard) the epitome of what is *wrong* with academic philosophy: abstract, dogmatic, and presented in incredibly dense and difficult prose.
12. This term is derived from J.-P. Sartre (1956) *Being and Nothingness*, translated H.E. Barnes (New York: Philosophical Library).
13. Pratchett, *Hogfather*, p. 365.
14. Kierkegaard, *Fear and Trembling*, pp. 34–6.
15. S. Kierkegaard (1941) *Concluding Unscientific Postscript*, translated D.F. Swenson and W. Lowrie (Princeton: Princeton University Press), pp. 179–80.
16. J.-P. Sartre (1957) *Existentialism and Human Emotion*, translated B. Frechtman (New York: Philosophical Library).
17. J.-P. Sartre (1956) *Being and Nothingness*, translated H.E. Barnes (New York: Philosophical Library), p. 631.
18. Kierkegaard, *Fear and Trembling*, p. 34.
19. Pratchett, *Hogfather*, p. 423.

Bibliography

Hume, D. (2003) *A Treatise of Human Nature* (New York: Dover).
Kierkegaard, S. (1941) *Concluding Unscientific Postscript*, translated D.F. Swenson and W. Lowrie (Princeton: Princeton University Press).
___ (1941) *The Sickness Unto Death*, translated W. Lowrie (Princeton: Princeton University Press).
___ (1985) *Fear and Trembling*, translated A. Hannay (New York: Penguin).
Nietzsche, F. (1968) *The Will to Power*, translated W. Kaufmann and R.J. Hollingdale (New York: Random House).
Pratchett, T. (1996) *Hogfather* (London: Victor Gollancz).

Pratchett, T. and S. Briggs (1997) *The Discworld Companion* (London: Gollancz).

Sartre, J.-P. (1956) *Being and Nothingness*, translated H.E. Barnes (New York: Philosophical Library).

____ (1957) *Existentialism and Human Emotion*, translated B. Frechtman (New York: Philosophical Library).

Part IV   Logic and Metaphysics

12 On the Possibility of the Discworld

Martin Vacek

The Discworld is possible! At least according to modal realism. It is one "point" in the phase space of consistent universes. Modal realism is a thesis according to which this world is not the only world in reality. The world we are part of is but one of a plurality of worlds, and we who inhabit this world are only a few out of all the inhabitants of all the worlds.[1] Phase spaces deal with everything that *might* be, not what is. There are other worlds, other alternatives to the world we are part of and, believe it or not, some worlds are exactly like the Discworld. And the reason is straightforward: our world could have been otherwise.

The "could have been" problem, or the problem concerning modality, has been bothering philosophers since antiquity. Philosophers have always had trouble understanding notions like possibility, necessity, and contingency. Although the notions seem to be indispensable in our everyday talk, it took a while to give a comprehensive story of how they function. And at the core stands the idea of a plurality of possible worlds.

Possible Worlds

It is a matter of fact that philosophers aim to explain various phenomena and make them comprehensible. Sure, people love engaging in fictional stories. But philosophers need something beyond it in order to take fictions seriously. They look for reasons and justifications for accepting the existence of such strange things in the same way as a craftsman looks for reasons to create a hammer. Before someone makes a hammer he or she thinks about the pros and cons of making it and considers whether it is worth the effort. And the same holds for philosophers. Before they accept some theory they need to see that it works. That means that it should help them in their philosophizing and be at least as effective as the theory they were using before. They must also see reasons to prefer one theory rather than another when it comes to its simplicity and explanatory strength. And it turns out that the possible-worlds framework provides the resources for dealing with a whole host of difficult problems.

According to the plurality of worlds every way the world can be is a way some world is. To explain, think about our world. Every single thing in the world has some properties and stands in some relations to other things. Consider:

(1) Our world is not a flat world, carried through space on the back of a giant turtle.

Apparently, any of us would agree that the proposition is truth-apt, that is, it has truth-value. Moreover, whether (1) is true or false can be easily decided. We can simply scrutinize our world by means of various experiments and observations and decide whether (1) is true.

The situation is, however, different with another kind of proposition. For example:

(2) Our world *could be* a flat world, carried through space on the back of a giant turtle.

Again, any of us is inclined to say that the above proposition is either true or false. Yet, the difference between (2) and (1) is that there are no *actual* experiments and observations that would verify or falsify (2). For, according to actual scientific discoveries, science tells us what *is* but does not inform us of what *could be*. Nonetheless, we construct thought experiments about what science might have looked like if the universe had been different, or if the history of science had followed a different route.[2]

Due to the difference between (1) and (2), philosophers found the idea of the existence of merely possible scenarios—ways the world could have been—useful for philosophical analysis. Namely, they say that our world could be a flat world just in case such a scenario is possible. Or:

(2*) Our world *could be* a flat world, carried through space on the back of a giant turtle, if and only if our world *is* the flat world, carried through space on the back of a giant turtle *in some possible scenario*.

The goal of the move from (2) to (2*) is to translate the possible proposition into a factual proposition holding in some possible scenario—*possible world*. Doing so, we can say under which conditions modal propositions are true, false, necessarily true, or necessarily false. Namely, a modal proposition is true if its non-modal version holds in at least one possible world; necessarily true if its non-modal version holds in every possible world; false if there is at least one possible world at which its non-modal version does not hold; and finally, necessarily false, if there is no possible world at which its non-modal version holds.

Possible (Disc) Worlds

An especially influential theory of possible worlds, although not the only one available,[3] says that possible worlds are as real and concrete as the actual world. This theory has been proposed by American philosopher David Lewis. Lewis announces his theory—*modal realism*—in the following words:

The world we live in is a very inclusive thing. Every stick and every stone you have ever seen is part of it. And so are

you and I. And so are the planet Earth, the solar system, the
entire Milky Way, the remote galaxies we see through tele-
scopes, and (if there are such things) all the bits of empty
space between the stars and galaxies . . . Likewise the world
is inclusive in time. No long-gone ancient Romans, no long-
gone pterodactyls, no long-gone primordial clouds of plasma
are too far in the past, nor are the dead dark stars too far in
the future, to be part of this same world . . . nothing is so
alien in kind as not to be part of our world, provided only
that it does exist at some distance and direction from here,
or at some time before or after or simultaneous with now.[4]

Two paragraphs later he continues:

Are there other worlds that are other ways? I say there are.
I advocate a thesis of plurality of worlds, or modal realism,
which holds that our world is but one world among many.
There are countless other worlds, other very inclusive things.
Our world consists of us and all our surroundings, however
remote in time and space; just as it is one big thing having
lesser things as parts, so likewise do other worlds have lesser
otherworldly things as parts. The worlds are something like
remote planets; except that most of them are much bigger
than mere planets, and they are not remote. Neither are they
nearby. They are not at any spatial distance whatever from
here. They are not far in the past or future, nor for that matter
near; they are not at any temporal distance whatever from
now. They are isolated: there are no spatiotemporal relations at
all between things that belong to different worlds. Nor does
anything that happens at one world cause anything to happen
at another. Nor do they overlap; they have no parts in
common, with the exception, perhaps, of immanent universals
exercising their characteristic privilege of repeated occurrence.[5]

Thus, according to modal realism, there are infinitely many
possible worlds because there are infinitely many variations

our world might go through. All of them are real and concrete. They are parts of different spatiotemporal systems such as our own and contain different inhabitants. According to some of them I do not exist, in some of them I have a twin, some of them lack our laws of nature, and, surprisingly or not, some of them are like flat planets resting on the backs of four huge elephants which are in turn standing on the back of an enormous turtle.

The Metaphysics of Possible (Disc)worlds

One of the main principles of modal realism is the principle of plenitude. Roughly speaking, the principle says that there are no "gaps" in logical space or, even more informally, that no possibilities are left out of reality. So, for instance, if there could be a dragon and there could be a unicorn there could be a dragon and unicorn next to each other. By the same reasoning, if we can consistently construct a fiction in which there is a planet in the shape of a disc, the moon of which is slightly closer to the world than the sun, contains glowing plants which feed the lunar dragons, contains trolls, witches, a seven-foot-tall skeleton with tiny points of light in its eye sockets, etc., a denial of the existence of such a possibility would mean a gap in reality.

The thesis of this chapter is that the Discworld, as we know it, is nothing but a result of such a *recombination* and, *a fortiori*, exists. Since any recombination of parts of different possible worlds yields another possible world, a world that is a flat planet that rests on the backs of four huge elephants is not an exception. For, there is no contradiction in saying that such a world came in to existence because of some blip on the curve of probability; that it contains creatures of various kinds; that laws of nature are different from those in our world; that it changes its spin from time to time or that each season occurs twice as much as in the actual world.[6] There is nothing in modal realism's theoretical apparatus that would prohibit it.

So, according to modal realism possible worlds are spatiotemporal systems, quite like planets (much bigger though). Philosophers have introduced them in order to play some theoretical role, namely to make notions of possibility, necessity, or fiction clearer. As we are free to say that "the Earth does not rest on the backs of four huge elephants" if and only if the world is such that it does not rest on the backs of four huge elephants, given possible worlds theory, to say that "it is possible that a world that rests on the backs of four huge elephants exists" is equal to saying that "there exists a possible world such that it rests on the backs of four huge elephants."

Given the above we can preliminarily conclude that if the possible-worlds approach is the best approach to the "could be" cases and possible worlds are conceived as really existing, we have reason to believe that the Discworld does exist. Moreover, under the assumption that modal realism is the best theory of "could be" situations, the Discworld is as real as the actual world and contains inhabitants as real as we are. Trolls, witches, or fire-breathing dragons are not only words in Pratchett's stories, they are as real and concrete as we are.

However, a problem may arise if we ask what exactly is going on in different possible worlds. Since they are isolated spatiotemporal systems, there is no connection between them, whatsoever. We cannot travel from our world to the Discworld and look at what is going on in it. What we can do is rationally describe it and fantasize about it. How, then, could such worlds be important for us when it comes to possibility? How relevant are different possible worlds for us if there is no causal connection between our world and other possible worlds? And finally, can the Discworld represent a real alternative to our world? Put otherwise, could we live in the Discworld? Since, as we saw earlier, philosophers accept possible worlds just in case they help in solving philosophical problems, much more should be said about their real philosophical impact.

Are Possible (Disc)worlds Philosophically Useful?

The most fundamental and persistent objection to the philosophical importance of the Discworld is the fact that its existence is irrelevant to modal truths about our world. Let's suppose that the Discworld exists and, as the theory assumes, its existence helps us to understand modal features of our world better. A dilemma arises. Since the possibility of *our* world to be a flat world has something to do with *our* world—recall that we are thinking about what is possible for our world—and, on the other side, the Discworld is causally isolated from our world, modal realism seems to lead to deadlock. How can the Discworld represent a possibility for our world when it is so far away from us?

Modal realists developed a strong theory around the "possibility" cases. As already mentioned, in the core of the theory is the claim that there exist concrete possible worlds. The worlds do not overlap and so every possible world has its own inhabitants. Next, possibility is to be understood in terms of "going on" in some possible world, and necessity is understood in terms of "going on" in every possible world. Applied to the "Discworld case," it is actually true that our world is not flat. But, at the same time, it is true that it *could* be. It could contain trolls instead of people or talking dogs instead of this-worldly dogs. Given the definition of possibility as a truth in some *possible* scenario, this means that there exists a concrete possible world according to which the actual world is flat rather than round, contains trolls rather than people, and talking dogs rather than silent ones. But again, our world as well as the Discworld, although they both exist, is isolated. Nonetheless, for modal realists there is one kind of relation that exists between worlds—the *similarity* relation.

The similarity relation is a relation between worlds that share the same properties. Something is qualitatively similar to something else if the two share the same properties. For instance, two red things are qualitatively more similar (when it comes to colors) than a blue and a red thing, since to share the same color contributes to the overall similarity. The same goes for shape, smell, taste, density, etc., because if individuals share the same properties they are more similar than individuals that do not.

So far, so good. However, the variety of properties that individuals (including big worlds) do and do not share indicates that it is not just one similarity relation that enters into the modal story. On the contrary, we have many and varied similarity relations. Some similarity relations differ from others because they put different priorities on different aspects of intrinsic or extrinsic qualitative features. With respect to intrinsic qualitative features, the similarity holds in virtue of the way things themselves are. So, it does not matter in which environment I am in order for me to have five fingers on my left hand since things around me do not contribute to the constitution of my body. On the other hand, some of my properties vary from situation to situation; these are extrinsic features. I am in front of my computer now, so I have the property of being in front of my computer. Once I stand, however, I lose that property and obtain a different one, say being behind the same computer. And so the latter sort of properties—the extrinsic ones—are possessed by individuals as a result of standing in, or lacking, relations to other things.

Let's illustrate the variety of similarity relations with an example. According to Pratchett's stories, trolls in the Discworld are humanoid life forms. They usually consist of metamorphoric rock, but some of them are made of sedimentary rock or diamond. Although they are stones all the time and become sluggish during the day they do in fact have brains. Some of them are clever and under certain circumstances able to do serious mathematics and quantum counting. Also, they have dispositions to unhealthy behavior, or they can gain nutrition from mineral matter and even get drunk in certain circumstances. In addition, they have developed their socio-political system based on the authority of the biggest rock, and their society consists of various tribes. Some troll tribes have their own spoken language, worship gods, and play a variety of games (including a sort of soccer and chess). So:

(3) Someone could be a troll.

Having (2*) in mind, (3) would mean that:

(3*) Someone could be a troll if and only if someone else *is* a troll,

which means:

(3**) Someone could be a troll if and only if there exists a possible individual that *shares* some important properties with him or her and the possible individual *is* a troll.

The question now is what exactly are the relevant properties that matter in deciding whether "someone could be a troll" is true? If it is the shape of body and its constitution that matter, we would reject (3) as plainly false. Someone simply could not be a troll as there is no similarity relation regarding bodily composition. Actual human people do not have shapes, organs, and limbs similar to Pratchettean trolls. We cannot say that they share the same properties. However, if we take the social constitution and social behavior as the relevant features, it turns out that someone could be troll.

Possible *worlds* also bear similarity relations to each other. And again, similarity relations come in degrees. A world that is exactly like the actual world except that it contains more people is more similar to the actual world than a world that contains trolls, like the Discworld. Although both worlds are logically possible—we can imagine them and write stories about them— one of them is more similar to the actual world. A world that shares the laws of physics with the actual world is more similar to it than the Discworld, which doesn't. Yet, both of them are (unrestrictedly speaking) possible. Due to the indeterminacy the similarity relation brings into the theory a lot of quite incredible worlds could be real. It does not mean, however, that they do really present philosophically substantive alternatives. Rather, philosophically more appealing are the considerations of what differentiates various—however incredible, but still consistent—possibilities.

Differences between various degrees of possibility raise serious issues in philosophy. Modal realists draw a strict distinction between the absolutely unrestricted use of the existence predicate—as in the case of logic and mathematics—and restricted modalities. It starts with the idea that there is one kind of possibility that is absolutely unrestricted, and various kinds that are not. For instance, the actual laws of nature, as opposed to the laws of logic, are not absolutely true since we can imagine a situation in which the Law of Gravity fails. In the language of possible worlds, there (unrestrictedly) exists a possible world that invalidates the natural laws of the actual world.

Now, if it could be shown that Pratchett offers us a vision of a world relevantly similar to ours, the Discworld would not be mere fiction. Rather, it would straightforwardly contribute to the modal profile of our world and present thus a real possibility. But how should one approach the question?

Natural Laws

The suggestion here is that the closeness of possible (Disc) worlds is to be analyzed in terms of the match of physical facts of the worlds. This means that the Discworld is similar to our world just in case it minimizes changes in *physical laws* and maximizes matches of matters of *fact*. And so it is physical laws that turn out to play an indispensable role in evaluating the Discworld as an alternative to our world. The problem, however, is that unless we know what the laws are we cannot decide whether the Discworld can do the job of representing the possibility. So the basic question is: What is it to be a law?

For Lewis, the laws of nature are best defined via "best-system" theory of natural laws. All we try to do is to fit the world into a deductive system that systematizes what is true in the world. Briefly, the identity of such systems is determined by their axioms; and any logical consequence of the axioms is a theorem of the system. Lewis writes:

> A contingent generalisation is a law of nature if and only if it appears as a theorem (or axiom) in each of the true deductive systems that achieves a best combination of simplicity and strength. A generalisation is a law at a world i, likewise, if and only if it appears as a theorem in each of the best deductive systems true at i.[7]

Lewis continues:

> I take a suitable system to be one that has the virtues we aspire to in our own theory building, and that has them in the greatest extent possible given the way the world is. It must be entirely true; it must be closed under strict implication; it must be as simple in axiomatisation as it can be without sacrificing too much information content; and it must have as much information content as it can have without sacrificing too much simplicity. A law is any regularity that earns inclusion in the ideal system. (Or, in the case of ties, in every ideal system.)[8]

And finally:

> Take all deductive systems whose theorems are true. Some are simpler, better than others. Some are stronger, more informative than others. These virtues compete: An uninformative system can be very simple, an unsystematized compendium of miscellaneous information can be very informative. The best system is the one that strikes as good a balance as truth will allow between simplicity and

strength. How good a balance that is will depend on how kind nature is. A regularity is a law *iff* it is a theorem of the best system.[9]

A rather simplistic version of the laws of nature says that the laws are the winners of a "competition" among all collections of truths. Apparently, there are different types of truths. We have simple ones like "this is red," "that is green," and so on. But some truths are more important in a sense that they say something substantial about the world we live in. For instance, they say that there exists a force of attraction between all masses in the universe, that any two objects are attracted to one another, that the force of attraction is proportional to the product of their masses and inversely proportional to the distance between them. Such truths say something stronger than the truth that this or that is green.

And that brings us back to the motivations for thinking about the Discworld as a philosophically relevant story. It was not the fantasy that gave raise to the possible-worlds theory. Rather, it was an attempt to elucidate and analyze various problematic philosophical concepts people use in their everyday lives. For instance, we use concepts like "fictional," "possible," "incredible," "magical," or "necessary" as meaning different things depending on different circumstances. For instance, we all agree that it is not possible to fly from New York to London in one minute, since the laws of nature do not enable us to do so. Neither is it possible to square a circle since, by definition, a circle cannot be squared. We do differentiate between the above impossibilities, nonetheless. In the former, it is impossible to fly from New York to London in one minute, but were the laws of nature to be otherwise, we could make it. We simply can imagine that under some (possible) circumstances people could develop a plane that would take us from New York to London in one minute. Since our imagination is almost without limitation, situations we can imagine abound. This is not so in the latter case, though. For, we cannot think about a situation in which someone squares a circle. Mathematics, as opposed to physics, cannot be otherwise.

The aim of philosophical investigations is to systematize our pre-existing opinions about various kinds of possibility, necessity, fictionality. This means that philosophers should provide us with an orderly system that respects our intuitions with respect to different degrees of similarity between worlds and, consequently, various kinds of possibility.

We can thus preliminarily conclude that possible worlds display different qualitative features and that their similarity and dissimilarity come in different degrees. Modal realists say a little bit more about the closeness of worlds and its context sensitiveness, yet admit that there is no one true measure of similarity. Only certain kinds of matches of *facts* are relevant and not all such matches are equal. So in order to identify the philosophical utility of the Discworld's existence, we should scrutinize its qualitative and factual features. In other words, although it still may hold that similarity consists of innumerable similarities and differences, there must be some properties due to which we intuitively adjudicate some modal sentences as true and others as false.

How Similar is a Globe to a Disc?

In his *Counterfactual Dependence and Time's Arrow*, David Lewis says a little bit more about the closeness of worlds, yet admits that there is no one true measure of similarity. He presents a list of desiderata in determining which kinds of matches are important. The following are constraints on the closeness between worlds:

(a) It is of first importance to avoid big, widespread, diverse violations of a physical law. For instance, a world that violates the Law of Gravity would not count as close enough and should be ignored in the analysis.

(b) It is of second importance to maximize the spatiotemporal region throughout which a perfect match of a particular fact prevails. Here, the Discworld is close by to the extent that it has a large region of perfect match of matters of fact while such a match does not come at the expense of a large miracle.

(c) It is of third importance to avoid even small, localized, simple violations of a physical law. In this case, an occurrence of, say, a flying witch counts against the similarity since relevant worlds should minimize the occurrence of "small miracles."

(d) It is of little or no importance to secure approximate similarity of a particular fact.

One way to look at the similarity between the Discworld and the actual world is to consider our very commonsensical picture of reality. Interestingly, the relation between common sense and reality is usually very direct in the Discworld as well as in our world. Common sense tells us what the universe seems like to creatures of our particular size, habits, and disposition. For instance, it tells us that the Earth is flat, that if it wasn't flat, things ought to roll around or fall off and so on. The *fact*, however, is that the Earth isn't flat.[10]

Common sense dictates to the wizards of Unseen University that Discworld is flat—and it is. A way to verify it is to go to the edge, as Rincewind and Twoflower do in *The Colour of Magic*, and see.[11] Modal realists also maintain that philosophers come to philosophy already endowed with a stock of opinions and it is not the business of philosophy to undermine them. In this context, Pratchett adds:

[The Roundworld] began, in various ways, to *resemble* Discworld. The apes acquired minds, and their minds started to interfere with the normal running of the universe. Things started to happen because human minds wanted them to. Suddenly the laws of nature, which up to that point had been blind, mindless rules, were infused with purpose and intention. Things started to happen for a reason, and among these things that happened was reasoning itself. Yet this dramatic change took place without the slightest violation of the same rules that had, up to that point, made the universe a place without purpose. Which, on the level of the rules, it still is.[12]

However, what runs Discworld is deeper than mere magic and more powerful than science. It is narrative imperative that plays a role similar to that substance known as phlogiston, once believed to be the principle or substance within inflammable things that enabled them to burn. Narrativium is part of the spin of every atom, the drift of every cloud. It is what causes them to be what they are and continue to exist and take part in the ongoing story of the world.[13]

The Discworld is a flat planet supported by four elephants. They are supported by a giant turtle. There is no support for the turtle as it simply swims through space. Discworld is a consistent, well-developed universe with its own kinds of rules, and convincingly real people live on it despite the substantial differences between their universe's rules and ours. Many of them also have a thoroughgoing grounding in "common sense," one of science's natural enemies.[14]

The Discworld exists at the edge of reality as an impossible blip because the gods enjoy jokes as much as anyone else. It also has one not-too-far-away Sun and magically recycled oceans falling over its edge. It changes its spin from time to time, contains two of each season, has 13 months, and time is rather hard to measure. Three features of the Discworld's physics are crucial, however. First, there is narrative causality—the power of stories—which determines what is happening on the Discworld. Things happen because the power of stories wants them to happen. Due to that power, history repeats itself. People experience the same situations again and again. They play the same roles and instantiate suspiciously similar patterns. On Discworld, things happen because narrative imperative makes them happen. There is no choice about ends, only about means.[15] The second quite pertinent scientific feature of the Discworld is its unique life force. In contrast to the actual world, life at the Discworld is "a very common commodity." Almost everything has a disposition to come to life, including stones, storms, buildings, trolls, and chess figures. The only thing necessary for such an awakening is appropriate circumstances. Third, there is the power of belief. Any single thing that is believed can exist because belief is sometimes a sufficient condition for something's existence. Gods, ghosts, souls, or Death can (and in fact do) exist because people have strong beliefs in them.[16]

Given the above, we can think about the Discworld in two quite different ways. It definitely is a *logical possibility* as there is nothing that would contradict the idea of its existence. Its existence is ensured by the recombination principle together with the ontological commitments of modal realism. Moreover, if we interviewed some spokesman for common sense here at the actual world and at the Discworld about what their worlds are like, we would be surprised how many facts look the same.

On the other hand, its "scientific" profile puts it too far away from the actual world and, a fortiori, it does not provide relevant data for evaluation of physical possibility. Since it is *physically impossible*—that is, it is too dissimilar to the actual world with respect to the laws of nature, people's constitutions, animals' behavior, or substantial differences between their universe's rules and ours[17]—it does not present a relevant philosophical datum. Since it does not belong to the selected collection of possible worlds sharing the same laws of nature, its existence is irrelevant for the physical character of our world. Speaking unrestrictedly, Pratchett's Discworld logically exists since there is nothing that contradicts the idea. As we saw, however, a more fine-grained analysis requires us to put some restrictions on the modalities at issue. As far as we think about physical possibility, the Discworld is not possible as it violates our natural laws extensively.

This does not mean, however, that Pratchett's visions of justice, belief, or human behavior should be ignored. On the contrary. There are historical, legal, epistemic, deontic, and doxastic modalities that are best analyzed in a possible-worlds framework. And since speaking of various restricted modalities assumes various incompatible similarity relations, the *physical* impossibility does not exclude the Discworld from the analysis of history, law, knowledge, obligations, and beliefs, respectively.

Notes

1. D. Lewis (1986) *On the Plurality of Worlds* (Oxford: Blackwell), p. vii.
2. T. Pratchett, I. Stewart, and J. Cohen (2002) *The Science of Discworld*, rev. edn (London: Ebury Press), p. 11.
3. According to some philosophers, one concrete world only—our world—and abstract surrogates play the same theoretical role as concrete possible worlds; see Lewis, *On the Plurality of Worlds*, p. 137; J. Divers (2002) *Possible Worlds* (London: Routledge); T. Sider (2002) "The Ersatz Pluriverse," *Journal of Philosophy* 99(6), pp. 279–315.
4. Lewis, *On the Plurality of Worlds*, p. 1.
5. Ibid., p. 2.
6. T. Pratchett and S. Briggs (2003) *The New Discworld Companion*, 1st rev. edn (London: Gollancz), pp. 128–9.
7. D. Lewis (1973) *Counterfactuals* (Oxford: Blackwell), p. 73.
8. D. Lewis (1983) "New Work for a Theory of Universals," *Australasian Journal of Philosophy* 61, pp. 343–77, p. 367.
9. D. Lewis (1994) "Humean Supervenience Debugged," *Mind* 103, p. 478.
10. Pratchett et al., *Science of Discworld*, p. 85.
11. Ibid.
12. Ibid., p. 17; my emphasis.
13. Ibid., p. 10.
14. Ibid., p. 12.
15. Ibid., p. 262.
16. Pratchett and Briggs, *New Discworld Companion*, pp. 131–2.
17. Pratchett et al., *Science of Discworld*, p. 12.

Bibliography

Carroll, J.W. (Spring 2012 Edition) "Laws of Nature," *The Stanford Encyclopedia of Philosophy*, ed. Edward N. Zalta: http://plato.stanford.edu/archives/spr2012/entries/laws-of-nature.

Divers, J. (2002) *Possible Worlds* (London: Routledge).

Lewis, D. (1973) *Counterfactuals* (Oxford: Blackwell).

_____ (1979) "Counterfactual Dependence and Time's Arrow," *Noûs* 13, pp. 455–76.

_____ (1983) "New Work for a Theory of Universals," *Australasian Journal of*
Philosophy 61, pp. 343–77.

_____ (1986) *On the Plurality of Worlds* (Oxford: Blackwell).

_____ (1994) "Humean Supervenience Debugged," *Mind* 103, pp. 473–90.

Pratchett, T. and S. Briggs (2003) *The New Discworld Companion*, 1st rev. edn (London: Gollancz).

Pratchett, T., I. Stewart, and J. Cohen (2002) *The Science of Discworld*, rev. edn (London: Ebury Press).

Sider, T. (2002) "The Ersatz Pluriverse," *Journal of Philosophy* 99(6), pp. 279–315.

13 Pratchett's *The Last Continent* and the Act of Creation

Jay Ruud

In his book length study *The Postmodern Fairytale*, Kevin Paul Smith observes that Terry Pratchett is "always pointing out that humans do not live in the real world, but an imaginary one of their own creation."[1] At the beginning of his twenty-second Discworld novel, *The Last Continent*, Pratchett makes the following observation:

> People don't actually *live* on the Disc any more than, in less hand-crafted parts of the multiverse, they live on balls. Oh, planets may be the place where their body eats its tea, but they *live* elsewhere, in worlds of their own which orbit very handily around the center of their heads.[2]

From the very beginning of the novel, then, Pratchett seems to announce that one of his major themes will be perception as human reality: the idea that the only reality we can know is what our own senses tell us about the world in which we live, and how our minds interpret that sensory data. Immediately after this statement, Pratchett suggests that truth, as we perceive it, depends largely on creativity and imagination—on the stories that we choose to believe, for, as he says, "all tribal myths are true, for a given value of 'true.'"[3] Thus the novel is essentially about epistemology and aesthetics—about art (like the tribal myths) as a reflection of epistemology, or of a certain view of epistemology.[4]

Put succinctly, Pratchett is introducing two particular propositions in the beginning of his novel, which the novel itself then goes on to illustrate. First, he seems to argue that

> Any individual truth is truth of the world as one perceives it.
> Art (e.g. tribal myths, a Pratchett novel) is an expression of the truth of the world as one perceives it.
> Therefore individual truth is reflected in art.

Furthermore, since the world in which we live is only inside our heads and art is an expression, in some concrete medium, of what is inside our heads, it could be argued that

> Epistemology is the formal study of the way one perceives the world.
> Art is a physical manifestation of the artist's perception of the world.
> Therefore art is a physical manifestation of epistemology.

While such concerns are not unusual in contemporary literature, what is somewhat more surprising is that Pratchett's exploration of epistemology as it develops in the novel in fact parallels the spirited epistemological debate between realists and nominalists in late medieval philosophy, a debate that centered chiefly on the question of whether or not universals had a real existence. The novel further explores the importance of imaginative creativity, and does so in a way that once again recalls the ideas of medieval thinkers. But it should come as no great surprise to find Pratchett making use of medieval philosophy rather than, say, classical or Enlightenment arguments, for his Discworld, peopled as it is with dwarves and trolls, gnomes and werewolves, is in many ways a parody of Tolkien's essentially medieval Middle Earth; hence the use of medieval ways of thinking about epistemological questions (likewise in a largely parodying manner) is hardly out of place within the imaginary boundaries of the Discworld.

288

Accordingly this chapter will examine Pratchett's view of the value of art (including literature) as implied in the novel through the depiction of two contrasting "creator gods." Because these figures embody characteristics familiar to nominalist and realist thinkers of the late Middle Ages, I will first discuss characteristics of the epistemology and aesthetic concerns of nominalism and realism, then suggest how the two gods of the novel reflect those concerns, and finally suggest which point of view Pratchett seems to favor in his final assessment of the creative process as the novel represents it.

Nominalism and Realism

Drawing their definition chiefly from Aristotle, medieval metaphysicians defined a universal as something that individuals held in common: both roundness and redness, for example, in the case of individual apples; the physical characteristics of "horseness"—shape and form as well as characteristics like power and speed—in the case of a pair of stallions. The debatable question was whether these universals had any real existence apart from the individuals that held them in common. This problem became more significant when applied to epistemology, when Aristotle described the universal as the intelligible form of the individual, its essence, which was the only thing about the individual that the intellect could know directly.

There is certainly no space here to discuss the various differences among individual medieval philosophers all categorized loosely as "nominalists." Generally, however, nominalists denied the extra-mental reality of universals, except as linguistic terms. Only individuals exist in reality. Marilyn McCord Adams summarizes the position of representative nominalist William of Ockham (c.1287–1347) this way:

> Ockham regarded the view that universals are real things other than names as "the worst error of philosophy," not

primarily on grounds of ontological parsimony, but because he found it contradictory.[5]

Or, as Ockham himself declares, "if we take the term 'universal' to mean that which is not one in number, as many do, then, I want to say that nothing is a universal."[6] Unless, of course, one is using a universal as a linguistic term:

> A spoken word, which is numerically one quality, is a universal; it is a sign conventionally appointed for the signification of many things. Thus, since the word is said to be common, it can be called a universal. But notice it is not by nature, but only by convention, that this label applies.[7]

The implications of these precepts for the creative imagination are far from sanguine. It is difficult to describe carefully a nominalist view of aesthetics, usually defined as the study of principles related to the consideration and appreciation of beauty, particularly in the arts. Ockham has left no direct discussion of the nature of art or of literature, but his arguments concerning language might be used to infer a distrust of the value of literary art—of those "tribal myths" that Pratchett asserts the truth of. If the intellect cannot directly know universals but only particulars, then how does language express meaning? In the sphere of language, words—like universals—are only mental concepts, and a word like "dog," expressing the idea of the general category of dogs rather than a particular dog, is an abstraction at one remove from another abstraction. In Ockham's *Prologue to the Expositio super viii libros Physicorum*, he says that:

> The real sciences are about mental contents, since they are about contents which stand for things; for even though they are mental contents, they will stand for things. Logic, on the other hand, is about mental contents that stand for mental contents.[8]

If science is concerned primarily only with "terms" or mental concepts, and if logic only with terms that stand for other terms, then how far from reality indeed is literature, with its metaphors and similes and terms that stand for terms that stand for other terms? The human activities of art and literature must, for nominalists like Ockham, be highly suspect paths to any kind of truth (unless they are informed by divine revelation).

This cannot be said of the realist position. Naturally, as in the case of nominalists, there is no single version of realism, and there are varying degrees of faith in the reality of universals. But essentially, realists believed that the human intellect could directly know only universals—the intelligible "forms" of things rather than individuals. The most influential realist of the scholastic era, St. Thomas Aquinas (1225–74), was chiefly interested in how human beings "come to have cognition of first principles," as MacDonald remarks,[9] principles he was absolutely convinced existed extra-mentally. Since those first principles are abstract universals, and since human beings, as MacDonald describes us, are "by nature unified corporal substances whose natural access to the world is through the bodily senses,"[10] the problem arises as to how corporeal substance can commune with abstract essence. Aquinas accepts the Aristotelian solution of abstractive cognition.

He begins with the assumption that our intellect is simply not constructed in a way that allows it to know individuals directly:

Our intellect cannot know the singular in material things directly and primarily. The reason for this is that the principle of singularity in material things is individual matter; whereas our intellect, as we have said above, understands by abstracting the intelligible species from matter.[11]

Now of course it is the case that our senses do perceive individuals, but they store up these sense impressions in a part of the mind known variously as the imagination or fantasy, which includes sense memory. The stored images, which Aquinas calls "phantasms," are then acted upon by what medieval philosophers called the "agent" intellect, which abstracts the universal form from the particular individual phantasm (Aquinas uses the terms "essence," "quiddity," and "form" to mean essentially the same thing, as he explains in his treatise *Being and Essence*).[12] That form is then stored in the potential intellect, which perceives and understands the universal form, and ultimately stores it in the memory. The process in Aquinas's description works thus:

> The human intellect . . . is a power of the soul, which is the form of the body . . . And therefore it is proper to it to know a form existing individually in corporeal matter, but not as existing in this individual matter. But to know what is an individual matter, yet not as existing in such matter, is to abstract the form from individual matter which is represented by the phantasms.[13]

Unlike Ockham and most nominalists, many realists did argue that universals have a real extra-mental existence. Even for Aquinas, who is generally considered a moderate realist, universals existed apart from corporeal matter, as he makes clear in *On Being and Essence*:

> Whenever two things are related to each other such that one is the cause of the other, the one that is the cause can have existence without the other, but not conversely. Now, we find that matter and form are related in such a way that form gives existence to matter, and therefore it is impossible that matter exist without a form; but it is not impossible that a form exist without matter, for a form, insofar as it is a form, is not dependent on matter.[14]

This view cannot help but affect the realist view of aesthetics, just as Ockham's views had implications for his attitude toward language and, by extension, literature. Aquinas, speaking of aesthetics, argues that the apprehension of beauty is an intellectual activity, involving our perception of the form of an object:

> Beauty relates to the cognitive faculty; for beautiful things are those which please when seen. Hence beauty consists in due proportion; for the senses delight in things duly proportioned, as in what is after their own kind—because even sense is a sort of reason, just as is every cognitive faculty. Now since knowledge is by assimilation, and similarity relates to form, beauty properly belongs to the nature of a formal cause.[15]

Thus for Aquinas, beauty is a matter of perception, and so aesthetics, commonly defined as the consideration of beauty in the form of art, is related to epistemology: the creative artist produces an object or a text whose form is perceived as beautiful by its consumer.

The Handyman God and the Doodling God

Allusions to these two philosophical camps occur in two specific passages in the text of *The Last Continent*. These scenes involve contrasting depictions of two "creator gods." The first of these is the busy god with the extensive toolkit, encountered by the wizards of Unseen University on an otherwise deserted island at some point in the far distant past. This scene is contrasted with the later appearance of a second creator god on the Australia-like continent of Fourecks itself, who spends his time drawing simple pictures on a stone wall, pictures that become complex living creatures as soon as he has drawn them. I shall refer to these two deities henceforth as the "Handyman god" and the "Doodling god." These gods represent, respectively, the nominalist and the realist positions in the late medieval debate over universals.

That Pratchett makes the authors of these contrasting epistemological possibilities gods should be no real surprise. Despite his avowed atheism, Pratchett habitually makes use of gods in his Discworld series. Indeed, as Elisabeth Gruner says, "religious belief is of central thematic concern [to Pratchett], even if the gods believed in are frequently ridiculous."[16] And the gods often act in a ridiculous manner because their devotees—whose faith gives them life—believe that this is how gods should act: since for Pratchett it is human beings who create the gods, each of these creator gods is the mythic product of the humans who perceive them. Human beings with a particular way of looking at the world will imagine gods whose created universe begs to be interpreted in that particular way.[17] Thus, building on the two earlier propositions with which Pratchett began his novel, these deities might be explained in this way:

> Epistemology is how we perceive the world as created.
> The world as created takes on the character of the mind that created it (i.e. "god").
> Therefore epistemology is how we perceive the mind of god.

Or, to be more clear:

> Epistemology is a formalization of how we perceive the mind of the god whom we believe in.

That it is Ponder Stibbons who first comes across the Handyman god is also to be expected: Youngest of the major wizards of Unseen University, and technically the Head of Inadvisably Applied Magic, Stibbons is a tinkerer and handyman himself, who invented, among other things, the impossibly complicated computer Hex. Though in many ways Stibbons is the most practical and least batty of the wizards, he also at times seems to put too much faith in technology and innovation. Naturally, rather than continue with his fellow wizards, he wants to stay on with the Handyman god and become his apprentice.

In the wizards' meeting with the Handyman god comes the first indication that the gods of this book stem in part from medieval philosophy, though this first allusion has nothing, in fact, to do with the question of universals. It appears, rather, in Stibbons's initial conversation with the Handyman god after meeting him on that island long in the past. The god is in the midst of a project involving an elephant, trying to fit the creature with wheels. Stibbons says to him:

"You don't think just, you know, moving the legs about would be simpler?"

"Oh, we'd never get anywhere if I just copied earlier ideas," said the god. "Diversify and fill all niches, that's the ticket."[18]

The idea of a god who desires to fill all of the "niches" in creation, making sure that all creatures that can exist will in fact exist, is a formulation of what Arthur O. Lovejoy has called the "principle of plenitude." This principle, derived from the Neoplatonists' doctrine of "emanation," was applied to the Christian God by St Augustine, though Augustine's own position is less extreme.[19] For Augustine, God could not have made a universe of only the highest or most perfect beings, for without a plenitude of creatures the range of God's creativity could not be displayed, and certain good things could not exist without such variation—generosity, for example, could not exist if there were no one to receive it.

Pratchett's answer to the Augustinian principle of plenitude is quite simple, and comes from the lips of Ponder Stibbons, who, watching the Handyman god trying to put wheels on an elephant, asks: "But is lying on your side in a mud hole with your wheels spinning a very *important* niche?"[20] The principle is further undercut by the Handyman god's own obsession with creating thousands of species of beetles, an obsession that

Stibbons hopes to wean him from until he discovers that the god's secret ambition, anticipated as his greatest triumph, is the creation of the cockroach.[21]

This Handyman god is seen by many readers of *The Last Continent* as essentially a god of evolution, and is referred to as such in *The Science of Discworld*.[22] He is precisely the kind of "scientific" god that someone like Ponder Stibbons would emulate. Like evolution, the god has no particular goal in mind: he only wants to fill the niches—niches in the chain of being that leads to what Ponder Stibbons, at least, considers the crown of creation, human beings. But it would be more accurate to call him the god of intelligent design, because he seems to function largely as Pratchett's ironic commentary on the fundamentalist notion of an intelligent designer responsible for the universe: if in fact evolution can be explained by the notion of such a designer, then why does that omniscient god seem so incredibly inept? Some 99 percent of his creations have already failed and gone extinct, and if human beings are indeed the apex of his creation, then why does he spend so much time creating thousands of species of beetles? Prachett's handyman god debunks the concept of intelligent design by presenting such a creator in all of his bumbling foolishness. Stibbons, though, has a nagging belief in intelligent design, and suggests to the Handyman god that the ultimate purpose of evolution may be to produce a creature capable of understanding the whole process.[23] But the island god, wanting nothing to do with so-called "higher" life forms, responds:

> "Dear me, the purpose of the whole business, you see, is in fact to *be* the whole business. Although," he sniffed, "if we can do it all with beetles I shan't complain."
>
> "But surely the purpose of—I mean, wouldn't it be nice if you ended up with some creature that started to *think* about the universe—?"
>
> "Good gravy, I don't want anything poking around!" said the god testily. "There's enough patches and stitches

in it as it is without some clever devil trying to find more, I can assure you. No, the gods on the mainland have got *that* right, at least. Intelligence is like legs—too many and you trip yourself up. Six is about the right number, in my view."[24]

Modern science has generally been nominalist in its world view in the sense that it relies on inductive reasoning (beginning with particular things with a physical existence in space and time, and forming generalizations or "universal" kinds of statements about groups of individuals), as opposed to deductive reasoning (beginning with precepts or general truths—universals—and applying those to particular cases). In an extreme way the Handyman god reflects this focus: what most clearly identifies him as representative of a radically nominalist point of view is his process of making only a single representative of each species of creature he designs: there are, in his world, no universals, only individuals.

Since Pratchett's interest in universals is chiefly a product of his exploration of epistemology, the point of the Handyman god is his perception of created species. The fact that he can conceive only one individual representative of each species exempts him from conceiving of even the "common nature" that the most moderate of realists might postulate. He represents, therefore, the mind that cannot know universals, but directly knows only individuals. But his perception allows for very little imagination—there is little creativity in his creation. He hasn't yet figured out, for instance, that more creatures of the same species could be produced through the vehicle of sex.

Pratchett has produced in the Handyman god a *reductio ad absurdum* of this particular nominalist position. If the intellect could directly know only individuals, then we humans would all be in the situation that the Handyman god finds himself in: Any individual we ran across would have its own properties and attributes, and would be absolutely unique, at least as far as our understanding was concerned. And it could be truly said of every one of us that we couldn't see the forest for the trees. We too would lack imagination. But this is a position that Pratchett cannot embrace. Pratchett's gods themselves are imaginative creations. As Kevin Paul Smith has noted, "in Pratchett's world, gods and other anthropomorphic personifications . . . exist only because people believe in them and die when belief in them ceases. It is easy to forget sometimes that stories have power not just to represent, but to change the world, something that Pratchett is intensely aware of."[25]

The actions of the Doodling god contrast rather sharply to these. First, the wizard who encounters this god is the Bursar— in many ways the direct opposite of Stibbons; for if Stibbons seems to be the sanest of the wizards, the Bursar is by all accounts the least in touch with reality. As Pratchett says, "the Bursar was . . . quite accustomed to the presence of people who couldn't be seen or heard by anyone else, and had spent many a pleasant hour in conversation with historical figures and, sometimes, the wall."[26] All of this made him, in Pratchett's phrase, "depending on your outlook, the most or least suitable person to encounter deity on a first-hand basis."[27] Assuming, again, that human beings believe in the gods that they can conceive of, this Doodling god is the least "scientific," the least bound to the physical world, that a god can be—and thus is encountered by the wizard least in touch with the material world.

The Doodling god has no great laboratory or set of sophisticated tools, but rather simply breaks a branch off a dead tree, chars its end in a fire, and then walks to an overhang sheltering the vertical wall of a small cliff:

> Someone had drawn a tree. It was the simplest drawing of a tree the Bursar had ever seen since he'd been old enough to read books that weren't mainly pictures, but it was also in some strange way the most accurate. It was simple because something complex had been rolled up small; as if someone had drawn trees, and started with the normal green cloud on a stick, and refined it, and refined it some more, and looked

for the little twists in a line that said *tree* and refined *those* until there was just one line that said TREE.

And now when you looked at it you could hear the wind in the branches.

The old man reached down beside him and took up a flat stone with some white paste on it. He drew another line on the rock, slightly like a flattened V, and smeared it with mud.

The Bursar burst out laughing as the wings emerged from the painting and whirred past him.[28]

The description of the Doodling god's creation of trees or birds suggests an ideal form present in the mind of the god, transferred into individuals by the god's will once the ideal forms are loosed into the physical world through the medium of the drawings on the wall. In this, the Doodling god's process of creation exemplifies the kind of world that exists in the mind of a philosopher whose epistemology was radically realist, even Platonic, as Aquinas describes Platonist epistemology:

The exemplars of all creatures existed in the divine mind. It is according to these that all things are formed, as well as that the human soul knows all things . . . but since besides the intellectual light which is in us, intelligible species, which are derived from things, are required in order that we may have knowledge of material things, therefore this knowledge is not due merely to a participation of the eternal exemplars, as the Platonists held.[29]

Here, the Doodling god holds the exemplar, the universal, in his mind, and manifests individuals in the real world through his representation of the fairly abstract form of that individual represented in the rock drawings.

Creating Gods

Shortly before the novel's climax, then, Pratchett has presented two contrasting images of creation, inspired by two contrasting ways of comprehending that creation. The climax itself, however, involves the hapless wizard Rincewind's application of the creative process to the alleviation of the water crisis on the continent of Fourecks. Rincewind re-enacts the process of divine creation within the created world; in doing so he emulates the role of the artist, of Pratchett himself—who also re-enacts the divine creative process in the creation of the Discworld. James Brown first pointed out Pratchett's use of this connection:

> In *The Last Continent* the myth of the rain-bringer who restores barren land to life is particularly associated with an idea of art. It is an idea that Coleridge had proposed: that in representing the world the artist in some sense reiterates the process of Creation.[30]

Consider this particular crisis. In the same way as modernist classics like Eliot's *The Waste Land* and Hemingway's "Big Two-Hearted River" and *The Sun Also Rises*, Pratchett makes use of the Grail Knight and his restoration of fertility to the wasteland, an archetypal motif with roots far back in the Western literary and folk tradition. The restoration of fertility is itself another creative act, like the creation of poetry and art. As an archetypal narrative motif, the myth of the wasteland is to literature what the intelligible forms are to cognition in realist epistemology: the essential truth that is embodied in the individual narrative. Within the story itself, Rincewind, the putative Grail Knight, who has sensed that the wizards of Unseen University are some-how trapped in the Last Continent's distant past, asks for some paint in order to draw on a cave wall. He decides "it was no good trying to be strictly true to life here; what he had to go for was an impression." When he finishes his work, Neilette says "you know . . . the way the light falls on it and everything . . . it could be a group of wizards," at which point the lost wizards appear.[31] Rincewind's impressionistic art, capturing the essence rather than the concrete individuality of the thing, proves to be salvation for Fourecks (and the wizards)—a bold statement of the power of art and literature to shape events and arrive at truth the way that, as Pratchett had said at the beginning of the novel, "all tribal myths are true."[32]

While Brown attributes this view of the creative power of art to Coleridge, there is a closer and perhaps even more likely source from whom Pratchett might have taken this idea: J.R.R. Tolkien. In his seminal essay "On Fairy Stories," Tolkien argued that human nature, though marred by the Fall, retained in the imagination what he called the power of sub-creation: the human being as artist is involved in a "Secondary Creation" and so mirrors the Creator God himself. "We make in our measure and in our derivative mode, because we are made: and not only made, but made in the image and likeness of a Maker."[33] Tolkien thought this was particularly true of the fantasy or "fairy-story" writer, whose creation was not a direct copy of the perceived world, but a true secondary creation. Thus Rincewind's act mirrors the creative act of the Doodling god, and Pratchett's novel mirrors the act of a realist god.

Seen in this way, Pratchett's view of art seems in line with the realist rather than the nominalist point of view. As Brown puts it:

> Repeatedly, as the rock-drawing motif recurs, Pratchett comes up with various ways of gesturing towards the idea of language or a form of representation that grasps not the appearances of things but their very essence . . . Then Rincewind has to draw in the same way in order to get the wizards out of the past, the bullroarer back to rain-making, and history back on track.[34]

As Brown describes Rincewind's representations, they sound like nothing if not the universal forms that exist in the mind of the realist perceiver.

But why should Pratchett, product of a post-Darwinian culture who has asserted "I have never disliked religion. I think it has some purpose in our evolution,"[35] give preferential treatment in his novel to a realist rather than a nominalist view of art—to the epistemology of the Bursar's god rather than Ponder Stibbons's? Aside from the association of Stibbons's god with the idea of intelligent design, Pratchett's concern seems to be with the importance of creative activity, of literary art, and with the kind of truth that can be expressed through that art of which Pratchett's novel is itself a prime example. With fiction, particularly with fantasy fiction, this truth can only be realized through what is essentially an interpretive act that, somewhat like the realist's abstracted cognition, finds the universal in the particular fiction, and then applies it to "real life."

Like most writers of contemporary fiction, Pratchett does not present his readers with neatly packaged answers or clear visions of universal truths as an Augustine or an Aquinas—or, for that matter, a Tolkien—would do. Truth is a matter of perception, of what goes on in individuals' heads—the "worlds of their own which orbit very handily around the center of their heads" he refers to at the beginning of the novel.[36] But some of those worlds are more functional than others, more creative, more satisfying, and perhaps more shareable, and those are in the minds whose perceptions are more realist than nominalist. But in the end, it would go too far to claim from this that Pratchett has been enticed into belief in the universal truths of an Augustinian God. After all, he is still a 21st-century author and still Pratchett. As he has said recently with regard to such speculations: "there is a rumour going around that I have found God. I think this is unlikely because I have enough difficulty finding my keys, and there is empirical evidence that *they* exist."[37]

Notes

1. K.P. Smith (2007) *The Postmodern Fairytale: Folkloric Intertexts in Contemporary Fiction* (New York: Palgrave Macmillan), p. 161.

2. T. Pratchett (1997) *The Last Continent* (New York: HarperCollins), p. 1.
3. Ibid., p. 2. Though this question is certainly not unique to medieval thinkers, the specific ways that Pratchett explores the question with his contrasting gods of *The Last Continent* recalls the way those questions were approached by medieval nominalist and realist thinkers.
4. The history of philosophical arguments concerning the relationship of art and epistemology is long and complex. One thing that is certain is that our experience of a work of art is in itself a perceptual activity, similar to but not identical with our mind's engagement with the physical world. But many thinkers go further and suggest that our experience of a work of art can *change* the way that we perceive the world. While Plato famously called all poets "liars" and insisted (particularly in Book X of *The Republic*) that the kinds of things that move us emotionally in a work of fiction, for instance, are in fact detrimental to one's character since they engage the audience with the vicarious experience of psychic conflicts and traumas but with no rational component. In his *Poetics*, on the other hand, Aristotle saw the experience of poetry, especially in the performance of tragedy, as beneficial to our character, both because he saw poetry as more "philosophical" than history (because it could teach us universal truths rather than particular ones) but also because the catharsis of poetry allowed us to purge undesirable emotions like pity and fear. Aristotle's was essentially the view that predominated during the Middle Ages and Renaissance. But by the Romantic period, artists began to emphasize the role of the imagination in epistemology—and, despite his interest here in realism and nominalism, that particular Romantic conception, expressed especially by Coleridge, seems also to have significantly influenced Pratchett, as will be seen later.
5. M.M. Adams (1989) *William Ockham*, 2 vols (Notre Dame: Notre Dame University Press), p. 13.
6. M.L. Loux (translator) (1974) *Ockham's Theory of Terms: Part I of the Summa Logicae* (Notre Dame: University of Notre Dame Press), p. 78.
7. Ibid., p. 79.
8. P. Boehner (editor and translator) (1957) *Ockham: Philosophical Writings* (London: Thomas Nelson), p. 12.
9. S. MacDonald (1993) "Theory of Knowledge," in *The Cambridge Companion to Aquinas*, edited N. Kretzmann and E. Stump (Cambridge: Cambridge University Press), p. 181.
10. Ibid., p. 182.

11. Thomas Aquinas (1947) *Summa Theologica*, translated Fathers of the English Dominican Province, 3 vols (New York: Benziger Brothers), I, q. 86, a. 1.

12. According to Aquinas, "since that through which a thing is constituted in its proper genus or species is what is signified by the definition indicating what the thing is, philosophers introduced the term quiddity to mean the same as the term essence; . . . Essence is also called form, for the certitude of every thing is signified through its form, as Avicenna says in his *Metaphysicae* I, cap. 6. The same thing is also called nature, taking nature in the first of the four senses that Boethius distinguishes in his book *De Persona et Duabus Naturis* cap. 1 (PL 64, 1341B)"; see Thomas Aquinas (1997) *On Being and Essence*, translated R.T. Miller (Fordham University: Internet Medieval Sourcebook), ch. I, par. 3, at www.fordham.edu/halsall/basis/aquinas-esse.asp#f2. (accessed 5 May 2014).

13. Aquinas, *Summa Theologica*, I, q. 85, a. 1.

14. Aquinas, *On Being and Essence*, ch. IV, par. 3.

15. Aquinas, *Summa Theologica*, I. q. 5. a. 4.

16. E.R. Gruner (2011) "Wrestling with Religion: Pullman, Pratchett, and the Uses of Story," *Children's Literature Association Quarterly* 36, Fall, p. 277.

17. In *The Science of Discworld*, Pratchett explains this way of looking at the world as "narrative imperative, the power of story" (p. 10), which he names "narrativium." Later he asserts that "humans add narrativium to their world. They insist on interpreting the universe as if it's telling a story. This leads them to focus on facts that fit the story, while ignoring those that don't" (p. 274). Thus they tend to create their gods in their own image. See Pratchett, T., I. Stewart, and J. Cohen (2002) *The Science of Discworld* (London: Ebury Press).

18. Pratchett, *Last Continent*, p. 209.

19. As Simo Knuuttila argues, "it is not clear whether or not Augustine assumed that there are empty generic forms, but he thought that the number of merely possible individuals was much larger than that of the individuals which occur in the world history"; see S. Knuuttila (2001) "Time and Creation in Augustine," *The Cambridge Companion to Augustine*, edited Eleonore Stump and Norman Kretzmann (Cambridge: Cambridge University Press), pp. 103–15, p. 108. But Augustine did use a version of this principle as a part of his theodicy. Why should God have made lower creatures? Why should he not have simply stopped with the angels? Why allow a diversity of creatures who live such different lives—some long and happy, others short and difficult? The answer, as Augustine sees it, is that the

diversity of creatures allows for the whole range of God's eternal ideas to be manifested in the world.

20. Pratchett, *Last Continent*, p. 209.
21. In *The Science of Discworld* (p. 300), Pratchett and his co-authors note the origin of this quirk in *The Last Continent's* evolutionary creator: The great biologist John (J.B.S.) Haldane was once asked what question he would like to pose to God, and replied that he'd like to know why He has such an inordinate fondness for beetles. There are a third of a million beetle species today—far more than in any other plant or animal group.
22. Ibid., p. 209.
23. Pratchett would probably consider the concept of intelligent design the product of the sort of narrativium described above. He and his co-authors sum up the real lessons of evolution in *The Science of Discworld*: "We think the planet's a great place. We grew up here. We were made for it, and it's just right for us ... at the moment. Tell that to the dinosaurs. You can't, can you. That's the point" (p. 364). In real life, that is in what Pratchett calls the "Roundworld," species adapt and thrive, a catastrophic event causes their extinction, and new species adapt and thrive. New species—not us, not the dinosaurs—are the end goal of evolution. "Life is resilient," as Pratchett says, "but any particular species may not be" (ibid., p. 300).
24. Pratchett, *Last Continent*, p. 211.
25. Smith, *The Postmodern Fairytale*, p. 162.
26. Pratchett, *Last Continent*, p. 324.
27. Ibid.
28. Ibid., pp. 325–6.
29. Aquinas, *Summa Theologica*, I, q. 84, a. 1.
30. J. Brown (2004) "Believing is Seeing: Silas Tomkyn Comberbache and *Terry Pratchett*," *Terry Pratchett*: Guilty of Literature, 2nd edn, edited A.M. Butler, E. James, and F. Mendelsohn (Baltimore: Old Earth Books), p. 296.
31. Pratchett, *Last Continent*, p. 366.
32. Pratchett, *Last Continent*, p. 2.
33. J.R.R. Tolkien (2008) "On Fairy-Stories," *Tales from the Perilous Realm* (Boston: Houghton Mifflin Harcourt), pp. 315–400, p. 371.
34. Brown, "Believing is Seeing," p. 298.
35. T. Pratchett (2008) "I Create Gods All the Time—Now I Think One Might Exist, Says Fantasy Author Terry Pratchett," June, at www.dailymail.co.uk/femail/article-1028222/I-create-gods-time–I-think-exist.html (accessed 25 April 2013).
36. Pratchett, *Last Continent*, p. 1.
37. Pratchett, "I Create Gods."

Bibliography

Adams, M.M. (1989) *William Ockham*, 2 vols (Notre Dame: Notre Dame University Press).

Boehner, P. (editor and translator) (1957) *Ockham: Philosophical Writings* (London: Thomas Nelson).

Brown, J. (2004) "Believing is Seeing: Silas Tomkyn Comberbache and Terry Pratchett," *Terry Pratchett: Guilty of Literature*, 2nd edn, edited A.M. Butler, E. James, and F. Mendelsohn (Baltimore: Old Earth Books), pp. 261–99.

Gruner, E.R. (2011) "Wrestling with Religion: Pullman, Pratchett, and the Uses of Story," *Children's Literature Association Quarterly* 36(3), pp. 276–95.

Knuuttila, S. (2001) "Time and Creation in Augustine," *The Cambridge Companion to Augustine*, edited Eleonore Stump and Normann Kretzmann (Cambridge: Cambridge University Press), pp. 103–15.

Loux, M.L. (translator) (1974) *Ockham's Theory of Terms: Part I of the Summa Logicae* (Notre Dame: University of Notre Dame Press).

Lovejoy, A.O. (1936) *The Great Chain of Being: A Study of the History of an Idea* (Cambridge, MA: Harvard University Press).

MacDonald, S. (1993) "Theory of Knowledge," in *The Cambridge Companion to Aquinas*, edited N. Kretzmann and E. Stump (Cambridge: Cambridge University Press).

Pratchett, T. (1997) *The Last Continent* (New York: HarperCollins).

——— (2008) "I Create Gods All the Time—Now I Think One Might Exist, Says Fantasy Author Terry Pratchett," June, at www.dailymail. co.uk/femail/article-1028222/I-create-gods-time–I-think-exist.html. (accessed 25 April 2013).

Pratchett, T., I. Stewart, and J. Cohen (2002) *The Science of Discworld* (London: Ebury Press).

Smith, K.P. (2007) *The Postmodern Fairytale: Folkloric Intertexts in Contemporary Fiction* (New York: Palgrave Macmillan).

Thomas Aquinas (1997) *On Being and Essence*, translated R.T. Miller, Internet Medieval Sourcebook, Fordham University, at www.fordham. edu/halsall/basis/aquinas-esse.asp#f2. (accessed 5 May 2014).

——— *Summa Theologica* (1947) translated Fathers of the English Dominican Province, 3 vols (New York: Benziger Brothers).

Tolkien, J.R.R. (2008) "On Fairy-Stories," *Tales from the Perilous Realm* (Boston: Houghton Mifflin Harcourt), pp. 315–400.

Index

Index

Index